SYMPATH

THE SENTINELS OF EDEN
~ BOOK THREE ~

CAROLYN DENMAN

ODYSSEY
BOOKS

Published by Odyssey Books in 2018
www.odysseybooks.com.au

Copyright © Carolyn Denman 2018

All rights reserved. No part of this book may be reproduced or transmitted by any person or entity, including internet search engines or retailers, in any form or by any means, electronic or mechanical, including photocopying (except under the statutory exceptions provisions of the *Australian Copyright Act* 1968), recording, scanning or by any information storage and retrieval system without the prior written permission of the publisher.

A Cataloguing-in-Publication entry is available from the National Library of Australia

ISBN: 978-1-925652-33-8 (pbk)
ISBN: 978-1-925652-34-5 (ebook)

Cover design by Elijah Toten

For Paul

Hope deferred makes the heart sick, but when the desire comes,
it is a tree of life.

Proverbs 13:12 NKJ

Author's Note

The Sentinels of Eden series is set in a fictional town based on Jardwadjali Country. I would like to acknowledge the traditional owners of that place. I also express my deepest respect for all Aboriginal Elders, both past and present, across this Great Southern Land.

This novel is a speculative fictional story that draws loosely upon the foundational beliefs of many religions and cultures, including Judeo-Christian and Indigenous traditions. However, I do not purport to represent or detract from either ontological perspective. What is known as 'The Dreaming' is the foundational belief system of Aboriginal communities in Australia and I value and acknowledge Indigenous ontologies and epistemologies. I present my narrative ever conscious that Australian Indigenous Society is the oldest continuous living culture in the world.

My desire is that this fantasy tale reflects the co-existence and interconnectedness of belief systems and that you enjoy it, always conscious of my deep respect for Aboriginal Country and Aboriginal Society.

Prologue

The standing stones reflected the colours of passing souls. Blues and greys and warm pinks and, in this place, many strands of gold decorated every personality. Annie was fairly certain that if there were stones like these on the other side of the boundary, the colours would be much less vibrant. She placed her palms against a sun-kissed rock twice her height, and closed her eyes. The memories were easier to catch here. The scent of them lingered, the same way the sun's warmth lingered in the stone long into the night.

Nayn had wanted her to come here. He'd seen her tears, taken Dallmin's letter from her fist and then taken her hand, leading her to this place. It was the only place she knew where Edenites sometimes felt an emotion that could have partnered her grief. They never felt grief, of course. Certainly never sadness. This place, though, was where they indulged in thoughts of people who had left. People they would not see for a long time. People they would miss. So perhaps they wouldn't be quite so confused by her tears if they saw her crying. Nayn was very wise.

One glorious night, many years ago, she and Harry had celebrated her mum's passing here, on this hill. It had been a night full of stories and singing, and the stones held the feel of her even now. Kiah Langley. Cherub appointed to hold the secret path, to protect Eden from fallen human greed. Annie pressed her cheek against the stone. Kiah Langley had not just been 'Cherub'. She'd also been 'Mum'. She had taken photos of every box construction Annie had brought home from kinder, and braided her hair on her first day of school. She'd yelled at Annie for using weed killer too close to the river, and always made her put her clothes in the laundry before she was allowed to turn on the telly. Her mum had taught her which songs she was allowed to sing in front of her school friends, and which were to be kept only for Eden, and explained that it was okay to teach her Eden friends whatever *Playschool* songs she liked. She'd also made up a lullaby just for the two of them. One with a pretty tune and words that made no sense, but that didn't matter because it was *theirs*, and she had been ready with it when her own precious Lainie had refused to go to sleep. Kiah Langley. Best in Show four years running for her home-grown peaches and her fruit pies. Kiah, the woman who had tried to take down an organised crime syndicate with one clever phone call, and had believed it would be all that was needed to keep Harry safe.

Harry had not been brought here when he died, so it was right that Annie should spend some time feeding these stones with her memories of him. She knew that somehow, by doing that, some of Harry's own memories would be drawn here too. Things she hadn't seen herself, and yet the stones still found them, and shared them. A gift to those left behind. Of course, Harry's own family had long since flown from this realm, so who was left for the stones to talk to? Perhaps she should bring Noah and Lainie here sometime, so they could add their memories of Harry, and re-live some of his. Of course, that would be tricky just now because Noah had built a great wall of rock in the cave between Nalong and Eden.

Annie looked up at the cliffs to the east. They towered even over this hill of stories. The Skin of the World ran along them, she knew. Passable only by Cherubim, like her. She could always follow Lainie out of Eden by climbing the cliffs like she had. Find Dallmin. Bring him home. What if he never returned? What if his stories drifted away, with no one coming here to celebrate him and feed the stones with his soul memories? If only she could talk to someone, ask for advice. She missed Harry. She missed her mother. Sometimes they felt so far away, exiled from her life with so many other memories. Other times, she felt she could simply turn her head and see them standing beside her, as if they'd never left.

Her tears darkened the colours where they ran down the stone. This was her fault. She should never have let Dallmin leave. It had simply never crossed her mind that Dallmin, *Dallmin*, could ever become tainted. What a mess she'd made of things. Dallmin was exiled, Lainie had died—again—causing Bane new levels of pain that Annie had been far too unpractised to guard against. She'd lasted less than a minute in Bane's presence before having to stumble back across the Skin of the World to breathe in Eden's soothing fragrance. And that boy, Jake, had run off with the holy sword.

There was more to this story. Annie could feel it, and had done so for many years. She had made a promise to her Guardian, but deep down she knew there was more than that promise holding her here. Lainie and Noah didn't know everything they needed to. Nayn was right to bring her to the place where she could feel her stories, and her mother's stories. Perhaps if she let herself remember, the stones would draw her Guardian's and Harry's memories here too, here for her to find, to feel, to live again. If she could pluck up the courage to face them.

Palms flat. Forehead pressed to the warm stone. Annie breathed in the colours, and remembered.

Chapter 1

According to her late grandmother's stories, Annie should have been able to wipe every last March fly from the face of the planet with a simple word or two. Pity no one had ever been able to teach her the right words. Every time she'd asked, her grandmother had assured her that the words were already inside her bones, sleeping until they were needed. With those words, she had the authority to move mountains. Power limited only by need. Her mother, in turn, had nodded, with a look that warned Annie not to disrespect the older woman by challenging the truth of her stories. Not that her grandmother had been losing her mind, or lying, just that her stories tended to contain a lot of allegories designed to teach moral lessons. *When you face your biggest challenge, you will unlock your hidden strength,* was a common tag line to those tales.

When yet another needle of pain jabbed into Annie's shoulder blade, her reflexive smack dislodged the March fly, but also sent her book spinning from her lap.

'Stupid feral torture beasts,' she complained to her best friend. 'Why do they even exist?'

Kelly ignored her, humming her favourite Hunters & Collectors song as she continued to squint at the surfers out past the breakers. Annie wished she'd pick another tune. 'When The River Runs Dry' had made her cry ever since its release two years earlier, and she could never get the words out to explain to Kelly why.

A fat black March fly hovered above Kelly's elbow, and Annie seriously considered using it as an excuse to slap her friend to stop her humming. *Land. Go on. I dare you,* she challenged. The insect flew toward her, hovering right in front of her face, as if it was preparing to fight back.

Her grandmother had insisted that all she needed to do to wake the sleeping words was to believe the right excuse. Cunning critters. They probably had a hive mentality. Controlled by a super-intelligent Queen Fly. With a plan. A diabolical strategy to sneak into the Garden of Eden and annoy the people there so much that they lost their temper and … Okay, no. Not even March flies could ever make that happen, but surely there had to be *some* way to justify wiping the creatures out. They weren't that important to the ecological balance, were they? She bared her teeth at the blood-sucker, and it flew off.

'Bloody things!' Annie smacked at a second fly that had started to feed on her foot while its colleague had distracted her.

Kelly spread her auburn hair around her shoulders like a silken fly-proof cape. 'You could always go for a swim if the flies bother you,' she suggested. Annie raised an eyebrow at her. 'At least stop swearing. It doesn't sound right coming from you.'

'I wouldn't swear if I wasn't being attacked by a squadron of demonic March flies. And anyway, it's not swearing. They drink blood, so they're bloody,' Annie said, burying her feet into the sand to cool them down and protect as much skin as possible from being stung. A sharp gust of wind blew a spray of fine sand into her face as she tried to dust off her book.

Kelly leant back on her elbows as if to invite a full-body sand-blasting. 'It comes with the territory, Slaps: beach, sand, flies, surf, boys. You get all or nothing. It's not a perfect world.'

Not a perfect world. The words bumped around inside the hole in Annie's chest. The hole that was only ever filled when she was on the other side of the hidden gateway. As a Cherub born into a human body, charged to protect the secret existence of the Garden of Eden, Annie knew a thing or two about perfect worlds, but she couldn't tell her best friend any of it. Besides, Kelly was having the time of her life. Growing up in Nalong seemed about as far from the beach as you could get, so naturally, Kelly craved it, pestering her dad to take her whenever possible, and the four-day weekend at the start of November was a welcome escape from school. The last break before exams.

Beach meant fun. Everyone said so. Every TV show seemed to include glorious montages of sexy girls eating Gelati and mumbling to each other about which clock direction had the best view, as cute boys with surfboards jogged past them. Somehow Annie had imagined that just sitting on their oversized towels out in the sun would magically give them golden glowing skin, shiny sun-bleached hair and enormous boobs. Instead they got dry peeling skin, tangled salt-encrusted hair and itchy insect bites that were big enough to have their own boobs. Even so, Annie could have ignored all that, except for one overshadowing problem. Beach, sand, flies, surf, boys, Kelly had said. The first four were in abundant supply. It was the 'boys' part that was making Annie nervous. Ever since she was little, her parents had assured her that one day she would meet her perfect match. He would be drawn to her, they'd said. He would protect her, no matter what. He would always know where she was. He could well be someone she had known for a long time and not taken much notice of. Even a fellow student, but maybe not. Someone local, because he wouldn't be able to live too far away from her without being sick all the time—although her father's bond with her mum had only started to kick in when he'd moved to Nalong at the age of twelve, so that wasn't a reliable thing to go on. Especially since Annie had already tested every boy within a hundred-kilometre radius of their small town. The test was pretty straightforward. If her Guardian was compelled to protect her from all physical harm, then a game of Slaps would surely reveal that quirk. The childhood game involved taking turns at smacking each other's hands, and you were only allowed to flinch away if your own hands were under genuine attack. Not one of Annie's opponents had ever hesitated to slap her hands, or even so much as pulled a sour face when she'd played with them. Not a single one had ever let her win, either. Okay, so maybe one. Dean Evans had stupidly assumed that losing on purpose might have made her more inclined to go out with him. Needless to say, it'd had the reverse effect. To her intense relief, a tiny nick on her fingertip with her compass during maths class had ruled him out before things had become too awkward.

Almost obsessively, she'd continued to challenge every new or visiting male student who so much as showed his face in town. It had earned her a stupid nickname, but not a Guardian.

She almost felt like she could pretend to be a normal girl. At least for a while. A girl who could indulge in letting boys flirt with her, and could flirt back without feeling guilty. How long could this freedom last before she was locked into a binding relationship? Binding, bonded. Bound, unable to breathe.

So now, squinting across the water at the three guys Kelly was ogling, who were straddling their surfboards and looking like they were arguing about something, Annie considered her options. They were surely not for her. Not here, over four hundred kilometres from home. Did that mean it would be okay to play a little? It was risky. What if she hit it off with someone, only to have to break his heart when her Guardian turned up to claim her? It would have been much easier if she'd known whom she was destined for—the person she had to avoid at all costs. That was the whole point of this trip, after all. It was the plan that her partner Cherub, Harry, had come up with. Leave town. Go far away. Let him scout around and see who got sick while she was gone. Then after Christmas she would return the favour. It wasn't the kindest of plans, but she was getting tired of being called 'Slaps'.

The boys were drifting back to shore, throwing glances their way, trying to be subtle. One guy—whose build reminded Annie of a Paddle Pop stick with legs—leant toward his friend with the shaggy golden curls and made some comment that caused them both to laugh, and the third guy to leap from his board and attack him. Much splashing and dunking ensued.

Kelly raised one knee, which by some bio-mechanical miracle seemed to enhance the outline of her already ample chest. 'If it *was* a perfect world,' she mused, 'they'd decide that the next set of waves weren't worth waiting for, and choose to paddle across in front of us to show off their tight abs to their best advantage.'

Annie smiled at her friend's self-confidence.

'Then,' she continued, 'they'd come ashore and pretend to be surprised that they'd drifted so far across the beach from where they left their gear. Of course, that would mean they'd be forced to carry their boards back past where we are sitting, giving them the perfect opportunity to show us how easily they can carry such long manly surfboards with their strong manly arms.' Her smile looked dreamy, accentuating the softness of her face.

'A perfect world, Kel? I'm not so sure. If it was a perfect world, we would already be in there with them, playing in the perfect surf, riding the waves with the dolphins and turtles, and no one would need to worry about showing off just to get noticed. The right person would notice straight away, no matter how rat-tailey your hair …' Her voice trailed away as one of the boys turned and stared at her, his frown barely visible under his scruffy fringe. Was his frown grumpy or confused? She could usually tell. Emotions were easy to judge. Usually. Perhaps he was too far away.

He flicked his pale hair out of his eyes and looked back out to sea, saying something to his companions. Their shoulders slumped, but whatever he'd said, they weren't disagreeing. Paddle Pop boy gave a sideways smile and knelt up on his board. The others followed and they started to scull across the breakers. Kelly looked smug. Tight abs tensed in rhythm with the rise and fall of the gentle swell of the waves.

Once they came ashore, the third guy, the one with tidy black hair and skin almost as dark as Annie's own, pointed back up the beach to a clump of trees that were an obvious landmark. The other two looked around, apparently surprised. Annie turned to her friend and blinked. Kelly batted her eyelashes, causing Annie to laugh away the remains of her tired waspishness.

Three surfboards were hefted by three strong sets of arms. Three pairs of board shorts clung to three pairs of muscled thighs. One surfboard dipped dangerously low as it overbalanced but was rescued by a quickly raised foot from the companion behind. If it was a soft-drink ad, they would have been jogging. But then, if it was a soft-drink ad, Annie was certain her bikini would have fit her better.

Also, if it was a soft-drink ad, the guy in the middle with the crazy hair wouldn't have stepped on a clump of kelp containing a dying blue-ringed octopus.

∼

'I'm fine. I don't need an ambulance, this is stupid. Leave me alone.' The guy's husky voice sounded a little bit strained, as if he was short of breath. He was sitting on the beach cradling his left foot and prodding at the red mark where the tiny brown octopus had chomped on him. About the size of Annie's palm, the squashed little sea creature lay twitching on the sand by her feet. It had been all but dead even before it had been trodden on. It had probably washed over from the rock pools around the other side of the point. Already its blue rings were fading to grey, as if it was running out of batteries. A bit late to flash its warning colouration *after* it had been stepped on, poor thing.

'I can't even feel it,' the guy continued. 'I'm fine, I promise. It's barely even bleeding. Cam, you should go and tell Dave not to bother.' Dave—the Paddle Pop guy—had bolted off to call an ambulance, his long legs scattering sand behind him as he'd raced to save his friend.

For a moment, Cam looked unsure of what to do, until Annie caught his eye and shook her head. Then he clamped his hand onto his injured friend's shoulder to prevent him from trying to stand up. 'Lucas, you know we won't take any risks with something like this.'

'Have a drink of water,' Annie offered, handing Lucas her bottle. It was an automatic reaction. Drinking water made you feel better when you were sick, or tired. It was her mother's solution to everything she ever complained about, so it was comforting just to hear the words. 'Have a drink of water' meant that someone knew what to do. 'Have a drink of water' meant that you couldn't possibly be about to see a complete stranger fall down dead on the beach right in front of you. Didn't it?

Preoccupied with staring at his foot, Lucas took the bottle and gulped down a few swallows. Then he frowned, and peered more closely through the clear plastic at the brownish water inside. She'd forgotten about that. He probably wasn't expecting to be offered Nalong River water. Snatching the bottle back and hiding it behind her, Annie tried to look casual.

'Er, thanks. I think,' he mumbled. He glanced at Kelly, who was hovering nearby, fiddling with her necklace and chewing her lower lip, and then looked back at Annie. 'Really, you don't need to stay. I'll be fine. This is all just a precaution. It hardly got me.'

Kelly crouched down to look him in the eye, as if assessing his state of mind. 'I think we're the ones who are supposed to be keeping you from panicking, not the other way around. Perhaps we should move you to the shade while we wait for the paramedics?'

Something flickered in his eyes as he followed Kelly's gaze toward the nearby tree line, and Annie felt his stab of alarm.

'I don't think we're supposed to move him, Kelly. I'm sure it won't take long for the ambos to get here, but do you think you could race home and find a bandage? If octopus bites are anything like snake bites, then we should probably use compression.'

Kelly didn't hesitate, racing for the sandy track that rose between clumpy shrubs and tussock grass, and Lucas watched her go with a look of irritation. It was all starting to get a bit serious, and he clearly didn't find that very comforting, so Annie tried to soothe him with her gaze the way Harry's dad used to do when she was little. He didn't look very soothed. His breath was getting heavier, like he'd been running, and he kept rubbing his lower leg.

'Don't do that,' she admonished, pulling his hand away. His skin felt unnaturally hot, almost electrified. It reminded her of the time she'd grabbed at the wrong strand of wire to climb through a paddock fence. The jolt of electricity had squeezed her muscles even tighter, despite her reflexes trying to snap her hand away. 'Just let it go numb,' she said. 'If you massage it, the poison will only spread faster.'

His eyes widened at that, as if saying it out loud had suddenly made it all real. The look he gave her was fierce, and held a generous dose of shock, but she knew he wasn't angry with her. It felt more like he was primed for a fight he didn't expect to win and yet was committed to anyway. His emotions were an open book to her now. Mostly because she had forgotten to let go of his hand. She dropped it awkwardly and looked away, trying to look calm and patient, which didn't last long. He was scared. More than scared—panicking, and she was helpless to block it out. That surprised her because she'd been practising a lot in the past year and thought she had it under control. She no longer flinched when people got upset and their negative feelings spiked into her. She had learned to block her empathic gift almost reflexively. She'd had to. But as Lucas started to lose all feeling in his left leg, his fear slammed through her defences like a tractor through a spider web. Before long his right leg went numb too and he couldn't move it, and she had to grab hold of his right hand to stop him from slapping and pinching at himself.

After a few more minutes, Paddle Pop Dave returned, gasping for breath after his sprint, and assured them that help was on its way. Practically on his tail, Kelly raced across the sand with a first-aid kit cradled under her arm, panting far more heavily than she had in all the years of PE Annie had shared with her. Full of impatience, Annie watched as first David, then Cam tried to bandage Lucas's foot. Both attempts ended with dangling loops of crumpled bandage interspersed with sections so tight she thought the poor guy's toes were going to pop. Cam dropped the roll as he tried to unwind it to start again.

'Okay, my turn,' she said, snatching the mess away from Cam's trembling fingers. It was full of sand so she shook it out and began to roll it back into some semblance of usefulness. It only took a minute to apply the bandage properly, with even pressure from his toes to above his knee. Dave looked like he wanted to hug her.

Lucas breathed a sigh of grateful relief too. 'Wow,' he said, plucking at the dressing to test the tightness. 'Do you keep your bedroom as meticulously tidy as this?'

'Why are you interested in my bedroom?' No no no no. That was not what she'd meant to say. Now he was blushing. Annie cleared her throat and tried again. 'My bedroom floor still has so much Lego on it I can't make it to the loo during the night without bruises, and I haven't played with Lego since I was nine. I do vacuum occasionally so I have no idea where the Lego keeps coming from. Maybe under my bed. I only know how to do this because my horse ran through a fence last year and copped a gash that ran from below his hock almost down to his fetlock. I had to dress it every day for a month. The trick is to extend the bandage much further than you think you need to and keep the pressure consistent. It also helped that you weren't trying to kick me.'

Sometimes, when she opened her mouth, random babble fell out.

'You have a horse?' Dave asked, craning his neck to squint through the scrub at each car that appeared from around the bend in the road, and scowling at each one that stubbornly refused to be an ambulance.

'Four of them. And a turtle, sixteen chickens, two cats, four cows and a few hundred sheep.'

'Oh.' He squinted at another car, and said nothing else.

So much for a conversation starter. Dave was too busy fretting to really care about the answer to his own question. He stood guard with his arms crossed over his chest, clearly at a loss as to what else to do. Cam wasn't much better, prodding at the octopus with a stick and throwing nervous glances at both his friends. Lucas smiled and lay back as if he wanted to sun bake, and asked Dave what he thought they should buy for dinner, but Annie wasn't fooled by his casual attitude.

Worried, she gave up trying to block him out and *allowed* herself to feel what he felt. Tears welled as his distress overwhelmed her, but she blinked them away before anyone noticed. He wasn't going to die, and he wasn't alone. Kneeling next to him, she took hold of his hand again and looked him right in the eye, ignoring Kelly's raised eyebrows. *I will not leave you alone*, she promised silently. Lucas stared right back at her as if questioning her boldness, and yet he didn't pull away. His fear was sharp and icy and enormous. Too big to hold back, and far too easy for her to classify. Annie couldn't read thoughts, but his fears were so specific, and each one was clearer than words on a page. The heavier his bones became, the more his panic grew as he wrestled with his disobedient muscles, lashing out with every ounce of his strength only to have his efforts smash back at him with terrifying *nothingness*. No movement. Every breath a conflict as dire as Armageddon, and each one harder than the last. He was feeling as if time itself was trying to pull him under, slowing his movements, his breath, his blood, as if it wanted to drag him behind the rest of the world. And if time slowed too much, the ambulance would never arrive …

If only she had a different gift. If only she could talk him into trusting her, the way Harry could, or better still, calm his fears the way Harry's dad had been able to. What was the point of being able to read his emotions if she couldn't soothe them? Still, whatever she was doing seemed to help. She could tell, because the more of his fear she allowed in, the less he seemed to feel. So she swallowed it all, bit by painful bit, and squashed it into a tiny ball inside her chest. He watched her the whole time with eyes the same deep indigo as the warning colouration of the doomed octopus, and she wondered in passing if maybe it meant the same thing.

Within a few minutes they were surrounded by a crowd of well-meaning onlookers offering all sorts of advice. Someone suggested that they move Lucas onto his side to make it easier for him to breathe, and Kelly spread her towel out so they could roll him onto it. Cam gripped him under his shoulders while Dave grabbed his knees, but the moment Annie let go of his hand, his sudden burst of panic sent her reeling.

Lucas convulsed, and then vomited, barely missing Cam's feet.

'Mate. Try harder next time. You missed,' Cam joked, but the look he threw Dave was full of worry.

'Sorry,' Lucas whispered.

'For missing?'

'For the mess.'

Dave pushed Cam aside and then got to work. 'No biggie, Lou. That's the beauty of sand. Look. All buried.'

'Sorry you all had to see that,' Lucas said. His face was very pale.

Kelly gave him her best sparkly laugh. 'Hardly your fault,' she assured him. 'It was probably Annie's revolting river water that caused that.'

Lucas looked up at Annie, like he wanted something from her. Perhaps some reassurance that Kelly was right. There was sweat running down his face.

'Try to relax,' Annie told him as his friends arranged his limbs to make him more comfortable.

'Can't move anything,' he gasped, 'so I can't get much more relaxed than this, can I?'

He was smiling and it must have sounded like a flippant wise-crack to the others, but his glazed eyes kept seeking hers, pleading for a genuine answer as if he knew she'd done something unusual. So Annie took his hand again and drew his panic away … which was when he passed out. The heavy ball of emotion she was holding for him unravelled in an instant and flew out of her mouth with a small sharp cry that thankfully went unnoticed among the swear words Dave was yelling as he tried to get Lucas to wake up. She let go and sat back, letting the sand warm her suddenly chilled fingers. There was nothing else she could do to help him, and she was too drained to even block out the anxiety and dread emanating from everyone else. That was not good. What if he died right there in front of them? What would everyone feel, and how could she possibly defend herself against such strong reactions? Annie had been there before. Feeling her own smothering grief, and then being crushed by someone else's. She glanced around. So many people. If she didn't protect herself from this, she would sink back into that abyss and never come out. She found herself scuttling backward through the sand, away from the sticky web of emotions that swirled faster and deeper than the nearby water currents, and yet she couldn't stop staring at Lucas's pallid face. He'd been so afraid of being alone, and she'd made a promise, even if he hadn't heard her say it. He was surrounded by caring, concerned expressions, but not one of these people understood what he felt. Not like she did.

This time when she took his hand in both of hers, no one looked at her strangely. Like her, they could only watch and wait to see if he would live or die. Nothing could feel stranger or more disturbing than that. No one spoke.

Everyone seemed to be studying the rise and fall of his chest. The way the rhythm slowed. The way it became harder to tell if it was moving at all, even though he was bare-chested. Dave swore again, and Annie noticed a tear rolling down his cheek, accompanied by a bursting bubble of despair and fury that she couldn't shield herself against, so she had to shut her eyes to hold in her own tears. She shifted her grip until she could feel Lucas's pulse with her little finger, and her heart thumped harder as if it could show *his* heart how it was supposed to beat. Strong and fierce, not fluttering like a butterfly newly emerged from its cocoon.

All her attention was focused on the unsteady flow of his blood as she willed his heart to fight the poison. Willing the butterfly to test its wings and fight free from the chrysalis it was trapped in. It had a job to do, a life to live. All it had to do was to fight for it. His pulse fluttered again. One beat, two … three, four, barely there. One wing free, the other dragged behind the ongoing flow of time. The fluttering slowed, and then stopped.

One second. And another. Still nothing.

That happened sometimes, didn't it? Annie had watched lambs being born, the ewe straining and pushing and just as it was time for the final effort, she would stop for a rest. Chicks did the same thing, pecking with soft beaks at hard shells and then the long pause, as if giving up, or deciding whether this life business was really going to be worth all this effort.

Three seconds. Four. Five. *Come on, Lucas.*

Annie bit down on her tongue to stop herself from crying out. This wasn't happening. His pulse would return, he would wake up, and she would feel something from him again. Better to feel his anguish and fear than this complete numbness. Everyone else's emotions beat against her, and her only method of blocking them out was to focus everything she had on feeling for his pulse, but it was gone.

Six seconds, seven …

She bit down harder, tasting blood, wanting to feel something to offset his paralysis, wishing she could use her pain to fight the poison that blocked his.

One fragile wing fluttered against her fingertip. The barest beat.

Annie crushed her tongue with her teeth. *Feel something!* her mind screamed.

Another flutter.

Wake up and feel something, she ordered, wishing she had the authority to command this stranger with the bright eyes and crazy hair who had smiled at her instead of watching where he was walking.

A soft thump, and then another, and with the flow of blood came a surge of warmth into cooling flesh. Warmth and life.

Chapter 2

It felt like such a long time until the anticipated sound of sirens finally cut through the soft crashes of breaking waves. As the ambulance approached, all the bystanders released their anxiety into its care, letting its brash wail take over the job of expressing their alarm at the situation.

Lucas was breathing, but not very regularly.

The paramedics in their navy overalls and pockets stuffed with paraphernalia were brusque and sympathetic as they shooed everyone aside so they could give him extra oxygen. As the blue slowly faded from his skin, they asked Annie for his name and personal details. She looked to Cam, who answered them in a shaky voice. Lucas Gracewood, from Melbourne. Staying with Cam's family with their other friend, Dave. No idea what his blood type is but he definitely has ambulance insurance because they play soccer together and the club makes all the players take out insurance. Then Paddle Pop Dave explained that he had called Cam's mum from the payphone, who in turn would have called Lucas's parents, who were probably already on their way. It would take them a few hours to arrive.

After Lucas was finally stretchered off the beach and loaded into the ambulance, one of the officers headed back to bag the guilty sea creature, while the other one turned to Annie and reassured her that Lucas would be fine so long as there were no additional complications. He said that even in the time they had been working on him there had already been some improvement, which was a very good sign. Instead of trying to explain that she didn't even know him, she thanked the man and then turned to Cam with an apologetic shrug. He didn't seem bothered by the paramedic's assumption. As the sound of sirens began to fade, he turned to Kelly.

'Thanks for hanging around,' he said.

Kelly flashed her dimples right back at him, and Cam's face finally took on the same attentiveness that most guys had around her. He paused for a moment, and then stood a little straighter and cleared his throat.

'I'm Cameron, by the way. I kind of forgot to introduce myself earlier.'

'Kelly Taylor. And this is Sla … Annie.'

Annie cleared her throat in belated warning. They weren't in Nalong. There was no need for anyone to know her nickname here.

'Salami?' Cam raised one dark eyebrow.

The look Annie threw her friend could have cut through a Besser brick, but Kelly glanced away as if she hadn't noticed.

'Annie,' she corrected. 'Annie Langley.'

'Well, thanks, Annie. I know Lucas appreciated having someone to … you know.' He looked down at his bare feet, shuffling them on the scorching car park bitumen.

She shoved Kelly over a bit so Cam could share the patch of shade they were standing on. It was easier than acknowledging what it was he was thanking her for. The last ten minutes had been pretty surreal, and now she felt hideously embarrassed at the fact that she had barged her way in so intimately. How could she possibly explain that her empathic gift had left her no choice?

Kelly saved the awkward moment as easily as she did everything else. 'Do you need a lift to the hospital? My place is right across the road. Vicky … my dad's, ah … girlfriend, would be happy to drive you, I'm sure.'

'You live in Apollo Bay? Not just here for a holiday?' Cam asked.

Kelly's face fell. She hadn't quite come to terms with the answer to that particular question. 'I don't live here yet. I mean, Dad wants us to move in with her and her daughter, Sarah, but our other place hasn't sold.'

Dave returned then, lugging an Esky and a couple of bags up the beach to where they were standing. Annie hadn't even noticed when he'd left. Cam jumped to help him, apologising for leaving him to carry it all on his own. As soon as he was relieved of his burdens, Dave sat down on the Esky, stretching his long legs out and resting his head in his hands. His hair, almost as pale as Lucas's, was sweat-plastered to his cheek.

'Cam, I told your mum we'd find our own way back to town. I thought it would be better if she went straight to the hospital. Someone should be there with him. I didn't think about the boards, though. How are we going to carry three of them?'

Cam turned back to Kelly. 'Could we leave them at your place? Just till tomorrow?'

'Of course,' she replied, 'and we'll see about a lift, too.'

⌒

'Cam, is that you? Surf's up. Get me out of here. Talk to your mum, will you?'

Two hours after being rushed to hospital, Lucas was standing by the window of the ward, trying to look over the tops of the trees and houses at the ocean beyond. From where she was skulking in the doorway, Annie could see plenty of water, but not the beach. There was no way he'd be able to assess the quality of surf from the limited view he had. He was leaning against the glass looking a bit unsteady, and yet the simple fact that he was standing up at all helped her chest to unclench the ball of fear she was still minding for him. Cam must have felt much the same because he pushed past her to enter the room, straightening his shoulders. Lucas still didn't tear his gaze away from the window.

'They're keeping you in overnight. As they should, Lou. Do you really think my mum would be able to face yours if she talked them into letting you out?' Cam threw a t-shirt onto the end of the bed, presumably one that Lucas had left on the beach. At least he would be able to get out of the stupid hospital gown. Pity, really, because the view from the back, with those badly done up cotton ties, was intriguing. 'No surf for you today, but we've got your back,' Cam said with a grin. 'You went to a lot of trouble to get their attention so we thought we'd better introduce you to the girls you wanted to talk to earlier. This is Annie, and Kelly.'

Lucas spun around, gripped the back of the cotton robe a bit tighter and tangled himself in the drip line that connected his hand to the silver pole he had forgotten about. The plastic bag of fluid swung around in protest, which he ignored because he was too busy staring at the strangers lingering uncomfortably in the doorway. At least, Annie felt uncomfortable. Kelly looked quite at ease with the fact that she had talked her way into coming in to see him once Sarah, her older sis-ter-to-be, had graciously dropped them at the front of the hospital. Annie had followed her in, hoping that if she stayed quiet enough, no one would notice her.

Kelly stepped over to him and grabbed the bag of fluid to stop it swinging. She had thrown on a pair of denim shorts and a loose translucent white shirt that was knotted at her waist. Her bright blue bikini top showed through from underneath. Back in the car, Cam had noticed it. Kelly had noticed him noticing and had smiled. But now as she helped untangle the drip line, Lucas hardly even glanced at her, and Annie felt a small spike of annoyance from her friend.

'You look much better,' Kelly told him with one of her sweetest smiles. It was the smile that usually got her out of the worst sort of trouble. That same smile had once caused a full-on brawl between two of the hottest guys at school, and even then she hadn't really comprehended just how powerful it was. When Annie had sat her down and tried to explain it to her, Kelly hadn't believed her because Annie couldn't reveal that she knew what people were really feeling. Kelly's smile made guys feel valiant. Poor Lucas must have still been partially numb in some way though, because he just turned back to stare out the window again.

'I keep trying to tell you, I'm fine. The doctor said the octopus mustn't have had much toxin left in its bite because the effects didn't last long at all. By the time I arrived here I was breathing fine and my arms and legs were tingly again. They didn't even really believe that I had actually been paralysed until they questioned the ambos again. None of them seem very concerned. I'm sure if I argue enough they'll let me go.'

Annie gripped the doorframe. Should she tell someone that his heart *had stopped*? And yet here he was, shuffling his bare feet back to the window, stretching up to catch a glimpse of the breakers, blue eyes full of life and longing.

'Your mum is on her way,' Dave reminded him. 'Cam's right, she won't be too happy if anyone cuts any corners. Wait and talk to her if you want out.'

Lucas grunted. 'I can't believe she's driving all the way down from Melbourne. She'd better not try to make me come home. We have two more days and I fully intend to spend them in the water.'

Dave laid a hand on his shoulder. He topped Lucas's height by a full head—and Lucas wasn't exactly short. The fact that Dave was so thin and lanky made him look even taller somehow, as if his bones had stretched and were still waiting for his muscles and skin to catch up. It was his open friendliness that really caught Annie's attention though. Dave's whole demeanour screamed of honesty and loyalty. He looked like the sort of friend who would do anything for you without a second thought. He would probably have carried Lucas all the way to the hospital in his arms if he'd had to. She was surprised he hadn't tried to suck the poison right out of his foot.

'They won't let you surf for a while, Lucas. Just in case. Sorry.' Poor Dave looked miserable at having to tell him.

A spike of angry rebellion flashed from his friend. Apparently, Lucas was as obsessed with being in the water as Annie was with staying away from it. Where had her emotional shield gone? She wasn't even touching him.

'Maybe we can do something else?' Cam suggested, tilting his head not so subtly at Kelly, clearly hoping he would be happy to let her distract him from the surf.

Blue eyes met Annie's for the briefest of moments before Lucas glanced away toward the window again. 'Fine,' he acceded, sounding more irritable than Annie knew he actually felt. 'Just don't let them take me back to Melbourne early.'

It turned out that Lucas only managed to talk his mum out of taking him home when Cam's mum offered to let her and his sister stay with them. And once again, Kelly managed to charm her way into their plans, dragging Annie along like a faithful sidekick to the beach the following day. Annie was a bit grumpy about it, because she *liked* the three guys and found herself getting caught up in Kelly's enthusiasm. None of them were for her. She knew that. But what if she was wrong? Getting all flirty was not a good idea.

Luckily, things weren't too awkward when they met up, because there were more people. It was the Monday before a public holiday, and when Kelly had realised that Sarah wasn't working, she'd invited her along. Both she and Kelly had been good about spending time getting to know each other the way their respective parents clearly hoped, but so far it had all felt a bit … staged. The beach was home to Sarah though, and she seemed comfortable hanging out there.

The other newcomer was Lucas's sister, Lily. At just fourteen years old, she had everyone eating from the palm of her hand. She had shoulder-length hair the colour of polished pearl, blue eyes like her brother's, and such a precocious sense of humour that somehow, within the first ten minutes of meeting her, everyone felt united in defending themselves from her falsely innocent teasing.

Annie spluttered at the girl's offhand question. 'Just because we come from the country doesn't mean we don't know how to swim,' she answered. Aghast at the completely naïve look on Lily's face, she almost missed the amused looks the boys threw her. So, Lily was faking her ignorance.

'It's okay if the ocean frightens you,' Lily said. 'It's a pretty dangerous place. My brother nearly *died* yesterday when that octopus tried to strangle him.'

'Strangle?'

Lily wasn't listening because she'd taken the opportunity to nick her brother's surfboard and was waddling down the beach with it balanced badly under one arm.

'Hey, I never said you could use it!' he cried, getting up to chase after her. Both Dave and Cam stepped in front of him, arms crossed, blocking his path to the water. Behind them, Lily laughed and launched herself straight into the icy waves, lying on the board and squealing as the first chilling breaker engulfed her.

'If you get so much as a big toe wet, I'm dobbing!' she called back at him.

He swore at her with his mouth mostly shut.

'Dave, you should come in. Check out this next set,' she taunted, paddling out to sea.

Two heads turned to look wistfully over shoulders as both Cam and David appraised the surf. It was clean, and swelling nicely.

'Go. Just go,' Lucas grumbled, shoving at them. 'I can't stand having you both sulking. Just don't complain if I eat all the snacks. And promise me we can come back at dawn tomorrow.'

The doctor had given Lucas a strict twenty-four-hour ban on swimming when he'd released him that morning. Lily had explained that if he broke it, their mum would pack him off home in an instant—with some additional undesirable repercussions thrown in. Lucas sighed as Sarah grabbed her own board and headed for the water. Kelly also stood and began to tie her hair back, shucking off her shorts as she prepared to follow. That was too much for his poor friends. No way were they going to stand around on the beach while the three girls got all the good waves.

The backlash of envy Annie expected to feel from the abandoned invalid never came. Instead, all she felt from him was … wariness?

Oh. Right. He was stuck with just her to talk to and it was awkward. After all, what was he supposed to say to the girl who had intruded so brazenly at a time when he could hardly breathe, let alone move away? She had held his hand and stared him in the face for a good ten minutes. It had felt like the right thing to do at the time—in fact the only thing to do—but she had no clue as to how he felt about her interference.

To make herself look casual and content, she rummaged through her bag for her book and opened it to a random page, covering her legs with the long skirt she'd remembered to wear to keep the flies off.

At least thirty seconds passed before he even moved a muscle.

'Are you really afraid of the ocean?' he eventually asked in his husky voice, coming to sit beside her on Kelly's towel. 'You don't seem the type to be easily frightened.'

Annie licked her lips and peered at him out of the corner of her eye. He wasn't looking at her, but was staring out to sea. His wavy hair stuck out in the breeze, glowing golden brown with summer reflection. Melbourne boy. Never even heard of Nalong. Not for her. Surely not for her.

'I'm not frightened. I love swimming. My dad taught me to surf a few years ago, before he died.' Pain and grief welled, as usual, and as usual she wrapped it up in a blanket of numbness and shielded it, the same way she did with other people's emotions. Lucas opened his mouth to speak, but she didn't want to hear it. She didn't want to hear that he was sorry. What a silly thing to say. 'The beach just reminds me of him, I guess. It's not as much fun as I remember,' she explained, cutting him off.

'That's terrible.'

She rolled her eyes and looked back down at her book. She wasn't fishing for pity; she just didn't want him to think she was afraid.

'I mean, it's terrible that you don't enjoy the beach anymore just because it reminds you of fun times you had with your dad.'

She swung around and glared at him.

He glared right back. Pale blue eyes—brighter now that he wasn't dying—locked onto hers in blatant challenge, and although she tried to find the feeling of righteous outrage she was entitled to, it had fled into hiding somewhere. Having him look at her like that just reminded her of the day before, when his panic had almost pulled them both under. It was difficult to remember she could breathe, as she relived what Lucas had felt. No air. No feeling. Everything numb. Fear like needles spiking through her.

'You're doing it again,' he whispered, searching her face.

He knew. Somehow, he knew what she'd done. How? No one had ever seemed to notice anything before. Then again, yesterday's trick was something new. She hadn't just shared his emotions, she'd lifted them away from him. A March fly bit her on the elbow, breaking the spell as she smacked at it.

'Sorry. I couldn't help … I mean, I never meant to—'

'Thank you.' He waved another fly away. 'I don't know exactly what you did, but whatever it was … it helped.'

Not for her. He was not for her.

'I didn't do anything,' she lied. 'You really were very lucky, you know. You were bitten by one of the most dangerous creatures on the planet.'

'Maybe it was the manky water from your bottle that saved me.' The smile he gave made her pulse go all wiggly. It spoke of shared secrets and whispered promises.

'Perhaps it was,' she said with a laugh, wondering what her neighbour Harry would say to that. Who knew? Maybe Lucas was right. A second later, she realised what she'd said, and was startled that she had even jokingly hinted at the idea that the water could be anything interesting at all. This boy was not for her. 'Do you go back to school on Wednesday?' she asked, changing the subject.

'Yeah, unless I can convince Mum that I should stay home just in case. It might be worth a shot.' Idly, he brushed another fly from her arm. His fingers felt warm, his touch vibrant.

Annie shook her head and grinned at him. 'You can't have it both ways, Lucas. You can't spend the weekend convincing her that you're well enough to surf and then pull a sickie in time for school. Besides, you're in Year 12, right? Exams must be getting pretty close. After that, you can surf all you want.'

With his elbows resting on his knees, he fiddled with a shell he had picked up, following its blue and brown spiral pattern with his fingertip. 'Will you come back here? Over summer?' he asked, staring at the shell as if it was the most intriguing thing in the world and he really couldn't care less if she even answered the question or not. His emotions couldn't lie though. There was a nervous anticipation that she was struggling to block out. So unfair. He was almost flirting. Almost. But that was okay, wasn't it?

'No,' she said firmly, to herself as much as to him. 'I'm staying in Nalong over summer.' And forever more, she added silently. She had a duty there, and had been away for too long already. Time for a reality check. She could dream all she wanted about flirting with boys, but she didn't have to be stupid about it. Summer romances were not for her.

'Damn stupid flies!' he snarled, tossing the shell away and waving his hands about aggressively. That was how she knew she had shut him down effectively. She had done well. Used the right tone of voice. Closed. Final. No veiled hints that there was any hope whatsoever of seeing each other again. No one likes to be rejected, even in such a subtle way. That was why he was irritable. Or was it?

The others returned eventually, shaking water and sand all over them and babbling about how spectacularly Dave got wiped out. As they recounted each and every wave they'd caught in guilty detail, Annie sat back and studied the envious set of Lucas's shoulders. He hung on every word, glancing between his friends and the ocean, but every now and then his hand would flick out and swipe a March fly out of the air. Before it could land on her.

⌒

Crisp ocean gusts sent summer promises through the gloom as Annie crept out at dawn on Tuesday morning. She had to find out, and there was no time to be subtle about it because she was due to return home that afternoon. Even if she hadn't needed to be back for school the next day, she still couldn't have stayed longer. Her ties to home were not negotiable. She was already starting to feel like her bones were being pulled down into the ancient earth. Another couple of days away and she knew the nausea would start to kick in. There was no choice. She had to go home as planned.

Stealthy as a kelpie with a bone to hide, Annie reached her hand back through the bedroom window and wound it shut as much as she could, her shoulders relaxing when Kelly continued to snore on the other side of the room. After sharing a room with her, she'd been confident that her friend slept deeply enough for her to make a clean escape, yet it was still nerve-racking. She'd left a scribbled note to let Kelly know where she'd gone, telling her that she'd unsuccessfully tried to wake her to come along. Some things were important enough to lie about, even to your best friend.

A straggly rose bush tried to prevent her from leaving. She unhooked it from her shorts with finicky precision and yet still not enough patience. The world was just beginning to lighten to a sleepy glow, not giving quite enough visibility to avoid tripping over the edge of the garden bed, but somehow she managed to save herself from sprawling face-first into the rhododendrons. Finally, she found her way out of the narrow strip of jungle that ran along the side of the house and stepped confidently out onto the footpath.

'I thought you might—'

'Aaaagh!'

'Sssh. Do you want to wake up the whole street?'

The voice came again out of nowhere. Peering into the shadows, Annie just made out the shape of someone carrying a surfboard under one arm and a towel over her shoulder. It was Sarah, and she was laughing.

'Where's Kelly? Isn't she coming?' she asked.

'Coming where?' Annie asked. As if it wasn't obvious.

'She won't be happy if she finds out we left her behind. You'd better go and get her. You can go back in through the house though. It'll be easier than the way you came out.'

'Are you kidding? What if—'

'They won't care. I often surf at dawn. You really know nothing about life on the beach, do you? I left a note to say I'm taking you both, but if you don't hurry I'm going without you. I work two jobs, Annie. I don't get many days off and I'm not wasting this one.'

'You left a note? How did you know—'

She arched an eyebrow and hitched her board. 'Oh, come on, I wasn't born yesterday. They leave this morning. This is our last chance to see them. I don't know about you, but I have a phone number I need to get. See? I even brought a Texta. A good one that won't wash off in the surf.'

Annie's bleary eyes blinked at her in confusion. Sarah had just finished her first year of uni with great results, and then announced that she was dropping out because economics was too boring. To Annie she seemed so … worldly. Far too mature and confident to be interested in flirting with high school guys. Of course, they would only be a year or two younger than Sarah, and she'd been chatting a lot to Paddle Pop Dave the previous day. Annie should have paid more attention.

Putting her board down with a sigh, Sarah took Annie by the shoulders and gave her a gentle shove toward the front door of her house. 'Go and get Kelly. And a towel. And a jumper. You're freezing. The sun won't be warm enough for a while yet, and if you swim you'll be even colder. Go, Annie. And try to hurry a bit, please? We're wasting good waves.'

Was Sarah this bossy to everyone? She sounded like Harry's mum used to.

Five minutes later, Kelly was bouncing ahead of them down the footpath, tripping over her thongs in her enthusiasm to stalk their three new acquaintances. How was Annie supposed to find out what she needed to with Kelly and Sarah hanging around? She needed to talk to Lucas alone, somehow.

The guys were already out in the water by the time they arrived, shivering in the morning breeze. The sunrise was glorious, stretching orange streaks up over the point and glittering its way across the water toward them. The fresh light begged to be fully appreciated, so Annie only hesitated briefly before stripping down to her bathers and joining the others for a quick swim. Perhaps it was her craving for Eden games that motivated her, because her tiredness faded and all she wanted to do was to get into the water and play. Icy waves washed away her nausea and lethargy and most of her shakiness as she left Kelly squealing in the shallows. Yearning to be submersed, she dove in as soon as it was deep enough, knowing full well that it wasn't the right type of water she so desperately needed. Hoping that it would be close enough. It was. For now. Deliciously freezing, all her muscles seized up and every nerve-ending screamed in sensory overload. A wave threw her backward with indifferent violence, tugging her loose hair in twenty different directions. She found the sand beneath her feet and came up spluttering and laughing. Backlit by the pinkish sky, she saw the next wave just in time to duck under it the way her dad had taught her. Laughter morphed to tears and then back to laughter as a sudden flood of memories and conflicting emotions tugged at her even more forcefully than the waves did. He had held her tightly around the waist, lifting her safely above the water when she was afraid, and later, he'd held her hand as she began to gain confidence.

'*The waves might smash you down,*' her dad had told her, '*but your feet will always be attached to the ends of your legs, and you can use them to feel for the sand. As soon as you know where the ground is, all you need to do is push it away.*'

Why had they lost him? Why? Harry had once told her they were cursed. Doomed to die young, so that the secret would be easier to keep. Just two Cherub lines, small families, short lives. The fewer people who knew about Eden, the easier it would be to keep it safe. Cherubim had children at a young age, and then once an heir was born, it was unusual to have any more. Harry's parents had both passed away when he was nine years old, leaving him to be raised by his great-uncle on the farm next to Annie's. She had only been seven when they died. Just old enough to remember his dad, Geoff, singing songs to her in his deep voice, soothing her with eyes like the night sky. It had been less than two years since her own dad had died, and already she'd begun to lose the sharpness of her memories of him. In another few years, what would she be left with?

Over and over, Annie let the waves throw her around, tumbling her any which way they liked, scrambling each time to use her feet to find the sand and push. She would not be cursed. She would fight. No matter how many times the waves crashed over her, she would fight. She had no intention of dying young. There was a way to beat the system.

All she had to do was to make certain she didn't have an heir. Only, to do that, first she had to find out who it was she was supposed to be producing an heir with, and stay the hell away from him.

'Do you realise how far out you are?' a voice called from somewhere to her left. Lucas was lying on his surfboard, paddling toward her. Her heart leapt and sank at the same time, which hurt a lot. It was just a coincidence. So what if he came to say hello? It didn't mean anything.

'The waves are getting bigger, I think. Are you sure you're okay out here?'

He was just being polite. He couldn't possibly be the one.

'Want a lift?' he asked, facing into the next wave so that a heavy spray washed over him. He flicked his fringe out of his face with a jauntiness that dared the ocean to try harder. He was wearing a wetsuit that fit him very, very nicely.

Annie pursed her lips. *Did* she want a lift?

No. Bad idea. What if he really was The One?

Yes, she did, because he was gorgeous.

Yes, she did, because she had told herself over and over that she would not tie herself to some boy just because they were supernaturally destined to be bonded together. She could jump on anyone's surfboard if she felt like it. She had absolutely no intention of marrying young, having a baby, then dying because she'd fulfilled her purpose.

She wasn't just breeding stock.

She refused to be cursed.

'Are you worried about my safety?' she asked lightly, trying to sound like she was teasing.

'No, but your lips have turned blue and I'd hate for you to freeze just to prove that you aren't scared of the ocean.'

She climbed on board, as nimbly as she used to when it was her dad giving her a hand up. Lucas seemed surprised that she was able to do it without tipping them over. She knelt on the front of the board while he sat on the back, letting the waves drift them back toward the shore. Of course, now that she was up out of the water, the wind bit at her like it wanted to round her up and herd her back to Nalong where she belonged. The sun had fully risen now, promising a perfect balmy day ahead, although the ocean breeze was coming straight out of Antarctica. Belatedly she noticed that Kelly had already left the water—or perhaps she hadn't actually got any farther than the freezing shallows. She was huddled in her towel watching them with an expression full of curious anticipation. As soon as they got near the sandbank, Annie jumped off and held the board steady.

'You don't need to get out. Make the most of the time you have left,' she suggested, trying not to let him see how badly her teeth were chattering.

'If I'm really going to make the most of the time I have left, I'm going to need to get out,' he corrected, peeling off his ankle strap.

Ah, crap. Now he really was flirting. How awkward. And wonderful. But bad. Definitely bad. No, not bad. It was exactly what she'd wanted. She needed to talk to him alone and sort this out once and for all.

'In that case,' she managed to say calmly, 'maybe we should go for a walk.'

Waiting on the sand, Kelly was holding up Annie's towel in open invitation as they waded out of the shallows with giant heavy steps. Lucas got to her first and placed his board on the sand beside her as gently as if it was a sleeping baby.

'Can you mind this? Annie and I are going for a short walk.'

Kelly's head bent to peer around him as she sought Annie's face. Her pretty brown eyes were packed so full of silent questions they looked ready to explode. 'Sure,' she said, handing Annie her towel.

'Thanks, we won't be long.' He walked back down to the shoreline where the sand was firm, expecting Annie to follow.

The towel was rough and nicely distracting until Annie finished drying off, and then there was no excuse to delay further. Suddenly she felt like she was being led to some unknown lair by the Pied Piper. She *wanted* to go. And she needed to, she had no choice, but where would it lead? Still, maybe she was wrong about him. Maybe this was what it always felt like when boys flirted a little. After all, she'd never planned to spend her entire life avoiding boys altogether.

When Lucas realised how far behind she was lagging, he turned, walking backward as he unzipped his wetsuit and peeled his arms out of the sleeves. He was no weedy teenager waiting to grow into his bones. His sculpted arms made it obvious that he spent most of his time nowhere near a computer screen or telly. Annie let out a little involuntary whimper, then her feet started moving and she meekly followed them.

'Please watch where you're walking,' she begged. 'I thought you would have learned your lesson after the other day.'

Startled by the reminder, he tripped over the clump of kelp he had been about to step on, then stopped and waited for her to catch up.

'How are you feeling, by the way?' she asked, genuinely curious.

'Perfect. Completely back to normal. Everyone fusses too much.'

'Fusses too much?' She leant in to whisper, just in case the fickle ocean breeze carried her words where they shouldn't go. 'Are you aware that your heart stopped beating for a few seconds?'

His face drained of colour. 'Are you sure? I mean, if it was just for a few seconds, then maybe you were mistaken.'

Annie said nothing.

'Please don't tell anyone. I'm perfectly fine now, I promise. Actually, I feel great. Full of energy. The ocean must do me good. All this swimming seems to have even fixed my dodgy ankle.' He gave a wry smile. 'Came out of a bad tackle in our last soccer game for the season and it's been aching ever since—until now.'

Hmm. Good, but … hmm.

'Here,' she said, handing him the towel. 'Speaking of fussing, you should probably dry off a bit. I wouldn't want to risk your sister's wrath if I brought you back looking as blue as a Smurf.'

'Surfer Smurf was always my favourite,' he said, drying his arms and shoulders and then rubbing the towel through his hair.

'Yeah, well, I'd advise you to stay clear of blue things for a while,' she suggested.

'Like the ocean? No way. Wild horses couldn't keep me away from it.' He draped the towel back around her shoulders like she was a small child, pausing for a second as if he was about to gather her into his arms to warm her up. Maybe she should have listened to Sarah and brought a jumper. Deftly, she side-stepped him and kept walking, clutching the towel under her chin with one hand. She didn't know what to say to him. Her dad had loved the beach too, but they'd hardly ever managed to visit it.

'It was good to see you swimming this morning,' Lucas said, walking close to the edge of the water.

Her feet suddenly became very interesting. 'You were right. What you said yesterday. Dad would be pretty annoyed at me if he found out I'd been sulking.'

'I don't think sulking is—wait, your dad *would* be annoyed at you?'

There was a defiant glint in her eyes as she clarified. 'He's dead, but I'll see him again eventually, and if he finds out I wasted most of this trip sitting on the sand when I could have been swimming ...'

'Sorry, I didn't mean ... of course you'll see him again ...' The bluish tinge in his cheeks changed to pink.

'My mum keeps talking about him as if he's just gone away for a short trip. Like she expects to see him again any day. I guess her confidence has rubbed off a bit.'

They walked on in silence for a while, letting the feeble morning sun think it was warming them up.

'Are you okay, Annie? You seem kind of tired.'

Looking down, she noticed his fingers were twitching. She groaned. This would all have been so much simpler if she'd had no idea what was probably happening. She was reading way too much into every word, every gesture. It was making her crazy.

'I'm exhausted,' she admitted. 'Maybe because I woke at dawn,' she continued with slightly less honesty.

'Why did you?' he fished. She refused to answer. A seagull skimmed the water beside them, kindly giving them both something to pretend to look at. He cleared his throat. 'Anyway, don't you farm types always wake at the crack of dawn?' he asked instead, to ease the awkward moment.

'Not when we're on holidays.' A sneaky wave crept up from behind, bathing their ankles in icy bubbles.

Lucas stared straight ahead for a few moments. 'You leave today too.' It was a statement, not a question. Annie gave a single firm nod. He stopped walking. 'And it's highly unlikely that we'll ever see each other again.'

Now how exactly was she supposed to respond to that? Although his voice sounded composed, a symphony of conflicting emotions radiated from him, making it hard for her to focus. He felt nervous, and self-conscious, and frustrated, confused. The most prominent emotion, however, was edginess, a yearning that he was fighting hard to suppress. So she helped him. It would have been easier if she'd been brave enough to touch him, but that would have been counter-productive. Concentrating hard, she started to gather his emotions together like they were lost lambs, so that she could deal with them safely in private later, but she was too clumsy—and far too slow. While his piercing eyes searched for answers, she could only reflect back the emotions she was stealing from him. She was caught completely off-guard as her tactics backfired and he stepped forward, pulled her gently toward him with his hands deliciously burning on her neck, and kissed her.

Stunned sweetness answered the yearning for closeness and healing that they both felt, and Annie's human body double-crossed every reasoned thought in her head. Heat blossomed in her chest, spreading out through her limbs and making her skin tingle as a myriad of tiny insect bites and minor bruises disappeared. He was the whole world. Timeless and perfect and thrilling and terrifying … He was a whole new part of her, just begging to be explored. He was what she had been hunting for. Lucas Gracewood was her Guardian, assigned to protect her from all physical harm. Beyond a shadow of a doubt, it was him. Her feet had found the sand. All she had to do now was push. And it was the hardest thing she had ever done.

'Stop!' she cried, not having to feign her distress as she shoved him away. Despite her resolve, her push felt rather feeble, yet he staggered back dizzily and almost fell. 'Stay away from me. I don't want this,' she begged. Frantically she tried to take away his swirling emotions, but everything she took, she also felt, making it almost impossible to do what she had to do. She did it anyway. She was *not* breeding stock. She wanted a good long life of freedom, with no one compelling her to do anything. Some of her destiny was unavoidable, but not all.

Sand flicked around as she turned and ran back up the beach to where Kelly was waiting. She refused to look back but she could see Cam coming in from the water, trying to look casual. It was obvious that he had witnessed the awful scene, and she hoped he'd know what to say to his friend because what she'd just done to him was tearing her apart.

'I'm going back to the house,' she gasped to Kelly as she gathered up her clothes and shoes. Shaking sand from her shorts, she rummaged around in the pockets until she found what she had hoped she wouldn't need. She handed her friend a plain lumpy envelope, silently begging that her grandmother's trick would work. 'Could you please give this to Cam? Tell him not open it, and not to give it to Lucas unless he asks for it.' It was a long shot, but it was all she had to offer. Lucas wasn't getting anything else from her. Not ever.

'Wait, Slaps, hang on. Did I just see him try to kiss you?'

Annie was in no mood to talk about it. Choking on the scrunched-up mess of stolen and stymied emotions that were lodged in her throat, she ran away just as her tears smashed their way through her fragile state of mind.

Chapter 3

Lucas ran his fingertip along the open zipper of his wetsuit, using its plastic teeth to offset the numbness he felt. He watched Dave wave his decorated arm around in triumph and do a little victory dance that kicked sand up everywhere. A fair amount of it flicked straight into Lucas's face where he sat, but he didn't complain.

Dave's forearm was adorned with a series of giant numbers in thick black marker that ran from wrist to elbow. Lucas visualised him showing off Sarah's phone number to everyone in school the next day and almost smiled. Almost.

Across the street, Kelly and Sarah were walking away, chatting as they headed home. Kelly glanced back at them, causing Dave to stumble to a sudden halt and try to look casual. The girls were still close enough that Lucas could see Kelly smile as she said something to her soon-to-be sister. She'd clearly caught him celebrating. Cam cracked up laughing.

'Laugh all you like,' Dave gloated. 'I don't see either of you two sporting a new tattoo. How long do you think I should wait before I call her?'

'Oh, I dunno,' Cam said, grinning as he shook water out of his ear. 'You only got a phone number. Lucas already got the smoochies.' His light voice was full of teasing, and yet there was a subtle wariness too. He sounded concerned, and Lucas knew he was fishing for some sort of reaction from him. He had none to give. His dizziness had faded now, but he still felt … disconnected. It was as if he was watching a movie and none of it felt real. None of it mattered.

Dave's eyebrows rose to his hairline. 'Wait, Lucas? He kissed Kelly? I don't believe you. No way, she—'

'Not Kelly,' Cam replied. His eyes were still on Lucas, watching him, waiting for an explanation.

'Annie? Are you kidding? She's *way* out of our league. I mean, she was polite and all, but she hardly said two words to anyone yesterday. I assumed she was, well, off the market …'

Lucas groaned and buried his face in his towel. What he'd done was inexcusable. Dave was right. Annie probably had a boyfriend already. How was it that his friends had automatically seen that and he hadn't? He hadn't even thought to ask her. No wonder she'd been so angry. What the hell had he thought was going to happen when he pounced on her like that? Looking back now, he began to feel mortified by his actions. It had seemed so natural at the time. He'd felt so hungry for her … and the thought of never seeing her again … and now Dave was sporting Sarah's phone number on his arm. The probability of them meeting any of the girls again was still slim, but not nearly as impossible as it had seemed half an hour ago. And now, whether she had a boyfriend or not, he'd well and truly blown his chances.

'Actually kissed her?' Dave asked. 'Are you sure?'

Lucas jerked his head up to glare at his friend. What sort of a question was that? But Dave was asking Cam, not him.

'I'm right here, you know,' Lucas objected.

'Sorry, Lou, it's just that you normally … I mean, you never …'

Cam laid a hand on Dave's wrist to silence him and then sat down on the sand to look Lucas in the eye. 'What Dave's trying to say is that, well …' he scratched his head, 'to be blunt, you're usually, kind of … all talk and no action. When you said the other day that you wanted to surf this side of the point, we wondered why until we noticed you watching those girls. Since then you've been, well, all action and no talk. Surprisingly, I find myself missing the talking. You never said a thing about Annie, and yet you could barely tear your eyes away from her yesterday. I noticed it, even if Dave here was a bit distracted. I was rapt when you plucked up the guts to speak to her this morning, although I never expected you to … She didn't react so well, I take it?'

'Do you blame her? What was I thinking, Cam?'

'I have no idea, because you haven't been *talking* to me. She's certainly got you in a spin. You really like her?'

'I guess, I mean, she's …' He took a deep breath and swallowed hard.

'Yeah. She is. No question,' Cam agreed.

'But then when I try to talk to her, I …' His friends leant in a little closer, with puppy dog looks on their faces. 'When I talk to her I feel nothing. Like I couldn't care less. But I know I do, and so it's very confusing. I can't really explain it.'

'Oh.' Dave looked disappointed. 'Then why did you kiss her?'

Lucas closed his eyes. He'd kissed her because he'd needed to. He could still feel her presence, as if she was sitting right next to him. She was like a magnet, pulling at him, calling to him, which was a lie. She'd run away, and was angry with him. He lifted his head toward where he knew she really was. Back at Sarah's house, probably letting her friends cheer her up by making cruel jokes about him over breakfast.

'Don't regret kissing her, man,' Cam protested. 'Even just one good moment with a girl is better than a lifetime of regret. Life's too short. Take a chance, I reckon, and if she says no, well, you've just seen the worst that can happen. So what?'

Lucas and Dave stared at him.

'All right, so just 'cause I'm useless at following my own advice, it doesn't mean the philosophy doesn't hold,' Cam clarified.

'Yeah, but I didn't really give her a chance to say no.'

An awkward moment passed.

'Oh, mate.' Cam shook his head. 'Not cool.'

His friends were scowling at him, and he had no excuses to offer them. How had he misjudged things so badly? She'd seemed … well, that was the problem right there. Although she'd *seemed* to be enjoying his attention, he barely knew her. What right did he have to assume anything? He wasn't *that* sort of a guy. Was he?

'No,' Dave said, crossing his arms.

'No what?' Lucas asked.

'No, you shouldn't follow them home to try to apologise. You messed up, and I guarantee she would prefer it if you just left her alone.'

'She told me to stay away from her,' Lucas admitted, staring at nothing.

'Then maybe you should listen to what she wants,' Cam agreed, tucking something small into his towel before rolling it up to shove into the bag they were all sharing. Something about it snagged Lucas's attention. It was intriguing, but Dave distracted him before he could ask about it.

'So then how long do I have to wait before I can call Sarah?' Dave asked again, grinning at the numbers scrawled across his wrist. Cam groaned and threw a wet towel at his head. It was going to be a very long trip home.

Chapter 4

The current tugged at Annie's t-shirt half-heartedly. Usually by the start of summer, the spring rains would have swollen the river at least up as far as the giant tree root, but today she had to settle for clinging to the slippery rock near the fallen gumtree. She closed her eyes and let the song of the river soothe her jangled nerves. There were words folded into the music that danced right on the edge of her senses. Every now and again she felt she could understand some of them. They spoke of birth and growth, of deep mountain roots and melting ice crystals. They echoed the cry that stars made when they were born. Words like that could weave galaxies together and solve the mysteries of time, if only she could catch and claim them. Easier to catch a single drop of water as it flowed past in the current.

On the other side of the riverbank, a tired wattle tree dripped its spent blossoms, showering the surface of the water with tiny yellow pompom boats. Life flowed all around: singing, flying, swimming, burrowing, nesting, brooding, feeding. Moving. Always moving. Upstream a few metres, Harry had a thick piece of rope wrapped around his hand. The other end had been tied to a tree up near the bend, so that it stretched out along the centre of the river course, holding him in place as he floated, relaxed, on his back. It was one of their favourite sections of the Nalong River where it flowed through the state park south-west of Annie's farm. The river was quiet and slow here, as if it had worked hard to make it southward through Harry's farm and then Annie's, and needed a bit of a snooze before turning east to head into town.

It had only been a few days since Annie had returned from the beach, and already she was restless. Her mum could see it. She knew she was itching to cross the Skin of the World, but she still had two weeks of school left before she could escape to Eden. Maybe she should drop out like Harry had, and help more on the farm. It wasn't like there was really any point in finishing school. No matter how much she dreamed of having a normal life, she was doomed to stay in Nalong. Alone, probably, now that she'd pushed her Guardian away.

That was what she'd wanted though, wasn't it? To be left alone to choose her own partner. How would that even play out? What would happen if she decided to marry someone other than her Guardian, or not marry at all? Times were changing, but she wasn't confident she'd be allowed to change with them. She wished her grandmother was still around to talk to. It wasn't like she could approach her mum with the idea that she might not want to be pressured into such an intense relationship. Not this soon after her mum had lost her own partner.

Harry noticed her mood. 'I'm sorry, Annie. I tried everything I could think of. No one reported to the hospital with gastro, and they wouldn't tell me anything at the doctor's surgery. Privacy regulations, apparently. Although the receptionist did tell me all about the time the fish and chip shop caused a spate of after-hours emergency visits. I'm never eating there again.'

'Never mind. Thanks for trying.'

'We knew it was going to be a long shot. Did you at least enjoy yourself at the beach?'

She opened her eyes again, but couldn't look at him. Guilt nearly made her cave in and tell him everything, and yet she just wasn't ready to say the words out loud. She'd found her Guardian, her soulmate, and rejected him before she'd even had a chance to find out what sort of person he was. Even though that had been the plan all along, it didn't make it any easier.

'The first three days were great, but, you know, homesickness kicked in. I didn't hit the nausea stage but I was pretty tired. How about you? Did Uncle Willie have any luck looking for a new farm hand?' Uncle Willie was now in his late sixties, and had already had some fairly major heart surgery. Despite Harry's decision to work at home instead of finishing school, he and his uncle still needed more help if they were going to have a hope of improving the farm's infrastructure the way they wanted.

'No luck at all,' Harry answered. 'All the locals have their own places to take care of, and people aren't exactly beating down the doors to move to Nalong. We're out of money. I think Uncle Willie wants to sell up.'

Annie spat out the mouthful of water she'd nearly inhaled and sat up. 'What? No way. You can't sell the farm. You need to guard it!'

'From what? Rabbits? Come on, Annie, no one's going to find the cave. It's been hidden away for thousands of years, and it's on your place anyway.'

'Yes, but you need to stay—'

'I'll stay on as a farm hand. It'll be fine.'

Farm hand? Not even a little bit fine. A primal, deep anger flared inside Annie's chest. 'And what if the new owners decide to turn it into some sort of … tourist resort, or put a hotel on it or something? We can't have people just wondering around exploring.'

Harry looked at her with a placid gaze that held the secrets of an ancient God-kissed race. Technically her eyes did too, although she couldn't quite carry it off the same way he did.

'Do you really think anyone would be stupid enough to try to open a tourist resort here? We can't even get a reliable phone line.'

He was right, but that was beside the point. 'But it's your land. Your *home*. You can't sell it.'

'We don't have a choice, Annie. The banks won't lend us any more money. We're in debt up to our sweaty armpits. Your place is only running okay because your dad …' The hand gripping the rope was tightly clenched as he pulled himself upright.

'My dad what?' She stood up in the water with her hands on her hips and water dripping from her tangled hair.

'Your dad took out a whopping big insurance policy when he married your mum. Uncle Willie told me. Your dad was smart enough to plan ahead. Not like my parents.'

'Because he knew we were all cursed,' she muttered. Harry couldn't refute that, so they waded over to the bank and sat quietly for a few minutes, brooding. Summer's heat was only just beginning, and already the trees looked exhausted. Even the ones close to the water.

Eventually Annie realised that there really wasn't any way of phrasing her question that wouldn't hurt his pride. 'Have you considered asking my mum for help?'

'No way. It would be stupid to put your farm under even more financial strain to save mine.' River water dripped from his hunched shoulders, highlighting all the muscle he'd developed from the effort he was putting in to run the farm. He deserved better.

'Maybe she can help some other way,' she suggested, bracing herself for his reaction. As expected, a flare of anger shot out from him as he clenched his jaw.

'I don't want to hear about those stupid family legends, Annie.'

'You know they aren't stupid. Being Cherubim must involve more than having a Guardian. Why are you so afraid of the idea that we might be able to do … other things?'

'Because if they were superheroes, my parents wouldn't be dead.' He tore out a clump of tussock grass in a fit of redirected aggression. 'Dad wouldn't have ended up in jail and Mum …' A shudder ran through his frame as he came close to saying what was never to be spoken of. It was a taboo even greater than that of Eden, in some ways. The one time she had plucked up the courage to ask why Geoff Doolan had been arrested, her mum had only said it was because he didn't listen well enough to his instincts, and refused to elaborate. Annie didn't push her because talking about it upset her too much. Harry seemed to think his dad had been the victim of a racist judicial system, but couldn't give her any details because his uncle was always vague about it when asked. Perhaps Uncle Willie didn't fully understand it himself, which made sense if it had something to do with protecting the secret of Eden— which his uncle knew nothing about. Harry had once suggested that his dad may have been unable to get the words out to refute whatever charge they'd laid against him. He had lasted for almost six months in jail in Melbourne before he'd collapsed. *Six months* away from Nalong. Annie always struggled to last more than a week. Ruby, Harry's mum, had died not long after. She was found at the base of one of the tallest office buildings in the city. At least she'd had enough presence of mind to leave home to do it rather than risk being found by her son. Maybe Harry was right. Maybe they were cursed.

Harry stared at the river as he spoke. 'Either Dad had no power, or he was too stupid to know how to use it.'

Such intense pain, and grief, and anger—Annie drew it in, using the new trick she'd found to help keep Lucas calm on the beach. 'I'm sorry.

You're right,' she said, wanting nothing more than to ease his distress. 'We'll find another way.'

A moment passed. Then another. Finally, Harry opened his hand and let the grass fall into the river. 'I'll go to the bank myself,' he said. 'See what I can do. I'll be twenty in a few months so maybe now they'll take me a bit more seriously. Maybe I can convince them to lend us enough to tide us over for another year.'

'If anyone can, you can,' Annie encouraged, amazed that her trick had worked so well.

He let out a resigned grunt as if he was reluctant to use the gift he knew he had. 'People trust me, Annie, but that doesn't mean I can talk them into lending me money. We haven't turned a profit in ages. I can try to consolidate some debt, but if things don't pick up soon, you need to accept that we'll have to sell.'

The idea was unthinkable.

'And what if you can't? Sell it, I mean. The Taylors have had their place on the market for almost a year with no luck. Kelly said there's been so little interest that her dad is thinking of staying if he can convince Sarah and her mum to move here.'

He shrugged. 'Sarah? Is that her step-sister?'

'Will be, as of January tenth. The wedding will be in Apollo Bay. I promised Kelly that Mum and I would be there. Is that okay?' It felt ridiculous to have to ask permission from Harry to leave town, but he needed to know not to make plans to leave himself. Someone needed to stick around in case the rabbits tried to invade Eden. Or the March flies.

'I guess. Where am I ever going to go? Although I'm starting to think we might have to leave town to track down these elusive Guardians of ours. They sure seem to be taking their time about turning up. Mum and Dad met when they were six years old. What if we've missed them somehow? Maybe they both died as children or something.'

Or something. 'Fine by me,' she evaded. 'Then I can choose my own partner. How can it not bother you that we don't have any say in this?'

'Because I remember how my parents used to look at each other. Yours too.'

'And how did that work out for Mum?'

'Are you saying she would have been better off with someone she didn't love as much?'

'Maybe I am.'

Harry looked at her. And kept looking.

'No, I'm not,' she relented. 'It does frighten me, though. That bond is so powerful. I don't want to lose who I am.'

'Annie, that would be impossible. You're the most …'

She waited, basking in his burst of affection, but whatever he was about to say got locked away.

'You know what frightens me?' he said instead. 'The idea of having to meet girls *without* supernatural assistance.'

'Oh, because it's so hard when they start telling you the first story that pops into their head, even if it's about food poisoning at the fish and chip shop, just so they can engage you in a conversation.'

His laugh was like a cool compress on a fevered brow. He made it so easy to be herself. She laughed with him, and wondered. She could do that. She could go there. He would too, she was sure of it. He was Harry and she loved him. It would be easy, and safe. They knew each other so very, very well. It wasn't a bad option at all, except …

'Your Guardian is out there somewhere, Harry. And I can't wait to meet her. I don't care if we need to start placing ads in the papers. We'll find her somehow.'

He gave a sideways smile, wriggling a bit in his wet clothes. 'And so is yours. It'll all work out. It always does, somehow.'

Yeah, but not well. They were all cursed.

Chapter 5

Plink. The stone hit the glass right in the middle. Lucas waited in the dark. Despite his agitation, a part of him still took satisfaction in the fact that his aim had been perfect. It was a tricky thing to do from the angle he was on. Cam's mother had grown a perfectly clipped hedge right under the window, and he knew she would notice if he squashed even one branch. Especially now when the house was up for sale. In front of the hedge was a pristine garden bed filled with various sorts of prickly flower bushes. Were they roses? They looked like roses, but he'd thought rose bushes were sort of … taller. These were all flat. And prickly. The point was that he couldn't stand on them and he couldn't climb past the hedge easily.

He threw another pebble. *Plink.* The faint moonlight was barely enough for him to make out the edge of curtain as it was pulled back.

'Cam! It's me. Let me in. I'm not climbing your drainpipe.'

'Lucas?' came a rasping whisper as the window was opened. 'Seriously, couldn't you just send me flowers and chocolates like everyone else? I dunno if I want to let you in. I have to wash my hair, and get my beauty sleep.'

'Shut up and open the door. I need something.'

'At two o'clock in the morning?' A deep sigh floated into the night. 'Hang on, I'll be down in a sec.'

As the curtain dropped closed, a cloud drifted in front of the moon, plunging the lawn into almost complete darkness. It was a good thing the garden was so tidy or he would have ended up in a rose bush for sure. As it was, he would have to ask Cam to rake out a couple of footprints before his mum called the police complaining of stalkers.

The front door opened almost silently and he could see Cam framed by the dim light coming from the bathroom down the hall. His friend pretended to twirl his short hair around one finger and lifted the hem of his boxer shorts suggestively. His mock alluring pose made Lucas smile despite his roiling stomach. All week he had felt sick, barely keeping down what little food he forced himself to eat. His mum had taken him twice to the doctor, and thorough checks had assured her both times that there was no longer any evidence of toxin in his system. Whatever was wrong with him now had nothing to do with the stupid octopus. Both doctors had vaguely suggested that his system was just recovering from the trauma, and that it would fade in a few days, but it hadn't.

'Not tonight dear, I have a headache,' Lucas said, kicking off his thongs and pushing past his best friend to head upstairs to his room. He'd spent enough time in Cam's house to avoid the creakiest steps and was certain he made far less noise than the sleepy oaf following behind him. He pushed open the door to Cam's bedroom and didn't even bother turning on the light because he already knew where it was. He just didn't know *what* it was.

The door closed as Cam finally caught up. Then the light came on, blinding them both for a few moments.

'What are you looking for?' he whispered loudly. 'The good magazines are—'

'Not interested in your revolting habits, Cam. I need … something. Please. I need it.' Now that it was so close, the pull was even clearer. Not stronger, exactly, just clearer. He opened a drawer and started tossing things out at random. 'I thought you were supposed to be clearing stuff out for the big move. What's this drawer meant to be for anyway? It's full of junk.' An old money box, a handful of pens, a Mars bar, a Cub Scout woggle, a Rubik's cube and a used tissue flew over his shoulder and on to the bed.

'Um, well, I keep it stocked just in case any of my friends want to drop around in the middle of the night to mess up my room. Hey, Mars bar! Score. I wonder how long that's been in there?' Shoving the rest of the collection unceremoniously to the floor, Cam flopped back on to his bed and unwrapped the chocolate. Lucas made a mental note to try to remember that when Cam finally reached the end of his time on Earth, to stock his coffin with chocolate just in case he got peckish after they buried him. He would never stop being hungry. Never. A couple of old birthday cards from a grandmother or aunt followed the rest of the junk onto the carpet.

'This. This is what I came for. What is it?' Lucas narrowed his eyes at the crumpled blank envelope, and then looked over at his friend, who was shovelling down the chocolate as if worried he might not stay awake long enough to finish it otherwise.

'That envelope? Oh, yeah, I forgot all about it. It's yours,' he mumbled with his mouth full.

'Mine? Where from?'

'Kelly. Or probably Annie, really. She told me not to give it to you until you asked for it. Are you asking for it?' he smirked, batting his eyelashes.

Lucas froze, trying to piece together what was happening. 'Annie gave you something to give me and you forgot about it?'

'Well, I didn't really want to bring up the subject again, to be honest. You're the one who said you wanted to forget all about it. In fact, I think your exact phrasing was "if either one of you so much as mention her name again I'll nipple-cripple you both". Not a risk I was willing to take, my serious friend.' Arms were crossed defensively over his chest after he took another bite of caramel goodness.

'But what is it?'

Cam shrugged his shoulders.

The envelope was ripped open with nervous haste, and a smallish shell dropped out onto Lucas's palm. It was smooth and round and had a blue-grey stripe that spiralled around to its peak. It was the one he'd been fiddling with on the previous Monday, the day before he'd made such an idiot of himself. Just holding it made him feel … content. And not sick. For the first time in days he didn't feel like curling into the foetal position and groaning like a footy player who'd been kicked in the goolies. He snatched Cam's chocolate bar away from him and bit into it, suddenly starving.

'Hey! Oh, never mind. Have it. Why not? What's mine is yours, apparently. So what is it, anyway? A shell? Cute. Weird, but cute. Girls, man. What the hell goes through their brains? I just don't get them. They're like another species.'

'What do you think it means? Did she give it to Kelly to give to you to give to me before or after I made her think I was a total sleezebag?'

A door opened down the hall somewhere and footsteps approached. They both froze, hoping that if they stayed quiet, whoever it was would go back to bed, but the bedroom door slowly opened and Cam's dad stepped in, clutching Cam's mother's yellow bathrobe around his bare chest. All three of them stared at each other awkwardly for a few seconds.

'When you start bringing girls,' his dad mumbled, 'try to be a bit quieter.' The door shut softly behind him as he retreated again.

'I'd better get going,' Lucas said, tucking the shell into his pocket. 'Sorry if I got you into trouble.' He threw the Mars bar wrapper in the bin under the desk and gave Cam a vague sort of wave. His friend grunted and crawled back under the covers.

Chapter 6

'We're staying, Slaps!'

Annie was caught up in an affectionate headlock the moment she stepped off the bus. She spat out a mouthful of Kelly's auburn hair and then hugged her back. 'Staying?'

'Vicky agreed finally. She got her transfer approved and she'll now be Nalong's Maternal and Child Health Nurse. Mrs Wise has been waiting to retire for about six decades anyway. I swear she was measuring babies back when Nalong had a working train line. Sarah told Vicky she didn't really care where they live since she's planning to travel next year anyway. We're going to keep the beach house and rent it out to tourists. We can still use it when we want. It's perfect! I get to stay here *and* go to the beach in the holidays.'

Annie had a flashback to the first day of primary school as Kelly spun them both around in a circle. It came with a surge of nostalgia so strong she felt like dragging her friend straight to the monkey bars. 'You mean I get to keep you? Kelly, that's the best news I've had in ages. But I thought you wanted to get out of Nalong?'

'Apollo Bay isn't exactly the big city either, you know. If I'm not going to get a mega shopping complex then I may as well stay here. At least until school finishes. Can you believe we've only got one more year?' She cast her gaze over the surrounding school buildings with a glint in her eyes that made Annie wonder if her friend had an empathic gift of her own. Still, it was a look that seemed to have been spreading around the senior students like a contagious disease over the last couple of weeks.

'Yeah, actually, one more year feels like forever,' Annie said. 'Do you think anyone will notice if I ditch these last three days? We're not really doing anything important anyway.'

'I'll notice. You're not leaving me to cover for you like last time. You *will* attend the sleepy hot afternoons of boring videos the teachers show us because they're too lazy to plan anything decent. You *will* come to Speech Night and you *will* bring lollies on the last day to share, like everyone else. Besides, Vicky and Sarah are coming up on the weekend. I'm supposed to be showing Sarah around town. I need you. Please don't disappear yet.'

'Disappear?'

'Like you do every year at this time. Visiting cousins, or camping, or Walkabout, or whatever it is you do. Every year, without fail. You always ditch me until Christmas. It's okay, you know. I think it's cool to have those traditions.'

Walkabout? No, that … oh, close enough. Annie took a few short breaths. It felt dreadful to have to be evasive with her best friend, but she could hardly explain where it was she really went, and why every moment spent here was torture, knowing that in just a few more days she would be able to cross the Skin of the World and lose herself in Paradise. 'Well, it's holiday time,' she said, walking toward the locker bay. 'It's normal to go away. Isn't it?'

'I suppose.' Kelly followed her, untangling a bronze lock of hair from her bag strap. 'Promise me you'll at least make it to Speech Night on Friday.'

A groan escaped Annie's lips, and she nearly turned and headed for the hills straight away. They would throw a party for her in Eden. They always did. There would be sugarnut cakes and music and dancing so wild that it would melt every earthly care back down to its natural proportion. Or she could stay and sit through school speeches and awards and photos of the new staff room kitchen that the Parents and Friends committee had subsidised that year. 'I can't, Kelly, really.'

'What? Why not?'

'Because I don't want to.'

Kelly stopped and gave her a look that would have had any of the boys in class sobbing for forgiveness. 'If you don't come, I'll tell your mum you kissed Lucas.'

'No, Kelly, you can't! Please, you don't understand. She can't know. Please don't tell her anything. *Please.*' She grabbed Kelly's hands in a death grip, panic flooding her system. Her mum couldn't find out what she'd done. She'd never understand.

'Wow! Okay, I won't. Don't have a spak-attack. I didn't think it was such a big deal. I mean, come on, it was only a little kiss. I'm sure your mum would understand. Apparently even old people were teenagers once.'

Annie winced. 'No one says "spak-attack" anymore, Kel. It's really offensive. And my mum is not old.'

Kelly laughed. 'Well, true. I mean seriously, she doesn't look much older than we are. She must have a seriously good skin routine. Remind me to ask her about that.' They started walking again. 'Oh, and if you really don't want your mum knowing anything about Lucas, you'd better warn Sarah and Dave not to say anything at the wrong time. They're both coming for the New Year's Eve picnic.'

'Dave?'

'The tall one. Remember? He's been looking for any excuse under the sun to visit Sarah. She's invited him up for a few days after Christmas. I can't believe Vicky agreed. I hope her parenting approach rubs off on Dad a bit more.'

'She's probably trying to compensate for remarrying by giving Sarah whatever she asks for. You could probably milk that too if you're clever about it.'

'Probably,' Kelly agreed, dumping her bag in the bottom of her locker. 'Did you want me to invite Cam and Lucas? I expect Sarah would prefer to have Dave's full attention without his mates to distract him, but I'm sure I can talk her into it.'

Using all her self-control, Annie fought very hard not let Kelly see her reaction. She could feel her heart shudder with panic. At least, she told herself it was panic.

'That would be a very bad idea. It might be a bit hard to explain to Mum how we know each other. She'll ask questions. She's nosy like that. I really would prefer not to see any of them ever again. Sorry, Kel. You do what you want, of course, but please don't think I have any interest in any of them.' Although her words came out much calmer and more reasoned than expected, she still had to lean for a moment against her locker to let her stomach settle. If Kelly knew how strongly just hearing Lucas's name affected her, she'd never let it rest.

As her friend continued to waffle on about her New Year's Eve plans,

Annie reconsidered her options. Even if the talisman was working, it would wear off eventually. At some point she'd need to find an excuse to send him a fresh one, and even then, how long could she get away with it for? She knew he'd still be drawn to her, even with the proxy to mitigate his separation illness. She needed to leave as soon as possible, because as soon as he no longer had school to keep him busy, she was certain he'd come and find her. She had to get away to where the bond wouldn't work, before it got hold of him any tighter.

Chapter 7

Ekala laughed at Annie's frustration when the bat colony flew off yet again. The creatures were supposed to be guiding them out of the cave system, only they seemed unable to grasp the concept that the human woman and Cherub girl were too large to follow them through the same narrow cracks that they used. Ekala had needed to entice them back four times today already—if it was indeed daytime. Even with all the glow worms, there was barely enough light for Annie to see her hand in front of her face, and keeping track of time in Eden was already a pointless exercise. All she knew was that her knees throbbed from crawling over so much rock, and her neck ached. She considered taking another bite of the luscious piece of Living Fruit that was tucked into her sash. Somehow it was still fresh, even after the three days they'd been scrambling through the tunnels. Or was it longer? Ahead of her, Ekala picked up the pace, so Annie had to settle for breathing in the therapeutic scent of the leaves that Ekala had threaded onto a necklace for her. She didn't want to be left behind in the dark, and Ekala would have no concept of why that might be an issue, so she wouldn't think to wait.

After a short while, Annie noticed the air become warmer. The scent of something other than limestone and bat poop wafted in on a welcome breeze. Surely soon, they would get to wherever it was Ekala wanted to take her. A glint of yellow caught her eye. Reflected light from ahead. As they squeezed through the next suffocating hairpin, the light became so strong that Annie had to blink several times to understand what she was seeing. Fine webs of gold stretched along the tunnel wall, a myriad of delicate laneways drawing together to guide them on. Onward and upward. The gold seam grew thicker and brighter as it hungered for the light ahead. Ahead of her, Ekala kept crawling at the same steady pace, whistling an intricate song that echoed behind them with undiminished chirpiness. Annie imagined the song floating all the way back to where they'd entered the cave system, and travelling all the way ahead as well, as if it could traverse time itself and be everywhere at once while she had to struggle and fight to get past every twist. Finally the passage grew wider, and taller, and just as Annie was about to lose patience and push past her infuriatingly cheerful friend, the tunnel spilled out into bright moonlight and luscious greenery.

Cheers and whistles exploded all around her, and she nearly jumped right out of her skin. The entire village was here, as far as she could tell. Apparently waiting for her to emerge.

'Joy to you, precious friend,' Ekala whispered in her ear, using the English she had insisted on learning on their journey through the tunnels. 'Do you like it?'

Annie tore her eyes away from the many smiles that greeted her, and looked around. They were in a huge natural amphitheatre, filled with so many butterflies it was hard to see anything else. Giant white flowers hung from vines that stretched between the biggest Trees of Life Annie had ever seen. The walls of the ancient crater towered over the giant trees, leaving a circle of silver moonlight high above. Everything under the canopy of rock was wreathed in tendrils of mist. Beside her, a tree frog the size of a kitten clung to a moss-laden tree trunk.

This is … I have no sign for how beautiful this is, she replied. *How did everyone get here before us?*

We came over the pass between the twin mountains, Beltana explained. *I lost my necklace in the snow and had to go back many hours to find it. I thought I was going to be late!*

Ekala laughed. *Again, Beltana? You tie too many trinkets to it. The feathers and shells are pretty, but what do you need all those rocks for?*

Memories, Ekala. Each one has a story.

Then I will find you a stronger cord to use. So you can't drop it in a snow drift.

Annie cut in before they could get too carried away. The two of them could talk for hours. *You all travelled through the snow? Why would you choose to do that?*

The Fruit is about to change colour again, so we know you'll be leaving again soon. We wanted to surprise you with a party here in this pretty place, Beltana said. *We have hot food ready for you both,* she added, spinning so fast that all the butterflies resting on her arms flitted away.

Annie took a moment to breathe in nothing but pure joy. There may have been snow high up in the mountain pass, but down in the crater, the warm night air caressed her lips with the flavour of moonlight and mist. She was surrounded by beauty, peace, and the unrelenting love of her Eden family, who never ceased to spoil her rotten. She wished she could stay forever.

Hot pink stars burst into showering sparkles above Nalong's lake, just as a champagne cork burst from a bottle and a toddler burst into frightened tears. His older sister clapped and cheered with innocent excitement as she watched the pre-midnight fireworks appetiser. Sprawled on a picnic rug on the footy oval, Annie watched both reactions and tried not to dwell on the tragedy of the toddler's fear. Somehow, she had to shake off her post-Eden melancholy.

It had only been two days since her mum had dragged her back home to help with the sheep sale, and so she had to remind herself not to jump up to cuddle the crying toddler. Even at the age of two, the boy would be wary of strangers, and wouldn't appreciate Annie's reflexive response to his distress. Besides, fresh from Eden, it wasn't a good time to draw attention to herself in any way. Usually they tried to wait at least a week before risking contact with the Nalong community when they returned. It was plain common sense. Don't swim straight after eating a big meal, don't run with scissors, never play with matches, and don't appear in public until you could at least remember to wear shoes and speak out loud. Annie had indulged in a longer than usual trip this year and her mum had explained that people were starting to get nosy, asking where she'd been all summer, and that the lies would only get bigger if she didn't make an appearance at the New Year's Eve fireworks. At least they'd thought to spread their rug at the edge of the well-lit oval, so Annie could stay out of everyone's way while her mum did all the socialising. Better to sit still and stay quiet, and imagine she was still perched in the top branches of a puff blossom tree, covered in blue pollen with hungry whisker-bees tickling her ears.

Another bang in the sky startled her thoughts back from Paradise, and she opened her eyes in time to see the terrified toddler fall over. Electric-blue sparkles rained down and their reflections sizzled across the surface of the lake. Hugging her knees to her chest, Annie looked past the fireworks to the stars beyond. They were the same stars, and if she blocked out the sounds of the crying child and the couple arguing over who had forgotten to pack the tomato sauce, she might be able to get back to her dreams of home. Perhaps if she drew away a sliver of the little boy's fear …

'You're here!'

Annie jumped like she had a firework explode under her feet. That would teach her for trying to take in someone else's fright.

'Slaps, I was worried you were going to miss the wedding. You're normally back by Christmas. Your mum said you were away with family. When did you get back?' Kelly's arms were laden with a bottle of Passiona, two plastic cups and a box of Cheezels, all of which she dumped into her friend's lap before sitting down with her on the blanket.

'Day before yesterday, but we had new stock arriving so I couldn't visit straight away, sorry. As if I would miss the wedding. Give me some credit.' In fact, it had been her mum's reminder about the coming celebration that had coaxed her away from her 'holiday' and back to the farm. The guilt she'd felt on her return—realising how much work she'd left her mum with—had been dreadful. Harry had been forced to cancel his fishing trip to help her on the farm. As if he didn't already work hard enough on his own place. She had never meant to go for quite so long, and although both her mum and Harry understood how easy it was to lose track of time, her ulterior motive for escaping for longer than usual was not enough of a reason to have left them with all the summer work.

Kelly poured her a cup of the passionfruit fizzy-drink, so Annie took a sip, gagging at the sweetness. When were people ever going to realise how much nicer fresh water was to drink? It was a moment before she noticed that Kelly wasn't drinking hers. Instead she was sitting with her legs crossed, watching her and biting her lower lip.

'What? Why are you looking at me like that?' She glanced down to make sure she hadn't forgotten anything obvious. Like clothes.

'I didn't think you were back.'

'Well, here I am. Surprise! What's the problem?'

'I would have warned you if I'd known.'

Although she should have felt panic, instead Kelly's words drifted through her brain like falling puff blossoms. Perhaps she was shielding her own emotions without even trying to. Defeated, she waited for her friend to announce her doom. Kelly mumbled it a bit.

'Sarah invited all three of them. Cam's parents wouldn't let him come, apparently his family are moving back to New Zealand next month and they're flat out getting ready. Lucas was supposed to help Cam run a garage sale, but he changed his mind at the last minute and decided to accept Sarah's invitation instead.'

Of course he did. Probably at about lunchtime two days ago. If wishes were horses, beggars would ride. But they weren't. Wishes were more like rabbits. No matter how hard you tried to catch one, they always managed to change direction at the last moment and escape. *Concentrate, Annie. Try to remember how to be subtle, and deceptive.* The Eden part of her shuddered in distaste.

'I don't care, really, so long as he leaves me alone. Just don't let Mum meet him. She always seems to know when I'm hiding something, and I'm a terrible liar—she'll know something's up. Why did Sarah decide to invite them all? You implied she'd prefer them not to come.'

'Oh, you missed heaps. Dave started sending her cards, and roses, and chocolates—the whole corny deal. It was like watching a bad sit-com. I guess it all got a bit too intense too quickly, which is why she invited the others. She said that inviting him up on his own to stay in our house would feel like she's committing to something she's not ready for.' She finally took a sip of her drink. 'Not long after you left, I was convinced Sarah was going to break up with him, but he's been pretty persistent. It's hard to ignore that level of dedication. In fact,' she whispered, leaning forward, 'it's a bit dark, but if you look carefully into the bushes over there, you can probably tell how dedicated they both are now.'

Annie couldn't bring herself to look. It was something she'd always had issues with. In Eden, physical partnerships were less common, and far more precious. Sacred, even. And her family's supernatural pair-bonding made them even more of a big deal. Something about watching partners kiss in Eden was … spiritual, and profoundly beautiful. In Nalong it was different—so casual and yet often so awkward. Perhaps it had something to do with her empathic gift. She often sensed feelings from one partner that weren't quite in sync with the other person's. No matter how much she tried to pretend that watching people kiss didn't bother her, Annie knew her friend thought she was a terrible prude. Unfortunately, Kelly also seemed to think that it was something she needed to be cured of, and took every opportunity to tell her about every casual fling and juicy piece of gossip she could. Some of it was even true.

'And your dad let her invite them all to stay with you?' Annie asked.

'He isn't really in a position to tell her what she can and can't do.'

'Of course he is. It's not her house.'

'Well, that's exactly where he went wrong. He gave us this long speech about how happy he was that we were all going to live together, and went on and on about how he wanted to make sure Sarah and Vicky felt that it was *their* home too …'

'… so he couldn't really turn around and use the old "my house, my rules" excuse to say no,' Annie finished.

'She totally played him,' Kelly agreed. 'I think I like her.' She opened the box of Cheezels and took out a handful. 'Although, I do wish she'd learn to be a bit more decisive. Do you know she's nearly cancelled her trip three times now?'

'Because of Dave? They hardly know each other. She worked her bum off saving for that trip,' Annie said, frowning.

'Which is why her mum keeps talking her back into going. Sarah keeps saying she wants to stay and start a business instead.'

'In Nalong? She must be nuts. Businesses are going bankrupt everywhere. What's she going to do, start a food bank for homeless farmers?'

Kelly knew better than to laugh at her cynical joke. 'Apparently, the type of business doesn't matter because all she needs is "her own special brand of confidence". If I'm completely honest, I have to say I'm a bit envious of her.'

Annie couldn't really refute that. If there was one thing she knew Kelly wanted, it was to have the confidence to step out into the world without people suspecting she'd grown up in such a small town that she'd never been in a queue longer than four people.

'So what do you want me to do about Lucas?' Kelly continued. 'I think he wants to apologise to you.'

Annie's groan of frustration was just too hard to suppress.

'What you need is a boyfriend,' Kelly suggested, biting a Cheezel ring from her finger.

Annie gaped at her.

'I mean a fake one. If you're absolutely sure you aren't interested. Although personally I think you're nuts. He can be my Patrick Swayze ghost if you don't want him.' Her eyes glazed over for a couple of seconds before she resumed speaking. 'My point is that if you really want him to leave you alone, just tell him you're already taken.'

'That makes me kind of cross, you know. Why can't I just say I'm not interested? Why do I need an excuse to say no to someone?'

Kelly gave her a regretful look. 'You could do that, I suppose. It's just that nobody likes to be rejected outright. He'd probably prefer to have a reason that doesn't leave him lying awake at night wondering why you don't like him.'

'Other people's insecurities are not my problem.'

The snorting laugh Kelly gave was not very lady-like. 'Annie, you are the most sensitive person I know. Other people's reactions are *always* your problem.'

She had a point. Stupid empathic gift. The hurt she'd stolen from Lucas when she'd fled from his kiss still bubbled and seethed in her chest. Perhaps living with a lie would be easier than living with any more of that pain. Besides, lies were a necessary part of her life. She'd done it plenty of times, to protect her secrets. The idea of lying to one of the few people who was allowed to know everything made her feel a little ill, though.

'Can you do it?' she begged, kind of pathetically. 'Could you speak to him? I told you I'm a hopeless liar. And I would rather not talk to him at all. Please, Kel?'

'Sure,' she said. 'No biggie. Wait here.' Taking another fistful of cheese-powdery jewellery, Kelly got up and started weaving between picnic rugs, back the way she'd come. Against her better judgment, Annie craned her neck to see where she ended up, but lost sight of her in the crowd.

The fireworks stuttered to a peppery halt. Lucas was in Nalong.

Actually here. Somewhere. She stared into the black sky, waiting for her eyes to adjust to the sudden darkness. A plover called plaintively, as if asking whether anyone else was still alive after the apocalyptic fire storm. Lucas. Here. Breathing away and existing and probably oblivious to the adorable way his pale hair curled down into his eyes. Somewhere behind her and off to her right, Kelly was talking to him. Lying to him. Pushing him further away. Annie hugged her knees a bit tighter.

Over to her left, Mrs Summerhayes and Mrs Middleton were sucking up to her mum for advice on their fruit harvests. Everyone knew that Kiah Langley's fruit won Best in Show every year. To stop herself from fretting, Annie began to hum a tune under her breath that Ekala had sung at her surprise party. It helped a little, until she began to imagine what would happen if for some reason Kelly couldn't find Lucas, and he came to find her first. And then how easy it would be for her mum to wander back over just as he arrived, and what she would possibly say when she was forced to introduce them to each other. Suddenly every surrounding movement became a messenger of doom in her overactive imagination, and she became hyper-aware of each person. The frightened child who was now snuggling into his dad's shoulder, growing sleepy. The irritated woman who'd been left to pack up on her own while the rest of the family were playing cricket. Dean Evans, from her class, who was trying to convince his dad to help him buy an old Commodore he'd seen advertised. Good luck with that one, mate. Their family car was a Ford Fairlane, and getting a Ford family to buy a Holden was like asking his dad to change footy teams. Everywhere, people were happy, cranky, bored, shy and jealous. It was too much, but she couldn't seem to stop herself from reading them, searching for the one she didn't want to find. Instead, her search revealed a familiar presence, calm as a mother hen surrounded by squawking chicks.

Harry. She jumped up and made a beeline for where she knew he was and a minute later she found him kicking a footy around with some friends. He felt her approach and passed the ball to Stumpy Johnson who had been begging to be allowed to join in.

'Hey, Annie, did you like the fireworks?' Harry asked, giving her a quick hug. Stumpy stared at him with the gigantic eyes of a twelve-year-old in total awe of his hero. Harry seemed to have that effect on people.

'They were nice,' she replied, but her body language must have betrayed her agitation because Harry grabbed her hand to stop her from speaking in sign. 'I could use some company,' she admitted, pulling him away from Stumpy's adoring gaze.

'Arn'cha gonna play anymore, Nargun?' the boy asked in a cracking voice full of disappointment.

'Priorities, mate. When a girl asks for your company, it's okay to drop the ball, but that's the only time, yeah?'

'Righto,' he mumbled, sounding a bit sulky as he ran his thumb across the laces of the footy.

Harry hid a laugh as he followed Annie back to her picnic rug.

'Nargun?' she asked idly while scanning the crowd for Lucas.

'My latest nickname, courtesy of Scotty. Could be worse.'

'Suits you better than he knows,' Annie said, pulling him down with her as she flopped down onto the rug. Then she finally gave in to what she'd been wanting to do all night and took off her boots. 'I didn't think Scott Henry knew any Indigenous stories.'

'We all read *Nargun and the Stars* in primary school, remember?'

'Oh, yeah.' Annie looked up at the stars, wondering how much of that story was based on reality. Australia had its fair share of supernatural beings, after all.

'Feeling a bit head-spacey?' he asked, rummaging in the box for some Cheezels.

'Yeah, I guess. I just need ...'

'My calming presence. I'm good like that,' he said around a mouthful of powdered cheese snacks. He picked up her unfinished drink. 'Here's to a glorious year, Annie,' he said, holding it up in a toast. 'I reckon 1992 will be an important one for us. No matter what happens, I'll always be here to ...' He paused, apparently unable to put his gift into words.

'Ground me?'

'I was going to say steal your Cheezels.'

Smiling, she leant against him, resting her head on his shoulder and closing her eyes. Sometimes he didn't need to look her in the eye to soothe her, just like she didn't need to read his emotions to know how he was feeling. They sat quietly for a while, letting the noise of the crowd blanket them in privacy. Everyone was talking and laughing and complaining about the music and telling each other what their New Year's resolutions were. At one point her mum came over to check on her and left again when she saw that Harry was keeping her company. If only Annie could convince her to take her home, but it was nearly midnight, and her mum looked like she was having fun. Or at least, fooling everyone really well. She deserved a night out, and talking to her friends was good for her. Going home could wait a few more minutes. Kelly hadn't returned, which she took as a good sign. If she hadn't been able to find Lucas, she figured she would have come back to let her know.

The noise grew more frenetic as midnight approached and people began to get excited for the countdown. Sparklers were lit. Poppers went off prematurely, sending tiny fountains of coloured paper everywhere. The countdown began, so Harry pulled Annie to her feet and she began to pay attention again. A tall figure passed by, bending his neck to whisper in someone's ear. It was Dave, and Sarah slipped her hand into his as they wove their way toward the lake. They stopped when the shouting chant got down to five. Four. Three. Two. One … Cheers and fireworks erupted in a wave of celebration.

And then Lucas was there.

Standing right in front of them with his bare feet and messy hair in his eyes and his hands in the back pockets of his shorts, watching her with a haunted expression. Bittersweet yearning caught in her chest and she couldn't tell if it was hers or his. She snatched it in, smothered it down.

Lucas looked down at her hand, where she was still clutching Harry's. The expression on his face looked utterly defeated, and it was apparently enough for Harry to know what it meant.

Harry looked quickly from him to her, then back again to Lucas with his mouth falling open.

Annie looked at them both, and chose.

'Happy New Year, Harry,' she cried, turning her back on the boy who had followed her to the back end of nowhere without even knowing why. And then she wrapped her arms around Harry's neck and kissed him fully on the mouth.

Chapter 8

Time seemed to freeze as Annie allowed her entire existence to shrink down to the simple act of connecting with her partner Cherub. All her life, Harry had been her anchor, her support, and her best friend. She knew him better than anyone, and he knew everything there was to know about her. So she threw everything she was into that kiss, and knew without a doubt that he would catch her. His initial shock melted within moments as he kissed her back, holding her as tightly as she held him. The kiss was fierce, and defiant, as if they really believed they could turn their backs on fate. At least for that frozen moment. It wasn't the perfect kiss, not by anyone's reckoning, but for all its dishonesty, it still had a deep authenticity. Their need for that defiance was real, and they both understood exactly what they were doing. No, it wasn't perfect, because a perfect kiss wouldn't have ended with Annie bursting into hysterical sobbing.

'Ssshh, it's okay, he's gone.' Harry clutched her head against his shoulder and held her up as she fell apart. 'Why, Annie?' he asked gently, once her sobs finally settled a little.

She squeezed him even more tightly. 'C— can't we just be cursed together? Why do we have to ruin more lives? I love you, Harry. Can't I just have you? Please?'

He stroked her hair and took a few deep breaths. 'If that's really what you want, then I'm all yours,' he promised, and then he pulled back and made her look at him. His velvet brown eyes held only sincerity and affection. 'I would do anything for you, you know that. Anything.' He almost soothed her into believing him, and it wasn't so much that he was lying, but his emotions told her that he simply wasn't so certain. There was someone out there for him. They both knew it, and knew that he couldn't escape it, any more than she could.

Closing her eyes to break his pacifying gaze, she shook her head. 'You say that now, but I could never keep you. I'm so sorry,' she whispered, feeling ashamed beyond belief. He let her cling to him while they slowly came to terms with their mutual decision. As much as they loved each other, some things were just never meant to happen.

'You're just not ready,' Harry said. 'I understand. It's okay, you can take as long as you want. Just because he's here doesn't mean you have to rush into anything.'

'But he won't be able—'

'I'll take care of it. I can do that much. I'll keep him away for as long as I can.'

Crumpling to the ground, she curled herself into a ball of sulky misery. 'He probably hates me. That should help a bit. He might never want anything more to do with me than absolutely necessary and I wouldn't blame him.'

Harry smiled and sat down, resting his wrist on one knee and leaning back on his other hand. 'So already you're conflicted. Do you want him to love you or hate you?'

'Neither! I just want to be left alone. Please, Harry, please don't let Mum know.'

'What? Why not?'

'How do you think she'd react if I told her I don't want a Guardian?'

'Probably the same way I am. With confusion. Bonding with a Guardian is supposed to be a good thing.'

'A good thing to lose your independence and identity? I need to be *me* for a while, Harry. Just me. Have you forgotten what happens once we find our Guardians? I haven't even finished school yet. This is the nineties. I refuse to get locked into marriage and kids at a young age like our parents and their parents did. I shouldn't have to be forced into that.'

The crowd around them was beginning to disperse. Now that the New Year had ticked over, most people seemed to want to just go home and get on with it. Except for the kids. They were all way too overtired to want to leave.

'Your mum would understand. She ...' Harry paused, thinking. 'No. She wouldn't. Not really. All she can see these days is how broken her life is after losing your dad. I think I see what you mean. You'll have to be very careful about this, Annie.'

'Exactly. I need her to only get good news for a while longer, especially if it has anything to do with Guardians. Until I'm ready to give her the news she wants to hear, she's better off not knowing anything.'

'Yeah. I agree. I just don't see how that will be possible. As soon as she sees the two of you together, she'll know who he is.'

'She can't even know he exists. Please, Harry. Promise me you won't tell her.'

'Okay. Settle down. I promise,' he said, peeling her fist from the front of his shirt. He held on to her hand, probably knowing full well that she was on the verge of tears again.

Out of the corner of her eye she could see Stumpy Jackson grinning like an idiot at the sight of them holding hands again and she vaguely wondered who else had noticed them kissing.

'Harry, I shouldn't have pounced on you like that. I had no right. I'm so sorry.'

He pulled her into another soothing hug and she concluded that his hugs were unquestionably part of his gift. He could probably heal all the world's problems with his comforting arms and gentle voice. Someone should give him a job at the United Nations. World Peace. Sorted.

'I'm not sorry. I've been wanting to do that for a long time now. I don't know about you, but I had to know.' Then he frowned. 'I never expected to do it in full view of your Guardian though. He might never forgive me for that.'

'Well, he'll just have to get over it. Or not. I don't really care. He doesn't know me. He can't just walk into my life and make judgments about whom I should and shouldn't kiss.'

'I never said he wouldn't forgive *you*,' he said with a smile. 'But you're right. He doesn't know you. If he wants anything to do with you, he's going to have to earn it.'

Chapter 9

'I've been offered a job,' Lucas announced once his parents finally stopped yabbering on about how short Lily's skirt was. His sister seemed to love the fact that they had forbidden her to leave the house, taking it as some sort of confirmation that what she had chosen to put on was probably going to have the desired effect. Everyone knew that she would get her way eventually, if not today then next week, or the one after. She wore their parents down with either overconfident persistence or just plain absurdity. It was hard to really discipline her when she so easily refuted each argument with her dead-pan humour. The look she threw him, though, showed Lucas that she didn't appreciate his timing. It would be much harder for her to talk them around if she had to compete with him being in their good books.

His mum handed Lily another pile of dirty dishes and turned to him, her eyes ready to soak in more details.

He swallowed, trying not to appear as nervous as he felt. 'I can start whenever I like.'

Silence. Now his parents were watching him, waiting for more. Lily just continued to stack the dishwasher.

'The pay isn't great, but it's better than nothing,' he said, trying to remember how he'd rehearsed it in his head.

'Do we have to drag it out of you? What's the job? Where?' his dad asked, turning down the television.

'Assistant Production Manager. They'd like me to work full time because they're pretty understaffed at the moment.' He grabbed a wet cloth and started wiping down the table. He couldn't remember if he'd ever done that before. He vaguely recalled seeing his mum do it once or twice, and it satisfied his sudden need to keep his hands busy and have somewhere to look other than at his mum. Unfortunately, it just seemed to make her suspicious.

'What exactly will you be producing?' she asked in a voice that sounded overly casual. Her eyes had narrowed somewhat.

He swallowed again. 'Raw materials for the textile industry.' At least he hoped that was what they did. He hadn't actually thought to ask, but it sounded better than 'raw materials for the meat industry'.

His mother looked slightly pacified. His father wasn't fooled. 'Like what?' he asked.

'Mmm … wool, I guess.'

His parents looked at each other and his mum got that little furrow between her eyes that meant she was fretting.

'Lucas, please,' his dad said. 'You're going to have to tell us more, you know that. What exactly would you be doing, and where is it located?'

Lucas sat down at the kitchen table and took a sudden interest in an old beetroot stain that had been there for as long as he could remember, scrubbing at it viciously. 'I'll be working on a sheep farm. In Nalong. They'll house me and feed me and I get some cash-in-hand every week.'

His mother's furrow turned to astonishment and even Lily stood up so fast she nearly knocked a glass off the bench.

'I've been looking for work for months here,' he added. '*Everyone* wants work over summer and there's nothing available. By the time I find something it'll be time to start uni and it'll be too late. They're desperate for people to work in regional areas.'

'They must be,' Lily mumbled, so he threw the wet cloth at her head.

He turned back to his mum. His reasoning had sounded a bit over-defensive even to his ears, mostly because he knew exactly what she was going to say.

'But it's so far away!'

Yep. There it was.

'You want to move out?' she asked, glancing over at the photo of him as a four-year-old, with infant Lily perched on his lap.

He winced. 'Of course not, but it's a job. And it won't be for long. Just a month or two, until uni starts. You'll hardly notice I'm gone.'

'Can I repaint the walls?' Lily asked. Everyone turned to her. 'In my new bedroom,' she explained with mock exasperation. 'I'd like purple walls, with mint green borders, and I'll need a new bedspread.'

'You're *not* having my room,' Lucas objected. 'And I haven't even accepted the job yet.'

'Do you really think it's a good idea?' his dad asked. 'I mean, cash-in-hand, who knows if they'll pay you on time, or at all? What sort of training will they give you? Will you be safe? How well do you know these people?'

Not at all, Lucas thought, wishing he could just go and curl up on his bed. His stomach was doing backflips, as it had done since he'd left Nalong the day before, and he had a growing suspicion that it wouldn't ease up until he found his way back there again, which made no sense whatsoever. Swallowing hard, he clutched the shell in his pocket. It calmed him slightly.

'They gave me an employment contract to sign. You can read it.'

His dad sighed.

'I think a job like this will round out my résumé nicely,' he continued. 'I have the grades to show I'm smart, and now this will prove that I'm not afraid of a bit of hard work.'

Lily laughed so hard she snorted. 'You don't even take the bins out without a fight. You won't last two minutes on a farm.'

Disconcertingly, by the thoughtful expression on his dad's face, her argument seemed to have helped his case.

'Your father's right. How do we know you'll be safe?' his mum asked as she poured herself a glass of white wine. He wasn't sure if that was good or bad.

'Of course he'll be safe,' Lily said. 'It's the country. No traffic, no muggings, less drugs … they only have snakes really, and apparently they aren't a problem so long as you watch where you're putting your feet … oh, wait …'

Lucas let his head flop down onto the table. This was not going according to plan.

Chapter 10

A low hum rewarded their efforts in a very satisfying way. The ancient fire-fighting pump chugged reluctantly to life as the diesel engine bullied it into motion. A shimmery vibration crimped the surface of the dam, making Harry smile.

'Yeah, baby! What'd I tell you? Impellers were jammed and it had a broken O ring. Simple to fix.' Lucas grinned at his handiwork, wiping grease onto his jeans.

'Simple. Now that you finally managed to put it back together the right way. Well, let's see if it's working,' Harry said and started trudging back up the dusty hill to the header tank. Behind him, he heard Lucas groan as he started to follow with heavy steps. It was the fifth time they'd had to make the trip up the steep embankment, and the heat was taking its toll. February was halfway over, but there would still be at least another month of dry weather, peppered with who knew how many more of these extreme heat days, before they could even begin to hope for the autumn rains.

Harry peered up at the sun. Still morning. Just. He'd been hoping to get the pump fixed long before the midday heat sucked the life out of everything, but the damn thing just wasn't playing fair. Behaving like a cantankerous old woman, the old pump simply refused to push water uphill, and continued to make rude noises at them, as if offended that they would even have the gall to ask her to defy the laws of physics.

'Stay down there, Lucas. I'll go,' Harry relented. 'We know the problem's not up the top. We don't both need to check.'

For weeks now, Harry had been testing Lucas out, pushing his temper, his work ethic and his stamina as much as he could. It had been a tough extended job interview, for something far more significant than just a job. Eventually he'd come to the grudging conclusion that who-ever it was Upstairs who had decided to give Lucas the role of being Annie's Guardian had probably known what they were doing after all. He was loyal, hard-working, mature beyond what even Lucas him-self probably realised, and ridiculously likeable. Likeable enough that Harry's natural jealousy was starting to give way to a subliminal desire to just head next door and slap his best friend on the back of her head for being so stubborn.

Before he even got to the top of the rise, Lucas called for him to stop. 'No good, Harry, it doesn't sound right. I'm switching it off again before something blows.'

Harry grumbled under his breath and sat down on the gravel to fan his sweaty face with his hat while the engine pattered down to silence.

'Wait up there,' Lucas called. 'I'm going to get some fresher water to prime the pump with. I think the last lot was too muddy. I should be able to start the engine myself now—I know what I'm listening for.'

The diesel engine was finicky, but at least it gave you subtle clues when you were flooding it, if you knew its language. Lucas was learn-ing, finally. The city boy didn't even bother to remove his boots this time as he took big enthusiastic strides into the murky water, holding the bucket up. Everything dried so fast in the Wimmera sun that they wouldn't weigh him down for long, and might even keep his feet a bit cooler for longer. It wasn't like he was planning to actually swim.

'Keep to the left a bit,' Harry called helpfully. 'There's a bit of a sink-hole to the right.'

Lucas stumbled forward with a splash, dropping the bucket.

'Possibly there's one to the left as well,' Harry amended.

Muddy water dripped from Lucas's hair as he spluttered and found his feet again. The boots probably weren't helping much.

'I think I found a yabbie!' he announced as he waded back toward the pugged shoreline, still not sounding cranky. Not much seemed to fluster him when he was outdoors working, which made Harry quietly hope that perhaps he wouldn't mind sticking around after all. The work seemed to suit him even if he did complain about being so far from the beach.

'Doesn't surprise me,' Harry responded. 'I was warned that you were good at attracting wildlife.'

Every muscle in Lucas's body tensed at the vague reference to Annie. He stopped walking, with the grimy water still up to his knees while his spare hand fumbled in his pocket for something. Harry had noticed it before. Usually when Lucas wasn't concentrating on anything particular, his eyes would drift to the south, toward Annie's place, and his hand would go into his pocket until Harry called his attention back. It had made him wonder.

'No. Wait, no,' Lucas cried, his voice rough. The bucket was discarded as both pockets were thoroughly searched. Whatever was supposed to be in there clearly wasn't.

'You lost something?'

Lucas didn't answer. Instead he spun around and tramped back into the water until he was chest deep, his head darting around as if he could see where the missing item had gone.

'I'm sorry, mate. Whatever it was, you've got Buckley's of finding it in there. Was it important?' Slipping a little on the loose scree, Harry made his way down to the water's edge.

There was a definite note of hysteria in his friend's voice. 'I need it. I can't lose it!'

'What was it?'

Stubborn silence lasted just a few moments until his distress won out. 'A shell. Just a shell. But I need it.'

Shaking his head, Harry waited for Lucas to look up at him so he could soothe him a little, but the new farmhand just stood with his eyes closed and head cocked to one side as if listening for something. With his eyes still shut, he began to walk forward, stopping every couple of steps to listen again. Harry watched on in astonishment. Finally, chest deep in the tan-coloured liquid that passed for water, Lucas reached down, putting his head under carefully as if trying not to disturb the water any more than he had to … and came up with a clenched fist and a smile bigger than the Luna Park entrance.

'Got it.' He grinned, shaking gritty water from his hair.

Harry waited until he clambered onto the cracked clay bank before holding his hand out in unspoken request. Lucas closed his fist protectively.

'I'm not going to hurt it, I just want a look.' Harry had to look him right in the eye before Lucas finally acceded, placing it in his palm and exhaling like he was relinquishing the keys to a fully restored 351 GT Falcon. The shell was small and fairly plain, creamy-brown with a bluish stripe spiralling around it. He looked inside. A blob of Blu-Tack was pressed into its opening. Harry pulled it out, and with it came a tiny scrap of cloth, dark brown and crumpled.

'Now that is seriously gross,' Harry mumbled. 'Annie gave this to you?'

Lucas looked away, ashamed. 'I don't know why I kept it, I'm sorry. When I found out that you and Annie … I mean, I kept meaning to throw it away, but … look, I don't know why she gave it to me!'

Lips pursed in distaste, Harry dropped the talisman back into Lucas's hand. 'You know that's blood, right? On the cloth?'

'I figured as much. Is she …' He stared down at it in conflicted distress. 'I mean, is she some sort of … a witch?'

Finally, Harry's legendary composure cracked and he laughed in spite of the panic and disbelief on his friend's face. 'No! Definitely not. Annie is a lot of things, but she's no witch. What did she say when she gave it to you?'

'Nothing. She had Kelly pass it to Cam. She must have had it ready before she ran off—' His lips snapped together as he cut off what he'd been about to say.

'She ran off?'

'Let's try the pump again. I'll get some more water.' Lucas deftly stuffed the scrap of dried blood back into the shell and squished the Blu-Tack in after it, shoving the talisman back into his pocket as he waded back into the dam to retrieve the bucket.

Harry decided to let the matter go. Sort of.

'If you want to give it back to her, bring it this arvo. Her mum's gone to Horsham to negotiate a hay sale so we're helping her shift the new stock out of the gully paddock.'

Harry walked his mount over to the dappled shade of a sugar gum, waiting for his best friend and employee to sort themselves out. The day wasn't getting any cooler.

Finally Lucas returned with the bottle of sunscreen he'd insisted on retrieving from the car. 'You're kidding me. An actual horse? A live one? Is that why I wasn't allowed to wear shorts?' He looked at the elderly bay stock horse with such horror that Annie turned to glare at Harry. Her expression said, *I thought you told me he was helpful.*

Out loud she said, 'Unfortunately we're all out of dead ones, so yes, you get Chez for the day. Give me the sunscreen. You couldn't have brought a smaller bottle? This won't fit in my saddle bag.'

'I'll carry it,' Lucas said.

'No, you won't,' Annie argued. 'You'll need both your hands. Just put some on now and leave the bottle here.'

'I've already lathered myself in the stuff. I thought you might need some.'

This time, when Annie turned to glare at him, Harry smiled back. He could see how irritating it could be to have a Guardian fuss over you.

'Your turn will come,' Annie mumbled to Harry while Lucas squirted way too much lotion into the palm of her hand.

'And until then, I'm going to watch and laugh,' Harry said.

Lucas walked over to Harry and offered him the bottle. 'What are you two talking about?'

'Nothing,' Harry said with a sigh, taking the sunscreen. 'Apparently I don't need to wait my turn.'

Annie chuckled and handed Lucas a helmet to wear before he could ask why they were being so cryptic. 'Put it on and stand here, next to Chez's shoulder. No, face his tail. Good, now put your foot in the stirrup here. It's not that high up, just stretch a bit. Blimey, your ballet teacher must have been hopeless … okay, now three good hops and jump up like you're going to lie across the saddle, and then swing your leg over and sit up slowly.'

She ducked back barely in time to avoid Lucas's boot hitting her in the face, and Lucas's reaction to the near miss nearly had him falling straight off the other side. Harry had to fake a cough to disguise his laugh.

'All right, so poor Chez now has a ninety-degree twist in his spine, but at least you're up,' Annie said.

Harry watched her place a hand on her Guardian's knee to help settle him down. It brought back memories of his parents. Any time his mum was stressed, his dad would place a hand on her shoulder, or arm, or back. It had always made his mum sigh in a way that used to make Harry pretend to cringe. What would it feel like to have that effect on someone?

Annie talked Lucas through the basics of where to find the go button, the stop button and the steering. She placed his hands correctly on the reins, and pushed his heels down and forward. It was like watching a guy teach a girl how to hold a pool cue.

'If you can surf, you can ride,' Annie assured the scarecrow in the saddle. 'It's exactly the same.'

They watched as Lucas walked Chez over toward the gate.

'Okay, maybe not exactly the same,' Annie amended. 'You don't need to use your arms to balance. Try imagining that you need to keep your sweaty armpits stifled. Just relax and let him carry you, and only steer when you need to.'

'My surfboard doesn't have teeth,' Lucas remarked.

'Your horse doesn't let you crash into things.'

'My board doesn't smell.'

'Your horse will warn you if you're about to step on a poisonous animal.'

Lucas paused, twisting his lips. 'Yeah, okay. You win.'

Harry laughed again, pulling his hat down low over his eyes and bridging his reins. This was a fun show to watch.

'Who are you trying to be?' Annie asked him, finally swinging into her own saddle. 'Clancy of the Overflow?'

'Yep,' Harry answered.

'Good. You can take the gully, then.'

❧

By the time the sun had faded to a friendlier strength, they'd rounded up the last of the stragglers and pestered them into moving from a paddock of short dead grass to one with slightly longer dead grass. In Harry's opinion, they didn't seem very grateful.

Lucas begged to be allowed to get down and stretch his legs and walk Chez back to the stockyards. Instead of explaining to him that the hills were a lot steeper than they felt on horseback, Annie agreed instantly, and then she took off at a steady canter. It seemed she wanted to talk to

Harry alone, so he nudged his tired horse into a reluctant trot to follow her. He glanced behind to see Lucas slide from the saddle to land on shaky legs, while Chez took a couple of sideways protest steps at being left behind his herd-mates. Lucas scratched his horse's wither like he'd been taught, which was enough to convince old Chez to behave. They would be fine. It wasn't like Lucas could get lost with Annie's magnetic trail to follow.

Hoof beats echoed, muted on the dry soil as if even the sound waves were too tired to bounce properly off the hillside. Harry caught up to Annie at the top of the next hill, and they slowed to a walk. It was far too hot for a proper race home.

'How did you go with the bank last week?' Annie asked, lifting the back of her saddle blanket to let the air cool some of the sweat underneath. 'Did you get to speak to a real person or did they just make you fill out a whole lot of forms again?'

'Oh, the manager was more than happy to meet with me. For some reason, he seemed to think it would make me feel better if he pointed out that he remembered Dad coming in to see him for the same reason ten years ago. Am I supposed to be happy that I'm not the first Doolan to suck at farming?'

'You don't suck at farming. Maybe he was just trying to reassure you that he'd helped get your family through difficult times in the past, and could do it again.'

The horses picked their way down a rocky gully with stilted steps and ears pricked forward, concentrating hard. There was a dried-up creek bed at the bottom. It was sad not hearing frogs tapping and chirping among the reeds.

Harry shook his head. 'It wasn't the bank that got them through. He showed me the records and asked if there was any chance I could do the same thing again. There was a massive lump sum repayment that cleared their overdraft—and then some. It came from a company called Celarsi Holdings; they're an umbrella company for a whole lot of smaller businesses that range from furniture imports to local green grocers. When I got home, I asked Uncle Willie what the payment had been for and he said my parents had sold off an asset. Some jewellery or something, he thinks. Unfortunately, the only assets we have left are the ones we need to keep the farm running.'

'Well, did the manager have any other suggestions? What about your business plan? It's a good one.'

'No go. I outlined my plan for drought-proofing and setting the place up to take more stock, but I guess Mr Anderson has heard it all before. Apparently we need to "improve our credit score" before he can consider lending us enough for such extensive improvements.'

'And how do you do that?' she asked.

'Make more money. I'll find a way.'

Annie leg-yielded across a little so that her stirrup clanked against his. He knew her gift laid all his emotions bare, and this was her way of letting him know she understood, without offering the blunt sympathy he didn't want. He believed that people got what they worked for, and if they didn't, they had to move on. There was no point either of them whining about it. And he had more work to do before he was ready to give up.

'*There* it is,' she said after a moment. 'I can feel it. That stirring pool of hope you have. I really respect that about you, Harry. You have a confidence that things will work out fine. Not like me. Sometimes, when I think of how well things always slide into place in Eden, I look at my life here and despair. Everything here is so hard.'

'Not everything has to be as hard as you seem to make it, Annie.'

She refused to acknowledge that, and so they rode up the next hill in silence. A light breeze sprang up that was enough to shoo the flies off their faces for almost two whole seconds, allowing them to briefly appreciate the sight of the river in the distance. Not too much farther to go. At the crest, Harry turned back to check on Lucas, only to find him resting on a fallen log, wiping his face with his Billabong tank top. He had Chez's reins hooked around his wrist and Harry winced at his lack of common sense. Luckily Chez wasn't one to make any sudden attempts to run home. Getting dragged by a horse was something that even Guardian reflexes wouldn't be able to help with.

'I thought Guardians were supposed to have super-stamina or super-strength or something,' Annie noted, following his gaze. 'Lucas is dead on his feet. He hasn't been sick, has he? I mean, he should be close enough to me now.'

Harry poured some water from his drink bottle over his head before answering. 'My fault. I did say he had to earn the right to get to know you, but I may have been pushing him a bit hard. And he hasn't been sleeping well.'

'Sleeping?' Her voice cracked, just a little. They both knew how closely Guardians were linked to their charges. 'I haven't been sleeping *that* badly. Is it true he won't sleep if I can't?'

'Maybe, but don't worry, it isn't you. We put some chicken eggs in the incubator last week and I gave him the job of turning them every couple of hours. He's been very diligent.' Harry kept a perfectly straight face.

'He turns them at night? You didn't tell him that wasn't necessary?'

'He didn't ask. He sets the alarm on his watch. It's kind of sweet.'

'Harry! You're supposed to be untainted,' she said with a soft laugh. 'When did you become so nasty?'

'Oh, like you've been any better, letting him suffer from separation illness without even telling him why.'

Her smile fled. 'I did not. I left for Eden as soon as I could, and stayed away as long as possible. The bond wouldn't have kicked in straight away. Surely it takes a while to get a proper hold. Besides, I gave him something just in case.'

'Yeah, I know. He showed me the shell today. Clever. You never told me about that trick.'

'It was Gran's little secret. She told me about it when your parents … well, she taught them how to do it, to make things easier when they were apart.'

Harry dipped his chin as the usual spike of grief hit him, only it dissolved before it could properly land, leaving him unexpectedly numb. It felt like he'd just lost a sneeze. He peered sideways at Annie, and noticed a tear running down one cheek. A tear that should have been his. It seemed she had more than one clever trick up her sleeve.

They started walking again.

'Lucas is supposed to leave for uni in less than a week. Will the shell be enough?' he asked.

'It will have to be. It's not like I can go with him.'

'Annie.' He tried to catch her eye. If she was going to use her gift on him, then maybe it was time to use his. He delivered his advice in his best pacifying voice. 'I think you should tell him the truth. He has a right to know.'

She gripped Pepper's reins so hard that the gelding tossed his head. Unlike her.

'I can't. I just can't do it. For so many reasons.'

'Such as?'

'Such as the fact that he's about to start an engineering degree. He has a life planned. How can I possibly tell him to give it all up?'

'Annie, you know better than to use that as an excuse. No one is asking him to do anything. You're the one limiting his choices right now by not telling him everything he needs to know. Tell me what the real problem is.'

'Do we really have to talk about this?'

'Only if you want my help. I'll always back you up, but I need to understand why we're lying to the people we care about. We already lie far too much as it is.'

'You care about Lucas? You've known him less than two months.'

'What can I say? He has a certain charm.'

She fiddled with the buckle of her reins, letting Pepper pick his own path between the clumps of gorse. 'You're going to tell me I'm being stupid.'

'You are being stupid. I already know this. So you might as well tell me why.'

She stared straight ahead as she answered, into nothing. 'I'm scared of it.'

'Of what, exactly?'

'The bond. I'm scared of how powerful it is.'

Harry slowed a little to let Pepper catch up. 'Since when is the promise of a deep soulmate connection a frightening thing? You know how happy your parents were. You, of all people, must have felt what it's like. You would have felt every precious emotion … oh, crap. You felt everything.'

Harry could have kicked himself for being so thick. It had taken Annie a long time to learn to shield herself from everyone else's grief when her dad had died. She'd been pretty messed up for a while. She'd felt everything her mum had. No wonder she was scared.

'I'm so sorry, Annie. That really isn't stupid at all.'

'Yeah, it is. It isn't like I don't know the saying. Better to have loved and lost, and all that. I can't help my emotions, though. If only *I* had someone to … never mind.'

Harry didn't know what to say. Or how to help.

After a moment she continued. 'I know it's inevitable. And I don't mind. Not really. It isn't like I want to escape him altogether. As I said at New Year's, I just want to have a chance to find out who I am first. Me. On my own. So that when … I mean, if anything happens to one of us, if the curse gets us, we'll have an identity that isn't tied to the other person, you know? I think that's been a big part of why Mum's struggled so much. She doesn't know who she is. They were so young when they met. Harry, why are you crying?'

'I'm not.'

'You are on the inside. I can feel it.'

'Who made you so damn wise, Annie? It's very annoying. You know you can't tell your mum about this. She'll blame herself.'

She rode up next to him again and took his hand. 'So you'll help me?'

'Of course. Somehow. Lucas might be hard to convince, though.'

'He doesn't even know me. To be honest, I'm not sure he even likes me. He spent the whole of this afternoon feeling frazzled and confused. He's drawn to me, and yet he doesn't actually enjoy being around me that much.'

Frazzled and confused? Harry wondered just how much she'd been using this new aspect to her gift, but decided it wasn't the right time to push her on it. Not directly, anyway. 'He still thinks we're together. I noticed you didn't do much to dispel that idea. Just how far do you want me to play along with that?'

'Why, can't we hold hands anymore? Is it weird now?'

'With your Guardian watching? Yeah, a bit. I keep thinking he's going to wollop me when I least expect it.'

'Good plan. We'll just make sure he does it when there are lots of people around. Maybe your Guardian will finally show up to defend you.'

'Maybe I'm not ready for her yet,' he countered. 'Or maybe we could match her up with Lucas and solve all our problems.'

Annie swivelled around in the saddle to glare at him so fast that Pepper stumbled sideways.

Harry rolled his eyes. 'I'm no empath like you, and even I can tell that was a jealous reflex. Not as quick to shield your own emotions, are you? Just be careful, Annie,' he said seriously. 'The only thing worse than being cursed to die young, would be to live a long life full of regret.'

Chapter 11

Each day that passed became more torturous. So far Annie had managed to avoid letting her mum anywhere near Lucas, despite her innocently curious questions about the Doolans' new farmhand. At least they felt innocent, but her small spike of emotion sent out little shoots of tremulous hope each time she brought up the subject. Annie knew that her mother yearned for her to find her soulmate, as did most parents, probably, but she ruthlessly pulled at her mother's feelings and left her a bit numb. It was better than letting her feel that hideous grief that shrouded her whenever she thought of her lost husband, and speculation about Annie's Guardian inevitably led to that.

On the day they'd moved the sheep, Lucas had returned the talisman to her with hardly a flinch, and without offering an explanation, or pressing her for one. Awkward for both of them. Since then, according to Harry, he often reached into his pocket for it before he remembered it was gone. The night before Lucas was due to drive his 'coffin on wheels' Datsun 120Y back to Melbourne, Annie replenished it. Luckily, she remembered to call Harry just before she stabbed her finger with the dress pin. He told her he'd try to distract Lucas by offering him a shot of bourbon as a thank you on his last night of employment. It must have been good bourbon because it took Annie four stabs to get enough blood to really soak the wad of silk properly and she spent the next half an hour looking out the window, afraid that her Guardian was going to come barging up the driveway to rescue her from the evil sewing box.

After she went to bed, she lay awake for a long time wondering if she was doing the right thing by letting him leave. She wanted to believe that she was taking the higher moral ground. She was helping him to escape Nalong and follow his own path, at least for a while. So why was it that all she could see when she closed her eyes was her father's face, filled with adoration and affection as he smiled at her mother?

Just after midnight she crawled into her mum's bed and let her wrap her arms around her like she was a tiny child again.

❦

Instead of catching the bus to school the next morning, she told the driver that her mum needed her on the tractor, and put up with the knowing look from him that meant he knew full well she was wagging. Still, it was better than having him wait around thinking she was just running late. Her mum probably would have noticed that. Once the bus was out of sight, she pulled her old bicycle out from the clump of ti-tree where she'd stashed it and began the long trek over to the Doolans' farm. She'd forgotten to ask what time Lucas was planning to leave and was terrified she might have missed him, but when she finally pedalled and puffed her way into Harry's home paddock, the little orange Datsun sedan was still parked near the rivergum on the front lawn. She jumped off her bike before Harry's dog, Bo, could bowl her over with his usual greeting.

'Hey, Uncle Willie,' she called out as she gave Bo's ears one last rub and pushed open the fly-screen. Harry's great-uncle was in his late sixties and getting a bit hard of hearing, so she didn't want to startle him. 'It's Annie. I came to say goodbye to Lucas. Are he and Harry out the back?' Even though she knew perfectly well where Harry was, it was a good habit to always ask.

The weathered man smiled a genuine welcome as she came into the kitchen. He was munching on a bowl of Corn Flakes and reading the *Weekly Times*, his gnarled brown hands showing early signs of arthritis. 'Yeah. They're checking on the mob down by the river. Lost a lamb the other day. Wanna know if it was foxes or wild dogs. You seen anything?'

'There are foxes everywhere,' she said as she pulled a stool out from the breakfast bar, 'but I haven't spotted any dogs since I shot that skinny black one down at the southern creek in the park last year. We've been okay since then. I'll have a bit of a look around though. Let you know if I find anything.' They didn't often get troubled by wild dogs because most of them found their way to Nalong's hidden paradise before causing too much havoc, but that one had been a real pest. Three lambs down, she'd had to send it to the other paradise realm. The hard way.

Uncle Willie grunted, satisfied. 'Your dad did a good job teaching you to shoot straight,' he said. 'I remember how obsessed he used to get about trying to rid the place of rabbits. He really hated rabbits.'

Annie sat down with a bump. She hadn't been ready for the reminder, or for Uncle Willie's sudden surge of grief. It happened that way sometimes. Something she said or did would remind people of her dad. Stray thoughts leading to gloomy memories. There, and then gone.

'Kettle's still hot,' he said after a moment. 'And the peaches you gave us the other day are perfect now.' He flipped to a new page of his paper while she made herself a cuppa.

It wasn't long before the boys came back in, Harry heading straight for the sink to get a glass of water while Lucas hung back in the doorway, frowning at him. Annie stopped munching on her peach and tried to work out why Lucas was feeling so annoyed.

'Hey, Annie,' Harry mumbled as he sat down on one of the bar stools. It swayed a little—it was probably older than Uncle Willie. The flash of annoyance from Lucas turned to indignation and she suddenly remembered what the problem was, so she leant over and gave Harry a quick peck on the cheek the way a girlfriend probably would. Harry glanced back at her apologetically for forgetting, but couldn't quite bring himself to kiss her back. Across the table, Uncle Willie's eyes went as wide as the Nullarbor and Annie felt her cheeks flush in response.

Harry took a sip of his water and then cleared his throat. 'Lambs are all okay, Uncle,' he said. 'We found a new fox burrow in a clump of gorse up near Storyteller Hill. I'll take Bo out later and see what he can flush out.'

Uncle Willie nodded. 'I might have a bit of a wander out in the park later. See if I can find signs of dogs.'

Annie felt her shoulders stiffen. They had to be careful not to arouse Uncle's suspicions about what else might be out there. She kept her eyes down and let Harry handle it, because it never went smoothly when they both jumped to dissuade him from going past the farm boundary.

'I'll come with you,' Harry said. 'Bo will be better at finding a dog scent than either of us will.'

A long pause made Annie look up to see Uncle Willie licking his lips. 'You have to stay and fix the mower, Harry. I'll take Bo.'

Something was off. Uncle sounded uncomfortable, almost nervous, the same way she usually did when trying to come up with a lame excuse to stop people from getting too close to business that wasn't theirs. She glanced at Harry, who had gone very still.

Lucas noticed the atmosphere and gave a snort. 'I already fixed the mower, Uncle. Take Harry with you. You don't need to find excuses to leave Harry and Annie alone together. I'm sure they'll manage that just fine.'

Uncle Willie grunted and went back to his reading, while Annie found herself looking anywhere other than at Harry. The toaster was really shiny today. Almost shiny enough for her to see the reflection of her blushing cheeks. She stretched out her gift but there was no further reaction from Uncle. His emotions felt stable enough to walk on, but then, they always did. Nothing ever surprised him for long. If aliens were ever to land in the front yard, he would probably just tell them that the kettle was still hot and then give them some fresh eggs to take home when they left. The false news that she and Harry were apparently an item was just another step in a journey, it seemed.

She and Harry. A thread of self-disgust began to unfurl. Her deceit was spreading to include Uncle now. If only she could just tell the truth, spit out the words that would scrub her soul clean again. She was not interested in Harry that way because there was someone else for him, someone perfect. And for her, there was … a jumbled mess of confusion.

Lucas perched on the edge of his stool, fiddling with the cuff of his cotton shirt. Harry had taken him into town to buy some proper clothes because his board shorts and tank tops hadn't done nearly enough to keep the prickles off. He looked good in moleskins. His blue eyes flicked up at Annie as if he could hear what she was thinking. She tried to look away. She really did.

'I thought you'd be at school today,' he said with a very slight hint of disapproval. It was all fake though. His emotions told her that he was pleased she'd come.

'I am,' she replied without remorse. 'If Mum asks, I'm at school. Right, Uncle Willie?'

'Righto, Annie.' Along with most other farmers in the region, Harry's great-uncle wasn't exactly strict about school attendance when the season got busy. It wasn't that he didn't value having an education, it was just that practical decisions would always outweigh idealistic ones. He was the last person to care if she skipped a day or two.

'I wanted to say goodbye,' she admitted. 'I take it you don't really have any plans to return?'

The whole room turned to Lucas, waiting for his reply. Even the fridge seemed to be holding its frosty breath.

The look Lucas turned on her yearned for answers. He had absolutely no logical reason to want to stay, but it was clear that a part of him still did. His eyes begged for a reason—one that he could use to justify his reluctance to leave—and she had a whopper for him, and yet she kept her mouth shut. After a few moments he shook his head.

'Well, if you change your mind, just head on back. We'll find plenty for you to do,' Uncle Willie offered. 'You're good with a pump. You go study your engineering and then come and fix the old girl properly. Make sure they teach you about proper diesel engines too, not just those fancy electric things. They're no good on a farm.'

Lucas looked a bit unsure how to reply to that. 'I'd better grab my stuff. I told Mum I'd be home around mid-afternoon.'

As he left the room, Harry glared at Annie with eyes full of admonition. 'I need to talk to you,' he said as soon as Lucas was out of earshot. 'Alone.'

Uncle Willie smiled into his newspaper. What a hideous lie this was.

Tossing the peach pit into the compost, Annie grabbed another from the box and then made herself follow Harry outside. They went all the way over to the rivergum to make certain there was no way Uncle Willie or Lucas could accidentally overhear. Its wide branches greeted them like treasured friends.

'You can't let him go without knowing anything. It's wrong, and you know it, Annie.'

Leaning against the trunk of the tree, she picked at some bark and sighed. Hours of tossing and turning the previous night hadn't made her decision any easier. It hadn't changed it either.

'It's better for him if he doesn't know. What he doesn't know, he can't regret. I can't offer him what I'm supposed to. Not yet. So leave it.'

'But why not? No one's saying you have to rush into anything. Just take it one step at a time, but you can't—'

'Yes, I can. I've made my decision so, please, just let it go.'

Pushing herself away from the trunk, she marched back to the front door just as it swung open and a giant duffel bag was shoved through it, followed by Lucas draped in plastic shopping bags filled with various bits and pieces he hadn't bothered to pack properly.

'Let me give you a hand,' she offered. 'Is there anything else to bring?'

'No.'

'Are you driving in thongs? All the way to Melbourne?'

He strode to the car without looking at her, dumped everything into the tiny boot and slammed it shut, and then kicked off his thongs and threw them into the back seat without a word. Annie crossed her arms. He was such a skeg. Even after all this time on the farm, he still looked for any excuse to go barefoot, as if he expected soft sand underfoot. Probably just as well he was heading back to the clean city footpaths where he couldn't step on something even worse than that octopus.

'I just turned the eggs. I hope they all hatch okay,' Lucas said to Harry, who had come over and was standing with his hands in his pockets, looking a bit grumpy.

'I'm sure they'll be fine. You've done a good job,' he replied. 'Wait here a minute. I'm going to go get your final pay. Let me know if you ever want a reference or anything, not that you'll need it with your qualifications,' he added, backing away toward the house and giving Annie a pointed look to emphasise his double meaning.

'I haven't qualified for anything yet,' Lucas replied, and Annie glared right back at Harry triumphantly. Her partner Cherub shrugged one shoulder, turned, and left them on their own.

Lucas leant back on the driver's door and fiddled with his car keys, still refusing to look at her.

Gathering her courage was like raking up dead leaves on a windy day, but eventually she fished the talisman out of her pocket and held it out to him without a word. The smooth little shell waited innocently between them like a child trying to make sense of a custody battle. Instinctively, his fingers began to twitch as he looked at it. He didn't take it.

'What do I want with that stupid thing?' he asked, sounding sullen. She wasn't surprised. Sullenness was about the only emotion she'd left him with, yet it still hurt.

'I suggest you keep it with you, for a while at least. You might need it.'

His irritation blossomed into straight-up anger and fear. 'What did you do to me? That day on the beach? When you said I was bitten by one of the most dangerous creatures on the planet, you didn't mean the stupid octopus, did you?' His bright eyes bit into her. She should have been able to shield that, or drain it softly away, but the way he was looking at her made it impossible.

'Nothing! I didn't do anything. It wasn't my fault.'

'What wasn't?' he challenged.

Stupid, Annie. Be smarter than that. She took a couple of deep breaths and tried to think. 'I just meant that it wasn't my fault that you got bitten. All I did was try to help you. I'm sorry if I butted my nose in where it wasn't wanted. I grew up *here,* Lucas. In the country. Where people help each other in an emergency whether they're best friends or complete strangers. I never meant to offend you.'

'Offend me? You know that's not what I—you know what? Never mind. Keep the stupid shell. I don't want anything to do with it. Or with you. You confuse the hell out of me, and I don't like it. Tell Harry I'm sorry I couldn't wait. He can keep the money.' Yanking open the squeaky car door, he slid into the driver's seat and started the engine, slamming the door shut again and causing the little car to sway. 'Damn,' he said, followed by some other words that were too muffled by the car window between them for her to make out. He clutched at the steering wheel and squeezed his eyes shut for an uncomfortably long time. When he wound down the window, his jaw was clenched so tightly she could hear his teeth grind. 'I've totally stuffed this up,' he said. 'I've been waiting weeks for a chance to talk to you alone—to apologise for my inexcusable behaviour that day …'

Annie tried to think of what to say. How could she possibly explain that she had tampered with his reactions to her? She'd *wanted* him to kiss her, right up until the moment when her brain had caught up and she'd changed her mind, at which point he'd let her go. He hadn't done anything wrong.

'I'm sorry, Annie. I should have asked first. It won't happen again.'

Then the car was moving.

'No. Wait! You have to take it. Lucas, please, just keep it for a little while—' She chased after him, trying to get close enough to toss the shell through the window, but he didn't slow.

And then Harry was there, planting himself in front of the car and waving a couple of twenty dollar bills at him, forcing him to slam his brakes on. If Harry had been bonded to a Guardian, she would have fainted at the near miss.

'I wish we could pay you more,' Harry said casually, as if he hadn't been listening to every word they'd just been throwing at each other. 'You've earned it. Maybe if you can come back after the autumn sales we can offer you a better rate?'

'Thanks for the offer,' Lucas said, leaning his elbow out the window, 'but I'll probably try to save up a bit more and go overseas. Cam keeps asking me to visit his new place in Christchurch. It's walking distance to a surf beach. Or else I might head to Europe like Sarah has. Maybe I'll get enough for a plane ticket if I sell this.' He patted the steering wheel fondly, and the car spluttered and almost died, so he revved it like he was punishing a recalcitrant seventeen-year-old Datsun, and then glared at Annie with tight lips as if it was her fault. 'Or maybe not.' He reached out and shook Harry's hand. 'I appreciate everything you've done for me, Harry, but I think I'd better stay away from Nalong.' He took a shaky breath and then looked up at Annie again, the set of his jaw showing an obvious effort to remain civil. 'I'm sorry I was so rude, Annie. I never meant to … I mean, I wish you both all the best in the future.'

The brief kiss they had shared shone behind his eyes, clear as the sun, and it coloured all his emotions. It stunned her. She'd almost forgotten how powerful it had been, all fire and longing, and so soft. His skin had felt so warm, and his breath like the sea … and then the car pulled away again, crunching on the gravel as he sped away down the driveway. Everything felt numb as she watched him go. It took a moment to remember that she was still clutching the shell.

'Annie, he said—'

'Overseas,' she whispered in a daze. 'Plane ticket.'

'Will the talisman be enough? It might not be enough if he goes too far—'

She opened her palm so Harry could see what she was still holding. Letting out a bewildered whimper, he pushed back his short hair and watched the car speed away.

'He could die,' she whispered. She could feel a single panicked tear run down to her lip. 'If he gets on a plane and then gets sick—they might not let him fly back, and he won't know …' Horror-struck, she watched the little orange sedan bump its way down the driveway in a cloud of dust. Her head began to shake as she realised the full danger. 'Call him back!'

'I can't. He won't hear.'

The little rust-bucket sped up even more, as if the driver felt the need to reach a certain escape velocity in order to leave her orbit.

'Hit me,' she sobbed, turning to clutch at the front of Harry's shirt.

'What?'

'You heard me. Hit me! We have to get him back. *Please.*'

'I'm not going to hit you. Are you crazy? I would never hit a girl. If you're changing your mind, just call him when he gets—'

'No. He won't listen because I made him too angry. It needs to be now, and we need to make sure he believes us. He has to feel a threat to my safety. This is not an ordinary situation, Harry. I would hit you if you begged me. Now, please!'

Looking more distressed than she had ever seen him, Harry cringed and slapped her gently on the cheek.

'Oh, for God's sake, Harry,' she cried, not even certain she was really blaspheming. 'Don't you get it? He could die if we don't get him back.' With every ounce of talent she possessed, Annie pulled every emotion away from Harry except his frustration at her for being so stubborn. She honed it down to its purest, unclouded form until it was free from all other reasoned restraint. 'Now hit me like I just insulted your mum!'

He took a deep breath and held it, clenching his fist. And then let it out again. 'I can't, Annie. I'm sorry.'

She ground her teeth. 'Fine. Pretend to hit me, then. Just aim it to the right of my head.'

'Will that work?'

'It will if you close your eyes and imagine you're trying to hit me as hard as you can. He should sense your intent. Hurry up! He's almost at the road!'

She watched him close his eyes and draw back his arm. The she lifted her chin and took half a step forward. His fist, when it connected with her jaw, felt like it could have taken her whole head off. Bone against bone sent pain exploding through her face. It hurt almost as much as

Harry's crushing spike of sickening guilt that she was too stunned to shield. Grass tickled her fingers and she realised groggily that she was on the ground. The sky spun gruesomely and one of her eyes refused to focus, but she rolled onto her side and pushed herself up, frantic to see if it had worked.

A massive cloud of road grit obscured the scene, but the unmistakable sound of squealing tyres made her expel a breath full of dust and tension. Squinting, she watched the poor abused relic of a car spin around and charge back.

'Annie! Are you okay? I can't believe you just made me do that! *How* did you?' Strong arms lifted her and held her up as she wobbled. The car sped up.

'Good hit,' she mumbled, checking to see if she still had all her teeth. Her tongue was bleeding and numb, so it was a bit hard to tell. Real pain was … very painful. The sedan drew closer, and was still accelerating.

'Um, Annie, I think we'd better move,' Harry said, backing away. She grabbed on to his wrist as tightly as her shaken muscles would let her.

'Don't,' she slurred.

'But, Annie—'

'*Stay.*'

The car was heading straight for them, bearing down like a wild pig.

'But, Annie, I don't want to be killed by a *Datsun*,' Harry wailed.

'Then stay behind me,' she grunted, standing as bravely as she could and suddenly hoping it wasn't all some terrible mistake. But then, if it was, why would the car have turned around?

Like a perfectly executed movie stunt, the sedan spun sideways at the very last moment and skidded to a halt less than half a metre from where she was wobbling. Behind her, her Cherub partner let out a muffled, non-Harry-like whimper. The door of the sedan flew open so violently it nearly bounced right back again. Lucas tumbled out, with his furious sapphire eyes locked on Harry.

'Okay, maybe now you should run,' she suggested.

Chapter 12

Harry made it about twenty metres before Lucas tackled him from behind and sent them both sprawling. There was a loud crack when they hit the dirt and Annie prayed that it was only a stick. The sound of a fist hitting flesh was less ambiguous.

'Stop, Lucas! Leave him alone. It wasn't his fault. I asked him to do it. Please try to listen!'

Frenzied scuffling left no room for her words to mean anything at all, so instead she launched herself into the fray, ignoring the stabbing pain that shot through her jaw as she landed in the middle of the tangle of flailing limbs. Lucas couldn't hurt her, even by accident. She hoped.

She was right. As soon as she touched him, a shockwave ran through him like he'd been hit by lightning and half a second later she was wrenched sideways by a pair of muscled arms around her waist. Next thing she knew she was flat on her back on the grass with Lucas leaning over her, one arm planted either side of her head forming a sort of protective cage. He was breathing hard and kept flicking his gaze between her and Harry. She had never seen an expression quite that … dangerous.

'Harry's not going to hurt me. I'm not in any danger, am I?' She lay as still as possible, and after spitting out a mouthful of grass and dust, so did Harry. They both knew how volatile Lucas was at that moment, and that's when Annie realised that she had been very, very wrong. How could she have thought that it was okay to let him feel such powerful compulsions without understanding why? Watching the way his body trembled, all her recent behaviour suddenly seemed inexcusably selfish.

'Lucas,' she said softly, reaching up and touching his cheek with her fingertips. 'Lucas, look at me.'

His flashing eyes burned when she turned his head to meet her gaze. He froze for a few seconds, torn between compulsive forces that he didn't understand, and then pulled away, trying to deny all of them. Annie pushed herself up and made a grab for his hand as he sat back. Boldly placing his palm against her rapidly swelling jaw, she gasped as fire spread from his fingers and burned right into her bones. Despite the countless stories that her parents had told her, nothing had prepared her for the deep intimacy of being healed by her Guardian. She'd expected the heat, but not the complete loss of all her emotional barriers. Everything Lucas was feeling slammed into her like a road train, scattering all sense of reason and control. Fear, confusion, yearning, anger, insatiable protectiveness—all of it hit her at once, and with it came the same aftermath that Lucas himself experienced. Both of them fainted.

As Annie blinked her way back to lucidity, Uncle Willie's wide nose and smoky quartz eyes took up almost her entire field of vision. When he pulled back, his black and grey curly hair was framed by the bright blue sky. The concerned look on his face was all she could focus on for a few moments, until the sudden return of memory made her yelp and sit up. Lucas was sitting beside her on the grass with a dazzled expression and a couple of leaves in his hair. Over by the rivergum, Harry was watching them from behind the trunk, possibly for protection. His shoulders relaxed when she caught his eye.

'You all right, Annie?' Uncle asked. 'I thought City Boy smashed you with his car.'

'What? No. I'm fine. I just fainted.'

'What are you all doing fainting on my lawn?'

'Harry hit her,' Lucas growled, looking as if he was barely restraining himself from going after him again. 'I saw … I know he … then I …' As the speech embargo kicked in, the poor guy looked like he'd bitten an icy pole with his bottom teeth.

'Harry would never hurt me,' Annie interrupted, before Uncle Willie could ask. 'Lucas thought he saw Harry have a go at me but he was mistaken, I'm perfectly fine. See?' She prodded at her face to prove it didn't hurt. To herself as much as everyone else. 'We were just play fighting, like we always do.'

Harry tilted his head around the tree trunk to blink at her. They hadn't played at wrestling since she'd accidentally poked him in the eye when she was eight years old.

Uncle Willie laughed. 'Is that why Harry's hiding behind a tree? Is he scared of City Boy, or you?' He pulled her up off the ground. 'You sure you're good? The car came awful close. I saw through the window. No wonder you fainted.'

'Yeah, I'm good,' she assured him, brushing grass and gumnuts from her back.

'Well, then I'll go and put the kettle on.'

The fly-screen door clattered shut as Uncle Willie left, leaving a silence that held everyone still except for Bo, who ran around in exuberant celebration of the fact that Lucas and Annie no longer appeared to be dead.

'He hit you,' Lucas insisted. 'Don't try to tell me I was mistaken.'

'I made him do it. He would never hurt me.'

'Annie, your face felt like it was split in two! That punch nearly broke your jaw. Your eye was … you should at least get some ice or something … that was no play fight …' His voice trailed off as his fingers brushed her cheek, searching for a wound he knew full well was no longer there. He just didn't have enough information to piece together what had happened.

'Of course it wasn't a play fight. I lied to Uncle Willie, but it wasn't Harry's fault either. It was totally mine—'

'Can you hear yourself? There is *never* a good reason to hit a woman … to hit anyone!' He glared at the Cherub behind the tree. 'Except maybe him.'

It was not going well. She tried again. 'But I asked—'

'You didn't ask for it, Annie! No matter what you said or did, you didn't deserve to get punched.'

'How about if I said "please"? You're not listening, Lucas. I *literally* asked him to hit me.'

'Tricked me into it, actually,' Harry mumbled, before snapping his mouth closed and sliding down to slump against the tree trunk. Annie almost expected him to roll over and offer Lucas his unprotected belly as a sign of submission, like Bo sometimes did.

'I needed to bring you back,' she explained to Lucas. 'I was wrong before. I couldn't just let you leave without telling you what was going on. You didn't even see him punch me, did you?'

Lucas stared at her, grinding his teeth again.

'You felt it, you didn't see it.'

His confused glower could have frightened off a Drop Bear.

'You're bonded to me, Lucas. You're my Guardian. You can feel when I'm hurt.'

'That's ridiculous,' he said, shaking his head, but he kept staring.

'You healed me.'

Lucas looked down at his hand as if remembering the searing heat they'd both felt. He rubbed his palm.

While Annie waited for him to absorb the truth, she tried to figure out what to do next. Harry would want to take him to the cave to show him the holy sword, but her mum would know as soon as they started heading that way. The thought of her finding out about Lucas made her stomach churn. That hadn't changed. She simply wasn't ready to handle that conversation.

Without even glancing at her, Lucas stood up and stomped back to his car and was about to get back in when he started swearing again. One of the front tyres was flat. He slammed the door so hard it looked like the car was about to tip over. Then he kicked at the disloyal tyre a few times in a fit of temper before disappearing back into the house. An inner door slammed a moment later.

She heard Harry sigh. 'Well,' he said, still slumped against the tree. 'That could have gone better.'

Chapter 13

Annie's Guardian brooded for about three hours. All she saw of him in that time was a brief appearance when he came out of his room to call his mum. He told her that he was having car trouble and that it might take a long time to fix. There was a pause, where she apparently offered to come and get him, but after a few drawn out moments of thinking about it he told her not to worry. He wasn't willing to leave without his car anyway so it wouldn't help. Annie took that as a good sign.

When the sun got too hot, Annie moved into the kitchen and made some sandwiches. Uncle Willie thanked her and took a couple with him as he left with Harry to search for wild dogs in the state park. It was the slowest day of her life. When she'd cleaned everything she could possibly find to clean in the kitchen, she started to vacuum the lounge. The Doolans' house was her second home and she often helped out wherever she could, both outside and in. Uncle Willie was a total clean-freak and was always grateful to have her do the chores Harry managed to avoid, but once the temperature passed thirty-two on the old thermometer on the lounge room wall, she started to wonder if going to school might have been the better option after all. With the Hoover running she completely missed the fact that Lucas was standing in the doorway watching her, until she turned the machine off and nearly jumped through the ceiling when he said her name.

'Jeez, how long have you been standing there?' she asked, trying to remember if she'd been singing out loud or just in her head.

'Long enough to hear most of "Mysterious Ways". I like your voice.'

Damn. She rallied quickly. 'I saw some bread rolls in the freezer if you're hungry. The sliced ham is still good and I picked a fresh lettuce. I'd stay away from the cold chicken though. It smells a bit funky. If you like, I know an easy way to check for sure.'

His eyes narrowed but he didn't ask. Instead he leant against the doorframe with his arms crossed, as if he was expecting her to do something he wasn't going to like.

So she did something he didn't like. She fished the shell out of her pocket and tossed it to him.

'I told you I don't want it,' he said, yet he plucked it easily out of the air anyway.

'You only said that because you don't trust me.'

'So?'

'I want you to trust me.'

He came to stand in front of her, his runners touching the Hoover between them. 'So tell me what's really going on.'

When he was so near, leaning over her like that, she struggled to think straight. The lines between his emotions and hers kept blurring. She wanted to push his shaggy hair out of his face so she could see his eyes better.

'I'm not sure where to start. First, I have to say sorry.' She stepped away and sat down on the old velvet settee so she could concentrate properly. 'I should have told you everything right from the start, but I chickened out. I thought maybe if I gave you the talisman, you could just go on with your life and forget you ever met me, but that was never going to happen.' She winced at how obnoxious that sounded.

'What did you mean before, about us being bonded? What exactly did you do to me?'

'Nothing! It wasn't me. I was just sitting on the beach minding my own business.'

'Until I stood on that creature.'

'You're blaming *me* for that?' She realised her voice was rising to a very unattractive frequency, and swallowed hard.

'Well, what *can* I blame you for?' he yelled straight back.

'How about for the fact that you heal far quicker than anyone else and would probably be dead otherwise? Or the fact that I stayed with you because I felt how scared you were and couldn't stand to let you feel so alone?'

He stared at her, speechless, and yet his emotions spoke loudly enough. He was obviously remembering what it had felt like, lying there on the sand, unable to move or breathe.

'I wasn't all that scared,' he said after a moment, sounding more confused than defensive. 'Why not? I remember being terrified, but then …'

'I didn't let you feel it. I took it from you so you wouldn't have to deal with that as well.' Admitting what she could do felt very peculiar. For most of her life there had been exactly three people she could have said those words to, and after her dad died, that had left her with two. And she'd told neither of them.

Lucas finally sat down. 'I think you'd better tell me everything.'

This. This was the exact moment. The one she and Harry used to laugh about, imagining how it would play out. Her parents used to love retelling their own story of when this had happened for them. Would she botch it as badly as her mum had? Probably.

'Genesis one to three. Those chapters pretty much cover it,' she said, reaching for the Bible that Harry had thoughtfully handed her before he'd left. How many years had she spent practising this little speech? She'd even memorised the whole of chapter three, word for word. In Old King James too, so it sounded more impressive. 'In the sweat of thy face shalt thou eat bread' had been an ongoing taunt whenever she or Harry had sprung each other doing something they weren't supposed to. Unfortunately, now that the time had come, all those beautiful phrases with their 'thees' and 'thous' and 'hearkeneds' and 'whences' just felt wrong. She was about to turn someone's life inside-out. Flowery language wasn't going to make it any easier.

Lucas actually looked a bit relieved when he saw what she was handing him. It had to be better than being handed a giant book of spells or something. He didn't ask any further questions but obediently sat back and began to read.

'Last time I opened one of these, it had more pictures. I distinctly remember pictures,' he complained.

Annie went to make some coffee.

❧

'Not human?' Lucas asked.

Annie took a moment to make certain her voice wouldn't waver. 'Correct,' she answered.

Above them the ceiling fan was dutifully churning the hot air into a nice thick soup. The curtains were closed against the sun, the windows open just enough to keep the air moving. Every few moments, the hot northerly wind sent the curtains flapping, as if pestering them to get to work dusting the back of the old armchair. Annie pulled her sweaty shirt away from her back yet again and raked another damp strand of hair off her face.

Lucas looked her in the eye. 'Cherubim.'

She nodded.

'You and Harry?'

'And Mum.' Her eyes widened as she remembered. 'You can't tell her!'

'That she's not human?'

'No! I mean you can't tell her who you are. Or that you're here. Or even that you exist. Please, Lucas. It's important.'

A new wave of frustration and confusion swirled around with the soupy air. Annie walked to the window again and peeked past the curtain, wishing for a sign that Harry was returning, which was stupid because she could feel that he was still quite a distance away to the west. Without his calming presence, she was making a shemozzle of things.

'Annie, stop pacing and sit down, will you? It's too hot.' Lucas put the shell down on the coffee table next to the two steaming mugs that neither of them had touched. 'You're not making any sense, so I'm going to make things easy. I'll ask you some questions, and you just stick with yes and no, all right?'

She sat.

'Good. Okay, so there really is a Garden of Eden?'

'Yes.'

'And you guard the entrance to it?'

'Yeah, I guess.' *Against rabbits and scheming March flies …*

'In Australia?'

She nodded.

'Near *here* somewhere?' he asked with a disbelieving laugh.

'Yes.'

A few seconds passed while that news flitted around the air like a butterfly on red cordial. It was too tricky to really grasp properly, so he eventually just moved on.

'Can I see it?'

'Resounding "no". Sorry.'

More heavy seconds passed by. Lucas watched her with serious, thoughtful eyes.

'Your job is to stop people getting in, so they can't eat from the Tree of Life?'

'Yeah. Only Cherubim are allowed in, and no one else is even allowed to know about it.'

Lucas nodded once. 'You mean other than you, me, Harry, your mum and Mr Doolan?'

'No, not Uncle Willie. He hasn't a clue.'

'And what happens if I tell other people?'

'You won't be able to.'

His eyebrows made a funny shape.

'Imagine telling Cam,' she suggested. 'What words would you use?'

Lucas shifted about in his chair as he tried to evade the sudden feeling of guilt that rose up to choke him. She left that emotion alone.

'Don't worry. You'll get used to it,' she told him. 'We all get it if we accidentally go to say the wrong thing at the wrong time. It's quite an effective little safeguard.'

Lucas picked up his coffee, probably just for something to do with his hands, which made Annie notice that she was fiddling with the end of her ponytail.

'So, um … what stuff can you do? Anything … magic?'

Annie made a rather rude sound. 'Trust me. Harry and I have tried. All we've got is a sudden case of ants in our pants whenever anyone wanders too close to the cave. Harry once got suspended from school for a week for bolting straight out of class three days in a row. There was a group of hikers camping by Dead Horse Creek and they kept heading too far north.'

'And what happened? How did Harry defend the cave?'

She tried not to scoff at the excitement in his voice. 'He told them that there was a really pretty track down to the south of the shale slides that was full of peppermint gums, so they would probably see koalas there.'

'That's all?'

'People trust Harry.'

Lucas conceded that with a nod that seemed only slightly disappointed. 'And what's the point of me? Why are we bonded?'

Her hair suddenly became incredibly fascinating, but she forced herself to answer. 'You job is to protect me. Like a bodyguard. That's why you always know where I am, and if I'm in any danger. I'm sorry, Lucas, but that's also why you get sick if we get too far away from each other. I gave you the talisman to try to stop that from happening. I was stupid to think that would work indefinitely. I guess it wore off.'

'It's stronger now. I can feel it,' he said, leaning forward to peer at the innocent looking memento of their day together on the beach. 'It has your blood in it. You topped it up, didn't you? That was why you wanted me to take it back.'

'And you still can. Now that you know, you can still choose what you want to do. No one's forcing you to stay.'

'Except God Himself,' he shot back, tapping the cover of the Bible on the table.

Inwardly she groaned at the fact that she was going to have to resort to using the same argument her parents had used when she'd said the same thing. 'God isn't forcing you any more than He forces moths to fly toward the moon. It's in your nature to be drawn here, but there are things we can do if you really don't want that.'

'Like trick me with a false moon? Like a flame?' he asked, picking up the shell and displaying it between his thumb and forefinger.

Great. Why hadn't she used a different analogy? Still. He wasn't wrong.

'That was why I had to tell you. Once you mentioned going overseas, I realised how dangerous it was for you not to know, but now you do. You're smarter than a moth.'

'Am I? Then why is it I have no clear sense of direction whatsoever?'

'Well, you did just get hit with some pretty heavy news …'

'I don't just mean today,' he admitted, tracing his finger around the spiral pattern. 'I've always struggled to make major decisions. I picked subjects at school based on keeping my options as wide open as possible, and I picked engineering because it was the best course I could get into with my qualifying score and because it leads to so many different career paths. If I left my options any more open they'd be doing the splits.'

She couldn't help laughing at that. He was so easy going, when he wasn't slamming doors and driving like a maniac. She nearly wished that she hadn't wasted quite so much time avoiding him. There had to be a way to sort out this mess, somehow. They just had to come to a clear arrangement. For that, she needed time to think.

'You should take your time in deciding what to do. I suggest you go home as you'd intended. Take the shell and let me know if you have any problems. Don't do anything drastic just yet.' Somehow, she needed to keep him away until she could come up with some semblance of a plan.

'But what about you? Don't I need to protect you?'

'From what? Harry's fist? I've managed just fine without you for nearly eighteen whole years …' It was the wrong thing to say. Suddenly every muscle Lucas owned went rigid at the reminder of what Harry had done. And he owned a lot of them.

His voice went as cold as the river in June. 'He should never have hit you. I don't care if you begged him to do it.'

'He wasn't aiming to hit me. He had his eyes closed and I stepped— you know what? Never mind. That's going to sound bad no matter how I phrase it. Just try to remember that he did it for you. To save your life, potentially.'

'I don't care! He hit—'

Lucas glanced down at his hand, which she had grabbed just as he'd launched himself from the settee in a fit of frenzy. Good thing Harry hadn't come back yet.

'Powerful, isn't it?' she said, trying hard to sound a bit arrogant. Unfortunately, arrogance was at the opposite end of the spectrum from how she really felt, so instead she just sounded sort of … petulant. It made no difference anyway because Lucas was busy staring at their hands as if trying to work out whose they were. His shoulders relaxed and he sighed. Skin on skin. Also very powerful. Awkwardly, she pulled her fingers from his and crossed her arms.

Lucas sat down again on the far end of the settee, and crossed his arms too. 'If he ever touches you again, I'll kill him. I don't care if he's the angel Gabriel himself.'

'So you do know your Bible stories,' she said.

'Only the ones with the pictures.'

Frowning at the way the spare tyre sagged when she let down the jack, Annie wondered again just how much of an active part God had to play in everything that happened to them. It was beginning to seem less and less likely that the poor little Datsun would ever get Lucas back to Melbourne. His door-slam the previous day had jammed something in the locking mechanism, and it wouldn't open, and now it appeared that the spare tyre had already lived a life of crime, skipped bail, and flunked its rehabilitation program. Perhaps he really was going to be forced to stay.

'You'd better put some more air into it as soon as you get to town,' she advised. Harry nodded in agreement, but Lucas just shrugged. Perhaps he thought that risking another flat was a way of keeping his options open.

He turned to her, fiddling with his keys. 'Shouldn't I at least have your phone number? You know, in case something happens?'

'To me or to you?' she asked. 'I'll be fine, Lucas. Call Harry if you need to. What on earth would Mum say if you called our place?'

Lucas and Harry looked at her as if waiting for her to answer her own question.

'We *can't* let her find out. You both promised. I'll tell her eventually, once we've all had a chance to figure out what we want. She won't understand if Lucas decides not to stay.' Her eyes begged Harry to back her up and play along.

It was all a bit messy. Her mum would be devastated if Annie admitted she was too frightened to give in to the bond with her Guardian. The bond was supposed to be a blessing, yet Annie had seen the other end of it firsthand. She'd felt what it was like to lose a bonded partner, and the idea of becoming so attached to another person quite simply terrified her. Yet how could she possibly explain all that to Lucas without admitting that Cherubim always married their Guardians? *One lot of bad news at a time,* she decided.

'Why won't she understand?' Lucas asked. 'Have any other Guardians ever decided not to stay?'

Annie was at a complete loss. Luckily Harry had her back. Again.

'You're the first one we know of who wasn't already settled here when the bond kicked in,' he said. 'Times are changing, Lucas. You don't need to feel bound to old traditions these days.'

'And Annie's mum would rather I stuck with convention.'

'Annie's mum still believes her girl needs a protector. I can under-stand why Annie might choose not to go along with that. Let the two of them sort this out between them, Lucas.'

The ground seemed to drop out from beneath Annie's feet. Nothing Harry had said was technically a lie, but Harry made her mum sound like a stuffy old matron. Nothing could be further from the truth. Of course, Lucas didn't question him. No one ever questioned the motivations behind anything Harry said.

'Fine,' Lucas said, turning back to her. 'I'll stay away from your mum. Feels a bit dishonest, though.'

If only people trusted her the same way.

'One more thing before you go,' she said to him. 'Kelly mentioned that Sarah might be coming home soon. She's not sure why, but it sounded like Sarah was a bit upset. Her mum just said that things weren't working out the way she'd hoped. Kelly thought maybe Dave would want to know.'

'Maybe she had trouble finding work. You can't live off your savings forever, especially not in Europe,' Harry suggested.

Lucas cleared his throat, and hesitated for a moment before reply-ing. 'I'll tell him, although I don't know if it matters. Apparently they broke up just before she left.'

'Oh,' Annie muttered. 'I hadn't realised. Sorry. I thought they were doing great. Kelly said they spent nearly the entire time together when her dad and Vicky were away on their honeymoon. She promised Sarah she wouldn't tell them that he'd stayed at their house.'

Kelly had also told her that Sarah had been almost impossible to live with during that time. Crazy-mental mood swings, crying fits and full-on tantrums. Kelly's new sister had seemed completely unable to make up her mind about what she wanted, changing plans constantly. Kelly had tried to be patient, hoping it was just the transition to a new town and new family that was sending her troppo, but she had definitely been relieved when Sarah had finally boarded the plane for London. That had been almost six weeks ago. Annie wondered what Kelly really thought about the fact that she might be heading home already.

Lucas opened his mouth as if he had more to say, and then changed his mind. He and Dave were pretty close. He undoubtedly knew more about their situation, as did she, and he was choosing not to blab. A little satisfied feeling of respect for him warmed Annie's chest. For the briefest of moments. Until he spoiled it.

'Well, I'd better get moving,' he said, throwing his bag onto the back seat before walking right up to Harry again. They were pretty much the same height, but suddenly Lucas looked as though he was towering above him. He stood so close that for a moment Annie thought she was going to have to intervene again. Bo barked once, softly, as a polite warning for them both to behave.

Lucas fixed his steely gaze on Harry's worried frown. 'You won't hurt her again.'

'Of course not.'

More seconds passed while Lucas waited for more.

Harry struck back with his soothing gaze. 'No matter what she asks me to do, I promise you I will never hurt her again. I love her.'

Lucas's sudden spike of jealousy caught Annie so off-guard that she missed the chance to snatch it away, but it lasted for barely a second and she realised that he must have suppressed it himself. Or perhaps Harry's pacifying gift had eased it away first.

Lucas glanced at her, with a good attempt at hiding how self-conscious he was feeling. 'Look, Annie, I know you two are destined to be together and all that, but I need to say something.'

Annie bit her bottom lip and kept her eyes on the Datsun's dodgy tyre. Anything to avoid looking at either of them.

'I don't care if you two are the only ones of your … species on the planet, or if God Himself signs your marriage contract. I still don't think he should take you for granted. If you ever feel unsafe …'

'You would feel it, Lucas,' Harry assured him. 'No matter how far away you are. You won't have to worry.'

Lucas turned his back on him and touched Annie lightly on the elbow. His blue eyes reminded her of the poor octopus, glowing with a primal warning system that would never falter, even until death. 'If he really wants you, he should have to earn it.'

Speechless, she gaped at him, while the only male member of her 'species' in the world clamped a hand over his mouth to try to contain his laughter. A snorty kind of cough was all that escaped. Somehow Harry managed to compose his face just in time as Lucas spun back to him.

'I agree whole-heartedly, Lucas. She deserves someone who will treasure her above all else.'

Lucas gave him a serious nod and then started climbing into his car through the window. Farm work had not done those abs any harm at all.

'Goodbye, Annie,' he said, looking disappointed as the engine turned over the first time. 'I'll let you know when I've figured out what to do.' He gripped the wheel. 'Thank you for giving me space to think. I really appreciate it.' But the feeling of resentment she sensed from him betrayed the fact that he would probably have preferred being told he had to stay. She was kicking him out, and they both knew it. They'd spent hours talking about it. Or at least, he'd spent hours trying to justify why deferring from uni wasn't such a big deal and she'd spent even longer telling him he was being ridiculous. There was no sane reason for him to leave everyone he knew, drop all his plans and move to Nalong. Once he did that, it would be very difficult to leave again. Even he could sense the truth of that. He'd finally agreed to go, but only after she'd told him bluntly that she wasn't sure that she wanted him hanging around her and Harry like a third wheel. That had been the dirtiest lie she'd ever told and it still made her feel a bit ill.

Finally, the Datsun pulled away and Lucas gave a pathetic little wave that was barely discernible through the cloud of road dust he left behind.

Chapter 14

There was so little useful information that Annie had been able to tell Lucas, that it didn't take long for him to start calling Harry with questions. Harry complained that he never knew what to say to him, not knowing how much she was happy for Lucas to know, and not really being able to talk freely on the phone anyhow. Phones were unreliable things when it came to real privacy, apparently, because they always made Annie's words stumble over each other whenever she tried to say anything to Harry that was even remotely related to Eden.

After about three weeks of fielding Lucas's calls, Harry turned up at her farm one morning, presumably to tell her off. She was kneeling by the strawberry plants trying to catch a pesky blue-tongue lizard when she felt him approach. She knew she couldn't avoid him any longer.

'Need a hand?' he asked, leaning over the chicken-wire fence that surrounded the veggie patch.

Searching under the strawberry leaves, she rummaged around and came out holding a grumpy looking reptile. It hissed and curled its fat body around her wrist, its little claws scrambling in the air like a cartoon character that had just realised it had run off the edge of a cliff. Pink strawberry juice was smeared along its jaw in undeniable evidence of its thievery. Annie breathed a sigh of relief for the fact that it really was a blue-tongue. She had been *fairly* confident …

'I thought rats were nicking all our berries, but it was you, wasn't it, you little troublemaker,' she admonished the wriggling creature. She handed the lizard to Harry and climbed back over the short fence. 'Sometimes I wonder why we bother at all. Between the snails, the bugs, the rabbits, the rats, the cockies and the lizards, everything gets to eat our veggies except for us. It's hardly worth the effort.' Complaining to

Harry was always very gratifying. He always listened so attentively, and like an old man in a teenager's body, he always had a wise or comforting comment that never failed to put her petty grievances into perspective.

'You're screwing him over, Annie.'

Not the comforting words she'd been fishing for. The frightened lizard latched its toothless gums onto Harry's finger, and she used the few moments it took to gently pry it away to madly try to come up with a decent argument. Unable to think of one, she cradled the bluey along her forearm and headed down the hill toward the dam so she could release it somewhere safe.

'He can do whatever he wants,' she snapped when she realised Harry was following. 'I told him to make his own decisions.'

'Good. I'll let him know. He'll be here by dinner. Tell your mum to set him up in the spare room.'

'Not funny, Harry. I won't do that to her,' she said, setting the lizard down on a rock. The sleek grey and brown reptile stared at them, probably wondering if its freedom was some sort of a trick.

'You can't keep him away forever.'

'So, what do you suggest?' she asked, rounding on her friend. 'The other day Mum asked me what I wanted to do for my eighteenth birthday. I told her I'd like to go for a holiday with her somewhere. Just the two of us. Maybe head to Melbourne for a weekend and catch a movie or something, like we used to.'

Harry shrugged. 'Great idea. I can cover things here. No problem. What did she say?'

'She smiled and said, "Perfect, we'll stay at the same place we did when Dad took us to see *Cats*". Then she burst into tears and retreated to her bedroom. She went Next Door during the night. That was four days ago.'

'Went Next Door' was their code for heading to Eden. It had simplified things numerous times when there was company about, and the habit stuck even when they were on their own.

The bluey tasted the air but continued to stare at them. Annie was certain it would have frowned if it'd had eyebrows.

'Wednesday night? I felt that, I think. I thought I was just sleeping badly. Annie, I'm so sorry. I had no idea she was still so … I mean, if I'd realised you were on your own I would have—'

'What? What would you have done? Left Uncle to supervise your lamb sale? You know you get a better price than he ever does. You're needed at home. Besides, I'm fine here. Everything's under control, more or less. I even got the roadside paddock sprayed, finally. It should be blackberry-free in a month or so. Oh, and you can let Uncle know that there *is* another wild dog around, but I know where it is so he can stop wandering around out in the park looking for it.'

Harry looked relieved at that. 'Good. He's been taking the four-wheeler out there the last couple of days. Not a word to me about it. Basic farm safety—always let someone know where you're going. He told me I sounded like my mum. So, you reckon you can find it?'

'Sure. I found fresh tracks near Skinny-dip Dam yesterday. I'll go out there this afternoon and deal with it. We really need a new dog here soon, even if it's something yappy and small—at least it might be able to warn me when there's a feral hanging around. Maybe if we get something stupid enough it won't be able to follow us Next Door and run away like the last two …'

'Annie—'

'Did I tell you I actually found Ferris last time I went? He came bounding up to me as if he'd never left, bouncing around without a care in the world. Absolutely no memory of the fact that he was bred to be a working dog. I asked him to come home but he just looked at me with his innocent doggy eyes as if I was insane—'

'Annie, stop.'

Harry's liquid dark eyes cut through her rambling as effectively as the opening beats of a rock concert.

'When did you last get to school?' he asked.

She glared right back, trying not to look guilty. 'Wednesday. I can hardly leave the place while Mum's away, can I? There's way too much to do here.'

'You're in Year 12.'

'Really? Are you sure? I must have lost count.'

'I thought you wanted to be a vet.'

'Pffft, as if that was ever going to happen. I can't last a week away from home without falling apart. Did you really think I'd survive a five-year uni degree? I just told Mum that to make her … happy.'

Harry scoffed. 'Happy? You know she'd be happy with whatever you decided to do. She's not like Uncle Willie. She understands. Sometimes I think you forget that she's been in your shoes—'

'No, she hasn't!' she shouted. 'She had both her parents, until they were old. Well, sort of old … They were a real family. She never had to spend every waking moment reminding *her* mother how to live. Do you have any idea how exhausting that is? Trying to constantly convince her that not everything revolves around the Garden? What if she disappears one day and never comes back? You *know* how easily that could happen. I'd much rather have Uncle Willie. Or in fact anyone I could at least rely on to want to stay in the same world as me—'

Harry's arms were around her in the next instant and he crushed her against his chest, letting her sob away all her fear and anxiety. He didn't say a word. He didn't need to. His gift wasn't restricted by mere words.

∾

'You're out of bread. And juice … and cheese. The only veggies you have are zucchinis … what have you been eating, Annie?'

'Cheese, and juice, and bread. That's why there are none of those things left. There are heaps of zucchinis still in the garden though. The rats haven't eaten all of them yet. Oh, and just so you know, we're also out of loo paper,' she warned, jiggling two teabags at once.

'No wonder Lucas keeps calling me,' she heard Harry mumble as he peered dejectedly into the empty coffee jar. 'I'm getting sick of hearing the stupid phone ringing.'

'Fine. I'll drive into town and get some groceries as soon as I've fed the horses.'

'Bad idea. There's a new cop in town. Young guy. Mike something. His entire job seems to consist of driving around and checking people's tail lights and licences. The other officers probably make him do it just to keep him out of the station so they can get the real work done. He's pulled me over twice already, once for the crack in my windscreen and then again for having too much dust on my back number plate. Seriously, dust! I'm not sure I'll be able to talk him out of a fine a third time. You've got Buckley's of getting away with only having a learner's permit and no supervising driver if he catches you. He won't care that you've been driving around your farm for years.'

Groaning, she handed Harry his tea and then stared out the kitchen window to the west, wondering if there was any chance at all of dragging her mother back home before she ran out of zucchinis and had to start eating hay. Or perhaps she should just do the same thing and disappear Next Door. The Garden pulled at her, making her feet jiggle around.

'Do you want me to try to bring her back?' Harry asked, genuine concern resonating from every line of his body. Only Harry could sympathise so convincingly.

'No,' she sighed. 'Her visits there do her good. When she gets back she'll be … better. And I need her to be better. Besides, they're getting less frequent. That's good, right?'

'But they're also getting longer,' Harry pointed out. 'You can't run this place on your own, Annie. Let me suggest to Lucas—'

'No way. He can't—'

'Just listen. Let me suggest to him to come back to work at my place. Then I'll be able to spend some time here, giving you a hand. There's no need for your mum to find out about him until you want her to. We can keep track of her and warn Lucas to make himself scarce if she comes over. We just need to pay attention to where she is, and you do that automatically now anyway, don't you?'

Annie stared into the murky depths of her tea, knowing that his solution was only a short-term one. It would buy maybe a few weeks at best. Her mother was grieving, not stupid, yet there really weren't a lot of other options. 'Okay, but it has to be his choice. Which means that you can't be the one to call him. I'll do it.'

Harry, who had been sniffing at his tea in distaste, tilted his head in silent query.

'You can be very persuasive, Harry. Even when you don't mean to be.' Annie looked out the window again, at the tree-covered hills that hid their complicated secret. There was something unnerving about the way the hills stared back at her, unchanging, unblinking.

'Well, in that case, I'm going to persuade you to let me drive you to town to buy some coffee. I can't drink this revolting dam water.' He emptied his mug into the sink, picked up his keys and waited for her in the kitchen doorway. 'And then I'm going to drop you at school.'

'No.'

'You should make it there by the end of lunch if we go now. At least you can pick up all the work you've missed. I'll help you tackle it tonight if you like, not that I can help you much these days. I just don't get chemistry.'

'No.'

A flash of annoyance crossed Harry's face. Unlike him, under normal circumstances. He was feeling it too—he just hadn't paid enough attention to it yet.

'Annie, I've been shooting that many foxes lately that I still have the rifle in my car, so I can go after the dog as soon as—'

'It isn't that,' she explained. 'Did Uncle Willie say what his plans were for this morning? I take it you told him you were coming straight here after doing the feed run.'

And that was all it took for Harry to notice what had been unsettling him. Suddenly they were pushing past each other to get outside. Annie reached the ute first and jumped in the passenger side. Her fingers trembled as she tied her hair back while Harry started the engine with an impatient roar. Tyres skidded on gravel as they took off toward the state park, toward where they could feel someone approaching the river from the far side, heading toward the place where a waterfall marked the start of a line of cliffs. Cliffs that were full of secret caves.

'Do you have a drink bottle in here anywhere?' Annie asked ten minutes later, pulling chip packets and hay band out from under her seat. Her head whacked against the window winder as they hit a particularly big hole in the track.

'Try behind the head rest,' Harry suggested, accelerating to the base of the next hill.

A lidless plastic Coke bottle was a major win. It only held a few ants. The day was hot enough that dehydration could become a major issue far too easily.

'He feels more to the south to me,' Annie suggested. 'We might have to leave the track now.'

'Almost directly south-west from here, I think. Only we can't leave the track yet. We have to get around the back of this hill first otherwise we'll get caught at the steep part of that little gully. It's too overgrown; we'll never make it through.'

'Why do you think Uncle Willie came out here? Do you really believe he's just after that wild dog?'

Harry squinted at the ruts ahead. 'Given that we can't get to this track from our place, he must have driven around the long way to explore this side of the river, which means he must be pretty determined to find the dog. He usually just takes the four-wheeler out along our back trails. Why do you ask? Why else would he be here?'

'I don't know, but there must be a reason he doesn't let you come along. He only comes out here when you aren't around.' The ute stopped so suddenly that Annie squashed the Coke bottle against the dashboard. Harry was glaring at her as if the whole situation was her fault.

'I keep finding reasons to stop him going,' he said. 'That's why he goes behind my back. It isn't surprising.'

'Harry, your rifle box is here, in the tray, remember? Why would he come all the way out here to hunt a wild dog without it?'

He began to drive again, without a word.

They stopped at the next creek crossing to fill up the bottle with bug-infested water. Better than nothing. Harry started driving again as soon as Annie had one foot in the door. 'Whoa, Harry. Careful. I don't think there's any need to rush quite so much. He hasn't moved for a while now so we should catch up okay.'

'Why hasn't he moved?'

'Maybe he's resting? It's stinking hot.'

The look on Harry's face could have darkened the sun. 'He's on the western side of this ridge. There isn't a decent tree anywhere near there, only dry shrubs and shale until you reach the creek at the very bottom, which is impossible to get down to. No shade at all. There are a lot of caves though, and not all of them are easy to see.'

'You know this place pretty well, don't you?'

'Of course. It's my home. It isn't just the nothing-zone that buffers Eden from the rest of this world, Annie. It's precious too, and ours to protect.'

Harry was definitely grouchier than usual. He almost sounded snappy.

Neither of them spoke another word, even after they reached the other side of the gully and found Uncle's Toyota trooper perched on a rocky outcrop as if it was just there to appreciate the view. Harry drove on, following the sense of someone much farther to the north. It took another half an hour of bush-bashing before they stopped, unable to navigate the rocky slope that marked the southern end of the great sweeping valley. Still without a word, they split up to begin searching the area for signs of Uncle Willie's passage. A few minutes later, Annie gave a single low whistle when she came across a scuff mark on one of the boulders. Then they began to call his name. He was no longer moving, no longer drawing closer to that place that had to be kept hidden, no longer able to be pinpointed with flashes of visions showing landmarks or scenery. Annie could feel that he was nearby, but the closest thing to a vision she got was an ominous feeling of darkness and stifling heat that was probably just a reflection of her worry.

They scrambled down the hill, over boulders and through patches of spiky flame heath, sweat soaking up the dust on Annie's face to form muddy tracks down her jaw. Flies were everywhere, each one dedicated to getting up her nose. She followed Harry down a short drop, scraping the backs of her thighs as she slid and scrambled for somewhere to place her feet at the bottom among all the smaller rocks and dry mulch. Her best choice was where a shrub had found precarious purchase on a tiny patch of dirt, only the shrub was more of a pile of dead sticks than a living thing. Was there anywhere better? How cranky was Lucas going to get if she drew a little blood? Too late.

'I see something,' Harry called back, finally breaking the silence that was the closest thing they ever really did to fighting. 'It's his hat.' He launched himself from a small outcrop, landing on the other side of what Annie now saw was a deep black hole between the boulders. His boots slid for a good three feet, sending a shower of pebbles plinking and echoing into the cave. That was when they heard the groan.

'Uncle?' Harry's voice held a quality to it that Annie had rarely heard.

'What took you so long?'

The reply was far too feeble, slurred, and farther away than Annie had expected. How deep was that hole?

'Are you hurt?'

'Yeah. A bit. Can't use my shoulder well enough to climb back up. Thought I was going to have to eat spiders for tea. I don't sup ...'

The rest of his sentence became a mumble of seemingly made-up words.

'Uncle?' Harry called.

There was no answer. Harry leant over to peer farther into the gloom and called again, but there was no reply. He braced his legs and shoulders against the opposing rocks, preparing to slide down.

'Harry, wait. If Uncle hurt himself falling in there, chances are you will too.'

The last thing Harry did before he disappeared into the black was turn and look her in the eye. 'Trust me.'

It felt as if the sun was telling her off for letting it happen. There was no breeze, unless you counted the air currents created by the wings of the hundreds of flies that had converged on her scent. They kept landing on her face, making it difficult to climb as carefully as she should. How long had it taken to clamber down to where they'd found Uncle's hat? It seemed to take three times as long to get back up again. And once she did, what was she supposed to do then? Go for help? That would take hours, and how was she supposed to stomach letting strangers get this close to the valley? No. She would have to get them out herself, somehow. First, water. Harry had hit his head quite badly on the way down the shaft, but had managed to call up to her that Uncle was unconscious. Without any obvious head trauma, dehydration was the most likely cause of Uncle Willie's condition. How many hours had he spent wandering around the tracks before coming far enough north to trigger their senses?

When Annie reached the ute, she honked the horn long and loud to let Harry know. Then she grabbed the Coke bottle she'd filled from the creek, along with the snatch-strap from under the driver's seat, and headed straight back down the hill again, pausing only to find a better route around the red-bellied black snake sunning itself on a rock. Rocks, sun, caves, and a creek below. Snake paradise. *Are you sure this isn't just a buffer zone around Eden, Harry?*

When she reached the cave again, she lowered one end of the snatch-strap down into the gloom. It took a long time for Harry to call out that it had reached him, and there was hardly any of it left over for her to hold. What was she going to secure it to?

'Did you get the water, Annie? Uncle really needs it.'

'I did, but your bottle doesn't have a lid. I can't get it down to you without spilling it all. Is he conscious?'

'In and out,' Harry replied. 'Delirious. Keeps talking about treasure.'

Annie sat down on a log wedged between the boulders above the hole. Treasure? Did Uncle Willie suspect something about Eden? If that was the real reason he had come out here, they had a problem.

'Let's just get him out of there. What do you need me to do? I hate to admit it, but I'm not strong enough to pull either one of you up on my own.'

'I'll help lift Uncle from down here. We'll just take it slow.'

Annie glanced around. Despite Harry's easy assurance, she knew she was going to need some decent leverage if they were to have any chance at all. The landscape wasn't promising. An ancient landslide had left a tumble of limestone and dead wood and not much else. Sticks and stones, caves and bones, all left to bake in the sun's seething waves. The rocks were hot enough to cook eggs on, and even the log she was sitting on was burning the backs of her legs. She studied it more closely. It had long since lost all its skin—the leftover heartwood smooth and diamond-hard, except for some old scratch marks that seemed too regular for natural damage. They reminded Annie of the chevron patterns that were carved into the tree in the park in town. The trunk was wedged firmly between boulders, and had built up a clot of dirt and dead wood behind it. A couple of poor bushes had attempted to take root in the precious patch of dirt, but hadn't found enough moisture to grow bigger than a foot or so before perishing. Annie yanked one of them out, easily. Sure enough, dirt crumbled down from the underside the log, making a gap where the roots from the bush no longer held the soil in place. Just enough of a gap to thread the snatch-strap through.

'I'm ready, Harry,' she called once she'd sat and braced her legs against the boulder below the log. With the strap wrapped once around the trunk, she was confident she could pull and then get the dead tree to secure the slack as they went.

It took a long time to get started, with Uncle Willie groaning and swearing until Harry finally got the strap looped under his arms. It wasn't a bad thing that the pain from his injured shoulder was keeping him awake, because at least he was able to put his feet in the right places as they climbed. After that, the only communication any of them had breath for consisted of the words 'pull', 'hold', and 'I *am* pulling!'

It was hot, slow, and exhausting, and at one point Annie had so much sweat in her eyes that she misjudged her grip on the strap and let it slip, her trembling arms just managing to catch the loose end as Uncle Willie's full weight was caught by the tree. The man's cry of pain echoed from the cave, and Annie's rasping apology was lost in the effort of pulling yet harder so she could help Harry get him back to the relative safety of the next tiny ledge. It was when she was readjusting the tightness of the loop around the log that she noticed movement out of the corner of her eye.

'Pull now, Annie. Uncle's losing consciousness again. I can't hold him.'

Annie planted her feet and leant all her weight against the strap, choosing to ignore the red-bellied black snake that had come to investigate the encroachment on its territory. It was the snake's prerogative. She understood how it felt to have strangers invade your sacred place.

Her shoulders and hands were cramping so much that she struggled to let go when she needed to, and struggled even harder to re-grip. The flat strap cut into her palms. It was designed for winching out cars with other cars. It wasn't the easiest thing to grip. In desperation, she wrapped it around her wrist, crying out as she felt it crack, but kept pulling.

'How much farther, Harry?' Her voice shook. The snake was above her now, easing down onto the dead tree with graceful strength.

'We're almost halfway. You're doing great, Annie. Keep going.'

Only halfway? Annie blinked more sweat away, and tried to watch the snake and concentrate on pulling at the same time, but the snake was behind and above her now. At any moment it could strike out. Surely animals occasionally wandered out of the Garden, and this was snake paradise after all, so perhaps it was an Eden snake. They didn't strike at people.

Her legs were shaking, so Annie grunted and braced them more firmly, and pulled harder. *No sudden movements. Don't look like a threat.* Hand over hand, she kept as steady a tension on the strap as she could, and ignored the flies that buzzed around her face. They pestered her relentlessly, in her eyes, up her nose, as if to warn her that there was danger close by. As if they wanted her to move. She held on.

A movement to her right, and a forked tongue flicked out, tasting her sweaty scent as the serpent slipped down off the tree and on to the rock beside her. It was so close. *Good thing Lucas isn't here. He would probably do something stupid about now.*

'Keep pulling, Annie. We're underneath an outcrop. If we can get past it, we can rest a bit.'

The snake coiled and rose to stare at her, revealing its crimson belly. Its scales looked like they had been formed from rubies, or like they'd been sliding across blood.

'Annie?'

She didn't speak. Didn't move.

Flies buzzed. The hot wind flicked at her hair, whipping it around her face and drawing the snake's attention. The snatch-strap quivered as Harry kept trying to climb.

I wish Lucas was here to do something stupid.

Black scales glistened in the sun, matching the polished obsidian eyes that pinned her. Overhead, a wedge-tail eagle circled, possibly wondering if it could steal the wriggling meal away from the Cherub below. *It's all yours, mate. Take it. Take it and gobble it up. This is a harsh, cruel world of predators and prey, and I don't belong here.*

The eagle flew away and left her to sort out her own mess. How long had she been frozen in this stalemate with the serpent? It felt like forever. Every muscle in her body was cramping from the strain of holding the tension in the strap and trying to stay very still. She wanted to swallow down her nerves, but her mouth was too dry.

The strap jerked again, too wildly, and the sudden release of tension threw her backward. A scatter of pebbles was dislodged where her shoulder hit the ground. The snake hissed, rose up and looked her right in the eyes, its neck flat.

She couldn't move. Couldn't even breathe. Sharp rocks dug into the back of her scalp.

'Annie? Are you all right?' Harry called. The strap twitched again and her fingers were too numb to hold it steady. The bottle of water tipped over as the strap smacked into it, sending rivulets of moisture into thirsty cracks of stone.

Like a whip, the snake struck. So close to Annie's face that she flinched, whacking her head on the rocks under her. A mock attack. A final warning.

Apparently, Harry had somehow made it past the outcrop because the snatch-strap remained loose in her hand. The snake turned its head slightly, toward the vertical cave. Snakes were mostly deaf, so it was unlikely it could hear Harry's voice, but it could feel the vibrations from the rope and clearly realised there was another large animal nearby. It hissed again, lowered its head and slid forward, right over Annie's sweat-damp ponytail. The end of its tail brushed her jaw before it retreated under the ancient tree trunk.

Everything felt sharp and bright. The sun, hot on her skin. The sky, looming over her. The air, dry and tangy with eucalyptus. Rocks below her, deeply resonating. Everything working together, struggling to nourish the plants which nourished the animals which nourished the land. All bonded by the need to survive. So much vibrant world around her. So real. For the first time in her life, the world felt as real and solid and precious as Eden did.

It was a good thirty seconds before Annie pulled herself together enough to sit up again. When she did, she looked up to see the eagle circle past again, and realised she had been wrong. She did belong here.

'Okay, Harry. I've rested now. Let's get you out so we can go home,' she said. Her voice didn't even sound shaky. *Home. This is my home. I am as bonded to this land as Lucas is to me. Snakes and all. And I will protect it with my life. This is who I am.*

Fifteen minutes later as the two of them began to drag Uncle Willie up the uneven slope, Annie looked back to see the serpent slide out from under the log and hunt for the remaining traces of spilled water.

Chapter 15

'No way!' she shouted down the phone line. 'Kelly, tell me everything. How far along is she?'

The jam sandwich Annie had made herself for dinner sat untouched on the table, ignored in favour of the drama unfolding down the crackly line that was her only connection to the outside world. Talking about normal human dramas had sounded like bliss when she'd first heard her friend's voice, but Kelly's news had crossed a significant boundary when the words 'Sarah's pregnant' had echoed around the receiver.

Kelly's voice was a bit shrill, as if she wasn't sure if she was supposed to sound happy or upset. 'She's nearly twelve weeks, but she looks like she's about twenty. The doctor scanned her. She's having twins.'

'Twins?' Annie repeated, sounding pretty stupid, so then she shut her mouth and let Kelly speak. After a couple of minutes of listening to the details of Sarah's monster bouts of morning sickness, she managed to formulate some semi-coherent thoughts. 'Is she certain, you know, that Dave's the father?' The very concept of having to even ask such a question felt surreal.

'Very. There was no one else. And she's told him, after much crying and arguing with herself. I've been cried on a lot in the last few days. Apparently, I'm a good listener, even if I'm not so good at offering advice. Luckily Vicky sorted her out or she'd still be pacing around trying to decide whether to let him know. I'm glad. Dave should know. It was the right thing to do.'

'Of course it was. How did he react?'

'He's ecstatic. He's here, actually. Lucas offered to drive him up here because he was a bit mental. Happy mental, but Lucas seemed to think he needed company.'

Yah. No kidding. Although she'd told Harry she would call her Guardian, two weeks had passed before she'd plucked up the courage to do it. Lily had answered, and explained that Lucas had been banned from using the telephone after he'd thrown it through the lounge room window in a fit of rage one day. She didn't need to ask which day that had been, or why he'd thrown such a tantrum. Since then she'd been too chicken to try calling again because it would have meant fessing up to him what had happened with the snake, and yet she knew that procrastinating was never going to work. Now he was in town. Did he even realise how quickly he was losing his freedom?

'What did Dave say to her when he arrived? Were you there?' she asked, trying not to think about Lucas at all.

'Oh, Slaps, it was so sweet. He walked in the door with a huge bunch of roses, handed them to her and then hugged her for the longest time. Then he said, "I'm here with you, and I'm yours, in every way, if you want me". We all got kind of weepy at that point. Even Lucas.'

Annie decided that someone had been watching too many daytime soap operas. 'And?' she prompted, hoping with all her heart that Sarah had made a real decision for once.

'And Sarah kissed him. Then they went outside to talk. For ages. That was *two days* ago, Slaps. I'm allowed to tell people now. Finally. It's been torture!'

'So, what will they do?' she asked, untangling the telephone cord from around her fingers and stretching to reach her sandwich.

'Not sure. Dave's moving in. He says he'll drop out of uni and get a job here, but Sarah wants him to see if he can still study at least part-time. Personally, I don't think that will happen. He's not stupid. If they're going to raise twins, they'll need more money than a part-time job will get them. Apparently his family are fairly well-off, or so Lucas tells me, but they've only met Sarah a couple of times. Who knows how they'll react?'

'What was Dave studying? I never even thought to ask.'

Kelly sounded relieved to be finally able to talk to someone. Her family had already doubled in size at the start of the year, and now it was about to get even bigger. It was strange to think that just a few months ago they hadn't even met Dave or Lucas, and now they were both fated to become family.

'He was studying business management. Not that he got very far into his course. I don't know how he'll go finding work in this recession, but he seems eager to try.'

'Do you think they'll move back to the city eventually?'

'Who knows? Sarah just wants to be wherever her mum is, which is fair enough, although she doesn't seem to be very good at committing to things long term. She likes to keep her options open.'

'Well, having twins is about as long-term a commitment as you can get, so she's going to have to learn ... Wait, did you say, "keep her options open?" Really?'

'I just meant that she'll only make decisions that don't tie her down. She doesn't like having to plan too far ahead. She loves Nalong. Didn't stop raving about the place when she first came here, but I honestly can't see her settling down here, or anywhere, in fact. Poor Dave.'

An uncomfortable feeling settled between Annie's shoulder blades. Like a fly that kept pestering her, all she could think of were Lucas's words: 'If I left my options any more open, they'd be doing the splits'.

'Slaps? Are you still there?'

'Yeah, sorry, just trying to take it all in. Kelly. Aunty Kelly. I can't believe you're somebody's aunty. You're going to have to send birthday cards every year with cash in them and buy them stupid t-shirts and take them to see Disney movies.'

'I can do that. And when they're older I'll pull them aside and pry into their love-lives and make them tell me all the things they won't tell their parents, but of course they'll be sweet innocent girls who won't kiss anyone until they meet some sexy guys on the beach one day and—'

'Did the scan say they were girls?' she interrupted before that sentence could go any further.

'Well, no. It was still a bit early to tell with the dodgy ultrasound machine that Nalong Memorial Hospital has, but of course they'll be girls.'

'What makes you so sure?'

'Because the mere thought of twin boys is making my brain want to implode, so I'm choosing to delude myself for the sake of self-preservation. That will work, right?'

Choosing to delude yourself. Sure. When doesn't that work?

'Slaps?'

'Sorry. I was just thinking.'

'You know you're zoning out, don't you? What's the matter? Is your mum okay?'

Annie sighed and poked unenthusiastically at her sandwich, wondering how long it would take for her mum to remember that she'd promised to cook tonight. Although she'd been much happier since she'd returned the previous week, she was still a bit vague about mundane things such as eating and hanging out washing.

'Mum's fine. She's still outside. Listen, is Lucas nearby? I think I'd better have a chat to him.'

Although Annie's gift didn't work through the phone line, she didn't need it to sense her friend's smugness. Kelly didn't even need to say anything. The way she was *breathing* even sounded smug.

'I'll get him. On one condition.'

'No, you can't listen in.'

'But you never tell me anything anymore. How am I supposed to know what's going on if I don't cheat?'

'Try doing what you always do,' Annie suggested. 'Wait until tomorrow and then pester me until I cave.'

High heels were apparently compulsory for any eighteenth birthday party, especially your own, according to Kelly. Four times her friend had dragged Annie around the shops before they'd found a dress she was satisfied with. The shopping itself was torture, of course, because the farthest they could persuade either of Kelly's parents to take them was Horsham, and there wasn't exactly much of a selection there, but secretly, Annie loved every moment of her friend's attention. In the end, they found a sweet little dress in deep red that was fairly plain, and at least it wasn't a rural town's leftovers from the early eighties. The part she loved most about the process, however, was that for a while at least, they could both pretend that they were still just teenagers without a care in the world other than whether or not they would find the right shoes to match her new dress. Not once did Kelly mention the fact that Annie was more often out of school than in it, and in return Annie didn't talk about the fact that three weeks ago Kelly had been kicked out of the bedroom she'd been in her whole life to make room for an entire new sub-family.

Now, as Annie wobbled her way along the gravel driveway that was in no way designed for heels, hurrying after her mother who was already in the car, she tried not to think too hard about what it would mean to turn eighteen. Even though her mum had been much more relaxed since returning from Eden, neither of them had brought up the idea of going away for the weekend again. Instead, Annie had booked a restaurant for a few of her friends, and for the moment she was more than happy for that to be all it meant to 'come of age'. Time to celebrate. Have her first legal drink. Watch her mother behave like a human being the way she did when other people were around, instead of moping about pretending to be happy and normal for her daughter's sake.

They weren't the first ones to arrive at the Thai restaurant. Through the window she could see three other guys from school talking to Mandy, who used to have swimming lessons with her before she moved to Ballarat, as well as Kelly and her parents, and Dave holding out a chair for an exhausted-looking Sarah. At fifteen weeks, she was really starting to show, and was attracting a good number of sideways looks from the locals at other tables who had obviously heard just enough gossip to be curious. Kelly was sitting next to her, reading the giant menu as if she didn't already know it off by heart. She squealed in dainty excitement when Annie walked in.

'Slaps! About time. I was starting to think we'd be celebrating my own birthday before you finally got here. You look perfect. Wow, look at your hair!'

Annie grinned. 'Mum spent ages braiding it. My fingers were cramping in sympathy the whole time. How do the flowers look?'

'They're gorgeous,' Kelly gushed. 'Nice work, Mrs Langley.'

'Thanks,' her mum replied with only a hint of frustration. She'd spent the last hour complaining that the only flowers left in their tired summer garden were dreary and pathetic, and that she wished she had thought to bring some back from Next Door. As if she would have actually done it. Very few objects were ever carried across the boundary between worlds, and never anything that was living. They talked about it all the time though. 'Wouldn't it be lovely if we took a tape recorder and brought back some recordings of the evening songs', or 'I wonder if

Pallano would like a telescope?' But they never followed through with such musings. The two worlds weren't meant to mix, not without a very good reason, and adorning Annie's hair with silver night blossoms wasn't exactly a priority in the grand scheme of things.

As Annie made her way around the table doing the obligatory round of hugs and helloes, she realised just how much she'd been missing her school friends. She greeted Kelly's dad and Vicky, and gave Dave and Sarah hugs, congratulating them again on their exciting news. Sarah gave her a look that clearly said she didn't think what they'd done deserved congratulations, but in the next moment, an even stronger emotion burst from her. Fierce affection and protectiveness bounced around the room so brightly Annie was surprised that everyone didn't turn their way, shielding their eyes and squinting.

'Okay, that was definitely not my imagination,' Sarah said, easing her chair back and prodding at her belly. 'When you hugged me, Annie. I'm sure I felt movement.'

Dave's eyes lit up like a kid catching his first glimpse of presents under the Christmas tree. Pure elation emanated from him, without the slightest trace of regret. If everyone she met felt as joyous as those two did right then, Annie decided she would happily spend all her time just basking in people's moods all day.

'Sarah, that's wonderful,' she congratulated. 'What an incredible feeling.'

'Well, it's about time I started to get some of the better ones. I've had enough of the nausea. What I can't get over is how I can possibly feel so foul and so hungry at the same time. Maybe one twin is hungry and one feels sick. Is that possible?'

'Should we start ordering?' Dave prompted. 'If you're hungry?'

Sarah rolled her eyes at his over-attentiveness. 'I believe we're still waiting on a couple more people,' she said, gesturing to the two empty chairs opposite where she was sitting.

'Actually, one of them has just arrived,' Annie's mum said, waving to Harry, who was walking past the restaurant window. Dressed in formal black pants, with a white cotton collarless shirt and hair freshly trimmed, Harry looked like he'd just stepped off a film set. He always had a relaxed, confident air, but the new clothes brought out something more. Something … gently regal. Annie had only seen him dress up four times before. Once was for his Year 10 formal dance, which had gained him a rather annoying stream of female followers from then until the day he'd walked out of PE and never returned to the school. The other times had all been for funerals. No wonder he hated dressing up. Annie felt honoured that he'd done so for her birthday.

As he walked in through the glass doors, squinting as his eyes adjusted to the paper lantern mood lighting, at least four other tables developed a sudden lull in their conversations. No one ever quite seemed to know why their attention was snagged every time a Cherub entered a room. The effect wore off once people got used to having them around, luckily, but being sensitive to the emotional atmosphere sometimes made Annie feel like she had toilet paper stuck to her shoe. Unwittingly snatching the attention of complete strangers would always be unnerving. Or did every teenage girl feel like that? Maybe it wasn't a Cherub thing at all.

It took a few seconds for the noise in the room to revert to its natural bustle as people tried to remember what they'd just been saying. Harry came and planted a fat kiss on her cheek and dropped a little yellow gift box in her lap.

'Happy birthday,' he said. 'Sorry I'm a bit late.'

'Thanks. And don't worry, we only just beat you here. Where's Uncle Willie?'

'Not feeling well. He sends his apologies.'

Annie couldn't help it. She closed her eyes briefly, feeling for the rhythms that provided a constant backdrop to her emotions, the rhythms that stuttered and grated her senses whenever someone got too close to the zone she was born to defend. It was like suddenly paying attention to the sounds of birds. All the little sparrows were settling down for the night though. There was nothing out of place.

Harry laid a hand on her shoulder. 'He promised me he would never do that again, Annie. Remember? And you killed that feral dog. He's not likely to go wandering around in the bush at night just because I'm not around to keep an eye on him.'

'You still believe he was looking for the dog?'

'That's what he said.' His voice was steady, but he wasn't meeting her eyes.

'He also said he fell into that hole by accident. Must have been a slow fall if he had time to take his hat off first.' She opened her mouth to say more when her mum coughed, and gave her a warning look. That was when Annie noticed how many people were listening in. 'Hey, you look great, by the way,' she commented instead.

Grimacing slightly, Harry tugged at his shirt as if it was choking him. 'I drew the line at wearing a tie. I don't love you *that* much.'

She laughed and then introduced him to Dave and Sarah. 'I should have thought to introduce you all on New Year's Eve, sorry. I guess I was a bit distracted.'

'Lucas told me your news,' Harry said, shaking Dave's hand and smiling at Sarah. 'Congratulations.'

Sarah just stared at him with her mouth slightly open. So maybe it really was a Cherub thing then.

'Thanks,' Dave replied, folding his long frame into his chair. 'Where is Lucas? I was hoping he'd be here tonight. I've hardly seen him since he started working for you again. He must really be enjoying the lifestyle. Personally, I didn't think he'd last a week on a farm—Lou's always been more of a beach-bum, and yet he didn't stop talking about Nalong when he came home. He even started buying the *Weekly Times*.'

'Lucas sends his apologies,' Harry said, shooting Annie an accusatory look. 'He would have loved to have been here. He just couldn't come.'

Because he wasn't invited. Annie glanced at her mother, but her attention was completely captivated by Sarah. It wasn't surprising. Sarah was pregnant, and her mum spent enough time in Eden to be influenced by the fact that a pregnant woman there was always the sole focus of everyone's attention. Luckily Sarah herself was still a bit dazed by Harry's entrance and didn't seem to notice.

'Open your presents,' Kelly demanded, flinging her sweet smile at Annie like a dagger. There was no arguing with that smile, even if she'd wanted to, so a few minutes later multiple balls of scrunched-up wrapping paper decorated the table along with a new bridle, a pretty blue blouse, an ornate photo frame with a picture of her school friends, a couple of movie tickets and a CD player. Apparently Dave was confident that the record store in Nalong would start stocking a decent selection of CDs one day. She opened Harry's gift last. It was a silver necklace, and hanging from it was a dainty tree of life pendant. Its leaves were all wrong, which was probably a good thing because she wasn't sure she would be able to bring herself to show it to anyone if it looked too much like the real thing. She beamed at Harry in awed gratitude. Where on earth had he found such a perfect gift? Her mum was fidgeting in her seat to have a look, so she passed it around for everyone to admire before letting Dave help her put it on.

Once the meals arrived, the conversation inevitably turned to the impending birth of the twins. It was good for Sarah to hear everyone get excited about it. Her emotions seemed to change from uncertainty and fretfulness to a calm sort of pleasure, like she was only just accepting that it was all right for her not to feel ashamed. It was as if the continuing banter helped to validate her hidden excitement about the arrival of two new humans, and the more she smiled, the more relaxed Dave became. Annie had only ever met two pregnant women in Eden, and the way they were cherished felt entirely natural, so the idea that Sarah could feel anything but treasured was utterly incomprehensible, yet her emotions couldn't lie. Just as well Dave was so enthusiastic, doting on her ferociously, because she was going to need a lot of doting on.

'I caught Lucas singing a lullaby to the baby chicks the other day,' Harry divulged in a soft voice, leaning across the table so only Dave, Sarah and Annie could hear him. Everyone else was busy bouncing baby names around, with regular input from the occupants of the other tables. 'He told me he was practising. I'm considering buying him a pair of knitting needles so he can make some booties or something.'

'Lou's more likely to knit them soccer strips,' Dave said, 'but somehow his cluckiness doesn't surprise me. Do you know what he said to the careers counsellor at school when we all had to have our interviews in Year 10? She asked what his first preference for a career would be, and he told her he just wanted to be a dad. We still haven't let him live that one down. Man, who would have thought I would beat him to it?' he mused. He placed his chopsticks across his empty bowl, leant back and stretched his long legs out as far as the table legs would allow.

Harry gave Annie a look that made her cheeks blush. She wanted to feel annoyed at the inevitability of her future. She was *not* breeding stock. But it was still kind of sweet.

'Was it a race?' Sarah asked.

Annie's head whipped around to look at her, worried that she might have been offended, yet all she felt from her was amusement. She was teasing him.

'Of course not,' Dave scoffed. 'It's never about speed. Cam and Lou would agree. It's always quality that matters.' Apparently, he could read her just as well as Annie could.

'If it's about quality, then how can you be so sure you've beaten him?' Sarah argued.

'Twins, Sarah. *Twins.* With the best human genetic material on the planet. No way could anyone ever beat that.' He gave her an exuberant kiss on the lips.

Again, Harry caught Annie's eye across the table. And winked, the naughty Cherub. Apparently in his mind, having a baby Cherub would beat human twins any day. Annie stuck her tongue out at him just as the waitress reached across from behind him to take their plates. She blushed, causing Harry to laugh as he reached across to help Sarah pass her plate to the overloaded waitress.

Their fingers brushed.

A flare of raw emotion hit Annie like a shot of straight whiskey as the plate fell with a clatter of cutlery. She couldn't even tell who it had come from, possibly both of them. They certainly both snapped their hands back as if they'd been burned, and from the looks on their faces, neither of them had a clue about what had just happened. Annie's mother did, though. She gasped, and let out a muffled cry that reminded Annie of a cat drowning in cream.

Excitement, thrill, anticipation, promise … confusion … despair. Powerful emotions slammed into her from three directions at once, and that didn't even include her own reaction.

One touch.

It couldn't be … could it? Ever since Kelly had mentioned the way Sarah liked to leave her options open, a fleeting thought had buzzed around the back of her mind. Now it stung with poisonous vengeance. Beside her, Sarah was staring at Harry like he'd just appeared out of thin air, while Harry was clutching the edge of the table with such a furious look on his face that she was worried he was going to hit someone. Luckily everyone else was staring at Annie's mum, wondering what had made her cry out, but she just sat frozen with her hands over her face. Numbly, Annie handed the plate to the waitress, with absolutely no clue as to how she was supposed to react.

One touch. Why hadn't she seen it earlier? No wonder Sarah had been staring at him all night. And no wonder her mum had been staring at Sarah.

One touch. Months too late. What had gone wrong?

Without a word Harry stood up and strode out of the restaurant, leaving behind a tangle of disconnected conversations as the whole room watched him leave.

Chapter 16

Go, her mum mouthed, wiping away tears and tilting her head toward the door.

Are you okay? Annie signed back as subtly as she could.

Her mum shrugged, sighed, and then bravely turned to the concerned faces around her. 'Sorry, I didn't mean to startle you all. I just remembered another gift I've had stashed away that I forgot to bring.' She laughed.

Liar. It was sad that her lie caused her far less guilt than telling the truth would have, and strange that hearing her lie so convincingly made Annie feel so proud of her.

Wishing she knew how to be unobtrusive, Annie rose and walked to the door. Kelly gave her a sad nod, well aware that Harry was upset by something, but kind enough to let her go and find out discreetly.

'So, Dave,' Annie heard her mother say, her voice quavering only slightly, 'I hear you're interested in business management. Have you ever considered farming?'

The cool air outside helped to clear Annie's head. Very few people lingered on the main street of their quiet town after dark, which was good because she was going to have to move fast to catch up to Harry and she didn't particularly want to attract any more attention than she had to. Forcing herself to calm down and concentrate, she focused on where he was. Damn, he could move quickly. Still, she was pretty certain he hadn't taken his car, and that was a huge relief because she didn't want to have to go back inside and ask for the car keys, nor did she want to risk getting caught driving without a licence. At least now that she was eighteen she would finally be able to rectify that little hassle. Resigning herself to an uncomfortable run, she headed down the main street after her best friend. He was making a beeline for the river, unsurprisingly. She soon got into a rhythm and felt that she was making quite good time until she rounded the corner of the pharmacy and was literally swept off her feet by an unexpected rugby tackle.

'Whoa! Hold on, I've got you,' came a husky voice she instantly recognised.

A pair of strong arms locked around her waist before she could fall flat on her face. Her Guardian had very quick reflexes.

'Annie, wow. You look … breathtaking,' Lucas exclaimed, supporting her while she regained her balance. He was wearing his usual shorts and thongs, despite the cool evening.

'Lucas, what are you doing here?'

'My job, apparently. Running in high heels is a bad idea.'

'Are you kidding me? You came all the way into town to prevent me from tripping over?' Anger coloured her voice because Harry was getting farther away and life was getting messier by the minute. She really didn't want to have to deal with Lucas just then.

His hands fell away. 'No. I just came to stalk you,' he admitted without out a trace of shame.

'Why?'

'Because you didn't invite me. So how else was I supposed to see you on your birthday? Did you like the necklace?'

She turned and kept running.

'Wait! Annie, I need to talk to you. Something weird happened at the jewellers. Where are you going?'

He was going to follow anyway, so she didn't bother answering.

Her stupid heels definitely did get in the way, so as soon as she got past the gravel and onto the grassy hill that led down from the bridge, she peeled them off and tossed them behind her. One of them hit Lucas. Possibly on purpose. He didn't complain—at least not out loud.

Harry was already in the water when they got there, waist deep in the murky current. Without hesitation, she plunged straight in after him, shooting Lucas a warning look that clearly requested some privacy. Soft mud squelched between her toes as she waded past the shallows to get to where the water was fresher. It was late summer, and the river was low and grimy, but it still sang sweetly in her ears and in her heart. Coming up behind Harry, she wrapped her arms around his waist and leant her head on the back of his shoulder. He was crying—despairing, and angry. As easily as breathing, she began to draw in his grief and slowly wind it into something containable, consolable. It worked for almost ten whole seconds, until he rounded on her, looking more furious than she had ever seen him.

'Stop it,' he snarled, gripping her shoulders and giving them a firm shake. 'Let me feel this!' White hot anger slammed into her far more painfully than the grip of his hands on her shoulders, shattering her defences like they were made of glass. 'You can't fix this, Annie!'

Before she even had a chance to open her mouth to respond, something shoved her roughly aside and Harry was rammed under the water. Two bodies thrashed about and she heard something that sounded like skin hitting skin before they both went under again. Of course Lucas had interfered, but she couldn't let Harry get hurt. Throwing herself at them, she tried to do the same thing she'd done the last time Lucas had tried to protect her. It was much harder in the water. No matter how hard she tried to get between them, she kept getting shoved aside. Muddy water splashed everywhere and it was too dark to really see what was happening. Frustrated, she lunged her way back to the riverbank as quickly as she could and then scrambled on her hands and knees in the mud, searching for something she could use. All she found was a loose rock about the size of her fist, so she stood up, closed her eyes, and dropped it on her bare foot. Raw pain blossomed, and was welcomed because it was followed by a blood curdling yell a second later and the splashing stopped.

'Please, Lucas, don't hurt him! He didn't mean it. Please just let me explain what's going on.' Annie wiped a bit of blood off her big toe, and held it up like it was a sugar cube being used to coax a nervous pony onto a horse float. Gross, but effective. Lucas stumbled toward her, so she started backing away from the water to put as much distance between him and Harry as possible. 'Harry, please, stop and think,' she called as she moved. 'If it really is Sarah, then she'll feel it if you get hurt. She won't understand. You need to calm down.'

Harry didn't look like he cared. He launched himself toward Lucas, intent on releasing all his anger on someone. Planting her feet firmly on the grass, she sucked away as much of Harry's fury as she could, knowing he would hate her for it but desperate to keep him from getting injured. She had never tried to pull so hard before, or so quickly, and his raw emotional violence dumped her like a giant crashing wave. Somehow, she found herself clutching at the ground to stop it and the rest of the world from spinning so fast. Her hip and head ached from her fall, and there was a sharp stick digging into her shoulder blade.

A moment later, fiery hands grasped her shoulders and sat her up, and the swirling landscape changed direction so fast that it felt as if the planet had been winding up for all those millennia and had just been let go. It was all Annie could do to stop herself from throwing up. Despite the spin, she forced her eyes to stay open. Lucas was crouched in front of her, the dim moonlight dappling his furious face and turning his blue eyes silver. A red welt ran from his left cheekbone to the corner of his split lip where Harry had hit him. Someone was holding a stick to his throat like it was a dagger, and when Annie realised it was her, she dropped it with a yelp. The violence that filled her was not her own.

For a moment they just looked at each other, while the moon and stars watched on indifferently. Then Lucas clasped his burning fingers around her foot where blood and mud welled together along the grimy wound. The pain of it dissolved like steam, leaving just an ephemeral memory of sweetness on her tongue as her body subconsciously recalled other healings she'd experienced. A crushed flower fell from her tangled hair and landed on the back of her Guardian's hand. He released his grip and listed to the left, so she steadied him as best she could, peering around his shoulders to see where Harry was.

The distraught Cherub was still standing knee-deep in the water, looking like a lost, forgotten child. He was staring at the moon in total despair, all anger gone, with his hands hanging limply by his sides. The anguish he felt was almost visible to her, but she let him keep it. He was right. She couldn't fix this. Certainly not by manipulating what he felt.

For a minute or so they all just remained where they were. Lucas was taking deep breaths and rubbing his eyes to clear the dizziness he'd earned by healing her, Harry was trembling in the river with tears running down his face, and she was watching them both, trying to anticipate whether the underlying aggression they were both feeling would erupt again.

Eventually, Harry's eyes sought hers. 'What did I do wrong, Annie?'

Her heart broke and suddenly he wasn't the only one crying. 'I'm so, so sorry,' she sobbed. 'It's my fault. I shouldn't have run away last year. If I'd been around, you would have met earlier, I'm so sorry, I—'

'Stop it, Annie!' Lucas interrupted. 'Stop apologising to him. I warned him if he ever touched you again—'

Ruthlessly, she pushed Lucas down and pinned him like a sheep needing its feet checked, but he didn't struggle nearly as much. Her knee on his chest probably helped. And also the fact that he couldn't push her aside without hurting her. Swallowing her pride and bowing to necessity, she revealed the truth she could no longer hide from him.

'Harry met his Guardian tonight. It's Sarah.'

Defensive savagery melted as her words sank in. Confusion took its place.

'Guardian? Like me? Why would Harry need a Guardian?'

Annie punched him on the shoulder. Hard. 'Don't be so sexist! Harry doesn't need a Guardian, any more than I do.'

'So what's the probl— Oh, sorry, I didn't think. They're bonded now? Like we are?' Understanding and sympathy darkened his bright eyes. 'Poor Sarah. Does she even know?'

'Not yet. It only just happened.'

'You can't keep it from her like you did with me. It's not fair. What if she gets sick? If you won't tell them, I will,' he declared.

'Them? No "them". Dave can't find out. You know that.'

He opened his mouth to protest and then flinched as he was hit with a gut-punching feeling of guilt that broke his resolve.

'But he's my best friend,' he complained, as if she was the one who'd made the rules. 'They're about to start a family together. Things are stressful enough for them without having to have secrets. How is she supposed to keep something as powerful as that a secret from her own partner? That can't be right. She can't be expected to be linked to one man in such a compulsive way and not even be able to tell …'

Defeated, Annie slid off him to give him some space while she waited for the penny to drop. It didn't take long.

'That's not the way it's supposed to work, is it?'

'We still make our own choices,' she insisted, suddenly unsure if that was a good thing. Sarah had been so indecisive that she had chosen without even intending to. Not making a real decision was still a choice in itself.

Lucas looked over at Harry, and then back to her, reading something else into her words. 'You've chosen him,' he surmised. 'You didn't even give me a chance.'

Ouch. That wasn't fair.

'You don't even know me,' she growled in return. 'Any more than Sarah knows Harry.' Picking herself off the ground, she turned away from him and waded back into the water, throwing her arms around Harry's neck, wishing she had something to say that would make things better. For their entire lives, they had lived with the promise of finding their perfect love-partners. Guardians who would protect them, heal them, support them, cherish and adore them with as deep a bond as they had seen their parents share. But now she had deliberately and repeatedly driven Lucas away, and Harry's Guardian was pregnant with twins to another man.

It was by far the worst birthday ever.

Chapter 17

Surprisingly, nearly everyone was still at the restaurant when Annie finally made it back there. They must have all been on about their fourth cups of coffee by then. Only Sarah and Dave had left, because apparently Sarah had lost her appetite for dessert and gone very quiet and Dave had insisted on taking her home. Annie's heart sank a little further when they told her. She smiled, nodded and sat down, trying really hard not to think about Sarah, and her 'own special brand of confidence'. Harry could have used some of that in his life.

'The river again, Annie? That was a new dress,' Kelly complained as she wrapped her own jacket around Annie's shoulders.

Mandy laughed. 'I guess she's learned her lesson. Don't leave your clothes on the riverbank where they can get nicked, right?'

Annie tried to decide if she cared enough to even ask. Mandy answered anyway.

'Don't you remember that time you and Harry wagged assembly to go for a swim and someone nicked your clothes? You both had to walk back to school in your underwear and scrounge spare clothes from the lost property box. You spent the rest of the day wearing some boy's sweaty shorts and a giant school jumper.'

Right. Of course. Apparently, that should have been a memorable experience, yet the only reason she remembered it at all was because Harry had been upset, convinced it was Mrs Clark who had stolen their clothes to teach them a lesson. What lesson? She'd spent much more time in Eden than Harry ever had. Underwear was plenty of cover. Harry had suggested that maybe that was why they needed Guardians. To remind them that clothes were important …

'So where is Harry?' Mandy asked after an awkward moment.

In a bad place. And about two kilometres to our west.

'He met a friend, and they went for a drink at Tully's.'

Her mother's sharp nod of approval felt a bit strange, luckily no one else seemed to notice.

Kelly brightened. 'Great idea. Let's join them.'

'I'm not really in the mood, Kel.'

'But it's your eighteenth. We *have* to go to Tully's.'

Annie couldn't think of what to say to dissuade her. She threw a pleading glance at her mum.

'The staff at Tully's know exactly how old *you* are though, Kelly Taylor,' her mum said. 'They won't serve you.' She pulled a bottle of champagne out from her bag under the table. 'That's why I picked a BYO restaurant,' she whispered with a wink. 'I've been waiting for you to come back, Annie, so I can offer you your first legal drink.'

Kelly looked rebellious, so Annie kicked her under the table. 'Good idea,' Annie said. 'Besides, I don't think Harry—and his friend—really want to spend the evening with *all* of us.' She gave Kelly a pointed look, begging her to take the hint.

Kelly's mouth made a little 'o'. She glanced at Annie's mum, and then gave a resigned nod.

Annie spent the remainder of the evening doing a terrible job of pretending that nothing was wrong. Much to her relief, everyone else left as soon as they thought they could do it without seeming rude.

On the way home, her mum asked whether Harry had said anything.

'You know him,' Annie answered. 'He'll talk when he's ready. I think he just needs some space for now.'

'We're all in a bit of shock, I think.'

'How is it even possible, Mum? I thought we were pretty much locked in to breeding up the next generation of Cherubim. How could Sarah fall pregnant with someone else?'

'She's human, Annie. There's no biological reason why it can't happen. In fact, quite the opposite. As I've warned you many times, we're all very fertile until the next Cherub is born, so she probably fell pregnant despite taking precautions.'

'How was she supposed to know? This isn't her fault. Or Harry's. What are they going to do?'

'I don't know. Maybe Harry should go Next Door. Until the twins are born,' her mum suggested.

'Maybe. But he's needed here. He doesn't like going for more than a couple of days. Even Uncle Willie starts to worry if he wanders off for too long.'

'Well at least they have help there now. You neglected to mention to me that their farmhand came back. Someone mentioned he and Dave are friends?'

Breathe. Stay calm.

'Yeah. Harry met him at the New Year's Eve barbeque and offered him a summer job, and I guess he liked it more than he liked studying. I don't know how long he's planning to stay.'

That was when she remembered just how close Harry and Sarah had come to meeting each other that night. Sarah had been just metres away when Lucas had shown up. Right there when she'd kissed Harry. Had she seen them? Had she been about to say hello and then changed her mind when they'd glued their faces together? Her selfishness had ruined everything.

The rest of the trip home passed in a haze. If her mum asked her anything else, she didn't hear it.

Staring out of her bedroom window that night, Annie watched the clouds block out sections of the starry sky as they drifted, and wished that she could block her own troubled thoughts the same way. Somewhere in the distance a fox barked, making her wonder how Lucas would cope on the farm without Harry around if he did escape to Eden. She should probably teach him to shoot—if he let her even speak to him ever again. What must he think of her now he knew the truth? She'd lied to him even after saying she wanted him to be able to trust her. She was still deceiving him, in fact, letting him think that she and Harry were together. The worst part was that he was right. She'd never even given him a chance. She'd accused him of not knowing anything about her, but whose fault was that? For months now, she'd been so terrified of ending up like her mother that she'd treated him like ... well, an inevitable curse to be held off for as long as possible. What she hadn't been brave enough to consider was how quickly things could go so very, very wrong. The thought of Lucas leaving, making the choice to follow his own path the way she kept encouraging him to, made her feel vulnerable. Which wasn't logical and she didn't like it. And why wouldn't he leave? He didn't know her, couldn't trust her, and thought that she'd chosen someone else over him. It would make perfect sense for him to go back to Melbourne, return to uni and meet someone who would treat him with the respect he deserved …

An hour later her pillow was soaked and her eyes were puffier than an Iced VoVo pavlova. She still couldn't sleep. Her damp and wrinkled red dress had left pink stains on her doona cover but she was totally unmotivated to do anything about it.

'Annie?'

The whisper was so soft she had to sit up to check if she was really awake, or if she'd just imagined it. It came again a moment later.

'Annie? It's me. I know you're awake.'

Oh, no. Not here. How dare he risk this? She went over to the window and opened it as quietly as she could.

'Stop stalking me,' she whispered, hating herself for trying to push him away again, and yet terrified of the alternative.

He put his finger to his lips, even more careful not to make a sound than she was, and then reached through the window and tugged at her hand. Bright blue eyes challenged her as he waited for her to choose, but she didn't really have a hope of resisting, not after all the guilt she'd been blubbering into her pillow for the last hour. As carefully as if she was one of his baby chicks, he balanced her as she climbed out, frowning when he noticed she wasn't wearing any shoes. As if he had any right to complain since he'd apparently lost his thongs in the river when he'd plunged in after her.

Eucalyptus leaves crunched pleasantly underfoot as Annie led the way down the hill. She didn't want to go too far in case her mum woke and noticed she'd left. Still, if she felt her near the river, she wouldn't think it strange, not after the events of the evening. The river was where they all went when they needed to think, and to brood. It was also loud enough to disguise the sound of talking, which could otherwise travel much farther in the night air than people usually realised.

Annie sat down on her favourite rock and dangled her bare feet into the water, shivering as she felt its crisp song welcome her. Now nearing the end of April, the nights were definitely getting colder, but the river was worth a little chill.

'You took Harry home?' she asked, already aware that he had returned from town, but fishing for information about how much had been said when she wasn't around.

Lucas nodded and sat down on the rock next to hers, with his feet tucked up. 'He wasn't in much of a state to drive. We'll have to go back for his car tomorrow. He really doesn't drink much normally, does he?'

'Not really his thing.'

'I can tell. Still, I think it was worth it tonight.'

'Just tell me he didn't get drunk enough to get sick. I don't know how quickly the bond kicks in and we can't risk Sarah suffering any more than she has to.'

'Don't worry. I'm well aware of that. So is he, now. He said to say thanks, for earlier, for stopping our fight. He's not cross with you.' In the moonlight, she could see his jaw clenching as he remembered Harry shaking her. She peered closely at his cheek and lip to see where Harry had hit him, but they looked completely normal. It made her wonder whether Guardian quick healing traits were ever noticed by outsiders. 'He also wants to apologise for … nearly hurting you. Again.'

Even getting the words out seemed to be difficult for him.

'Did he tell you why he did?'

'Yeah. For doing what you always do. For what you're doing now, in fact.'

Annie's breath hitched and she looked at him, horrified. He knew she'd been drawing away his feelings for her? Had it been so easy to tell?

'What makes you think—'

'You told me what you can do, remember? It explains a lot. Don't worry. I'm getting used to it now. I don't try to fight it anymore. It feels better when you take it away.' A trace of bitterness coloured his tone, and his voice was even huskier than normal.

Clamping her hand over her mouth, she struggled to contain the sobs that were threatening to escape. She was supposed to be the untainted one. What was wrong with her?

'It's all right, Annie. I understand why. You love Harry, and he's going to need you now more than ever. It makes sense for you to choose him. You've known him your whole life. I get it. I really do.' He sounded sincere, but his hands were trembling. Healing hands, capable of so much more. They were all she could stand to look at, those hands, because if she tried to look at those incredible blue eyes she would be lost. Already the pain of his bruised ego was almost breaking her, and yet she refused to block it out. She deserved to feel it.

'What will you do?' she whispered, terrified of his answer. Needing to know anyway.

'Do? You mean, will I leave?'

She gave a short nod.

'If you ask me to, but I can be useful here, I think. Harry said he might have to take off for a while, like you did, to make things easier for Sarah, but he can't leave Uncle on his own with his dodgy shoulder. Did you know the doctor called Uncle in for some more heart monitoring? He hasn't been right since the … incident out in the park. They've changed his medication again. And even if Harry does stay, Uncle doesn't cope well when they fight and I think it helps them both to have someone else around. I'd also like to be around for Dave. He's more scared than he lets on, and I could probably help to let Sarah know what to expect too. And since Dave isn't allowed to know, then someone will have to act as a go-between.' His words came out in a rush, as if he'd been rehearsing his argument to be allowed to stay. He held his breath, waiting for her response.

She could hardly believe he still wanted anything at all to do with Nalong or any of the people in it. 'Thank you, Lucas. You're right, but I'll understand if … wait. Did you say that Harry and Uncle Willie have been fighting?'

The poor guy must have been mighty uncomfortable in clammy shorts all night because instead of answering straight away, he wriggled a bit, and hugged his arms to his chest like he was cold. *He should really get out of those damp clothes …* Sternly exhaling the unhelpful train of thought, Annie leant forward and pestered him with only her glare until he answered her question.

'Fighting is a bit of a strong word,' he back-pedalled. 'Neither of them are really built to be argumentative. Forget I mentioned it.'

'Lucas …'

'Look, I don't know what the problem is and it's none of my business.'

'But you feel worried.'

'Stop prying into my feelings!'

'I can't help it. And if prying helps Harry then I'll use every trick I know. What are they fighting about?'

Lucas chewed on his lower lip, and then relented. 'It has to do with what the guy at the jewellery store said when we bought your necklace.' He began to pluck at his shirt cuff. 'Do you know him? Durante Diamonds is the name of the shop. George Durante.'

'Near the pricey hairdresser,' Annie offered. 'I've never been inside.' The jewellery store wasn't a place she ever had reason to go.

'Neither had Harry, but the guy seemed to know him pretty well. Greeted him by name the second we walked in.'

'That does happen sometimes,' Annie said. 'Apparently we can be very … noticeable. It's embarrassing when people know our names and we don't remember them.'

'Noticeable? That's one word for it.' He reached out and plucked a stray flower from her tangled braid.

'Keep going.'

He reached for her hair again.

'I mean with the story. What did Mr Durante say?'

'Oh. Well, he just seemed so … eager to please. It must be a difficult business to try to run in a town like Nalong, especially now with the recession, because he *really* wanted us to buy something. He offered Harry a half-price discount on anything in the store and then started showing us all his custom-made pieces—as if we could ever afford anything like that. He said if we ever needed anything made, he'd take care of us.' He gave his head a slight shake. 'Okay, not us. Harry. I might as well not have existed. When we picked out the pendant, he gave him a free chain to go with it. Does that sort of thing normally happen?'

'I wish. People trust Harry, but they don't give him free stuff.' Annie played with the tiny silver tree, feeling bad that she hadn't even thanked him for it yet. 'So what does any of that have to do with Uncle?'

'Nothing, really. It was the guy's parting comment that got me curious. He said he was really sorry about what happened to Harry's parents. He said he never thought it would go that far.'

Annie sat up straighter. Did George Durante have something to do with Geoff's arrest? 'Then what?'

'Then nothing. Harry tried to ask about it and the man pretended he hadn't heard. He slammed the door shut and flipped the sign to "Closed". It was kind of dramatic. Harry explained to me that his dad died in jail and his mum … took her own life. I had no idea. He went very quiet after that. He told me he needed some time alone and went to sit near the lake by that Carved Tree.'

'Yeah. He often goes there to think.'

'Well, after about half an hour of wandering around, I got bored and went to sit with him. He didn't seem to mind. When we got home, he sat Uncle Willie down with a cuppa and asked him outright to tell him exactly why his dad was arrested.'

'And?'

'And that was their first fight. Uncle said his dad was unfairly judged for trying to protect some of their heritage. He said no pretty plaque would ever make up for what they did to him. Harry tried to argue that there must have been more to it than that but Uncle …' Lucas looked away. 'Uncle yelled at him to stop pestering him about the past and concentrate on the work that needs to be done now. He *yelled*, Annie. I didn't know he could.'

'He did lose his niece.'

'Yeah.'

Behind them somewhere, a brush-tailed possum launched itself to another tree in a rustle of activity.

'I take it that Harry hasn't let the matter rest?'

'Of course not. And every time he brings up the subject, Uncle comes down on him like he's about six years old. He even tried to send him to his room. Clearly he's never had to discipline Harry before—he doesn't have a clue how to go about it.'

Uncle Willie must have had a backbone forged from pure titanium to be able to resist Harry's gift once he set his mind on something. Her Cherub partner could be downright stubborn, but usually for a good reason. 'Harry has a right to know.'

'And he's not stupid. He's been doing his own research.'

Annie smiled. 'Of course he has. What's he found?'

'No idea. He won't talk to me.'

'Which is why you're worried.'

Lucas nodded, fiddling with his fingertips. 'I need to stick around. Someone needs to be there to make sure they don't push each other too far. Uncle won't understand what Harry's going through.'

Hearing Lucas talk like that gave Annie an astonishing and unexpected buzz, like she'd just been smacked in the face with a piece of Living Fruit. His adorable shaggy hair—she could admire but ignore. His athletic frame and swallow-the-sky blue eyes—she was learning to resist. He had a laugh as open and generous as any of her Eden family, and she could pretend that wasn't so rare, but those words, and the genuine concern she felt from him … Lucas *cared* for people. For *her* people, as much as his own. How was she supposed to defend against that? The icy water had numbed her feet, and the aching cold was starting to creep past her knees, so she pulled her feet up onto the rock and tried to pretend that the cold could numb the new thing that was budding in her heart as well.

'I agree,' she said once she was certain her voice would sound right. 'You are needed here. Just let me know if you change your mind. I'll do whatever you need me to.'

His downcast expression and a heart full of yearning told her what it was he needed, and she left it alone. *Just this once.* He was making major decisions and it would have been unfair for her to take away the emotions he needed to make them.

'What I need is for us to be friends, Annie. I need to be able to talk to you. Harry agrees. Things are going to be complicated enough without him having to act as mediator between us. He thinks it's time to tell your mum about me.'

He looked up at her, and Annie could see the scene reflected in his eyes. See the moment when Lucas met her mum. He would smile, and call her Mrs Langley, and her mum would blink at him, and then smile back. At first her mum would be thrilled, but then …

'No.' Her hands clenched at the rock she was sitting on. How could she admit to him the real reason for her fear when she could hardly make sense of it herself? All she knew was that she wasn't ready. Not ready to commit to a bond that she knew would define her, and possibly one day break her. And how could she risk putting her mum through the anguish of watching the two of them grow closer together, while she was grieving for her own lost Guardian? And telling Lucas that whole truth would only convince him that they really did belong together.

'I can't. She won't understand why I can't choose you—I mean, she really won't cope.'

The lie tasted sour on her lips.

'You have no idea what it's been like since Dad died,' she continued. 'Don't you get it, Lucas? He was her Guardian. Any reminders of him, of what she lost when she …' Dimly aware that she was saying too much, she snapped her mouth and eyes shut. Warm hands pried her fingers from the rock, and she felt healing heat soothe her scratched hands. There was a safe intimacy in his touch that made her want to cry when he let go again.

'Okay, calm down. I'll stay as far away from her as I can, I promise. I'm sorry I mentioned it. I should have realised … I assumed she already knew about you and Harry.' He ran his hands through his shaggy hair and sighed. 'So many secrets. How do you live like this?'

'Not well,' she grouched, rubbing her fingers to savour the warmth he'd left there. If only she could have properly shared with him how things should have been. Not just for them, but for all of humanity. There was a place where there were no secrets, no lies, and no tears. A place where that first touch would have been celebrated by an entire village as the start of something precious and brilliant because people just weren't built to make the wrong choices.

Instead, everything was twisted.

Hold me, she begged without words. *Kiss me like you did that day.* She sat, unmoving, barely breathing in case her movements gave her away. *Even just a hug, or …*

Her Guardian's fingers slipped between hers, braving her reaction, just to comfort her, and together they crushed everything they were feeling between their palms.

They sat silently by the river for a very long time, and with each passing moment, Annie's conviction began to wear down. Perhaps her mum wasn't as fragile as she thought. Perhaps it was simply a matter of choosing the right time to break the news that her Guardian had found her. Perhaps she and her mum and Lucas could live happily together for years and years and beat the family curse. After all, Harry seemed to be cursed enough for the both of them.

Chapter 18

All her life Annie had been strictly warned about getting addicted to their other world, but she'd never really felt that it could be that big a problem. Not until her mother stopped listening to her own advice. Annie couldn't stop herself from constantly monitoring her mother's feelings, sensing how her heart hungered for simplicity and comfort. How she mourned the companionship she'd lost when she and her Guardian had risked it all … and lost.

Four whole days had passed after Annie's disastrous birthday and her mum hadn't said another word about Harry and Sarah, or about anything at all, really. This heavy grief terrified her. If this was her mother's reaction to the discovery of Harry's Guardian, then how would Annie ever be able to introduce her to Lucas? Still, she would have to do it soon. She'd been thinking a lot about what Lucas had said. He was right about the stress of living with secrets. She'd wanted time to explore her own identity without being intertwined with someone else, but it felt like all that had achieved so far was to establish how deceitful she could be.

They were cooking dinner. Even though it wasn't Annie's turn to cook, her mum had been so quiet that she was desperate to find ways to interact with her, so she helped her cut up the potatoes just to have an excuse to chat. It wasn't that her mum was moping, exactly, it was more that she was just so … disengaged. To anyone else she would have appeared completely normal, if a bit distracted sometimes, only Annie knew better. Each time her mum stared out to the north-west, turning her wedding ring round and round her finger, her longing became almost too much to bear. She was doing it again now, instead of cooking the mince that Annie had tactfully placed right in front of her on the bench.

'The Fletchers are having another baby,' she enticed, hoping her mum would at least pretend to care. Babies were usually a good way to draw her attention back to Nalong.

'That's wonderful.' Although her pleasure was genuine, her eyes didn't leave the window.

'James told me his parents have decided to build a new room for his baby brother or sister. He sounded relieved. I think he was a bit worried they'd be trying to kick him out to make room,' she joked, taking another spud from the colander to slice up. 'Mind you, he was also talking about moving to Sydney once school's finished. If I were his parents I'd hold off on the renovations until he's decided what to do. Imagine if they spend all that money only to have him leave town anyway?'

'James *should* leave Nalong. He's old enough now; he doesn't need his parents anymore.'

The words felt like a stab to the heart. Surely she didn't mean it. Did she know how much that hurt? Annie licked her lips. She had to ask.

'What do you mean, Mum? What are you trying to say?'

Her mum turned to her, biting her lower lip as if considering something. 'You're almost done with school,' she said. 'Do you think you'll go away to study after that?'

'How can I? And what would be the point? I'm needed here.'

A single nod of acknowledgment was the only response, because there was no arguing the truth, and a little piece of Annie's heart crumbled away. Was this really all she was? All she could be?

Her mum gave a sly smile. 'Once your Guardian turns up, I'm thinking I might move Next Door. I'm sure if we're clever about it, I can come back and visit pretty much any time. I have some fun ideas about how to fake my death. I had a long chat to the pharmacist today about what might happen if I accidentally took too many of those pills I was on last year. He seemed genuinely concerned.'

The knife slipped and Annie watched a blossom of red cascade across the potato she was clutching. It made a pretty pattern. A second later she hissed as her brain registered the sting, and then hissed again as potato juice seeped into the cut.

'Annie, your hand! Here, let me see that.' Suddenly business-like, her mum hauled her over to the sink and turned on the tap.

A nice long incision now adorned the base of her thumb, and the self-condemning words that Annie mumbled just under her breath would have had Kelly scolding her for sure. She couldn't afford to be so clumsy. Crimson water spiralled down the plug hole, and she wondered if Lucas would be able to follow the path her blood took as it spun through the drainage system and spread out underground in the back paddock. Would he become bonded to their farm now?

'I need you here, Mum. Please don't leave me.'

'Oh, sweetheart. Don't cry. I won't be leaving you. I'll be Next Door, whenever you need me. Please don't think of it as some sort of abandonment. Trust me, once your Guardian shows up, you won't want me to hang around here interfering. You're at an age where you'll want your independence, and you said it yourself, you can't exactly leave home. This is the perfect solution.' She flashed Annie a grin that was reminiscent of a time long gone. 'I'll still be available to take your daughter Next Door so you and your Guardian can have dirty weekends away, like my mum did for me.'

Annie waited, and it didn't take long. Her mum's face lit up, and then fell as her memories resurfaced. It was a good thing Annie had perfected her new trick so she could snatch the pain away.

'Well, my Guardian isn't here yet,' Annie lied.

Her mum sighed as she inspected the wound. 'I do wish he'd get a move on.'

The clock on the wall ticked like a countdown to a bomb blast, but Annie used its steadiness to try to slow her racing heart as she fought to keep her face passive.

'I have to say, I'm a little concerned, Annie. Society's changing so fast. Perhaps I should be sending you out of town more often. Or at least *into* town. He's bound to be drawn here, and yet I can't help feeling that if Harry hadn't spent every waking moment working these farms, he might have—'

'Stop, Mum, please,' she begged, pulling her hand away from her close inspection. 'Don't blame Harry. The only reason he had to work so hard over summer was because I bailed on you both. He had planned to take some time off, remember?' Cradling her hand in a tea towel, Annie reached up to get the first-aid kit from above the fridge, figuring it would be better to get the wound dressed before she had to answer the phone call she knew she was about to get. She opened the tin and sat on the corner of the table to rummage through it. 'The farms don't run themselves. Which is a hint, by the way. Can we please do some shopping tomorrow? The last time you left, I ran out of pretty much everything. You'll be gone for weeks this time, and I'm a bit sick of zucchinis. Also, I'd like to stock up on some summer fruits while we can still get the local stuff.' It was harder than she expected to unwrap a Band-Aid with one hand. Her mum pulled it out from between her teeth and finished the job with a frown.

'What makes you so sure I'm leaving?' she all but whispered, holding Annie's injured hand in both of hers and closing her eyes.

Annie snatched her hand away before her mother could read her. Kiah Langley was able to see flashes of people's memories, particularly ones that held significant emotional impact. It was similar to Annie's own gift, but more detailed, and she had more control over when she used it because it relied on touch. It had been years since she'd used it on her daughter; she usually respected her privacy a bit more. Annie might have felt offended, except she knew that her mum was actually justified in trying it this time. Annie *was* hiding something. Something that, as a good parent, her mother had every right to know about. Something that would also make her leave home. Permanently.

'I hate it when you go,' Annie said, 'but you have to get better. You're not much use when you're like this, and I still need your help around here.'

The guilt and hurt in her mother's eyes made her feel horrible, especially knowing how easily she could draw it away; however, that would defeat the purpose.

The phone rang.

'I'll get it,' Annie said, jumping from the table, except her mum was paying attention to things now, and was quicker than expected. When her mum picked up the receiver, Annie froze. He'd promised. Lucas had promised to stay away. It wasn't that bad a cut that he would risk her mum finding out about him, was it? Why had she been so careless?

'Harry wants to talk to you.'

Her breath released again as she grabbed the receiver. 'Hey, Harry.'

Her mum waited, listening.

'Yeah, of course I'll help. How much do you want her to know?' she asked, grateful that he was smart enough not to ask her outright what she'd done to make Lucas crazy this time.

She held her hand over the mouthpiece and turned back to her mum. 'Can I go to Harry's tomorrow? Dave and Sarah are coming to visit. He thinks it might be a good time to explain some things to Sarah, if he can get her alone. It would be easier if I was there too.'

'School?' she asked.

'Tomorrow's Saturday,' Annie reminded her.

Her mum nodded and turned back to the cooking.

'Harry, Mum says that's fine. Listen, why don't you come over for dinner tonight? We can talk about what we should tell her, and how. Make some contingency plans for if things get difficult. We're only having shepherd's pie—if we can salvage the potatoes, that is. Would you believe I just sliced my thumb when I was cutting them up? That's what happens when you get the shearing contractors to sharpen all your kitchen knives when they do their clipper blades.'

Somehow, she knew that down the other end of the line, Harry was rolling his eyes.

⌒

'I brought cake,' Annie announced as she pulled up to Harry's house the next morning. She unstrapped the Tupperware container from the back of her quad bike before giving Bo his obligatory belly scratch with her foot. Dave and Sarah had already arrived and were admiring the chicks that were pecking at the lawn in their little mobile cage. They had just about lost all their baby feathers and looked old enough to go in with the others, and she wondered if Lucas was being a bit overprotective. It would fit with his personality.

Lucas was standing by the front door, arms crossed, staring at her with his gorgeous blue eyes. After greeting Sarah and Dave with polite hugs, she mouthed the word 'sorry' to him and held up the cake as a clandestine peace offering. He beckoned her over, looking impatient, but she shook her head, hoping the others wouldn't notice their subtle exchange.

'How are you feeling, Sarah?' she asked, heading into the house and carefully keeping the cake between Lucas and her bandaged hand.

'Actually pretty good these days,' she replied. 'Not sick at all anymore. I almost feel like a normal human again.' She followed through the door with Dave not far behind.

Normal human. Annie winced at the irony. Sarah's newly awoken Guardian traits, not her humanity, were more likely responsible for making her body stronger.

Harry was in the kitchen with Uncle Willie, fretting, so she put the cake down and gave him a quick hug.

'You took your time,' he grumbled.

'I had chores. And the cake took ages to cook,' Annie said, wondering if she should draw away some of his nervousness. Uncle looked at them with a sort of wary expression. They weren't normally huggers, and he seemed to be unsure about what it meant. Were they a couple, or weren't they? Perhaps he'd noticed that they only ever acted like a couple when Lucas was in the room. Uncle Willie put the kettle on, while Annie took a knife from the second drawer to cut the cake with.

'Let me do that,' Lucas suggested, reaching for the knife with a falsely sweet smile. She grunted, holding it stubbornly for a moment before choosing to act like a grown-up and let it go. Honestly, it was just a little cut. Did he have to be so grouchy about it?

Half an hour later, the cake had been utterly demolished and yet no one was in any hurry to move from the kitchen. Dave and Lucas were telling everyone about the pranks they'd arranged the previous year for their end of Year 12 celebrations, including a tradition Annie hadn't heard of, which involved playing 'Eagle Rock' over the school PA system. When she realised there was partial nudity involved, Annie asked if either of them happened to have a recording of the song. The whole time they talked, Sarah kept sneaking edgy glances at Harry, who looked like he wanted to hide under the table. He was so quiet he didn't even join in the argument when Lucas declared he was going to save up for a Ford Fairlane he'd seen at a dealer's in town, even when Annie nudged his foot. She could have used his gifted assistance to talk Lucas into buying a Holden instead.

Annie tried hard to encourage as much light-hearted banter as possible, mostly at Lucas's expense, while using her own gift to dull the edges of everyone's tension. Uncle Willie sat in the corner, sipping at his second cup of tea and enjoying the show.

'So, Uncle, do you have much on this afternoon?' Annie asked, toying with the bits of cake she hadn't managed to make herself eat.

'Gotta pick up a new tractor tyre from a guy in Horsham. Tried to have the old one fixed, but that thing's been going since Adam was a boy. I probably should get moving. You need anything from town?'

'Nah, we're good. Thanks anyway.' Annie felt her shoulders relax. No need to have to think of some lame excuse to send him to her place to get him out of the way. She wasn't great at being sneaky like that.

'What about the rest of you? Anyone need anything?' It was automatic. Horsham was far enough away that it was common to put in orders if someone else was about to make the trip.

'No thanks, Mr Doolan.' Dave chuckled.

'Why are you grinning like a loony?' Uncle asked him.

'Since Adam was a boy,' Dave replied. 'I haven't heard that expression before. I like it.'

Annie noticed a subtle change in the dark cloud of despair she could feel from Harry. He was smiling at something behind her. She turned to see Lucas trying so hard not to laugh that he had tears in his eyes.

'Adam,' Lucas repeated when everyone stared at him. 'It's funny.'

Uncle Willie blinked at him. 'Yeah, well, almost everything around here is ancient, me included, so I get to say it a lot.'

'You aren't that old, Mr Doolan,' Dave argued.

'Now, no more of this "Mr Doolan" business. You call me Uncle like everyone else. I'm no bank manager. I'm a farmer. We're all farmers 'round here, so we're all family, so I can be Uncle, get it?'

Dave nodded, flashing his white teeth and looking thrilled to be considered one of them. Maybe Annie's mum was right to encourage him toward farming.

'Lucas, why don't you show Dave around?' Annie suggested. 'He can take my quaddie.'

'I get to ride a quad bike?' Dave asked, standing so fast he knocked a pile of magazines off the table.

It was easy to forget how excited city people got about simple things like driving over bumpy grass. 'Feel free,' she told him. 'Just watch out for the steep hills. You really don't want a three hundred-kilo machine landing on you if you misjudge a bump.'

He turned to Sarah, his green eyes uneasy. 'Will you be all right here if I go? What will you do?'

Sarah glared at him. 'I'm going to go to the dunny and wipe my own bum.'

'I've been a bit clingy, haven't I?' he said, not sounding at all bothered by her icy tone. 'Sorry. I'll get out of your hair for a few hours. I'm sure there are plenty of jobs I could help with while we're here.'

Lucas rubbed his hands together in anticipation. 'I was kind of hoping you'd say that. There's a great big tree that's come down on the fence near the river. I'll cut if you stack,' he suggested. 'Should be able to get enough of it moved to get the fence back up if I have help.'

Dave looked ecstatic at the idea. Crazy city folk.

The faded curtains were so thin and worn out that they did almost nothing to block out the late autumn sun. Annie closed them anyway once the quad bikes disappeared around the corner of the shed. Somehow it felt better to do everything possible to avoid anyone seeing them, even though there was no longer anyone else around.

Sarah sat down on the sofa and began to flick through a magazine, but it was clear that she wasn't really reading anything because it was a farm equipment sales magazine, and Annie was pretty certain she wasn't actually in the market for a new slasher.

On the other side of the room Harry was literally pacing, pretending to tidy up now that he'd washed and dried all the dishes. She almost felt like making some mess just to give him something to do, but decided it would be better to just get things over with while they had the opportunity. So she walked past him and stomped on his foot.

Sarah flinched and the magazine flapped its pages in a wild attempt to escape her grasp.

'What was that for?' Harry complained half-heartedly. He was so busy trying not to look at Sarah that she could have probably set him on fire and he would have only said 'ow' half-heartedly.

'Just making sure, before we do anything drastic. Do you want to tell her first, or should I just get the knife?' she asked.

'Knife?' Sarah held up the magazine like a shield, looking nervous.

Annie replayed her last sentence back in her head, wincing as she realised how it must have sounded. After all, Sarah didn't really know them *that* well. 'Relax, I'm not going to stab you. We just need to show you something.'

It didn't take long for her to retrieve the sharp carving knife from the kitchen, only then she felt incredibly awkward walking back with it. How was one supposed to carry a knife without looking threatening? Hold the blade? Too weird. Lay it across her palms? No, looks like someone's about to perform an animal sacrifice. Behind her back? Definitely not. In the end, she just sort of dangled it loosely from her fingers and almost dropped it. Thankfully Harry took it away from her before she could stress Lucas out again.

'Wait,' she said to him as he gripped the handle and took a deep breath. 'You'd better sit down.' She shooed him over to the couch and sat him down right next to Sarah, so the poor girl wouldn't be forced to exert herself. Then she snatched the magazine out of Sarah's hands and spread it out on Harry's lap. She didn't want to have to explain the blood. Sarah looked ready to bolt, but Annie knew she wouldn't be able to.

Harry looked up at Annie, his dark eyes despairing. Everything would change for Sarah once they did this.

'I'm sorry, Harry,' Annie said. 'I know this isn't how you always imagined it happening. You deserve a better story than this one.'

He closed his eyes against the grief, but she was concentrating too hard on keeping Sarah calm to be able to help him too.

'Oh, my God! What are you two doing?' Sarah demanded, blasting through Annie's attempt to steal away her panic.

'You'd better be quick, Harry, and don't make it so big that she gets too dizzy. It does need to be big enough to prove it to her though. Did you want me to do it?'

'Of course not. She'll kill you and Lucas will never speak to me again. Just let me concentrate. This is harder than I expected, now that I have to actually do it.'

Sarah made a grab for the knife but Harry was ready. He sliced the tip of his finger with a hiss and then tossed the blade onto the coffee table before she could interfere. Blood welled up and started dripping.

'What the hell is the matter with you people!' Sarah yelled, grabbing at Harry's hand with both of hers. Annie's eyes widened as she watched it happen. On pure instinct, Sarah ran her thumb along the length of the cut, leaving behind completely healed skin, stained only with a few drops of crimson proof.

She gasped and let go, her eyes going a bit glassy.

'Don't speak,' Harry advised, holding Sarah's elbows to keep her steady. 'Just wait until the dizziness passes.'

'I'll get some water,' Annie offered, hoping they hadn't done anything to put her at risk. It wasn't just in Eden that pregnant women were considered precious, after all. They'd talked about it for hours the previous night, and her mum had agreed that it would be far too dangerous for her not to know what was going on. A small cut had been the safest way they could think of to prove to her what she could do, and how powerful it was.

When she returned, Sarah was inspecting Harry's finger with wide eyes, but it was Harry's expression that really grabbed her attention. He was drinking in every feature of Sarah's face like he thought he would never get another opportunity. She had thought she knew every nuance of every possible emotion that Harry could ever feel, and yet this was entirely new, this excitement, and fascination. Frozen in the doorway, she watched her best friend's feelings awaken and unfurl. Such a delicate and fragile gift … she wanted this for him, more than anything.

'How did you do that?' Sarah asked him. 'I saw the blood. I still see it, only the wound is completely gone.'

'That wasn't me, and you know it,' Harry said. His eyes had taken on that look. The one that meant he could tell you that *Play School* was being cancelled and you would still just smile and think it was the best thing you'd heard all day. 'You healed me, Sarah. Thank you.'

'Me? I didn't do anything … did I?'

'Yeah, it was definitely you,' Annie said. 'You kind of acted on instinct. Do you feel all right?' She handed Sarah the glass of water. She didn't know if river water would have helped her or just risked unwanted germs, so she'd stuck to the normal stuff. It made her realise how many questions she had never bothered to ask her parents. How could she ask them now, when the mere mention of the Guardians turned her mum into a glassy-eyed shell of a person, who wanted to fake her own death?

Sarah took a small sip. 'I'm okay. Just confused. You both set this up, didn't you? With the knife?'

'We needed you to know what you can do,' Harry replied.

'You couldn't just have told me?' she complained with typical Guardian grouchiness.

'Would you have believed us?'

'Do I believe you now?'

They waited, hoping that she'd answer her own question.

She placed the glass on the coffee table. 'I'm going to need a better explanation. Clearly you expected me to do whatever it was I did, so start talking.'

Her apparent irritation was all based on nerves, and Annie didn't blame her. There were more lives than just her own to be nervous about and her jumbled emotions probably made even less sense to her than they did to Annie.

It took the better part of an hour to properly fill her in. Harry did a much better job than she had with Lucas, patiently waiting for her to ask questions instead of throwing everything at her at once. It was hard for Annie not to interfere. More than once, he had to turn his soothing eyes on her with an unspoken reminder that it was his job to explain the situation. Despite his uncanny patience and pacifying gift, Sarah still didn't take it very well.

'I'm *bonded* to you? That's ridiculous. Even if I did believe in all that Garden of Eden stuff, that's taking things a bit too far. Why would you choose to bond with someone like me? I'm already kind of ... bonded to someone else, in case you haven't figured that out. You say that I can't tell anyone else, but I don't have any intention of keeping secrets from Dave. I would never do that to him. Forget it. Undo it. Find someone else.'

It wasn't like they hadn't known that this part was coming, but it didn't mean they knew how to handle it. Even through Annie's strongest shield she could feel Harry's anguish. He opened his mouth to answer her and nothing came out.

So Annie answered for him. 'It can't be undone, Sarah. You are Harry's Guardian and always have been. It's built in. We have no control over it and no say in it—only in how we deal with it.' Putting it that way made it sound like some sort of a disease. Just as well her mum couldn't hear her talk like that, she would have been mortified. 'The bond was never designed to cause problems,' she defended. 'It's supposed to be a blessing.' And she was the world's biggest hypocrite.

Sarah buried her face in her hands as the meaning behind her words sank in. 'No, no, no, no,' she rasped. 'That's all wrong. We make our own destiny. Don't you get it? I had to stop clinging to that childish idea that there was someone out there who would make everything fall into place. I grew up and let that dream go when Dad walked out on us. There's no such thing as a soulmate. That was Mum's stupid mistake, not mine. Relationships take work, and hard decisions, and real commitment. They don't just happen by … *magic.*'

Annie looked over at Harry and allowed herself to feel what he did. The fragile emotion that she had felt unfurl earlier folded back in on itself … and broke her heart.

Sarah didn't speak so much as a single word to Harry for the rest of the day. The few questions she still had were all directed at Annie as short terse queries and were all to do with how she could escape the trap she now saw herself in. How far could she go without feeling ill? If Harry hurt himself, would she be forced to come and heal him or could she just ignore it? Would it all wear off after a while? Was there any way to pass the bond to someone else? Every second phrase was 'not that I believe it all anyway'. Annie decided that she mustn't have spent enough time in Eden lately because by the time the others returned, the pregnant woman was really getting on her nerves. If she was honest, she knew that was mostly because Sarah was reflecting her own bad attitude toward what was supposed to be an honour and a gift.

The second Dave walked in the door, coated in mud and sawdust, Sarah threw herself into his arms with the exuberance of a kid with a new puppy. As Annie knew she would, she tried to tell him everything. And as she knew she would, Sarah burst into tears instead.

'Ho! What's happened, Sarah? Are you okay?' Dave grabbed her elbows and searched her face for an explanation. All she could do was shrug and sniffle. He turned to Harry instead, except he had pretty much shut down about an hour earlier and just ignored him.

'She's fine, Dave. Just a bit emotional. Is that normal for her?' Annie asked with a false air of innocence.

'Well, yes … but—ow!' He jumped backward before Sarah could elbow him again.

'I'm not just a bag of hormones,' she snapped.

No one knew what to say. Lucas held up the coffee jar as a sort of peace offering, but Sarah grumbled something under her breath and then shoved her way past him out of the kitchen. The backlash from Sarah's flare of anger was enough to make Annie step toward Lucas in defence—as if she could somehow shield him from it. Why was Sarah even angrier with Lucas than anyone else? Perhaps it was the overly sympathetic way he'd been smiling at her all day. She was probably getting enough of those looks already. Or perhaps she thought he'd caved too easily, giving up his studies to come to Nalong. Or perhaps she just felt angry in general and was taking it out on whoever was closest. Whatever it was, the others didn't need any special gifts to pick up on her mood, and it didn't take long for Dave to suggest that he take her home. Sarah snatched her keys from his hand and stormed out, leaving Dave to splutter out a hurried goodbye and race to catch up. Her red Gemini did a fishtail as it turned out of the driveway, causing Lucas to sigh. Then in the next moment both he and Annie turned in response to the sound of a quad bike starting up. Harry splattered mud across the lawn as he took off toward the river.

'Should we go after him?' Lucas asked. 'Would it help if he hit me again? I could get him to hit me, I don't mind.'

Annie shook her head. 'Not this time, thanks anyway. I think he just needs some space. He'll let me know when he wants to talk.'

They stood on the front step watching Harry bump across the home paddock, scattering a flock of cockatoos as he over-revved the engine. It started to drizzle, the fine mist matching the sombre mood in a satisfying way. A mob of young steers up on the hill moaned for their mothers who weren't there to answer.

'Can I fix your hand now?' Lucas asked. She could see his fingers twitching again but he politely kept his distance.

'Nope. Sorry. Mum got too good a look at it. I can't risk her noticing if it disappears.'

'Can't you just keep a bandage on it? She won't know.'

'Are you asking me to deceive my mother?'

'Aren't you already doing that?' he countered.

'I won't risk it,' she said, ignoring his stupid sensible argument.

He clenched his jaw, just slightly, before replying. 'It's very uncomfortable for me, when you're hurt. Last night Uncle asked me if I'd been doing drugs because I couldn't sit still. In the end Harry took me out to the garage and showed me how to change the oil in my car, just to keep me busy. I ended up doing the ute and the tractor as well.'

Good to know. Next time she needed a job done …

'How is Sarah going to cope?' he continued. 'Farms are not the safest places to live. We're constantly getting minor injuries. The other day a cow stood on my foot and I'm sure I heard something crack. I had an impressive bruise for a few hours, and it hurt like—anyway, its fine now, but my point is that it's too easy for you and Harry to get hurt, and if we're too far away to help, it can be pretty awful for everyone.'

'You broke your foot? Lucas that's terrible! Are you sure it's okay? Did you get it checked out?'

The expression on his face could only be described as sardonic, and she glanced away in embarrassment. Apparently she had no right to be concerned about his injuries if he wasn't allowed to heal hers.

'Harry warned me not to let Uncle know how bad it was. I did ice it for a bit.'

She pouted at his foot in disapproval so he hopped up and down on it and then did a little moonwalk and spin to prove that it was okay.

'You're smiling. I thought you'd forgotten how,' he said.

'Well, there hasn't been a lot to smile about lately.' She closed her eyes and concentrated for a second. Harry was still moving. He hadn't reached the river yet. 'You aren't wrong. About us getting injured easily. Is it really that bad for you when I get hurt? I only nicked myself. Stuff like that happens from time to time to everyone.'

He blew out a breath that lifted his fringe. 'It hasn't been too much of a problem for me until yesterday. I felt it when you whacked your head last week, and that time when you had something in your eye, and I know when your muscles get sore. I can ignore those the same way you can. I'm learning not to get too distracted by the minor things.' He turned to her and crossed his arms. 'But, Annie, please don't wax your legs again without giving me a chance to get roaring drunk first.'

Horrified, she gaped at him, feeling her face flush.

'Oh, come on. Don't try to tell me you didn't know I'd feel that,' he said. 'Did you purposefully pick the one night I was in town with Dave, or was that really just a coincidence?'

It may have crossed her mind that it might be an inconvenient time for him, but it had served him right after he'd teased her about her pathetic knowledge of international sports stars. What did she care if some soccer player had cheated and used his hand instead of his head and scored a goal? What was wrong with using your hands anyway? She'd told him the guy should have just stuck to real footy and it would never have been a problem. Even Harry had struggled to settle the shouting match that had erupted at that point. A little bit of payback was entirely justified, and her legs had badly needed the attention so she could wear that new dress for her birthday. She hadn't realised he'd have been able to tell *exactly* what it was she was doing.

Annie slid down to sit on the wooden step and leant against the veranda post. She'd hoped that the bond might not tighten so much if they didn't spend too much time together, and that maybe Lucas could still escape somehow, for a while longer.

'The roof of the car,' she explained, avoiding his previous question. 'When I hit my head. It was when I was getting into the car. Just a glancing blow. I barely even noticed it at the time. I'm sorry.'

'Don't apologise. And don't drive yourself crazy trying not to get hurt, either. As I said, I can ignore it.'

'And Sarah? Can we do anything to help her to ignore it? How long did it take for you to get so tightly bonded to me, Lucas? Did you become more sensitive to me when you came back up from Melbourne? Was it better when you were farther away? Does the bond get stronger each time we see each other?'

He sat down on the step below hers and bit his lower lip. 'Are you sure you want to know?' He watched her almost shyly, as if her answer was incredibly important to him.

'Of course. I need to know as much as possible, especially if it can help Sarah at all.'

He picked at the flaky paint on the railing as he answered. 'The bond kicked in about as quickly as the toxin from that damned octopus, Annie. It hasn't changed over time, I've just become better at understanding it. I felt you, right from the moment I arrived in Apollo Bay, although I didn't know what it was I was feeling. You … pulled at me. Once I saw you, I couldn't ignore it any longer, and from the moment you took hold of my hand …' There was no shyness left in his gaze as he boldly wove his fingers through hers, mimicking what she had done on the beach. 'From that moment on, I've felt everything. No, don't look so guilty. You don't get it. I *feel* everything, as if I have new senses. It's marvellous. Although it did take me a disconcerting few weeks to get the hang of distinguishing which were your injuries and which were my own. You girls really don't exaggerate when you complain about the cramping, do you?'

Mortified, Annie groaned and tried to hide under her elbows, but he refused to let go of her hand.

'And I won't pretend that the whole thing didn't scare the shit out of me. I didn't have a clue what was happening. Strangely enough, it scared me even more the day you must have gone … what do you call it? Next Door? I felt as if I'd suddenly gone deaf. I didn't feel sick anymore, but it was eerie and uncomfortable to only have my normal senses again. When you came back I had to find you.' He ducked his eyes a fraction as he admitted, 'I was going to scream at you until you told me everything, except then …' He swallowed.

Then he saw her kissing Harry.

'I'm so sorry,' she interrupted so he didn't have to continue. 'I didn't realise it would be so strong. Always before, Guardians have been close by. Dad moved to Nalong when he was twelve years old, so he and Mum knew each other long before the bond really kicked in. I thought that if I stayed away from you, it wouldn't be so powerful. I wanted—damn, Lucas, no!' Snatching her hand out of his, she lifted the corner of the wound dressing her mum had so meticulously applied. There was no trace left of the cut underneath.

'Oh, no, I didn't mean it! I didn't even notice I was doing it. Annie, I'm sorry.' He crossed his arms, tucking his hands away before they could get him into any more trouble. He looked so distressed and repentant that she struggled to stay angry. It wasn't really his fault.

'What am I going to tell her?' she moaned.

He didn't reply.

Inwardly she cringed. There was no avoiding it now. There was only one thing she could do to hide the truth from her mother, and it was worse than merely deceiving her. She was going to have to manipulate her into going Next Door. Right after she'd worked so hard to guilt her into staying. It just wasn't fair.

Chapter 19

The following Thursday, Annie met the boys by the lake in town after school. She sat down next to Harry on the park bench and dumped her Santa sack of a school bag on the ground. A couple of text books threatened to fall out, but Harry caught them with his foot.

'What's Lucas doing?' Annie asked, watching him chase a ball around the dry section of the lake bed.

'Teaching the swans to play soccer,' Harry replied. 'Being the start of May, this is the only mud we could find, and apparently playing where there's mud is important. Makes it more authentic. Or something.'

'Right. Whatever.'

'Mostly I think he started playing so we could talk alone. He wouldn't let me leave when we felt you heading this way. He asked me outright if I was avoiding you.'

'And what did you tell him?'

Harry gave her a wry smile. 'Couldn't really tell the truth given we're supposed to be romantically involved, now, could I?'

'So you *have* been avoiding me.'

He took her hand in his. 'Not consciously. It's just …'

'It's just that you know I won't let you get away with keeping secrets from me.' When he didn't reply, she knew she was right. 'Lucas told me about what the guy at the jewellery store said. And that Uncle Willie is being a bit evasive. What exactly are you trying to find out?'

Pressing his lips together, Harry glowered at the Carved Tree in front of them. Its dead branches made it look like an evil parody of the Trees in the Garden. A roughly cut chevron pattern scarred its trunk. When he finally answered, his voice was wrapped around his barely contained tears. 'I want to know how this bloody tree killed my parents.'

Annie gripped his hand tighter. 'I asked Mum about it. She said that the council were planning to cut it down with the rest when they made this park, and your dad kicked up a real stink. According to traditional lore the tree is supposed to ward off evil spirits. Your dad got into a fight with the council workers and was arrested for stealing a bulldozer.'

'Stealing?'

'That's what they called it, but it was in front of everyone, in broad daylight. It wasn't like he was planning to get very far. He was clearly just trying to make a point.'

'Yeah, that sounds like Dad,' Harry said. 'But even a theft charge wouldn't have got him that much jail time, surely.'

Annie shrugged. 'Mum sounded pretty cross when I pressed for more details, and yet she was actually feeling worried. No, more than worried. Scared. I don't get it. Surely if it had something to do with Eden then we would be better off knowing the full story. When I used that argument she just said "No, you wouldn't", and refused to say another word.'

A loud squawk interrupted the sombre mood when Lucas kicked his ball into a clump of reeds. The black swan that had been nesting there charged at him with wings outstretched and Lucas ran backward so fast he lost a shoe in the mud. They watched for a minute or so while Lucas tried to figure out how to get his ball back without losing what was left of his dignity. Annie couldn't help smiling.

'I assume you tried to look up the public records at the library?' she asked after a while.

'Yes. He was charged with manslaughter, only he died before it went to trial.'

'*What?*'

'You heard me. I have the date it happened, and the name of the man who was killed, but I can't find anything else. The newspaper reports were really vague. "Killed in an altercation." They obviously weren't allowed to say too much before it went to trial. I tried to ask at the police station—they won't talk to me.'

Annie was stunned. Manslaughter. Geoff Doolan? The same Geoff who used to sing her to sleep in the old language and taught her how to help abandoned baby birds to survive even if they had no feathers yet? No wonder Harry was pushing for more answers.

'It's a small town,' she said. 'Someone must remember what happened.'

'I've asked around a bit. Even Mrs Keel at the milk bar wasn't able to find out details at the time. She said my family could be stubbornly private.'

'Yeah. Funny about that.'

With a triumphant yodel, Lucas ran up the embankment carrying his mud-coated prize.

'I thought you weren't supposed to use your hands,' Annie called out. Lucas grinned at her and started flipping the ball from his foot to his knee.

'Well,' she said, turning back to Harry. 'There's one person who knows something. I think it's time I went jewellery shopping.'

For some reason, Harry and Lucas both seemed to feel the need to sneak up to the little shop as if it might run away if it saw them coming. Nestled between a hairdresser and a dry cleaner's, Durante Diamonds had a sparsely bedecked window display and a lot of mirrors to make it look more sparkly. Rolling her eyes at the way Lucas was all but sidling up to the adjoining brickwork, Annie walked straight up and pushed open the door, which gave a rude buzz to announce her arrival.

A middle-aged man in a crisp grey suit came out from the back room. He had prominent cheekbones and small chin, and looked like he was about three weeks late for an appointment at the hairdresser's next door.

'May I help you?' he asked in a voice too deep for his chin.

'Yes. I want you to tell me about Geoff and Ruby Doolan.'

The man's shoulders slumped. 'Harry sent you to hassle me? I already told him I don't know anything. He misunderstood a comment I made. I hadn't seen him for a few years and I was struck by how much he looks like his mum. I was merely expressing my condolences—I never meant to open up old wounds.'

'So you knew Ruby?'

'No. She was my best customer, but still just a customer. Please leave now.'

'What did she buy?'

'Nothing, she—I'm sorry, Miss Langley, I can't help you.'

'You know who I am.'

He moved to the door, flipped the sign over, and then held it open as a blatant request. 'It's getting late. I need to close the shop.'

'Why do you feel guilty?'

For a second he paused, and his dark eyes clouded, and then his emotions flipped in defence. 'Your rudeness is not welcome here,' he snapped, grabbing her elbow to push her out the door. Of course, Lucas was ready and somehow got between them.

'Don't touch her,' he growled.

'Bloody louts! Get out of my shop before I call the police!'

And then the door was closed in their faces and locked.

Harry was leaning against the brickwork on the far side of the dry-cleaning shop, minding Annie's school bag. 'So, it went about the same as every other time I've tried, then.' He hefted the bulging pack and started to walk away.

Lucas shook his head in disbelief. 'You have no idea about subtlety, do you, Annie?'

She ignored him and called out to Harry. 'What did your mum sell him?'

Her partner Cherub spun and frowned.

'He said she was a customer, but didn't buy anything,' she continued. 'That means she either had him make something, or she sold something. Didn't she have a necklace she always wore?'

Harry put the bag down again. 'The gold one with the ruby. When I was little I asked why her necklace had the same name as she did. She told me that was why Dad gave it to her. It had her name so it must be hers.'

Beside her, Lucas got that sentimental look in his blue eyes that made people want to give him baby chicks to care for. 'And I only bought you a tree.'

'What should you have got me?'

'A knee?' he suggested, smiling at his own terrible joke.

Annie blinked at him.

'Sorry.'

She walked past Harry, scooping up her bag on the way. 'So what happened to the ruby necklace, Harry? Do you still have it?'

'No, I …' For a second he looked like he'd been hit with the speech embargo, he was that close to tears. 'I dunno,' he mumbled, looking away. 'I'll see what I can find.' They started heading back to Harry's car. 'Hey, Annie?'

'Yeah?'

'Did he really feel guilty?'

She took his hand as they walked. 'Guilty as sin.'

Chapter 20

Annie retied her pony tail and tried to ignore the heaviness in her limbs. There was so much to get done. She had to keep moving. Jobs that she had managed to put off over winter could no longer be ignored, and she was the only one around to do them. Her mum had been gone for three whole months. Three months of not having to worry about her running into Lucas. Three months free from her mum's heavy burden of grief. Three months of knowing her mum was in a place where she could rest and heal, which must have been working given how badly she seemed to have lost track of time. And three months of trying to run a sheep farm on her own.

After losing two lambs and a ewe early in the season, even Harry had finally agreed that Year 12 was going to have to wait. She needed to be around to keep an eye on things. The worst part about ditching school was having to explain to everyone why. She *really* hated lying. Her fake old Aunty June was at death's door, and her mum was the only one able to care for her over in Western Australia. The signed note she'd handed in at the school office said that Annie would only miss a week or two, and that she'd drop in to collect assignments as often as she could, and study at home. Not even Kelly knew that her mum had already been away for over two months when Annie had stopped going. At least they had prepared better for her absence this time. Annie was now an authorised signatory on all the finances, she had her probationary Driver's Licence, and she was registered at the sale yards to make deals. Even though she was the one who'd made those suggestions, her mum's enthusiastic agreement had hurt.

Luckily, winter was always a fairly quiet time, and she'd managed reasonably well on her own. Then once the spring storms had begun to kick in, Harry and Lucas started to drop in more often. Just to use up the leftover weed spray, or borrow the chain-sharpener, or so Annie could clean out her gutters without Lucas turning into an insufferable pain in the bum. They came to help out as often as they could during the day, but she never let either of them stay once the work was done. That would have been a very bad idea. Instead she spent the evenings studying until very late, which helped to distract her from the fact that she felt so alone. Her mother had left her, Lucas was out of bounds, Kelly was busy with schoolwork and a boyfriend that had come and gone in the space of three weeks, and Harry was, well, cranky. He snapped at her every time she tried to speak to him alone. He was mad at her for lying to Lucas, and when she accused him of projecting his frustration about Sarah onto her, it only made him withdraw further, funnily enough. He'd also mentioned that he'd had no luck finding the necklace, which lent weight to the theory that his mum had sold it to pay off their debt, but that hadn't helped to explain how his dad had been charged with killing someone just a couple of months later. Since then, he'd refused to discuss it. No talking about Sarah, no talking about fights with Uncle Willie, no talking about the farm finances, and absolutely no talking about his parents. She was losing him, and was desperate for any opportunity to make things right again. So when the boys turned up to ask her opinion on the old mare's cough, she was more than happy to let them follow her out after lunch.

'Did you try putting Stockholm Tar up her nose?' Annie asked, climbing up to stand on the old gate post. From there she could see most of the ewes where they grazed among the early patches of yellow cape weed. They looked almost frantic, the way they cropped at the new growth as if they'd never seen real grass before. Usually by this time of year the sheep would all be starting to fatten and get lazy again, but August had so far given only a couple of days of half-hearted rain and not nearly enough warmth. It felt as if the spring sunshine was arriving later every year.

'What's Stockholm Tar?' Lucas asked, climbing neatly up onto the post on the other side of the gate. Smiling, Annie watched him assess the stock, no longer needing to be told what to look for. Not counting the few weeks he'd spent attempting to be a normal uni student in Melbourne, he'd now been working for Harry for almost eight months. If he survived lambing season, he might just be able to be called a farmer.

Harry leant on the gate between them. 'It's made from pine tar. Like the stuff you put in the bath for kids with eczema. Do you remember? We painted some onto that chook that was being picked on.'

'That brown sticky stuff? That stank! No wonder the other hens left her alone after that. Why would you put it up a horse's nostril?'

'It has antiseptic qualities,' Annie explained, squinting at a ewe that was walking in circles. 'I dunno how that helps to cure a runny nose, but it does. Give it a go, Harry, you'll see. Stockholm Tar can fix anything.'

He gave a serious nod as he scraped a heavy clod of mud from his boot. The pathetic amount of rain that had fallen the day before had been just enough to produce a greasy layer over the top of the dry one and so half the road stuck to their shoes like thick clay.

'Annie, is that one okay?' Lucas asked, pointing to the circling ewe.

Harry smiled proudly up at her, showing off how well he'd trained his apprentice.

'Good question,' she said. 'She's a maiden, and expecting twins. I've been watching her for the last couple of days. She's digging now, see? She keeps moving away from the others, and then gets nervous and comes back to them again.' The ewe in question let out a confused-sounding bleat, lifting her head and tasting the air. 'When I checked her this morning, the lambs felt lower than yesterday. That was hours ago. I thought she might have had them by now.'

It only took a few more minutes of patience to see what she had been expecting. The ewe became very restless, and soon lay down. A small shine appeared at the base of her tail along with a flood of clear fluid. They watched for a long time and nothing else happened, so she eventually nodded for Harry to pass her the bucket and lambing kit she'd brought along.

'Wait here,' she told Lucas. 'I'll just have a look.'

He waited. She looked. She washed her arms and investigated further, and then she beckoned the boys over.

'One leg is back,' she told them. 'They have their legs tangled, I think. I guess it's time to teach you what to do, city boy.'

'Me?' Lucas asked, his husky voice cracking. He cleared his throat. 'I don't think so. I think it would be best to leave this to the experts. Should I go and call the vet?'

Annie shook her head, rolling up her sleeves. She washed her arms again in the soapy water from the bucket and put on a fresh pair of lambing gloves. A minute later she was pushing lamb one back gently and trying to unhook lamb two's front leg from lamb one's left elbow. It was rather tricky. The ewe clearly agreed. Closing her eyes, Annie concentrated on feeling where everything was, trying to make certain that she knew which legs belonged to whom and which way around they were all supposed to be. Everything was so tight and squeezy that her fingers were tingling from lack of circulation. Finally, something gave way and slid in the right direction, so she drew a foreleg forward as gently as she could. The rest was easy. She handed the floppy wet blob to Lucas and reached in for number two, letting out her breath when she saw that its colour was okay. Pulling out cute little white blobs was a lot more fun than what sometimes happened. She cleared out number two's airway while Lucas copied her with his own charge. He beamed when his lamb took a twitchy breath a second before hers did the same.

'Annie, you made lambs! That was incredible,' he whispered, placing his lamb with hers in front of the tired ewe. 'They look like someone dipped a couple of kittens in a bowl of rice pudding. They're all soggy.'

Annie peeled off her gloves and washed her arms again, trying to ignore the mud that was plastered to her hair. She smelled terrible.

'They're pretty weak, so they still might not survive,' she warned him.

Lucas flicked some of the soapy water at her. 'You're as bad as Harry. You worry so much about all the things that can go wrong that you forget to enjoy what goes right. Life is too precious to miss out on with that attitude. You did a good thing, Annie. You're allowed to feel a bit proud of yourself, you know.'

She looked at the lambs again. Even after being surrounded by sheep all her life, she still found the newborns to be pretty cute. 'Thanks, Lucas. Definitely your turn next time, though. I've got eight more due to drop in the next week or so and I'm kind of stuffed. I don't think there are any more twins, thank goodness, except maybe that one over there,' she said, pointing to a ewe that was chewing on a saltbush. 'And she's had lambs before.' With a heave, she lifted the new mother up onto her feet above the wet infants so she could reach them more easily. The exhausted animal just sort of stood there and swayed a little. So did Annie. The ewe sniffed at the twitching blobs warily.

'You have a prickle in your hair,' Lucas warned, reaching behind her to peel it away.

Looking down to see what else she had picked up, Annie noticed mud caked all the way down one leg and blood and fluid soaking her shirt. Nice. Attempting to brush the mud off just made it worse. She was a mess. Just because she was constantly trying not to accidentally flirt with him didn't mean she felt happy about Lucas seeing her covered in birthing goop either. She took a self-conscious step back. Unfortunately, she was a bit too hasty because the prickle he was holding was still attached and it snagged at her hair and tangled it even more. She winced, and their apologies crossed over and tangled as well. Emotions flipped around like fish on the pier and she struggled to sort out whose were whose. She tried to shield, and to stifle them, but she was so tired, and Lucas was so elated, and frustrated, and … and …

'Harry,' Lucas said, stepping back and crossing his arms the way he always did when he was annoyed. 'Annie needs you.'

'What?' they both asked, confused.

'You're her boyfriend, aren't you?'

Annie froze, narrowing her eyes at Lucas. He looked right back at her, and his eyes dared her to refute it.

Harry lifted his chin. 'I … yeah, okay … so?'

'So, look at her. She's a mess. She's just done the most incredible thing, and all she can think about is how messy she is. Can't you see that? You're *supposed* to be able to see things like that.'

He sounded far more irritated than the situation seemed to warrant, which made Annie think that whatever the real problem was, it was something that had been bugging him for a while. Surely he couldn't actually be annoyed at Harry just because she was filthy? Harry looked at her, as if questioning what he should do. She gave him a little shrug. She had no idea what was going on.

'You're supposed to kiss her,' Lucas growled, backing away from them both. 'That *should* be obvious. It's what boyfriends do. With only the slightest excuse, you're supposed to want to … but you never do. *Never.*'

Harry spluttered, 'I … we … not in public—'

'You're not *in* public.'

'You *want* me to kiss her? Here? Right in front of you?'

Annie groaned and started to pack stuff away. She was way too tired for this. Lucas was being ridiculous, and Harry wasn't covering for them very well at all.

'Well, someone has to.'

A warm hand caught hers and pulled her around. Lucas was *right there*. His breath filled her face, cutting through her shield like an electric shock. His eyes searched hers, giving her every chance to pull away and yet somehow she found herself reaching for him instead. His kiss was honest, and fierce, defying any attempt she might make to steal his feelings away. As if she stood a chance of being able to do that. Not when her own emotions reflected his so completely. How can you absorb something you're reflecting? Everything in her ached for him, and she could do nothing to draw away her *own* feelings. No tricks she could use. His arms wrapped around her, pulling her even closer, and they both revelled in the burn of healing that flowed between them, washing away her tiredness and dull aches. There was only one lucid thought in her head: *I belong here.* It felt right, and good, and even the thought of Harry standing nearby couldn't trick her into believing otherwise. Lucas was for her, in every way, and all three of them knew it. That was the moment she realised that she was no longer afraid of losing her identity to the overwhelming power of the bond with her Guardian, because the bond was part of her. It didn't define her, any more than it defined who Lucas was. It felt like the bond had taught her a new language to speak, a language that only Lucas could understand, but they were still her words.

When Lucas finally pulled back she breathed out, and her lungs protested against breathing in again without him touching her.

'I knew it. I knew you wouldn't be able to steal from me if I kissed you.'

His voice was soft, throaty and beautiful, and it was so close that she almost snatched it straight from his lips, but she let him explain.

'I remembered from last time. On the beach. I remembered how it felt to feel you, without you playing any of your dirty tricks.'

She flinched. 'Dirty tricks? You said you didn't mind. You said it felt better when I took it away.'

'Better for whom? I've changed my mind, Annie. I'm tired of these games. No more lies, no more secrets, and no more stealing. I can't do it anymore.'

'But Harry—'

'I bet you a thousand dollars that Harry's smiling at us.' His eyes blazed with confidence.

Annie took an indignant breath. 'Harry doesn't smile much at anything these days.' She peered around his shoulder to check anyway. He was right, sort of. The look on Harry's face was not exactly happy, but he certainly looked relieved, and satisfied. What a crazy situation.

'Then let's not make things any more complicated for him than they need to be, Annie.'

How long had he known that she and Harry were pretending? Just how much did guys gossip with each other anyway? Somehow she couldn't quite picture them whispering juicy titbits to each other over tea and sandwiches, but they knew each other pretty well now. Maybe Harry wasn't to blame at all.

'No more lies or secrets?' she repeated.

'And no more stealing. I want to feel everything. Good and bad. Let me take responsibility for my own emotions.'

Sprawled on the damp grass, one of the lambs was feebly attempting to find its feet despite the unhelpful vigorous ministrations of its mother's tongue. Soon it would be up and walking, freshly bathed and flicking its tail around as it sought out nourishment. The other lamb just lay there passively, waiting its turn, hoping its mother hadn't abandoned it completely.

'I'm not a poddy,' she mumbled, watching the lamb just sit there as its brother was rolled over with a loving shove.

'What?'

'I'm not a poddy lamb. I have a mother. She hasn't abandoned me yet, and I won't let her. Sometimes secrets are necessary.'

'Wait, Annie, I don't understand. Where are you going?'

'To get my mother back. I'm sorry, Lucas, but I can't let her find out about you. I need you to leave. Please, just stay away from me!'

Annie's tears, as she ran, burned with shame and grief.

Crystal clean water washed away the remainder of the blood from her hair. Purity radiated from everything around her—the water, the air, the plants, and even the sounds that everything made. All fresh, and entirely refreshing. For a while Annie just floated, communing with the River, remembering what it felt like to be alive and not exhausted. And not lonely.

Her mum was not too far away. She could sense her presence, just as she knew her mother would be aware of her arrival. It was wrong of her to have ditched Harry so rudely, leaving him to try to coax the ewe into caring for both newborns. It would be unhelpful to get distracted for too long here, so rather than get caught up with the rest of her Eden family, Annie chose to wait for her mum to come and find her.

'When are you going to remember that creeping up on me can't work?' she called out a little while later, floating with her eyes shut past the riverbank where her mother hid among some giant leaves. A moment later, a flurry of blossoms rained down from above. The ambrosial richness of mixed fragrances made her take an automatic deep breath—sweet, luscious Eden. Annie sat up and opened her eyes just in time to see her mum dump a second basketful of flowers over her.

'I've missed you, Annie-blossom! I was hoping you'd come and play. Wait until I tell everyone you're here. There's a party tonight. You have excellent timing.' Her mum leapt into the water and peppered her with kisses as if she was a child again. How easy it would be to just stay and bask in her love. There was nothing to shield here, no emotions to guard or to squash. The residual grief that always hung like a mist around her mother when they were on the farm was so thin here. It was easy for Annie to ignore. Here, her grief was hazier, ephemeral and gentle. Here, it was a natural part of who she was, and was no longer her defining feature.

'I'm not staying,' Annie mumbled into her mother's shoulder as she hugged her back. 'I came to get you. I want you to come home now.'

'Home? You wanted me to come here. You said so. And I like it here.'

Silt tickled Annie's toes as she waded toward the riverbank, scooping up a giant yellow flower on the way from the collection twirling around them in the water. It smelled of lemon and jasmine and fairy floss. 'Mum, you've been here for a long time. I've missed you.' *Be gentle with her*, she reminded herself. *Don't stress her out.*

'Then stay! I'll make you a cake. I have a new recipe. It has nuts in it, and syrup that comes from that tree with the blue-ish bark. You'll love it, Annie.'

'I need to go home. There are lambs. No one is there to look after things. I want you to come back and help me because I'm tired. And I don't want to miss any more school. Please?'

Kiah Langley sprang up out of the water, shaking out her long hair. 'A lamb? Already? And it survived? I don't believe you. If you want me to come home, just say so. There's no need to make up stories.'

'I'm not. You know how quickly time passes here. Why would I need to make up stories?'

'The lambs won't start dropping until August. I'm distracted, but I'm not stupid.'

Annie backed up her next words with sign language, to prove she wasn't playing around. 'Today is August nineteenth.' She pointed to the nearest Tree, and its deep rust-coloured Living Fruit, to remind her of what August even was. Her mum blinked a few times, so Annie figured she may as well get it all out in one go.

'We have paddocks full of lambs and more to drop. The insurance is due, I've had to buy in extra hay, and the washing machine is making weird noises. I've arranged to take on some store lambs from a farm that just went bust, but I don't know how much I should pay for them. If I stall them any longer, I'll lose the deal. I haven't been to school for three weeks and Sarah and Dave have just announced that they're planning to move back to Melbourne for the birth of the twins. If Sarah doesn't start believing us soon, Harry's going to have to either come here or follow them to the city, and you know how he feels about coming here. I need you to come home, Mum. *Please.*' So much for being gentle.

Without warning, her mother grabbed her left hand in both of hers, gripping it firmly. Annie was so shocked that she cried out and wrenched herself away, backing up so fast that she almost slipped back into the water. To use any form of physical force in the Garden was unthinkable, and she was taken completely off-guard. Her mum had tried to read her. Why had she allowed her mum to see how stressed she was? And her concern wasn't unfounded. Just what had she seen?

'What are you hiding from me, Annie?' she asked, hurt by the rejection.

'Why do you want to read me? Don't you trust me?'

'Why won't you let me read you? Don't you trust *me*?' she retorted.

She really wasn't stupid. Annie tried to gather some semblance of logic she would believe. 'Of course I trust you! But you're not ready to see everything yet. You've forgotten how harsh things are at home. You need time to adjust before you accidentally view reruns of what I watched on TV last night. Have you forgotten?' Five deep breaths sounded loud in her ears before she saw her mother smile.

'Of course. You've been watching *Twin Peaks* again, haven't you? You're right. I don't want to see that.' Her laugh was soft and relaxed.

Annie's toes unclenched. No trace of distress marred her mum's emotions. At least, no more than usual. So she hadn't seen what was still foremost in Annie's memory. She hadn't seen his adorable smile and the joy in his blue, blue eyes.

In the end, Annie agreed to stay in the Garden for the party. It was a passing, a 'moving across' party, and they were very rare. Although everything in her screamed that she should take her mum away before it started, part of her needed to see it for herself. To see whether people would really let go of a friend so easily. A friend they had all known for time beyond measure.

The lady had been travelling for a long time. Annie had never even met her, which was a huge relief because her Eden family was precious to her, and she didn't know what would happen if she had to say goodbye to any of them. What if she cried in front of everyone? At least if it was someone she didn't know, she might have some hope of holding herself together.

By halfway through the night she realised that she needn't have worried. Aya's passing was joyous. Full of excitement and anticipation. Incredible music filled the air all afternoon, and everyone danced with her. Her son was there. Annie had known him all her life, and she had never seen him so happy. He wanted this for her, and kept hurrying things along, which felt completely whacko. If she hadn't known better she might have assumed that Aya was just on her way to Disneyland for a couple of weeks. As the sun set, hugging the valley with its golden farewell, Aya said her last goodbyes. She had chosen to fly—as apparently most people did—and at least twelve other people jumped with her from a giant tree that overhung the canyon at the far end of the valley, yodelling and laughing as they tumbled through the air together.

Everyone else waited at the bottom of the canyon with fresh pieces of Living Fruit for those who wanted to return to the party. Aya was the only one who didn't choose to taste its sweetness.

After that, they all gathered together around the cremation fire and told stories of things she had done over the years, people she'd known, adventures she'd lived.

'They remember everything,' her mum commented with a slow shake of her head. Someone had just told the story of how Aya had once dug a tunnel that ran from the top of the valley to the Canyon of the Silk Owls. 'I remember finding that tunnel when I was little,' her mum said. 'I was determined to follow it the whole way, only Geoff brought a search party in to find me after a day and a half. There were mushrooms and weird plants growing down there. That tunnel must have been around for a really long time even then.'

'Geoff? You mean Harry's dad? You never tell me stories about the two of you.'

That is true, Beltana signed as she walked over to them, which was when Annie realised she must have been speaking in sign as well as English.

You have more stories to share? Beltana asked. *Annie is right. You have not told us enough, Kiah. So much of your time is spent in your hidden place and you never share those stories with us. You'd better get on with it, or we'll have a very short party for you.*

Her mum didn't seem to know how to respond, so Annie covered for her. Anything to divert Beltana's curiosity about where they spent most of their time. *She will create many more stories here, Beltana. Perhaps my mother will collect so many memories for you to carry on your necklace that you'll need a couple of matching bracelets to help spread the weight.*

Perhaps, Beltana agreed, laughing. *That is for her to decide. Or perhaps she will have her party in another place, like Geoff did, and others will tell her stories.*

When neither of them could think of a response, Beltana walked away to talk to Aya's son, who was tossing fragrant branches of dried herbs onto the fire.

'The reason I don't talk about Geoff is because I miss him,' her mum said once Beltana was far enough away that they could speak in private. 'He never got to have a proper party like this one.'

She turned away, and for a moment Annie struggled to remember why she shouldn't just let her. It was clear that her mum didn't want to talk about it. Then when she remembered, Annie's want became the stronger one. And she wasn't above taking advantage of her mother's Eden-compliant frame of mind to finally get some answers.

'What really happened to him, Mum? I think I'm old enough to know.' She sat down on a log that had been carved to look like a giant tortoise, and nibbled on a piece of blue-bark-syrup cake while she waited for her mum to decide whether to answer. The cake really was very good. Sort of nutmeggy and lemony at the same time.

'He was wrongly accused of killing someone. It was Ruby who killed the man.'

Blue-bark-syrup cake sprayed out across the wooden tortoise as Annie forgot how to swallow properly. When she recovered enough breath to ask, she kept her voice low. 'What man?'

'A man named Paul Dashner. He broke into their house and tried to kidnap Harry.'

It was a good thing there was no more cake left in her mouth by then, because Annie sat with her mouth hanging open, unable to believe what she was hearing.

Her mother sighed and sat down on the tortoise's giant knee. 'I suppose it's important for you to know what can happen, but I don't think it's a good idea to tell Harry. Are you certain you're ready to hear all this?'

Although Annie wasn't certain at all, she nodded anyway.

When Annie caught up with him the next afternoon, Harry was riding his four-wheeler back from his top paddock with a lamb tucked under one arm. With his shirt partially unbuttoned and his chest coated in a sheen of sweat, she thought he looked ready for a Mills and Boon cover shoot, except for the fact that the lamb had left little poo pebbles in his lap.

As she slid down from Pepper's saddle, her words came out all in a rush. 'Mum thinks you shouldn't know, but I disagree. Lucas was right. Secrets and lies can be unhealthy. Especially this one, because you'll keep digging until you find out anyway, and that's not a good idea.'

Harry turned off the engine. 'You brought her back?'

She nodded. 'I made her tell me everything. Well, as much as I could, anyway. There are still a lot of holes in her story. Like why they would go to that much trouble for the sake of a ruby? They aren't worth risking lives for.'

'She told you about my parents?'

'Hard to keep secrets in Eden. Where's Lucas?'

'Helping Uncle with tagging. They'll be busy for a while. What did she tell you?'

She loosened Pepper's girth and ran up the stirrups so she could lead him without them bouncing around. 'It was all about the necklace. Not about the Carved Tree at all.' She started walking, but Harry didn't move. He was waiting for her to explain. Problem was, now that she came down to it, Annie wasn't sure how to tell him. How do you break the news to someone that their mother killed a man?

'Annie, please.'

Her hesitation was enough to allow Pepper to stop and lower his head to graze. 'It isn't a good story,' Annie said.

'I'm already well aware of that.'

She nodded, gathering her thoughts so she could explain clearly. 'The ruby was an heirloom that's been in your dad's family forever. He had it polished and made into a necklace as a wedding gift for your mum. She sold it when the farm got into financial trouble.'

He shifted the wriggling lamb to the other hip and waited for her to continue.

'Your dad wasn't nearly as mad at her as my mum was. Mum was petrified people would start asking questions about where it had come from. I mean, how would a farmer with an Indigenous background have a ruby as a family heirloom? She was right to worry. The buyer sent someone to find out more. They wanted to know if it had been mined locally. Of course, your dad struggled to give them a straight answer.'

'Because it came from Eden,' Harry said.

'Your dad wanted to buy it back from them but the money had already been used to pay down debt and he couldn't reverse that. So he had to get it back a different way.'

'He stole it?'

Annie fiddled with the rein buckle. 'Not exactly. Don't ask me how an Eden artefact came to be here in the first place. Maybe rubies weren't a big deal at the time. Just something pretty. I once brought home a tail feather from a blue glitter-sparrow that Ekala had stuck in my braid. It can happen.'

Harry shifted the lamb again.

'The gem came from Eden,' she continued. 'So no one was supposed to even see it. Not that they fully realised that until it was gone. Apparently Ruby felt hideously guilty selling it, only she assumed that was because she was selling her wedding gift. She must have been very strong-willed to push through the embargo like that.'

'If she did it to save the farm, I'm not surprised.'

'Yeah, well, your dad somehow sent it back to Eden. When I asked Mum how, she just said "It was needful, so he did it", and gave me that same smug look that Gran used to give us when she told those stories.'

'Right. The legends. I thought we decided they weren't true?'

Annie shrugged. 'Well, however he did it, the people who'd bought it weren't impressed. Perhaps they really did believe there was a ruby mine around here somewhere, because they sent someone to find out.'

'Sent someone?'

'I think, in TV terms, you would call him a thug.'

'I don't remember that.'

'That would be because you and I were whisked away to Eden by my mum. Listen, can we go back to the house? I really think the rest of this story should wait until you're sitting down.'

'I am sitting.'

'Until I'm sitting down, then. This isn't easy.'

'Get on with it, Annie.'

She squeezed her eyes shut. 'They had no luck getting information from your dad, or any evidence that he stole the gem back, so they sent someone to kidnap you. As leverage to get information, or to get the necklace back. Your mum didn't let that happen.'

The lamb escaped Harry's slack hold and tumbled onto the grass, skittering away to go and look for its mother.

'There was a fight, and your mum killed him. When your dad took the blame for that, your mum tried to tell the truth. No one believed her. She just didn't seem capable of it, I guess. And your dad already had a criminal record.'

'Because of the Carved Tree protest? Because he drove off in that bulldozer?'

'And because he supposedly decked the driver of the bulldozer when he stole it, although Mum says that was crap. Anyway, the hearing was totally unfair, but it's hard to argue when the defendant pleads guilty to manslaughter.'

'Didn't he know what would happen? It was a death sentence!'

Damp grass soaked Annie's jeans as her legs folded beneath her, nauseated by the mere thought of spending time in jail away from Nalong. Pepper sprinkled bits of grass down the back of her shirt in protest at having to eat with a bit in his mouth. 'I guess he trusted your mum to protect you more than he trusted himself.'

Harry stepped off the four-wheeler, paced around it running his hands through his hair, and then stopped and kicked the kajeebies out of one of the back tyres in a fit of aggression. Pepper snorted at him.

The rest didn't need to be spoken. Ruby had done a crap job of protecting him after his dad died. It was clear to Annie that Cherubim didn't survive well without their bonded partners. But that was the last thing Harry needed to hear.

Chapter 21

'You can't keep letting them into the house,' Annie complained to her mum as she shooed the lamb back out the front door. How times had changed. It used to be her mum telling Annie the same thing, except that she usually had to remove various items of clothing from the poor creatures at the same time. Lamb two had thrived under her mum's care over the past three weeks, as had the other two poddies from this year's crop, but the real benefit was in the way her mum had adjusted back to life on the farm. Having to care for the helpless babies had kept her mind on her tasks much better than Annie's constant nagging would have done. Still, she was grateful that lamb one had bonded to its mother successfully. They were busy enough.

'You're late for school. The bus is due any minute,' her mum called out from the kitchen. Thrilled that she had noticed, Annie ran back in to give her a quick peck on the cheek before grabbing her bag and bolting from the house. Brisk spring wind blew through the sugar gums along the driveway as she jogged down to the gate, trying to listen for the rumble of the bus. Luckily the poddy lambs had discovered a fresh patch of green grass under the old trampoline and didn't try to follow. Hopefully soon her mum would agree to put them in the small pen behind the shed where they belonged, or they would have no garden left.

Halfway down the driveway, she heard the sound she had been anticipating, and put on a burst of speed, her feet rolling a little on the gravel. The bus appeared from behind a row of trees at the bottom of the hill and slowed to a stop … and then pulled away again.

'What? No, wait!' Annie stumbled to a halt. *Seriously? Couldn't he see I was coming?* Normally Mr Elliot was happy to wait at least a couple of minutes for her, despite his fake grumbles about it. Was it because he knew she had her licence now? They still only had the one car between them to use. She couldn't just drive to school and leave her mum with no transport. Why didn't he wait?

The answer became apparent as soon as she saw the sickly orange Datsun parked behind a cape wattle, neatly hidden from the house. Lucas was leaning against the driver's door, drumming his fingers on the roof.

'Did you just tell the bus driver not to wait for me?' she spluttered, panting a bit. She glanced back toward the house as if she could actually see that far. Would her mum have noticed the bus leaving without her?

'Would I do that?'

'Of course.'

'Then yes, I told him I'd take you in today. But you're not going to school.'

'You'd let me skip school? I find that hard to believe.' Lucas had not exactly made a secret of the fact that he wanted her to finish Year 12. His disapproval was worse than her mother's, and he had repeatedly offered to help her catch up on all the study she'd missed. With exam time looming close enough to smell, she'd even taken him up on his offer a few times, meeting him at the library in town. He'd been professionally cold each time, keeping his distance as she'd asked, and in return, she had left his emotions alone, even though that made it very hard to concentrate. Not to mention that she'd been as jumpy as a kitten each time anyone she knew saw them together—which was often.

'Dave rang me this morning. It's started. Actually, it started during the night. We need to go.'

Even the kookaburras seemed to stop their cackling at his words. Time hung, waiting for her brain to catch up with his news. 'Sarah?' she asked.

He opened the passenger door. Tucked into the back seat, Harry was busy shredding a newspaper into tiny shapes. Miniscule paper animals littered the floor and the seat next to him.

'Harry? What are you doing?'

His warm brown eyes flicked up at her, and he opened his mouth to speak, and then closed it again and kept on ripping. A tiny flower flicked from his fingers and floated down, finished, and then ignored.

'I think he's nesting,' Lucas suggested. 'It's a long drive to Horsham. I should have given him a bigger newspaper. Maybe *The Age*.'

Not long after Annie's mum had returned from Eden, Sarah and Dave had spent almost four days in Melbourne, first at Sarah's dad's house, followed by three and a half days in hospital when her nausea just wouldn't let up. Harry had been frantic, and yet Lucas had been adamant that he should stay put. Sarah had been clearly and repeatedly warned about what would happen, but she'd told Lucas that she didn't believe a word of it, and she went to Melbourne just to prove it. In the end she had rung Annie, in tears, begging her to send Harry down because the hospital wouldn't let her out while she was so unwell. A couple of hours later Harry had crossed Next Door, temporarily breaking their link, and she had called back to thank them and apologise. They had all returned home the following day but her doctor was concerned enough to book her in to the larger hospital in Horsham rather than let her have the babies in Nalong's tiny facility.

'Harry, you could just go—'

'No!' he barked, tearing the page he was holding right down the middle. 'I need to know she's okay. I won't run away.'

Annie winced. He had never put it quite so bluntly before. She knew how he felt about going to Eden. He had always avoided it, because it left Uncle Willie on his own, and it was way too easy to lose track of time there … and priorities. Since her mother had started escaping there and leaving Annie alone, his opinion had become even more obvious, and yet he had never before hinted that he thought it was a weak way out.

Lucas started the engine. Luckily the old dear was on her best behaviour, or Harry might just have turned the Datsun into another pile of confetti.

⌒

They waited very impatiently in a café not far from the hospital, and called through to the ward from a payphone down the street to see if there was any news. The nurse at the desk wasn't particularly forthcoming, so Harry talked her into finding Kelly, who gave them every horrible detail of Sarah's marathon of pain. If Kelly thought it strange that they had all dropped what they were meant to be doing for the day, she didn't mention it.

The tiny café was stifling after the first hour, not because it was hot, but because they kept getting annoyed frowns from the waitress every time Harry rained another confetti creature onto her clean lino floor, so eventually they just picked up a couple of copies of the local paper for him and headed out down the street.

The fragrance of freshly cut grass greeted them as they made their way to the old seating stand at the local footy oval. Aluminium mesh benches weren't the most comfortable things to lie on, but at least they didn't frown, and it was kind of fun watching Lucas doing backflips off them. He'd ditched his shoes, as usual, and after a few minutes of flipping himself over, he decided to take off his shirt so he wouldn't have to turn up to the hospital ward in stinky clothes. Or so he said. Annie wasn't stupid. He was showing off for her. What *was* stupid was the way she was allowing herself to indulge in it. He looked really fit. Full of energy and life and fun and all the things she usually only found on the far side of a secret cave. How easy it would be to get up and show him how it was done. She'd learnt more than a few fun tricks from her friends in Eden, and it was *very* tempting to flirt back. His technique wasn't quite right. He really shouldn't throw his head back like that.

He caught her watching, so she looked away and started rummaging through her bag for her school diary to try to work out if she was missing out on anything vitally important. It turned out she was, and she became so absorbed with trying to figure out when she could re-sit her chemistry test that she somehow missed the fact that Lucas had snuck a hand into her bag and had started flipping through her maths folder, until he gave a funny little grunt.

'What? What are you doing?' she asked him.

'You got an A on this.'

Annie lunged to try to snatch her test paper from his hands, only his reflexes were much better than hers. 'Give it back! Who gave you permission to nose through my stuff?'

He kept reading the teacher's comments as he pointed to the sky.

'Oh, come on, that was never part of the deal. Give me my test back.'

Harry glanced up from his craft project, but didn't come to her aid, so Annie lunged again for the paper. Lucas smiled and flicked it neatly out of her reach, spinning his legs around and somehow ducking behind her all in one graceful move. Then he held up another paper he'd somehow managed to pilfer from her open bag in the process.

'An A-plus on this one … biology? I thought you said you were still way behind on that?'

'I paid attention in class and caught up,' she growled. 'What did you spend *your* time learning at school, pickpocketing?'

He grinned. 'I'm naturally stealthy. It makes me good at everything, remember?'

'Give me my stuff back,' she demanded, wondering if he realised just how much his arrogance bugged her. It was the one character flaw in people that she had little patience for, because it was usually used to disguise low self-esteem, and she could always see right through it. It was a dishonest emotion, and those were rare—and even more twisted when it was all play, designed specifically to push her buttons.

'Make me,' he challenged, flicking his fringe out of his face.

'Fine.' She stood up, crossed her arms over her chest and took a sharp shallow breath in … and didn't let it out. Lucas didn't move. After a few moments, he narrowed his eyes. After about thirty seconds of her holding her breath, he started to look annoyed.

'Seriously?' he asked. 'Are you a toddler? Lily used to do this when she was three. It always freaked Mum out, but it never fooled me.'

Annie let her lungs complain to her, relishing the tight feeling, because it matched the tightness developing around her Guardian's eyes.

'I'm not giving in to petty threats, Annie. Turn blue if you must.'

Her vision got a bit speckly. It was rather pretty.

'Childish!'

Getting bored, she tried to run down all the things her human body was doing to try to override her disobedient brain. A bit more biology study to fill in the time.

'Harry, tell her how stupid she's being.'

Harry didn't even look up. He'd used the same trick himself once or twice, to get out of class. In fact, Annie remembered dizzily, he was the one who'd taught it to her.

Lucas swallowed hard, and she noticed that his own breathing was getting a bit erratic, as he felt exactly what her body was going through, but also had to deal with his own body's conflicting instructions.

The footy goal posts began to sway in the non-existent breeze. Four little sticks, like decapitated Chupa Chups.

Annie woke to the sight of Lucas's blazing blue eyes close to hers, slightly unfocused, and felt his hands cupping her cheeks with all the gentleness of branding irons. Her reflexive reaction was to gasp and reach her mouth toward his, but luckily he didn't notice because at that very moment, his brain apparently decided that it had had enough of all the incompatible signals and healing, and shut itself down for a few seconds.

Just as well Harry was ready for it, and caught him before he tumbled head-first down the steps. He sat Lucas down with his hands on his shoulders to steady him, and threw Annie a look of disapproval.

Sitting up brightly, she picked her papers up off the bench, straightened out the pages that her Guardian had crushed in his fist, and placed them neatly back into her bag, zipping it closed and sitting on it.

'You are completely mental,' Lucas mumbled.

'Only when people mess with my stuff.'

'I didn't think it was actually possible to make yourself pass out,' he said, blinking away his grogginess. 'When Lily used to do it, the doctor told Mum it was involuntary, and something that kids grew out of by the age of about six. I *knew* he was wrong.'

Annie glanced at Harry, but he'd gone back to fretting with the help of the newspaper, no longer interested in their squabble.

'We aren't tied as tightly to our survival instincts as everyone else,' she explained. 'Or so the theory goes. Harry's mum once told him that it was the reason we need Guardians. Or maybe she just said that to soothe his male ego. Either way, we tend to be very good at overriding our reflexes if we choose to.'

Lucas glowered.

'Cherubim also aren't very ticklish,' she added for good measure. It didn't help. He still looked furious. When she got up to make yet another call to Kelly for an update, he didn't follow.

❦

It was almost three in the afternoon when Kelly finally answered the phone with a delighted squeal.

'I'm an aunty!' she cried, her enthusiasm crackling down the phone line. 'Both boys! Liam and Caleb. Sarah wanted at least one Irish name, because her dad's family are from there, and Dave just wanted one start-ing with L and one with a C, after his two best friends. I think it's the first thing they've agreed on in weeks.' As always, her excitement level was directly proportional to the speed at which she spoke.

'Sarah's okay?' Annie asked, grinning at the expression on Lucas's face as he realised that Liam was named in his honour.

'She's fine, just really tired. Everything went really smoothly. Vicky said the doctor spent more time reassuring Dave than he did checking out the babies.'

Harry leant in even closer to hear what she was saying. It was very crowded in the phone booth. 'When do you think we can come in?' he called out over Annie's shoulder.

'Whenever you like. Sarah's asleep, but Dave's buzzing. He could probably use Lucas's company. You're all still in Horsham, right?'

'No way could we leave until we heard something,' Annie said.

'Then you'd better come on up here before Dave starts hugging all the nurses again.'

The babies were adorable. Somehow, even their slightly squashed faces didn't sully their perfection. Liam had a fine fuzz of blond hair already, like both his parents, and Caleb somehow looked full of energy, even fast asleep. Dave was ridiculous in his excitement, bouncing around the ward like a stick insect with ants in its pants while still trying to stay quiet so as not to wake Sarah. He hugged Annie so often that Lucas frowned. He frowned even more when he got hugged for the third time himself. Even Harry earned himself a manly pat on the back.

'Dave, mate, how about we go for a walk?' Lucas whispered. 'Let Sarah sleep in peace for a while. I think the nurses would like us to take the boys back to the nursery, too. They've had a big day. Your parents are still at least an hour away, so now would be a good time to get you something to eat. How about we find a phone and call Cam? You can tell him how you picked Caleb's name.'

The new father looked like he was about to protest, but Kelly hit him with her dazzling smile and started wheeling one of the cribs out. 'You'll have the rest of your life to play with them, Dave. Let the nurses take them for a while. Are you coming with us, Harry?' she asked. 'I'll shout you a Chiko roll.'

'No, thanks. Not hungry.'

An awkward moment passed while everyone waited for Harry to come up with a better reason for wanting to sit in the hospital ward with Sarah while she slept. He didn't give one, so Lucas took hold of the crib containing 'lamb number two' and herded everyone from the room with it. Annie moved as if to follow, and then hung back when they got distracted by Lucas singing the babies a lullaby version of the Hawthorn theme song.

As soon as they were gone, Harry sat down in the chair next to Sarah's bed. Annie drew the curtain shut around them and watched as he pulled a small gift box from his pocket and laid it on the bedside table. She knew he'd been waiting for months for an excuse to give Sarah the talisman. Even though the card said that it was from Annie as well, Harry had been the one to design the silver bangle with its clever latch and hollow interior. He'd been the one who'd pestered Mr Durante into making it, and he'd been the one to pay for it, with cash, tears and even blood.

With a hidden stab of grief, Annie watched as his face softened, again drinking in Sarah's tired features as if he thought he might never see her again. The new mother stirred. Without opening her eyes, Sarah's hand slid out from under the blanket, reaching toward Harry. He gripped it in both of his and she sighed deeply, finally able to fully relax. Annie doubted that she was even aware of what she was doing.

Chapter 22

No one could believe how quickly Sarah recovered from the birth of the twins. Well, almost no one. Whether she admitted it or not, Sarah must have realised that her Guardian healing abilities were helping her out. She even managed not to look tired. In fact, she seemed to attack motherhood with ferocious commitment, as if all her previous lack of direction—that should have been rectified by guarding Harry—was instead being compensated for by trying to win the Mother of the Year award. Visitors had to practically bathe themselves in straight Domestos before they were allowed within cooee of her precious darlings. Germy farmers were clearly the least welcome, because Annie only got to visit a couple of times in the first two months, and only because Kelly insisted she be allowed to come over to study. Lucas bragged that he saw more of the twins; he said it was because Dave needed a friend, and seemed to find every excuse under the sun to invite him around. Dave was definitely looking the worse for wear whenever Annie saw him at the shops, usually with his lanky arms loaded with nappies and various cleaning chemicals.

Harry kept his distance from them on reluctant advice from Lucas. Apparently Sarah cut him off rudely every time Lucas tried to talk to her about her role. As far as she was concerned, being a mother was enough of a duty to cope with, and no one disagreed. Still, a passing acknowledgment of some sort from her would have put Annie's mind at ease.

At least she was wearing the bracelet.

It was the first thing Annie noticed when she stopped by to pick up Kelly on the way to the cinema one Friday night. It was December, and school was finally over. Exams were over, Muck Up Day was officially cancelled but celebrated regardless, and the graduation dance had been survived without her mum catching so much as a glimpse of her Guardian-stalker who had loitered outside the venue to spy on anyone she danced with. Now that they were finally free, Kelly insisted it was time Annie remembered that there was more to life than study and feeding chickens, and declared that they deserved a night with Tom Cruise.

The second thing Annie noticed, as she was handed a whiney infant, was the hostility that radiated from Sarah the moment Kelly said where they were going.

'Did you want to come with us?' Annie asked her, wondering how long it had been since she'd last left the house. 'Could Dave mind the boys for one evening?'

'He could, only I don't want to go because Dave already took me to see it. It's a good movie. You'll like it.' She sounded much more relaxed than her emotions felt.

Annie draped Caleb over her shoulder and jiggled him. He smelled wonderful. Like milk and cuddles. So if Sarah wasn't envious of them going out, what was the problem?

'Are you meeting anyone there?' Sarah asked a little too casually, gathering up a couple of cotton cloths, a fluffy penguin and a tiny cardigan from behind the couch. There was a stuffed rabbit on the floor too, which Sarah kicked under the couch. What did she have against rabbits?

'No. It's just us tonight,' Kelly said with a twist to her lips. 'I tried to convince Miss I'm-going-to-die-a-lonely-old-spinster here to invite Lucas and Harry, but she refused to get the hint.'

Hint? What hint? Kelly had asked, she'd said no.

'Well, maybe it's time you gave up relying on Annie to set you up with Harry. Clearly she's incapable of sorting her own feelings out, so how do you expect her to notice yours? If you want my advice, you should look elsewhere, Kel. Harry would have let you know by now if he was interested. Maybe try to find someone who can see past his own neighbour for someone to spend New Year's with.'

Utterly speechless, Annie watched as Sarah escaped down the hallway and into her bedroom. Grief and frustration echoed back. It was unlikely that Kelly had time to notice Sarah's tears, but she certainly noticed Annie's, because they kept reappearing throughout the evening.

Annie kept well away from Sarah after that. In fact, she kept away from everyone. It was hard to believe that a whole year had passed since Lucas had arrived in town, and her mum still hadn't met him. There was no way her luck could last for much longer. On the odd occasion that her mum had needed to visit the Doolans' farm, Harry had always felt her approaching and found an excuse to keep Lucas away, but she wasn't stupid, and she was no longer so disconnected from what was going on around her. And Annie had run out of ideas. She did have a reprieve over Christmas and New Year, when Lucas went home to visit his family and she had her longed-for annual break Next Door. And given that school was finished forever, nearly everyone she knew was having an extended holiday out of town so she could take her time. It was nice not to have to worry that her mum might bump into him at the feed store while she wasn't around to keep an eye on them both. For just a little while, Annie could pretend that everything was just fine.

Chapter 23

A lone kookaburra cackled at Harry's ute as he turned into his driveway, as if it was scolding him for returning from town with so little. He wove between potholes, trying not to think about the three meagre bags of groceries he'd brought home. The sales assistant had sounded heart-broken when she'd told him that the supermarket no longer accepted personal cheques. It was a good thing Lucas had taken such good care of his hens so at least there were plenty of eggs for them to eat. Maybe he should dig out a recipe book and try to find a new way to cook them. He and Uncle Willie were both getting a bit tired of omelettes. Not that Uncle would complain, so long as they could still afford to buy tea.

When he crested the small hill near the house, he noticed two things. Firstly, someone had left a big box of veggies on their front door step, and secondly, the Langley's Holden Jackaroo was parked on the far side of the machinery shed. He knew Annie was still in Eden for her well-earned holiday, and it was Annie's mum he could sense nearby. It took a moment for him to remember to relax his shoulders. Lucas was still in Melbourne. For once, there was no need for Harry to whisk him out of sight. Still, what if Uncle Willie said the wrong thing? What would she piece together?

Harry parked the car and rushed into the house to put the food away. The phone rang, but he ignored it and headed back out, making a beeline for the shed. He wanted to know why Kiah Langley was here. Not that it should matter to him. It was Annie's ridiculous idea to keep Lucas a secret. He'd understood her reasons at first, but it had been over a year now. How long could this go on? All he knew was that when Kiah finally found out, he wanted to make damn certain that Annie was around. No way was he going to face that scene on his own.

Bo came trotting toward him as he approached the open side of shed. He could hear Kiah speaking to Uncle Willie, so he slowed to listen, figuring it would be better to know what he was about to walk in on.

'I promised you I wouldn't go searching again, and I haven't,' Uncle said, sounding a bit defensive. 'It was only ever a slim hope to begin with, although I'm convinced that gem must have originally come from somewhere nearby. It's not like I'm a greedy bugger. I only wanted to find one or two small pretty things so I could get our overdraft down a bit. Not enough to draw any attention. And I promised Ruby I'd keep Harry well away from all that crap. I haven't told him anything. Have you?'

'I let some things slip to Annie a while ago,' Kiah replied with a deep sigh. 'I expect she told him, even though I asked her not to.' She raised her voice a bit. 'Isn't that right, Harry?'

'Harry's back?' Uncle asked.

'You didn't hear his car pull up? Bo didn't bark at it, so I'm assuming that's who it is.'

Bo leant up against Harry's legs, unapologetic. Perhaps he knew he was only being used as a cover for Kiah's Cherub-senses. Harry scratched behind the dog's ear and then entered the dubious shade of the steel shed. It was out of the sun, but the air was hot and still, and petrol-laden. He saw Kiah kicking at a wheel brace, trying to loosen the lug nuts of the front tractor tyre. When he'd helped his uncle to change the one on the opposite side earlier in the year, it had been a bugger of a job. Kiah had sweat dripping down the side of her face. Uncle Willie did too. He looked exhausted and they hadn't even removed the old wheel yet.

'Hi, Uncle. I thought I told you to wait for me to get back to change it over. I know it's a front tyre, but I still think we should keep it on the tractor and pry the bead over the rim.'

'You always think you know best. And I did wait, until Kiah offered to give me a hand. You were gone for ages,' Uncle Willie said, dousing the rusted nuts with WD40 lubricant. 'Did you remember to buy tea?'

'No, they were out.'

Uncle Willie paused and looked up at him, brown eyes wide.

'I'm kidding, Uncle. Of course I bought tea. Hi, Mrs Langley. Thanks for the veggies.'

'No problem,' she said in a light voice that contradicted her frown. 'Annie's not due back until next week, and I can only eat so much. The tomatoes are going crazy this year.'

'I like tomato in my omelettes,' Uncle said.

Harry smiled. 'I like them with a nice porterhouse steak, too. I bumped into Anna McKenzie at the shops. They had a vealer break a leg last week. She offered to bring some meat around for us.'

Uncle beamed at the good news, but Kiah looked agitated and kept glancing at the door.

'I can finish this if you want to get going,' Harry said to her. 'Uncle, where's the new tyre? Still in the ute?'

'Yeah. I'll get it,' Uncle offered.

Harry took a step back toward the door.

'I said, I'll get it,' Uncle Willie repeated. 'These new meds make me a bit shaky, but I'm not so bad I can't roll a tyre a few metres. Stop babying me.' He stomped out before Harry could even apologise.

As soon as he was out of earshot, Kiah dropped the wheel brace and turned to him. 'Sarah's been trying to call you. Many times.'

'Why?'

Kiah just looked at him and waited.

'I'm about to get hurt?'

'When she couldn't reach you, she tried to call Annie. She sounded pretty frantic so I promised her I'd come by and stop you from doing whatever risky thing you were planning to do.'

Harry grunted. 'Changing a tyre is hardly the most dangerous thing I've done all day. She can't keep calling here every time I'm about to stub my toe.'

For a second, Kiah closed her eyes, like she was remembering something. When she opened them again, a single tear escaped, which she didn't even bother to wipe away. Annie was right to be worried about her if even the most passing reference to her lost Guardian evoked such a response.

'She sounded pretty hysterical, Harry, and we both know she'd try to ignore it if she could.' She wiped her hands on a dirty rag. 'Uncle told me about the calls you've been making. I thought I told you to leave it alone.'

'You think I might be in some sort of danger because I've been trying to find out who bought Mum's ruby necklace?'

Kiah's eyes widened, and she didn't answer.

'Here's an idea,' Harry continued, looking her in the eye. 'How about if you tell me the whole truth, I'll stop trying to tempt Mr Durante with the possibility I might have more gems to sell. He almost let something slip the other day. Something about my mum insisting the ruby had come from overseas. He used that word, "insisted". I know the ruby came from Eden. That's why they couldn't tell the police everything when Dad was arrested, right? Sounds to me like someone was digging for information about where the ruby really came from. Even Uncle Willie believes there could be more gems to find around here.'

Bo jumped to his feet, ears pricked, and trotted out of the shed.

'Harry, no. Tell me you didn't. Your mum gave up everything to make certain they had no reason to come back to Nalong. She did it to keep you safe, and now you just—'

Her words were cut off by five sharp barks from Bo. Someone was coming up the driveway. Bo could always tell, even when visitors were still on the far side of the hill, out of sight from the house.

'We need to go.' Kiah grabbed his elbow and pulled him toward the door.

He followed her out to see who was coming, just as Uncle Willie came back with the new tyre.

'Willie, you need to tell these people Harry isn't here,' Kiah said as they brushed past him. There was a deep timbre to the way she said it. An authority far less gentle than the tone Harry used when he wanted people to trust him.

'Righto,' Uncle replied. 'You know who they are?'

'You promised Ruby you'd keep Harry out of it. I think now's the time to fulfil that promise. Say whatever you need to, just keep them away from Harry and I'll sort out the rest later.'

Uncle nodded and set his jaw. He let the tyre fall and opened the passenger door of the Jackaroo. 'I'll come find you once I've sent them packing.'

'Wait,' Harry said as Uncle nudged him to get into the car. Bo barked again, hackles raised, even though the approaching car was still out of sight. 'Wait. If I've done something to put myself in danger, then I'm not leaving Uncle here to face the consequences.'

A slap to his cheek made his eyes water. The shock of it was far worse than the pain. Uncle had *hit* him? Impossible.

'You'll do as you're told this time, Pup, or I'll smack you into next week. Get in the car.'

Before Harry had a chance to even think, he was shoved into the passenger seat. The door slammed shut and then they were moving. He whacked his head against the side window as Kiah drove straight off the edge of the gravel and bumped them across the paddock toward the trees.

'We don't even know who it is yet,' Harry argued. 'Could be the McKenzies, dropping off the meat.'

'Sarah was crying, Harry.'

When they reached the line of stringybarks, Kiah kept driving, heading for the overgrown track that ran along the river. Somehow Harry knew she wouldn't agree to stop until they were far enough upstream for the sound of the water to mask the sound of the engine.

Almost an hour passed, during which time Kiah kept her car keys stuffed down her bra. Apparently she was well aware that Harry wasn't above trying to nick them and drive back to the house.

At first, they sat by the river and argued, until Kiah told him very bluntly that he already knew as much as she did about his dad's arrest. Then Harry insisted that no one would send a thug to kidnap a child for the sake of a small ruby, and they argued some more.

'If there's a chance these people suspect anything supernatural going on around here, then I need to know!' Harry had never come close to shouting at her before. She'd helped to raise him. It felt weird.

'So far they know nothing, and we won't have any problem keeping it that way if you just stay out of it.'

'Who are *they*, anyway?'

'No idea. Don't you think the police would have told us if they'd found out who sent that guy to kidnap you?'

'Couldn't they track down who Mr Durante sold the necklace to?'

'Of course. Celarsi Holdings, but then where did it go? It was never that simple. Someone was covering their tracks, someone with influence. Seriously, Harry, don't you think we've been through all this already? You need to let this go before someone else gets hurt.'

As one, they looked up the hill at the house in the distance. From where they were, they could barely make out the machinery shed. No way of telling if the visitors were still there. It had been too long. Uncle should have driven down to give them the all-clear by now.

'Time's up, Kiah. Either give me the keys, or I'm walking back.'

She nodded, fished around in her bra, and then headed to where she'd parked the Jackaroo among the ti-tree. She drove them back along the track much more carefully than before, while Harry tried to keep his ankles from bouncing. He felt like his legs were ready to get out and run without him if she didn't move any faster. Kiah paused at the tree line, scanning the area. No sign of anyone. Not even Bo.

When she finally pulled up to the side of the shed, Harry was already halfway out of the car. 'Uncle?'

Bo barked once, from inside.

'Uncle, is everything—'

Everything was not all right. Uncle was crumpled in a heap on the concrete floor, his curly black and silver hair covering his face, and limbs skewed. The wheel brace was lying next to him. Harry tried to call out to Kiah, but no sound emerged. His knees hit the floor hard, the pain of it welcome. Why had he allowed them to send him away? He brushed the hair from his great-uncle's face and his hand came away sticky with crimson mess. Uncle Willie's skin was pale, but not blue.

'Uncle? Can you hear me?' He felt his neck for a pulse. It was there. Gloriously beating.

'Is he breathing?' Kiah asked from behind him. Harry could just see her hand from the corner of his eye. It was trembling.

'Yes, but it's shallow,' he replied.

She left without another word, running for the house.

Harry rolled his uncle onto his side, arranging his limbs so he looked more comfortable, and then looked at the tangle of hair on the back of his head. With gentle fingers, he probed at the wound, uncertain if he was doing the right thing. What if his skull was so damaged he made things worse? There was a lump forming, and it felt firm, and wasn't bleeding too badly. A quick scan under his sweaty shirt revealed red welts across the back of his shoulders, and there were bruises forming above his left ear.

'Uncle, please wake up,' Harry said in a voice that sounded like he was a nine-year-old boy again. 'Don't leave me. Not you too. Please.'

He took his great-uncle's hand, and didn't let it go until the paramedics made him.

Chapter 24

It was hard for Annie to think through all the possible scenarios while she was running through the bush in the dry heat, trying to transition from Eden. Everything here was so scratchy and sweaty and jangly. 'I'm sorry, Harry. You'll need to explain it again. How did Uncle hurt himself?'

Harry tugged her along. 'He didn't. He has bruises on the back of his shoulders. Someone's clobbered him, Annie.'

A thick clump of bracken tripped her, and she only managed to stay on her feet and keep moving because Harry gripped her wrist to steady her. 'Why? Who would hurt Uncle?'

'I already told you. Pay attention. I stuffed up, okay? I should never have called Celarsi Holdings. Although it didn't get me anywhere at the time, obviously someone noticed. Probably because I told Mr Durante there were more gems.'

This time she did stumble to a stop, partly because her hair, soaked from the hurried river crossing, caught itself in a wattle branch and yanked her backward. Normally she was much more agile than this, but the terrain was so different to what she had been bouncing through just half an hour earlier. She struggled to unhook her hair and piece together what had happened at the same time. 'Why would you do that?'

'Because I wanted to know more, and he wasn't talking.'

'And Durante believed you?'

'He trusts me.'

'Damn, Harry. You can't do that to people.'

'It isn't something I can control, and don't you *dare* accuse me of exploiting my gift after everything you've done with yours.'

His backlash of anger slapped her already reeling senses, and she burst into tears. 'I'm sorry. I know. I ...'

Harry walked back to her and sighed. 'Annie, I understand this is a hard transition for you. You can still go back. In fact, I probably shouldn't have come to get you, but I needed to talk to someone, and Lucas is still in Melbourne.'

'What? He's going to *kill* me.'

'No, he isn't, because I already called him to explain. He's on his way.'

'He can't drive if he's sick.'

'Do you want to go back?'

'Of course not. You can't just rock up in the Garden to tell me that Uncle Willie's in hospital and not expect me to come home.'

'Then Lucas will just have to manage,' he said, holding the branch aside so she could escape from it.

'So what did the police say?'

Harry looked belligerent, and didn't reply.

'Look, I know you don't trust them after what happened to your dad, but you can't afford to be afraid of them. It wasn't their fault. Please tell me you called them.'

'Afraid?' He looked like he wanted to argue, and then thought better of it. 'I guess I am, a bit. But yes, we called them. They asked me a lot of questions that I couldn't answer, as well as some stupid ones, like if Uncle had been drinking.'

'Did you tell them about Mr Durante? And the necklace?'

'No.' He turned and started pushing through the next patch of ti-tree.

'Harry ...'

She hurried after him as best she could, but she couldn't convince him to talk about it any further.

The sun seemed to react to the increased tension as they rushed back downstream, and by the time they reached Annie's farm she could feel the backs of her shoulders burning. Her mum was waiting for them on the porch.

'You should have stayed Next Door, like I told you. Why did you bring her back? Get inside, both of you.'

Even though her mum's anger was directed at Harry, Annie still felt it like a jolt of electricity. She really needed to transition faster if she was going to cope.

Harry lifted his chin. 'You can't just lock us away, Kiah. You already know that.'

Kiah? She'd never heard Harry called her mum by her first name before. And his defiance seemed to shut her mother down. Annie tried to feel for a reaction from her, but there was nothing. Just … nothing. Like she'd passed out and was still somehow standing up.

'Mum?' Annie climbed the steps up to her and stared into her blank face. Her mother blinked. 'Mum, what can I do to help?'

'Nothing,' she said in an echo of her normal voice. 'Go and get dressed. Uncle Willie's awake, but sedated. I'm going to see what I can find out from him. Harry's going to stay here with you until I get back.'

Harry gripped the porch railing. 'I won't just—'

'You will! This time you'll do as you're bloody told and let me do my job. Whoever hurt Uncle is still out there somewhere and so I need to find out as much as I can about what happened. While I'm gone you'll lock the doors and not leave the house for any reason, understand?' As she spoke, her voice changed, becoming stronger and more determined. Her words had a depth to them, a deep authority that Annie could feel in the soles of her feet, as if the ground itself was backing her up. Harry took a small step back and swallowed. Her mum didn't let up. 'Now *get inside.*'

Annie fled, while Harry stood on the porch with his arms crossed and his boots planted just far enough apart to suggest that he was ready to stand in the way of a bulldozer. 'You have no authority over me, Kiah. I made this mess, and I'm going to fix it. And if we have to ask Uncle to talk about what happened then I want Annie to be there. I won't risk upsetting him.'

'I wasn't planning on *asking* him anything. I don't need to.'

'Can you guarantee that you won't stress him out? Because the doctor said—'

At the end of the hallway Annie squeezed her hands over her ears to try to block out the sound of them arguing. It was too much. She wished she could take it all away. All the anger, and the fear, only she had nowhere to put it because her heart was still too full of shiny memories. Like how she'd mastered her first luge run down Glass Canyon that morning and then taught Ekala how to say the poem that got you a free Big Mac.

'Please stop,' she whispered. They didn't hear her. Noise, noise, so much angry noise, and the ringing wouldn't stop. She stumbled into the kitchen just as her mum yelled at Harry to be quiet because she thought she heard the phone ringing.

'Yes, he's here, only he's busy yelling,' Annie told the woman on the other end of the line. 'I've tried to get him to stop, but he can't hear me. Are you from the hospital? Can I talk to Uncle Willie? … Oh. That isn't good.' She flinched when the receiver was snatched from her grip.

'Hello?' Harry said. 'Yes, it's me.'

His face drained of colour and Annie tried every trick she knew to block out what he was feeling. It didn't really work.

'I'm on my way,' he told the woman, and hung up. When he turned to face her, he had tears in his eyes. 'Your mum was right. I should have left you Next Door. This is too hard a transition.'

'I'll manage. You need me here,' she said, heading to her bedroom for some clothes, but her mum wouldn't move out of her way.

'Annie, you aren't leaving this house. I *want* you to stay here.'

She could feel her mother's petition like a soft nudge, easing her own desires into alignment with it. She could also feel Harry's need: his grief and anxiety. This wasn't Eden. She had to choose.

'Uncle Willie's just had a heart attack,' Annie explained. 'Harry is my partner Cherub, and my place is by his side.'

It had been a really long night. Time seemed to drag on at the best of times on this side of the Skin of the World, and this was anything but the best of times. Annie felt a very long way from Eden. Worlds away. In a building with a purpose that her Eden family would find utterly incomprehensible.

The medical staff had managed to stabilise Uncle Willie's heart pretty swiftly, and his prognosis was good enough that they had moved him from ICU to a quieter, private room with pink and grey floral curtains. He was still hooked up to a lot of machines. It was almost dawn and they were all exhausted, but out of the four of them in the room, Uncle Willie's exhaustion went way beyond needing a good night's sleep. As the electronic beeping sped up, Annie peeked out the door. The nurse wasn't at her desk. There was a drip alarm going off down the hall some-where, so she was probably attending to that, which was good because if she heard them talking again, Harry may not have been able to talk her into letting them stay. Only the fact that Uncle Willie's heart rate sky-rocketed every time Harry left his side had so far convinced the hospital staff to let them hang around. That, and the way Harry had unleashed his talent on them. He had explained in a gentle voice that Uncle needed all three of them to remain, and they had trusted him. That simple.

'Harry has to back off?' Annie asked as she closed the door again. 'Is that what Uncle's trying to tell us?'

'Exactly,' her mum whispered, and a moment later they all breathed a sigh of relief when the heart rate monitor began to ease up again. The bulky machine was clearly the focus of everyone's attention, but they were all trying hard to pretend it wasn't. Annie's mum glanced at her one last time, in case she'd changed her mind.

'I'll be fine, Mum. This is important.'

'I'm going to speak it out the way I see it, honey, as if it's happening to me. I can't concentrate on two places at once, so I might not be able to soften the descriptions.'

'I understand.'

With a nod to Harry, her mum took Uncle Willie's hand in both of hers and closed her eyes.

'Uncle,' Harry said softly, placing a hand on his shoulder. 'Uncle, you stubborn old ram. You won't sleep properly until you've told me what happened, will you? So if you have something you want to tell me, I'm listening.'

The injured man's eyes opened in defiance of the painkillers he'd been given.

'Pup? I kept my promise.' His words were slurred, dissolving into mumbles.

'Uncle.' Harry paused, as if gathering his courage, or conviction. 'Uncle, do you remember what happened? Who were they?'

On Annie's side of the bed, the heart monitor picked up pace, until Annie took Uncle's other hand in hers. Harry acknowledged her gift with a grateful half-smile.

Uncle mumbled a few more words. Incomprehensible. After a few moments, he stopped with a frustrated sigh.

'It's okay, Uncle. I can hear you just fine. Keep going. Tell me whatever you want me to know. Try to remember as many details as you can.' Harry's eyes locked onto Uncle Willie's, until the older man relaxed into the care of the three Cherubim.

Hardly any sound emerged when he spoke, and yet he seemed to trust that his great-nephew really could hear him, and Annie could feel his determination to pass on his warning. She began to draw away his fear and confusion, allowing him to let the memories flow. When his words fell away altogether, he didn't seem to notice or care that Kiah Langley's voice took over. Annie felt her mother's gift wrap around the words as they fell into her mind and settled there. Annie closed her eyes and extended her own gift out, so that the words melded with Uncle's emotions to form a solid connection she could follow. A connection she could use to immerse herself in the moment, almost exactly as Uncle had seen it …

As soon as the Jackaroo passed the tree line, Uncle Willie lifted the tyre and rolled it through the open side of the shed, figuring he was better off looking like he was too busy to entertain guests. Even between Bo's barking and his dodgy hearing, he could still hear the deep rumbling of the new car approaching. A vehicle with decent horse-power, crunching on the gravel outside. As he strained against the cross brace, he could feel his heart begin to race. Who were these people, and what did they want with Harry? He felt the nut start to shift, but then his sweaty hands slipped and he stumbled. Patience. He needed to stay calm and wait for the strangers to approach him, not jump up like some nervous loony.

He readjusted his grip and tried again, gritting his teeth at the effort. His own father had lived to eighty-seven years old—why was he so useless at just sixty-nine? The heart surgery he'd had five years ago had really messed him around. At the time, he'd been convinced he was as doomed as a gummy-mouthed wether, but it turned out that he wasn't entirely toothless. He'd fought back, and survived, and not left his great-nephew alone again. That counted for a lot. He just wished Harry hadn't been forced to quit school to pick up the slack where his weakened body couldn't cope. And since that embarrassing incident out in the state park the previous year, his new medication had helped with the dizzy spells, but made him weaker. He couldn't afford to be weak. Not now. He'd promised Ruby he'd care for her boy. With a grunt, he gave the wheel brace another solid shove, and was rewarded with a creak of sliding metal.

'You oughtta give that a spray with some WD40,' came a man's voice.

Uncle Willie looked up to see a man in a charcoal business suit and matching tie standing by the sliding door of the shed. What sort of idiot would wear a jacket in this weather? He had dark hair, cropped close to his scalp, and plump lips. Bo walked past him and came to sit next to the tractor, tongue hanging out as he looked to his master for instruction.

'Already did that,' Uncle replied, starting on the next wheel nut. 'You from the bank? I already told you guys. Got a good price for our wheat this year, but the money doesn't just appear overnight, you know. We had a few days of rain which delayed—'

'I'm not from the bank. I'm looking for Harry Doolan.' The man's voice was deep and crisp, as if it came from a cavern of ice that held nothing but disdain for the sun.

'Harry? What you want with him?' Uncle asked, standing up and wiping his greasy hands on his moleskins. He walked toward the stranger and peered around him to see a black Mustang parked next to Harry's ute. A second man was by the front door of the house, rummaging through the box of veggies Kiah had brought over. It looked as if he'd left his jacket and tie in the car and had rolled up his shirt sleeves instead.

'Can you tell me where he is?' the first man asked.

Uncle frowned. 'He's in town getting groceries. Can I help?'

The man paused. 'You're his great-uncle? William Lewis?'

'That's me,' he replied, standing straighter. For some reason, he found himself wishing he was closer to the tool box. Perhaps it was because Bo was pacing back and forth instead of leaning against the man's legs for a pat the way he usually would.

The man lit a cigarette. 'This is pretty wild country up here,' he said after he inhaled a lungful of poison. 'Not just paddock after paddock of boring. Some might call it pretty. All those hills behind the house.'

'My mob reckons this place is the source of all creation,' Uncle replied. 'And it's certainly prettier than the flatlands up north.'

'The source of all creation,' the man mused, casting his eyes up to the west where mountain tops shimmered in the summer haze.

Tree-tops rippled across the hills like anemones in the current, the grey-green slashed here and there by sheer cliff faces. A hot breeze sang secrets through the river gums, chasing out a flock of black cockatoos who shrieked ancient warnings across the valley.

The man sucked in another lungful of smoke. 'Well, that's clearly bullshit. But tell me, does your mob know any other legends? I've done some research. Apparently some stories are passed on from father to son. Sacred artefacts that only the eldest son can touch, or even speak about. Maybe Geoff Doolan had a story he only told his son. Maybe, I don't know, a story about some special rocks? Or caves filled with treasure?'

'Treasure?' Uncle smirked. 'Out here? Don't be ridiculous. Gold country is that way,' he said, pointing south-east.

'Not gold. Gems.'

Uncle Willie felt his chest tighten. 'I think you need to leave now.'

'My friend in town seems to think you might have something to sell. If that's true then it would certainly get the bank off your back. It wouldn't even matter if your grain sale fell through, then, would it? I mean, if AJ at Wimmera Grain heard a rumour about your previous dodgy dealings, and withdrew his offer ...'

'Previous dodgy dealings? I've never—wait, how do you know who's buying our grain? Have you said something to AJ?'

'Won't matter if you sell us a gem or two. I can make certain you get an excellent price.'

'We have nothing to sell. You've been lied to. Please leave us alone.'

'Why would Harry lie about having gems to sell? Unless he's trying to stick his nose into business that's best left alone.'

Bo barked twice in warning as the second man approached and tossed a tomato to his colleague.

The man in the suit and tie sniffed at the tomato like he was testing the fragrance of a fine wine. 'Farm fresh. Ambrosial, even. Perhaps this really is the source of all creation.' He took a messy bite, leaning forward to avoid dripping it on his white shirt.

The second man stood with his arms crossed and legs slightly apart.

'There are two utes here, and the bonnet of one is still warm. Did you just arrive?'

Uncle refused to answer.

'If Harry really is in town, like you say, then perhaps I should leave him a message instead. One that he can't misinterpret.'

'You leave my boy alone, hear me? Harry doesn't know anything.'

'Anything about what?' The man laughed, reaching under his jacket.

Uncle lunged for the wheel brace, but then froze as the man pulled a gun out from under his jacket. The second man casually walked past them and picked up the steel brace off the floor.

He hefted it in his hands, testing its weight, and then smiled.

An alarm beeped as the machine reflected the rising panic in Annie's chest. She drew in as much of Uncle's fear as she could, until she found herself flinching away from a brief touch to her shoulder.

'Annie, are you okay?' Harry stepped back to give her some space. He must have come over to her side of the bed while she still had her eyes closed. Her mum stood up and moved to the window, her face pale. The alarm thankfully stopped just as the nurse entered the room. No one spoke while she checked his vitals and added a dose of something to his drip line. She gave Harry a sympathetic smile as she left.

Harry leant down to whisper in his uncle's ear. 'Sleep now, Uncle. I'll be right here. No one can get to me here.' It was the only reassurance that seemed to have made any difference to him across the long night, and a minute later his breathing finally settled into a sleeping rhythm.

The three Cherubim headed for the tea room, which was more like a broom closet with an urn in it, so they could talk. Her mum shut the door behind them.

'I'll have to be careful how I pass the information on to the police. If I give them too detailed a description of the men they might not believe it came from Uncle, given how sedated he is. I already told them that Harry and I were down by the river when it all happened, so I can't pretend I saw the men for myself. I could call in an anonymous tip, but that's dangerous. Last time I tried that the lead detective wasted a lot of time looking for a witness who didn't exist.'

Harry handed her a Styrofoam cup of tepid water with a tea bag floating in it. 'Last time?'

She continued as if she hadn't heard. 'I don't know how clearly I described the men to you just then, and I need you to be able to recognise them. They were both in their thirties. Dressed well. Both had short dark hair. One of them had thick eyebrows and kind of a pouty mouth. The other guy had high cheekbones and a receding hairline. And a lot of muscle. The car is a black Mustang, so it should be easy to notice around here.' She ran her hands across her face, like she was trying to wake up a bit. 'If you see anyone like that, you call the police straight away.'

'And tell them what?' Annie asked her. 'That we got an evil vibe from them? It's a small town, but not that small. We can't just call the cops every time we see a stranger with a receding hairline.'

'Tell them you saw a hand gun.'

Annie and Harry flinched as the door to the tea room opened. Annie breathed again when she saw who it was. Harry didn't.

'Well, you took your time,' Annie said to Sarah as she stepped into the room.

The reluctant Guardian looked terrible. She was in a mismatched tracksuit and old runners, had bags under her eyes, and there was milky baby spew on her shoulder. She stood uncertainly with her fingers twitching, staring at Harry. 'Dave helped me with the two am feeds, and it took ages for them all to get back to sleep,' she said.

'I told you not to come,' Harry admonished. 'I'm safe enough here, aren't I?'

'You don't know what it's been like,' Sarah said. 'I tried to warn you, but you didn't listen.'

'All you said was that there was something wrong. A bit vague, don't you think?'

'Keep your voices down,' Annie warned. 'It's the middle of the night.'

Sarah turned and snapped at her. 'And don't you dare accuse me of taking my time. If you had a Guardian around, would you have left him freaking out all night, sick to the stomach with worry?'

Annie swallowed hard. Sarah wouldn't really tell her mum about Lucas, would she?

'I think we should let you and Harry talk alone,' her mum suggested, and Annie practically bolted from the room before Sarah could say anything else.

When they reached the hospital foyer her mum paused by the vending machine, looking for something to eat. 'We need some sort of a plan,' she said, fishing some coins from her back pocket. 'I need your help to convince Harry to stay with you at our place. I'll take care of his.'

Annie gripped the little silver tree that was nestled against her throat. 'Is that really necessary?'

'Well, he can't stay on his farm alone.'

He won't be alone. Not with Lucas there. 'Well then, neither should you. How about if I stay there with him?' Annie suggested. 'That will give Sarah an excuse to come over whenever she feels Harry is in any danger. She can pretend to be visiting me.'

Her mum rubbed her eyebrow and gave her head a little shake while the machine dropped a packet of Twisties into the tray. 'No way. It isn't safe.'

'It should be safe enough if Harry does what he's told and stops asking questions. The police will find those men soon. And if anything does happen, Sarah will give us plenty of warning.'

The new day began to glow through the automatic glass doors. Her mother was exhausted, physically and emotionally. 'You aren't staying there, Annie,' she insisted, handing her the Twisties, 'but I guess Harry probably won't agree to leave. He's become a bit stubborn lately.' She drew her jacket in a bit tighter. 'The police will find them.' She nodded, as if to convince herself, and Annie hoped like crazy that she wouldn't change her mind as soon as she was no longer around to steal away her worry.

Chapter 25

When Kiah finally plucked up the courage to push open the door to Durante Diamonds, enough adrenaline was coursing through her that she jumped at the sound of the buzzer. It was times like this that she really missed Geoff's calming influence, but then, if Geoff was still around, none of this would be necessary. She clutched her daughter's lunchbox in one hand and pretended to examine a velvet tray of rings, trying not to think about what her Guardian would have said about her coming here.

'Mrs Langley, nice to see you. How may I help you today?'

Mr Durante had certainly aged since she'd last spoken to him all those years ago. She'd rarely seen him around town since then. Did he ever even leave his shop? She could swear he was still wearing the same grey suit. She took a deep breath and smiled the sort of smile that her daughter would call a lie.

'I've come to get my wedding rings checked. I think the setting might be a bit loose.' She held her hand out for him to examine.

He only paused for a moment before picking up his magnifying lens from the counter and taking her hand in his, peering closely at the small diamonds.

'I assume you heard about what happened to Uncle Willie?' she asked, not wanting to waste her window of opportunity with small talk. The jeweller glanced up at her briefly before returning to his task with false concentration.

'You mean William Lewis? Your neighbour? No, I haven't heard. Is he all right?'

'No one calls him William. Everyone here knows him as Uncle Willie,' she corrected. 'He had another heart attack on Tuesday. We're collecting donations of money or meals to help Harry out while he's in hospital. Most of the shops along here have chipped in.' She gave Annie's lunchbox a bit of a shake so he could hear the coins she'd put in there.

'*Another* heart attack?' Mr Durante asked. 'He's had one before?'

'Five years ago, and the prognosis isn't great this time. I wish I knew what caused this one. He's been doing all the right things—unless you count drinking too much tea.'

'Well, you know sometimes these things can just happen out of the blue,' he said, pulling away, but not before Kiah 'saw' what she needed to.

'Sometimes,' she agreed. 'Not this time. I need to make sure they don't come back.'

The man flinched, yet recovered fast. 'Sorry, what?'

'Harry's just a kid. He lied about having more gems to sell. I need you to tell them he was lying. He knows nothing, and won't trouble them again. I guarantee it.' For a moment, she considered trying to flirt with him like they did in the movies, as an excuse to touch him again so she could read some more images, but the idea just seemed ridiculous. And there was a glass counter in the way.

'Now, Mrs Langley, I'm afraid I don't know what you're—'

Kiah smacked her hand down on the glass, hard enough to get his attention. 'Stop it,' she demanded. 'I don't need you to admit to anything. I just need you to pass on the message, got it? I know you can contact Mr Rosa.'

He didn't move, but his sallow skin paled even more. 'Where did you hear that name?' he rasped.

She leant across the cabinet. 'You have done Harry's family enough harm, Mr Durante. Passing on the message is the least you can do. Tell those blokes to back off—there are no gems here, and no one wants to revisit the past.'

It wasn't until much later, after she'd dramatically stormed out of the shop and fled to the relative privacy of her car to try to deal with the ramifications of the memories she'd seen, that Kiah realised that her parting comment could be misconstrued as a threat. She sat in the driver's seat, staring at the set of wedding rings on her finger, and wondered what her Guardian would say about all this. Mr Rosa and his employees had been responsible for the deaths of Ruby and Geoff Doolan. The threat of their return had prompted her Guardian to take the risk that had ended in tragedy three years ago. Now she knew that it hadn't been such a formless threat, because they had returned after all, and attacked Uncle. And now she had just drawn attention to herself. They would not stop until they had their answers.

Kiah knew exactly what her Guardian would have said if he was here: let them come. One day she would see him again and would have to explain her choices. It was up to her to deal with the threat this time, and she was in a unique position to act. The solution was simple, really.

The diamond in her ring sparkled, revealing the sun's colourful magic. In order to take up her Guardian's role, she would take on his defiance. She would have to become as strong as diamond.

Let. Them. Come.

Chapter 26

Not only had the confrontation put too much strain on Uncle Willie's heart, but his cracked ribs and punctured lung made it difficult to treat him properly. After four days and three more cardiac episodes, Annie noticed that the doctors had stopped talking about how long it might take to stabilise him enough for surgery. His heart was sustaining new damage with each setback and it became apparent to everyone that he probably wouldn't be coming home. The only person who seemed to be able to ignore the verdict was Uncle. He insisted that Harry bring in the new market reports on grain and stock sales even though he was too sedated to read them, and every time Harry left for some much-needed rest, Uncle would ask the staff to pass on another message to the police. Some minor detail about the car he'd remembered, or a new theory about who might have been responsible for the attack.

'I've never felt anyone so tired, and yet determined,' Annie whispered to Lucas and Harry as they waited in the corner of the ward. 'He won't rest.'

'Hurts to … rest, Sunny,' Uncle mumbled from his bed. 'It's my … heart that's … cactus, not my … ears.'

'Sorry, Uncle.'

'Sunny?' Lucas asked, pouring Uncle a glass of water and freeing a straw from its paper cocoon.

'He called me that when I was little,' Annie explained. 'Years ago.'

'Too many … years,' Uncle agreed, speaking very slowly past the sedatives. 'She used to be … sunny, once. Before her … dad died. She was … almost as funny as my Harry.'

Harry cleared his throat. 'I'm still funny. I laughed the other day when I watched Lucas try to iron a bed sheet.'

'Laughing at someone else doesn't mean you're funny,' Annie remarked. 'You used to make actual jokes, once.'

The way Lucas frowned suggested that he found that hard to believe. She didn't blame him. Harry had changed. He needed Eden, needed to heal and revive his soul in the blissful Garden, but even if he stopped being so stubborn about going there, he would never leave while he was needed here.

Uncle smiled. 'Remember … when Harry … dressed that scarecrow up … in …'

It was taking longer and longer for him to push out his words, and whatever he said after that was lost in a mumbled haze of unpronounceable painkillers. Annie's gift was centred around emotions, and what she'd been feeling from Uncle since the attack was something off-kilter. She now recognised it as the unique blend of emotions that came with intense unrelenting pain and exhaustion. Even now as he drifted to sleep, that pain didn't let up, nor did his worry.

An arm was placed around her shoulder, and she was drawn into a hug. Lucas wiped a tear from her cheek without a word.

'Why won't he let go?' she whispered as softly as she could. 'It hurts him so much. I don't understand. I know it must seem obvious to you, but it isn't to me. He could just go …'

'He won't leave me,' Harry explained. 'Not while he thinks I'm in danger. Perhaps Guardian traits run in his family. Maybe that's where Mum got them from.'

'Or maybe he just loves you,' Lucas suggested.

Harry sucked in a deep breath to ward off his tears. 'Or maybe he's just a stubborn old man.' He took hold of Uncle's hand, limp on the crisp white blanket. 'If you didn't have to worry about me, would you choose to let go?' he asked his sleeping uncle.

No one answered him, but Annie knew the truth. Harry did too, and when he turned to her, she looked away. 'No,' she whispered. 'Don't ask me to do that.'

'Please,' Harry begged. 'He shouldn't have to go through this anymore.'

'It's not fair!'

'I disagree. Give him a fair choice, Annie. If he knew I had a Guardian, if he knew I would be safe, then what would he choose?'

Lucas gasped. 'You can't tell him … *How* would you tell him?'

'We don't need to tell him. Please, Annie, I'm begging you.' Harry's whole body shouted his intense appeal to her, pressing her own will into the same shape as his.

'Oh,' Lucas said. 'You want Annie to use her gift.'

She turned to Lucas, curious about how he'd react to such an idea. After a few moments of coming to terms with what Harry was proposing, Lucas swallowed hard and then nodded. 'If his fear for Harry really is all that's holding him here, then that's bad. If you take his fear away, and nothing happens, then at least he can rest easy. If taking it away allows him to let go, then that's the right thing to do. You won't be choosing anything for him, Annie. All you'll be doing is releasing him from a restriction he shouldn't have, to allow nature to take its course.'

'Are you certain about this, Harry?' she asked. 'Take some time to think it through.'

'I've been thinking of nothing else for days,' he said. He lifted his great-uncle's hand and kissed his knuckles. 'Uncle? Can you hear me? Uncle, wake up.'

The man stirred and sighed. His eyes were glazed, but they did open.

'Uncle, tell me again what you always tell me. Where will your life end?'

'It doesn't matter where,' he mumbled. 'I belong to the Earth, and she'll take me home.' He wriggled a bit, like he wanted to sit up. Annie was amazed at his strength of will. He refused to let his Harry down, not even to rest. She felt his determination warring with his pain, along with a growing sense of despair that she wished she could deny. A despair that flavoured his next words. 'And when she does, I'll have my boy by my side, and I'll know he's safe. Promise me you'll stay safe, Pup.'

'Of course, Uncle. You can trust me. I'll be safe.'

Uncle Willie sighed.

'Sleep now. I'll see you later.'

No one spoke while Uncle's breathing relaxed back to sleep, until eventually Harry turned to face Annie, deliberately keeping his eyes down, away from hers. She knew what that meant. He was trying not to use his gift to coerce her in any way.

'What better final wish could he have?' he asked her in a hushed voice. 'To have his boy by his side, and know he's safe. I'd give just about anything for a chance at that.'

Out of the corner of her eye she saw Lucas start to cry, and did her best to shield him out. Harry's chance at a family was not gone. She wouldn't give up on it yet. Even if Sarah chose to stay away indefinitely, then Annie was darn well going to drag Harry by the ear to Eden and make him stay there until he met someone worthy of him. No matter how long that took. He would *not* die alone.

'Please, Annie,' Harry continued. 'In this time, and this place, this is the right thing to do.'

With or without his gift, she still trusted his wisdom and integrity. *Do. Don't think too hard. Just do.*

It hardly took any effort for her to draw away the worry from the mix of emotions that swirled around Uncle's chest with each shallow breath. She wished she could replace his worry with the joyous anticipation that Aya had felt on her last evening. But her gift didn't work in reverse. Still, the relief and contentment he felt was enough. His Harry was safe. He no longer felt the need to struggle to stay and protect him. He could rest.

As she knew it would, the heart monitor made a terrible noise. Annie couldn't cry.

It was a hard funeral for Annie to sit through. She couldn't quite get her head around the concept of death, let alone the bittersweet emotions that filled the tiny church when they handed out cups of tea in the middle of the service to honour Uncle Willie's favourite tradition. There were a lot of strangers paying their respects: family and friends from up north. Enough new faces that her mum didn't look twice at the young man with the shaggy fringe crying in the back row—not even when Dave sat with him and spoke quietly into his ear.

Annie didn't last through the full service. She snuck out ten minutes before the end and found a tree to hide in. It was a stupid move. If Lucas followed her and her mum saw them together ... but she couldn't help it. She couldn't shield everything, not when everyone was reacting to everyone else's sorrow.

When he didn't come, she cried. She cried because he was respecting her wishes, and knew how important it was to her that her mum not find out about him, and she cried because he was in Nalong and not safe at home, far away from strangers with guns. She cried because she needed him to hold her, and he didn't, and it was her fault, and she cried because Uncle was gone and she missed him already.

She was still crying when Kelly came out to find her.

'Annie, are you okay?'

'Not really.'

She kicked off her black heels and climbed up to sit on the branch below Annie's. 'Do you need a distraction? What can I do?'

Annie scrubbed at her eyes, remembering all the times Kelly had helped her after her dad had died. Kelly was a far better friend than she deserved.

'A distraction would be great. Thanks, Kel.' She wiped her nose with the tissue Kelly handed her. 'Tell me about Charles and Di. Do you think they'll get back together?'

⬆

Eventually, when the service ended, Kelly offered to take Liam for a walk while Sarah and Dave took turns trying to settle his cranky twin. Kelly asked Annie to come along, but she refused, and pulled herself together enough to go and find Harry instead. She held his hand, and didn't let it go for the rest of the afternoon. Not even when people came to shake it. Not even when he placed the wreath made of gum leaves and native berries on the coffin as it was lowered into the ground. Not even when an elderly relative came and spoke to him in a language they had never taken the time to learn properly. The woman seemed disappointed when she had to translate into English, especially since she had come to remind him to spend more time learning the old ways. He told her that his uncle had taught him many things, and he promised to visit her soon. She nodded, apparently satisfied that he would do his duty to his people.

They lingered by the grave for a long time, until everyone else had left and the hot wind had wilted the flowers. They didn't speak, and didn't cry. Annie felt Harry's pain and loneliness, and she didn't shield it. Slowly and delicately, she drew it in, but didn't steal it. Instead, she simply shared it. What he felt, she felt, and after a while, it hurt a little less.

'No. No way. There must be something you can do,' she argued, gripping his elbow to try to make him turn and face her.

Harry ignored her and kept walking, not caring that she was practically drawing blood. They both knew she couldn't really cause him pain, not without all sorts of unwelcome consequences.

The main street of Horsham was crowded, for a weekday, and if she hadn't been able to feel where he was she might never have noticed him walking away from the real estate agent's office. He was carrying a plain manila folder, filled with documents that she knew meant trouble.

Lucas had clearly thought it important that she knew about this particular trip into town, because he'd asked Kelly to call and invite her to go shopping with her. Kelly had assumed that he wanted to trick her into meeting up with him and had happily played along, the traitor. But when Lucas had met them outside Target, he'd pulled Annie aside and told her what was going on. Harry had met with the bank manager that morning, and was planning to head straight over to the agent's office immediately after. By the time Annie caught up with him, Harry had already finished there.

'You can't sell the farm! It's our responsibility to care for it. We can't have just anyone living so clo ...' Her tongue tried to do a backflip rather than form the next words. It was incredibly frustrating.

'It's done, Annie. There's no other option. Even I can't convince the bank to lend me any more money. Uncle tried his best to fix our finances, but with only the two of us we just couldn't run enough stock to make ends meet. And after his first heart attack, no one would insure him anymore. There's nothing left. I can't even pay Lucas.'

After everything he'd been through, this just wasn't fair. He'd worked so hard. He'd done nothing wrong. The recession and the family curse had simply beaten him down.

'I'll do what I can to screen the buyers,' he said, 'and hopefully they'll let me stay on and work. Otherwise, I'm kind of hoping you'll help me out a little.'

Finally, he slowed down and let her catch up.

'Of course I will. We can fix up the old cottage if we need to, but Harry, I thought things were better with Lucas helping. You had more stock this year, and cut more hay. You did so well at that sale—'

'The sale fell through. I've found another buyer, but it's too late, the bank is shutting us down. Please don't make this any harder than it already is. If I had another choice, you know I'd take it. Besides, I'm starting to think it might be better if I disappeared altogether. It might be safer for everyone.'

Annie stopped so suddenly that a young girl bumped into her from behind. Was Harry actually thinking of going Next Door? Indefinitely? This was not like him at all. Things were bad.

'Sarah might still choose you, Harry. Give her time.'

This time he was the one to stop and cause the traffic jam. It was a good thing they were so noticeable to people or else he would have been run over by a kid on rollerblades. What were all these people doing here?

Harry ran his fingers through his hair and moved to the side of the footpath, leaning against the window of an op-shop. 'It's not going to happen, Annie. Dave asked her to marry him.'

Annie gaped at him, unable to think of a thing to say.

'She told him she wasn't ready,' he continued.

A tiny weird little noise escaped her lips that apparently meant 'thank goodness'. Harry lowered his eyes. 'She said she wanted to be sure he wasn't just marrying her because of the twins. As if she doesn't know how much he adores her.'

'Well, that's a good sign, isn't it?'

'No, Annie. A good sign would be if she'd told him "no". A good sign would be if she looked me in the eye every now and then. A good sign would be if she agreed to talk to me … at all … ever.'

'I'm so sorry—'

'No. You have to stop apologising for what's happened. It wasn't your fault. It wasn't anyone's fault. Sometimes things just don't go right, but I have to believe that not everything will go wrong all the time. Even I can't be that unlucky.' The pale yellow folder in his hand suggested otherwise. They both stared at it for a quiet moment.

'So, what happens next? How long do you think it will take to sell?' Her stomach churned at the thought of strangers living in Harry's house. Too close. It would be far too easy for the new people to go wandering around where they shouldn't. The uncleared south-western corner of his farm was close enough to Eden that her spine always shivered whenever she'd felt Uncle cross the river down there.

'I'm not selling all of it,' Harry said. 'I'm giving a big chunk of it to you.'

'*What?*'

'Everything west of the river. The solicitor has already drawn up the papers. All we need is for the surveyors to verify all the measurements and for your mum to sign her part. It won't change the sale price much because people are only really interested in the land they can use.'

Before she had a chance to react to his announcement, a shrill yelp from behind startled them both. She turned in time to see a face she recognised, framed with short blond hair and eyes full of mischief and indignant complaint. Lily was being yanked unceremoniously backward by her brother, who deftly snatched away the water pistol she was aiming at them. Annie noticed that the footpath had magically cleared.

'Oh, come on, Lou!' Lily complained. 'They need it. Can't you see how horribly serious they look?'

Instead of replying, Lucas just aimed the plastic toy right back at her and squirted her squarely on the chest repeatedly, which made her squeal.

'Lily? What are you doing here?' Annie asked, giving her a brief, damp hug as an excuse to use her own body to shield the girl from further attack. Lucas fumbled and almost dropped the pistol. Even aiming a fake weapon at her was clearly beyond him.

'Lucas promised he'd let me come up here over the holidays,' she said, shaking the water from her shirt. 'School starts next week, and I'm holding him to his word. He promised me a country-style barbeque on a working sheep farm on Australia Day. Didn't he invite you?'

'Australia Day? Really?' No wonder everyone was rushing around before the shops closed.

'It's tomorrow, Annie,' Kelly pointed out as she caught up to them with her arms loaded with shopping bags. 'I know you don't really celebrate it, but people do have time off work so Lucas invited everyone up to the farm. Did he really not tell you? Maybe it's payback for not inviting him to your birthday.'

'Everyone?' she asked, suddenly feeling her pulse under her ribs.

'Mum and Dad are here too,' Lucas admitted, swinging the pistol around his finger before handing it back to his sister. 'Even Dave's family are coming up from Melbourne in the morning. We've been here for a year now, Annie. They're all curious.'

He was right. Even if he hadn't told them about the attack on Uncle Willie, they still had every right to want to know what was going on up here. It must have been dreadful for Lucas to have had to justify to his family why he chose to drop out of uni to work on a sheep farm. A bankrupt sheep farm. She'd never even thought to ask him about how they'd taken it.

'How long are you here for, Lily?' she asked.

'Until Sunday. Lucas promised he'd teach me to ride a horse.'

Annie's Guardian refused to acknowledge her sceptical look.

'You are coming tomorrow, aren't you?' Lily asked. 'I bought water pistols. And gummy bears.'

'Mum and I have to get the hay in. It's a big job, Lily.'

Lily's face fell. 'But … gummy bears.'

Blue eyes, so like her brother's, struck Annie with a force not unlike Harry's soothing gift. Except they were anything but soothing, and Annie's own gift proved the authenticity of Lily's disappointment.

'If we're done early enough, I'll think about it.'

Lucas beamed, but Annie grabbed his elbow and pulled him all the way over to the other side of the street. They looked back to see Lily and Kelly whispering to each other and giggling.

'Lily's going to give me a hard time about this.' Lucas smiled. 'A private conversation with you. She'll be nosy.'

'So?'

'Good point. Can we at least give her something worth teasing me about? Maybe if I can make you smile …'

'Or maybe you can tell me why you've put your family in danger by bringing them to Nalong. What if those guys come back? Do you know how worried I've been, knowing that you and Harry are on your own? Why would you risk this?'

'You're worried about me?'

'Of course I am. The police have found no trace of them.'

'Because they've left town.'

'They might come back.'

'Not if Harry behaves himself.'

'They're criminals, Lucas. You can't rely on them to be fair.' It was hard to growl and whisper at the same time, and even harder to stop herself from trying to smack him when he laughed at her. So she didn't. He avoided her easily.

'Okay, sorry. Look. I understand what you're saying, but I didn't really have a choice. I couldn't put my parents off any longer without telling them everything, and if they knew about the attack, I would have no hope of being allowed to stay in Nalong. I might be nearly twenty, but they still have their ways to try to get me to do as I'm told. And I don't want to have to completely ruin my relationship with them if I can avoid it.' He glanced back at Lily, who was trying to squirt Kelly with the water pistol. 'Just until Sunday. What are the chances of those guys coming back this week? Just a few more days and then my parents will go home to where it's safe and never have to find out because I'll make sure Harry never even *thinks* of chasing down any more information. It will all work out fine. It has to. We have bigger things to take care of than petty criminals, Annie. You and Harry shouldn't have to worry about ordinary things like that. Trust me. It will all work out fine.'

Before she had a chance to splutter out any of her indignant arguments, he ran back across the street, nicked Lily's water pistol again, and chased his sister down the street with it, laughing as if he wasn't feeling anxious at all.

Chapter 27

The after-dinner conversation with her mum made Annie feel like she was walking barefoot through a patch of stinging nettles. When she'd explained that Harry had put his farm up for sale, her mum had gone very quiet for a few minutes, and then flipped around and started asking for every detail. How much was he selling for? Had Uncle Willie's estate been finalised and the title to the property transferred into Harry's name now that he was old enough? How was Harry feeling? Did he need company? Would it help if he felt more needed? For Annie, every response felt like a blow, and every word was tentative. In the end, she had to reveal that Harry was expecting visitors for lunch, and so they couldn't possibly ask him to come over in the morning to help shift the end-of-season small hay bales before the day's heat was due to kick in.

'Visitors?' her mum asked, but Annie pretended not to hear. Her mum was still under the impression that the Doolans' farmhand had left for good, since Harry could no longer pay him, and Annie hadn't corrected her. Yet she knew that time was running out. Her mum would find out about Lucas eventually, and then she would either crash into another depression, or leave for Eden permanently. Probably both.

Annie didn't sleep well that night. It was too hot and there were too many things to be nervous about. Her mum wanted to leave her. Harry was talking about leaving for Eden as well. Kelly was planning to move to Sydney for uni. Uncle was gone, her dad was gone … and with each parting, she felt as if another piece of her childhood was dissolving into distant memory. Who would be left to remember it with her? Without the people she grew up with, who would she even *be*?

There was much to celebrate about Australia, but by the time the scorching sun had fully risen, it felt as if the land was punishing its residents for being thoughtless enough to choose to do it on the anniversary of something so devastating. Annie decided that if forty-four degrees Celsius made for an authentic country-life barbeque, then Lily was going to be over the moon well before lunchtime. She wondered if Lily would have been so enthusiastic about other country-life realities, like having to wake up at sparrow's fart to bring in hay bales before the predicted late thunderstorms could ruin them. The up-side was that once the last bale was finally stacked, her mum declared that they deserved the rest of the day off. Annie hugged her a thank you with trembling arms, feeling totally wrecked, almost wishing she hadn't refused to call Harry to come over and help.

By then it was late morning, and the stifling northerly wind had stolen the energy out of everything and was using it for joyriding, tossing dry leaves and empty feed buckets around like disposable playthings.

'We should go into town and see a movie,' Annie suggested once they'd cooled off a little by having cold showers and then locking themselves in the lounge room with the overworked air conditioner. 'I checked. The cinema is open today.'

'And will be packed out, being a public holiday,' her mum replied, lying back and draping her legs over the end of the sofa. 'Personally, I'm happy to just veg out here for a while and read. Or sleep. I could happily sleep.' She balanced a glass of iced water on her forehead and closed her eyes. 'You have your licence now. You can go out if you like.'

Annie wondered why it was that teenagers were always so eager for independence. Any day now, her mother could fall apart again and disappear. She wanted to cherish each moment she had until then, but her mum kept pushing her to manage on her own. It wasn't fair. She *liked* the nest. Did her mum have to keep prodding with her beak to prompt her to fly? Still. She'd told Lily she'd consider going to the barbecue. And Lucas … well, his smile had said it all. If she was honest with herself she'd probably admit that the real reason she was trying to pike out of it was because she was nervous about meeting his parents. What was she supposed to wear?

The old air conditioner hissed and then groaned, and Annie groaned with it. Honest or not, she couldn't escape the fact that today was going to be difficult for Harry. Sarah would be there, as well as Dave and his family. What had Lucas been thinking, inviting them all? Reluctantly, she said she would head over to Harry's. Her mum picked up a magazine, barely even acknowledging her as she left.

So hot you had to boil the kettle to get a cool drink. So hot the flies were on strike. So hot the chooks were laying hard boiled eggs. Gripping the steering wheel, Annie ran through every colloquial hot day simile she could remember to distract herself from fretting when she saw all the cars lined up on the shady side of the zincalume machinery shed. One of them was a very clean white BMW. Dave's parents? When she got out and walked past it, she noticed an Aussie flag stuck to the back window, and for a moment Annie let herself daydream about how much simpler her family's job must have been in the days before that flag meant anything. Certainly, their authority would have been clearer, more open to the community. Less need to explain why certain things should be kept hidden, and why some stories were not for sharing. How lovely would it have been to only have to keep secrets that lifted her up toward the sacred, not secrets that weighed her down.

The grass behind the house was dry and crackly, all but dead because it was kept so sensibly short to reduce the risk of fire. Under the shade of a small stand of pine trees, an old wooden picnic table had been given the company of six white plastic chairs, all the kitchen stools, and a vinyl-backed picnic rug. Lily was in full swing with her water pistol, and as usual, she'd manipulated everyone into joining her. And there were a lot of people. Sarah and Kelly were so intent on using the water fight to release all the suppressed irritation they felt for each other that they barely acknowledged Annie's arrival. Lucas certainly noticed her, and Lily noticed him noticing. What that meant was that the first time Annie met Peter and Naomi Gracewood, she was wearing sensible denim shorts with an olive cotton shirt that clung to her in all the wrong ways due to the drenching she'd just received from their daughter.

The Gracewoods were lovely, and from the way Peter started juggling three of the freshly picked nectarines she'd brought along, she could see where Lily got her bubbly sense of fun from. She could also see evidence of Lucas's playful smile. Her Guardian's crazy curls clearly came from his mother though. Mrs Gracewood's long wavy hair would have made Cindy Crawford cry with envy.

Unfortunately, they probably thought Annie was a bit of a dimwit from the complete lack of coherent words that she was able to produce for the first half hour or so until her nerves settled down. Luckily everyone else talked enough for it not to be too uncomfortable. The Gracewoods had known David Ashbree's family for years, of course, and since the twins had been born, Mr and Mrs Ashbree had made considerable effort to spend time with Kelly and Sarah's parents too. They were like one great big happy family. Just like the one Annie had always dreamed of having.

They ate snags, bacon, and Doolan Farm's choicest lamb cuts with Harry's famous potato salad. Eggs that Lucas proudly declared he'd grown himself were fried on a spare hot plate that Harry had placed out in the sun. So hot you could cook an egg on the bonnet. That one wasn't so much a simile as it was genuine weather reporting.

'So, Annie-from-next-door. Lucas tells me you've just finished Year 12. With terrific results in biology, I hear. What are your plans for this year?' Naomi Gracewood handed Annie a plastic cup of orange fizzy drink.

She took a sip to give herself time to adjust to the sudden buzz of questions that blossomed inside her head. Lucas had talked about her? Had he mentioned that she'd barely scraped a pass in most of her other subjects? Had he told her about the amount of school she'd ditched and that she'd almost driven herself crazy overcompensating for it? What else had he said? His mum was feeling concerned, and curious, which wasn't exactly surprising, but it made her feel as if she was being checked out. Paranoia was not just for humans, apparently.

Somehow, she dredged up a believable smile. 'I have a farm to manage. There's only Mum and I, so I won't be able to study in the city.' Why did that suddenly make her feel inferior? It had never bothered her before.

'Could you study by correspondence?' she asked without so much of a hint of arrogance.

Annie breathed a little easier. This wasn't about her at all. She was still hoping to get her son's career back on track. 'Of course. There are lots of options available. More and more courses are being offered each year. Maybe even engineering.'

She laughed. 'Am I that obvious?'

'No. I just happen to be wondering the same thing you are. Has he decided what he wants to do yet?' Annie could feel her heart beating faster, and forced herself to take slow breaths. Harry couldn't afford to pay him anymore. There was a very real possibility that she was going to lose him altogether. Why would he stay?

'No, I haven't,' Lucas declared from right behind her. Fanta splashed everywhere, just missing Mrs Gracewood's shoes. 'How come so jumpy?'

'Because we're talking about you,' his mother admonished him. 'How many times have I told you not to sneak up on people?' She leant a little closer to Annie. 'Sometimes I think he was born with an extra gene dedicated to stealth.'

Lucas gave a short laugh, but there was an underlying tension to it, like it was a little bit forced. In fact, from the moment Annie had arrived he'd been tense, and every word that came out of Lily's mouth seemed to bug him. Was he really that anxious about letting his parents meet her? Despite her initial nerves, Annie found that she really was thrilled to finally meet them, and she wished with all her heart that she could reciprocate, and introduce them all to her mum.

'Sorry, Annie. I didn't mean to be sneaky,' he said. 'I just came to ask Mum if she'd like a tour of the place. Dave's dad wants to go for a drive around. Did you know he grew up in East Gippsland? His family ran a dairy. He said this place has good soil and he wants to see the river.'

The last part wasn't framed as a question, but Lucas was looking at her for permission. She nodded.

Nearly all the visitors chose to go once they realised that a swim was on offer, so Annie tossed Dave the keys to her ute. Once they'd all decided which ute to climb onto, and Lily was threatened with being left behind if she refused to stay seated, Dave and Harry drove off down the laneway. Lucas and Annie were left with just Sarah and the sleeping babies.

'Right,' Sarah said, once the cars were out of sight. 'I'll leave you two alone. I'm going to check on the boys.'

'Wait, Sarah, please,' Lucas begged, blocking her path to the front door. 'I need to talk to you.' Her icy stare nearly cancelled out the heat-wave, yet he ploughed on ahead anyway. 'I need to know how serious Dave is about this plan of his.'

The open look of distress on her face showed that she knew exactly what Lucas was asking about, but Annie was at a complete loss.

'You know him, Lou. Once he has his mind set on something, he can be very difficult to divert. Unlike some people.'

'What's that supposed to mean?' he asked.

'It means that he won't sit back and wait for other people to make up their minds. When he wants something, he gives everything he has for it.' She tried to push past him, but Lucas wouldn't budge.

'Something, or someone? Exactly what are you implying here?'

Sarah glanced over at Annie, and back at Lucas. 'How long are you going wait for her to decide she's ready? If you want her, you should fight for her.'

'Fight for her? She's not a trophy, Sarah. She's a person, and she's perfectly capable of making up her own mind about what she wants. Aren't you, Annie?'

For a moment, Annie was too offended to respond, until she took the time to examine Sarah's emotions more closely. There was anger there, sure, but it was paired with an equal amount of shame. Why shame? She caught Sarah's gaze, wishing she could read her thoughts as well.

'You think Harry should fight harder to win you over,' Annie guessed. 'Sarah, he wouldn't ever do that.'

'But if he did,' Lucas said, 'she'd be able to spread some of the blame for hurting Dave.'

Sarah's face paled. 'No, that's not what I … this isn't about me.'

For the past few months, Lucas had been trying to support both Dave and Harry. It seemed that the emotional tug-of-war was finally starting to crack his patience. He looked Sarah right in the eye. 'This is entirely about you. You act like all your choices have been taken away. Like you're being punished, and forced into a life you don't want. The truth is, you *want* someone to tell you what to do so you can have some-one else to blame.'

'How do you know I'm not being punished?' Sarah bit back. 'I didn't exactly behave like a perfect little Christian, did I?'

'You haven't been punished for anything, Sarah. You've been

choosing your own path all along, and the consequences have been complicated, but I would hardly class Liam and Caleb as any sort of divine punishment, would you?'

Whatever Sarah's next argument would have been went unheard, as her emotions flipped over themselves too fast for Annie to untangle.

'Dave, Harry, your parents … everyone's been doing their best to give you as much freedom as you can get,' Lucas continued. 'They've all made sacrifices for you and you've been too self-pitying to even notice. Get over it and make a decision.'

Annie almost staggered back from the flash of pain that Sarah felt at his words.

Lucas must have noticed her distress, because he glanced at her and then sighed. 'I'm sorry, Sarah. That was harsh. You have some difficult decisions to make, and if I'm totally honest, I couldn't even tell you what I would do in your situation. Dave is besotted with his boys, and with you. And you're right. He'll fight for all three of you with every-thing he has. So my question still stands: how serious is he about this?'

A timid breeze blew stifling air into their faces, and then died again. Sarah looked up at the old house, with its faded paintwork and cor-rugated iron roof, as if weighing it up. 'It's been less than a day, but I reckon he's made up his mind.'

Lucas followed her gaze. 'He's always been the most decisive one of our group.'

Annie was tempted to admit that Dave and Sarah probably com-plemented each other in that regard. His decisiveness balanced out her constantly changing mind-set.

'And how likely do you think it is, really?' Sarah asked.

'It's looking more and more like that will depend on you.'

Sarah sat down on the edge of a giant ceramic flower pot whose inhabitant had long since shrivelled into an untidy pile of dry sticks.

'Well, that's where things get tricky then, don't they?' Sarah sneered, gripping the edge of the pot. She sounded cranky, and yet that wasn't her predominant emotion. Mostly she felt confused, and apprehensive. 'He'd be stupid to do something like this without some sort of com-mitment from me, but it's clearly in everyone's best interest if he does. Especially mine. I need to stay in town, apparently, and so this is the best shot I have of keeping my family together. Did Dave's dad say anything this morning? You were all tucked away in the study for a long time.'

Another hot gust of wind tugged at Annie's hair, and she automatically took a deeper breath, but it disappeared too fast, leaving her dissatisfied. Although she wanted to know what the two Guardians were going on about, they were both so much on edge that for once she decided to just shut up and listen.

Lucas walked to the edge of the porch. 'He was quiet, but in a good way, I think. He asked for the tour, which got Dave pretty excited. He did ask a lot of questions about irrigation, and whether we had a licence to take water from the river. Harry was pretty blunt about what he thought of that, and explained all about the bore water system we have instead,' he said, coming back to stand next to her.

Annie frowned. Take water from the river? No way. That was sacrosanct. But would the new owners agree? And why would Dave's dad …

Sarah sighed. 'He suggested we try more mixed farming. Grow some canola and barley as well as the wheat. And run a lot more stock.'

Annie didn't remember moving, but suddenly found herself backed against the front door as if determined not to let anyone through. 'We?' she gasped.

Lucas watched her with his lips pressed together, obviously worried about her reaction. Even the sharp scented air around her seemed to be waiting to see how she'd react.

The pieces clicked. '*Dave's* thinking of buying this place?'

Her Guardian took her hand with a firm grip, and yet he somehow seemed unsteady, as if the rest of him was trembling. 'Harry is offering it to him at a ridiculously low price. Enough to pay out his debts and that's all. He says he'd prefer to sell to someone he knows.'

'He didn't mention anything to me yesterday,' she argued, her mind busily trying to wrap itself around the idea.

'That's because I only suggested it to him last night, after talking to Dave. For months now, Dave's been saying that he'd love to buy a farm one day. He had a whole five-year plan laid out. Apparently your mum started him off?'

Annie nodded, remembering how well her mum had held herself together when they'd first found out who Sarah was. She'd been smart enough to start planning ahead straight away, to try to convince Dave to stay in town.

Lucas continued. 'He has a bit of money saved up for a deposit, although still not nearly enough. He rang his dad last night for advice, and to ask for help. That wasn't easy for him.'

'His parents are considering guaranteeing a loan,' Annie surmised, wishing she could have done the same for Harry, but most banks only accepted immediate family members for that, and Harry would never have let her do it anyway. Putting her farm up as security was out of the question. That little patch of the planet was theirs to serve. Hers and Harry's. They couldn't risk letting the bank have a hold over it. End of story.

Sarah nodded. 'They're considering gifting us a fair chunk of money too. Enough to kick-start the business properly. More fencing, more stock, fix some of the infrastructure. Harry outlined exactly what's needed. If he hadn't been so far behind the eight-ball to start with, he really could have drought-proofed the place years ago, and made a heap of profit on the …' Her voiced trailed away as she met Annie's cold stare. As if Annie wasn't well aware of every difficult business decision Harry had been forced to make over the last few years.

Lucas deftly shifted the conversation. 'So how do *you* feel about it though, Sarah? Living out here? Dave's even more nervous about what you think than he was about having to make that phone call to his dad.'

The faraway look in her olive eyes as she gazed toward where the others had gone reminded Annie of her mother. Which of them was she thinking about? Dave or Harry?

'I belong here,' she whispered, sounding as surprised by her admission as they were. 'It feels more like home than where I grew up. All my dreams are set here.' She looked like she was about to cry as she glanced back at Annie. 'I've just realised that they always have been. How weird is that?'

Annie had nothing new to tell her.

'I can't even escape it in my dreams,' she continued.

Sarah knew what her choices were, and what they meant. There was a reason her gaze was constantly being drawn to wherever Harry happened to be. Annie's own eyes drifted southward, drawn just as compulsively toward her home. Her heart thudded in her chest with what she saw, and she snatched her hand out of Lucas's tense grip.

'Escape? This isn't some horror story that you're trapped in, and you don't have to wait for anyone else to make your decisions for you,' she told Sarah while looking at her Guardian. He flinched at the double implication. Those were the last words she wanted to utter. What she wanted was to fall to her knees and beg him to stay, except something else was suddenly far more urgent, and so she needed to be very careful. And quick. 'I'm sorry. I shouldn't be taking this out on you. I need some space to think about this,' she said, turning and walking away. Somehow, she kept her steps slow. 'Alone,' she added as Lucas started to follow. A shiver ran down her spine as she noticed the agitated way he shifted his feet while he tried to think of a reason to argue, which only made her more determined to hurry.

As soon as she had gone around the corner of the house, she bolted for the garage. Harry would know. He would have felt it at the same moment she had. He would make the call. She hated that she couldn't do it, but if she had … if she'd told Lucas and Sarah what she'd noticed …

Harry's dirt bike started beautifully. She remembered the day he'd proudly turned the engine over for the first time. Uncle had taught the two of them how to recondition the second-hand machine. It had been their ongoing project for quite some time and they'd done a great job. As she shot off down the driveway she caught a glimpse of Lucas as he sprinted after her, on foot and far too late.

Chapter 28

Kiah was dozing on the couch when she heard a car approach. She opened one eye, and then two. Perhaps Annie had popped back home for something. Only, it didn't sound like their ute. The rumble of the engine was too low. In an instant, Kiah was up and peeking out the net curtains to try to catch a glimpse of the car through the trees just outside the home paddock gate. As the black Mustang pulled into view, she uttered swear words she hadn't heard since the shearers were last in town. She raced for the kitchen and picked up the phone, her fingers hovering over the dial pad as she tried to decide who to call. The police would take at least forty minutes to arrive even under full sirens, but no way was she going to call the Doolan farm. She tried the Nalong police station anyway, but the line was engaged. Part-way through her second attempt she heard the front door open. Perhaps townies weren't so crazy to keep their doors locked after all. Still holding the receiver, she stretched the cord so she could peer around the corner into the hallway.

'Kiah Langley?' Even though the man who entered wasn't wearing a business suit, his thick lips and buzz cut were unmistakable.

'Who's asking? I don't remember inviting you in.'

'That phone message you left for my boss was invitation enough. You probably want to put the phone down, Mrs Langley. Best if we sort this out without official assistance. Where's your daughter?'

'Not here. She's at a barbeque,' she told him. Her hand shook as she replaced the receiver. This was real. These people had attacked Uncle. She'd seen it. This man didn't know that, though. And where was his friend with the receding hairline?

'You're too early,' she said to him. 'I expected you to wait longer. Isn't this a bit risky? The police are already hunting for you.'

'You're right, it is risky,' the man said. 'My employer initially told me to wait a few weeks, but then last night he had one of his nightmares. You gave him a nightmare, Kiah. I'd love to know how you did that. He even tossed around the idea of coming out here himself, and he hasn't involved himself in the messy legwork for decades.'

'Maybe he has a guilty conscience. He won't thank you for making it worse by attacking me.'

The man laughed. Not a soft, arrogant laugh. His laugh was so open and natural that Kiah found herself almost smiling back.

'What would be the point of attacking you? What would that achieve? Unless, of course, you need to be *persuaded* to tell me what you know.'

'I know enough to send your employer to prison. Why would you need the details? The deal was that if you stayed away from this town, I would keep my mouth shut. Was that not clear enough?'

The man walked past her, into the kitchen, poured himself a glass of yellowish tank water from the tap and then sat down. He took a couple of gulps and then rolled up the sleeves of his crisp white shirt. Surely he didn't mean her any harm if he was dressed like that. Who would wear a white business shirt to beat someone up? Of course, that could simply mean that he would go straight for the gun option instead, although he didn't appear to have it on him anywhere.

'You're either making an empty threat or a dangerous one. My employer wants to know which. I'm also supposed to ask you where his necklace is, and if there are any more gems lying about the area. You people can't seem to be able to coordinate your answers.'

'Seriously? Not this rubbish again. As I explained to Mr Durante, Harry lied about having more gems to sell. He got suspicious about what happened to his mum, and thought he was being clever. You should have just ignored him.' Kiah walked over to the fridge and pulled out a jug of filtered water that had slices of home-grown lemon floating in it. She poured herself a drink and then put the jug away again. She took her time savouring the chilled refreshment. It was, after all, a ridiculously hot day.

The man twitched his lips. Not quite a smile. 'And what was young Harry suspicious about, exactly? The police told my employer that Ruby Doolan chose his office building to jump from in order to make some sort of symbolic protest. As if she actually believed her husband could *murder* one of our staff members and no one would lay charges against him.'

Cold stung the tips of Kiah's fingers as she gripped her glass. 'Harry has learned his lesson. It's time you learned yours. Stop sending people out here to extort information that doesn't exist. The necklace isn't here, there have never been any other gems, and I'm the only person left in this town who knows what really happened to Ruby Doolan. I would die before I let Harry find out anything that might put him in any danger.'

'You're the only one? That makes things simple, then.'

It was too early. She hadn't yet had time to prepare any false evidence against Mr Rosa and his 'employees'. How was she supposed to have them charged for her fake murder if they actually did murder her?

The man stood up, walked to the fridge, and took out the jug of lemon water. He took a long gulp from it and then poured the rest over his head, using it to wash the sweat from his face. Apparently he didn't care about keeping his white shirt clean. Water splashed everywhere, running across the lino floor and under the table.

Kiah's voice sounded calmer than she felt. 'I don't believe Mr Rosa would be too impressed to be implicated in yet another murder investigation. What was it about that ruby that still warrants such risk, anyway?' She watched the condensation running down the side of her glass. *Go on, say it. Say that there's something intriguing about the gem. Say something that I can use.*

'Mr Rosa,' the man repeated. 'May I ask where you heard that name?'

'You can ask, but I can't speak the words you want to hear.'

For a long moment they stared at each other. Kiah knew she should have felt more nervous; instead, her blood seemed to slow within her veins, like she was turning to stone. Unbreakable. Unmoveable. Something flickered behind the man's eyes, almost as if he recognised that there would be no point in challenging her authority on this.

'It was never just a ruby, Kiah,' he said eventually. 'You backwater farmers never knew what it was you had.'

He grabbed her wrist and pulled her from the chair, and as their skin touched, Kiah was hit with all the memories she never wanted to see. Ruby had been like a sister to her, and this man had watched her die, and now she did too. *Never just a ruby?* His words should have been enough for her to act, but she couldn't seem to focus on anything other than the sight of her friend falling. Screaming. Pain shot through her shoulder as she was hauled out of the kitchen and back to the lounge room.

'Another murder? What proof do you have of any murders, Kiah? Now would be the time to tell me everything. I'd like to be able to tell my employer that there's no reason to ever return to this shit-hole town.'

She couldn't answer. Her mind was too busy trying to scramble for words she could use. She needed to end this nightmare.

'Still not talking? I suppose there is one simple way to be certain there isn't any evidence left lying about. I don't even need to know what evidence you think you have.' He threw her onto the couch, squashing the magazine she'd been reading before she'd dozed off earlier. She could see his hairy chest through his wet shirt. Words. Where were her words? He put his hand in his pocket and pulled out a couple of cable ties. She lunged for the door, only to be yanked back by her hair so violently that she fell onto the coffee table. It broke under her, and she scrambled to grab something she could fight back with, but the man was too fast. He grabbed her wrist again, and then smacked his other fist against her face. Bright spots exploded into pain. She fought back with all the energy she had. Her elbow connected with his shoulder, and her knee hit something that made him grunt, but then he managed to grab her other hand, and twisted it around so that she had to either stop moving or dislocate her own shoulder. For all the sheep she'd wrestled over the years, none of them had ever wrestled back. And none of them were bigger than she was, either. She was pretty strong, but it wasn't enough.

She heard laughter from the hallway, and looked up to see two other men standing in the doorway. For someone who was always immaculately dressed in suits for work, George Durante sure let loose on his days off. Or perhaps only on days as hot as this one. He wore a thick gold necklace, which looked out of place with his blue tank top and black shorts, and certainly didn't go well with the gun the other man had pressed up against his temple.

'Need a hand, Fourby?' the armed man asked. 'She looks like a lot of work for such a hot day.'

'I told you to wait in the car,' Fourby replied, tightening the cable ties around Kiah's wrists. She kicked him as hard as she could in the shin but he didn't react at all.

'It was too hot. Mr D here actually passed out for a minute. I suppose the stress doesn't help. I thought I'd better get him some water. So what's the deal? Did she have anything interesting to say?'

Fourby grunted. 'Nothing we didn't expect. She's going to have a nap on the couch now. The young man at the pharmacy warned me that those meds the doctor gave her for her depression could make her pretty sleepy. Especially if she takes too many of them at once. It's nice, in small towns, the way people will tell you just about anything when you start chatting. A lot of people seem to be pretty concerned about Mrs Langley here. She hasn't been the same since her husband died.'

'I'm not on medication anymore,' Kiah said, still trying to wrench herself out of the man's grip. 'My doctor was happy for me to stop. I never even finished the last lot I bought.'

'Well, isn't that handy? So where are they, then? Kitchen or bathroom?'

Kiah's eyes widened and she clamped her mouth shut.

Fourby sighed. 'Still being unhelpful. Never mind. I happen to have a good supplier of such things.' He fished around in his pocket and pulled out a plastic bottle filled with small white pills that she'd hoped she'd seen the last of. She had nothing against following medical advice, except for the fact that she wasn't ever supposed to need it. Each pill she'd swallowed had been a doubly cruel reminder of her loss. Eventually it had been Annie who'd suggested that time spent in Eden would work much better than the pills did.

As the medication was forced down her throat, Kiah kicked and spat and coughed and screamed, until something soft was pressed against her nose and mouth. Her next breath burned. The one after that didn't smell of anything at all, and then the room began to spin and darken.

'What a shame the pills will make her so sleepy she won't hear the fire alarm go off. Perhaps if it burns hot enough, the only thing left among the ashes will be our missing diamond.'

She should have felt more frightened by Fourby's chilling prediction, yet all she felt was confusion. *Diamond? What diamond?*

But there was no one left to ask, and no voice left to ask with, so her question floated away into grief and shadow.

Chapter 29

'Out! Got 'im!' Kelly shouted, raising her index finger to the sky as Bo caught the ball on the full in a magnificently dedicated leap from the riverbank.

'Hey, that doesn't count,' Dave complained, swinging the cricket bat around in protest.

'Of course it does,' Dave's mum announced when everyone turned to her for adjudication. 'Don't be so species-ist. Bo has as much right to play as anyone else. He certainly has the skill.'

'Fine. His turn to bowl then,' came the grumbled response.

Bo and Lily were wrestling for the tennis ball in the shallows, firm friends already. Lily seemed almost to be winning until she slipped on a rock and was forced to loosen her grip for a split second, long enough for Bo to leap onto the riverbank with his prize. Water sprayed everywhere as he shook himself.

And there endeth the game, Harry thought as he watched his dog lie down in full defensive mode, the ball wedged between his paws and his eyes shifting between Lily and his master. With a regretful sigh, Dave dropped the cricket bat onto the pile of abandoned shoes and jumped in for a fully clothed swim with the rest of the fielding team. Lily waded back out on to dry land, her wet thongs squeaking against her feet. She made one last lunge for the prize but was nowhere near fast enough to catch a six-year-old Koolie who regularly kept mobs of up to three hundred sheep in line. The star athlete trotted toward Harry where he sat on his favourite log and looked up lovingly, with complete doggy trust that his master would help to defend his prize to the death if need be. Harry held his hand out for the slobbery ball. He was born for such tasks after all.

His throw deliberately sent the ball as far upriver as possible, so that by the time Bo swam into the deeper, faster current, he would be able to retrieve it and still paddle back without ending up too far downstream where thick scrub and sinkholes lined the riverbanks. Perhaps he should clear a little more ti-tree away on this side. It tended to creep its way back up the hill if he left it for too long. Harry shook his head. Not his problem for much longer. What happened to the farm in the future would be beyond his control. If the new owners decided to clear the entire south-western corner that was currently pristine bushland, he would be powerless to complain. His eyes drifted to the thick line of trees that marked the northern edge of the buffer zone between farmed pastureland and the precious patch of the Langleys' property that needed to remain hidden. Annie was right. The idea of anyone making that area any more accessible made his skin crawl, but he could see no way to retain any influence over the land he was bound to.

Harry was not usually violent. In fact, other than the night of Annie's eighteenth birthday when he'd punched Lucas, Harry had only ever hurt two people before. One was on his last ever day of school, when Stumpy Johnson had been set upon by a couple of Year 9 cowards. They seemed to think Stumpy's eagerness to join in any ball game on the go gave them licence to teach a nine-year-old a hard lesson. Luckily one good shove, followed by a look that felt as if it could have told the moon to start spinning backward, had taught both the bullies a better lesson. The other person Harry had punched had literally begged him to do it, and he still hadn't forgiven Annie or himself for it. Since Lucas had been around though, he'd been conveniently available whenever Harry had needed to let off some steam, and the previous night's conversation had been another close call. When Lucas had first suggested his idea that Dave and Sarah buy the farm, the fury that exploded inside Harry's chest had been almost impossible to control. The idea of David Ashbree living in *his home*, with *his Guardian*, was a tough one to swallow. Not that he disliked the guy—it was simply that Dave had everything Harry had ever wanted, and now it looked like he was also going to get everything Harry already had and loved. Yet he couldn't deny that it was a good solution. From a practical standpoint, at least, it was perfect. Sarah would be settled close by, and not be pressured to move out of town. Harry would clear his debts without having to sell to any of the larger operators who might strip the land for every cent of profit they could squeeze regardless of the impact on the area, and with a bit of luck, Dave might be gently influenced to leave certain areas of the property alone. From a practical standpoint, selling to David Ashbree was a simple decision, but practical could also be heartbreaking.

Perhaps, once the details were all finalised, he would escape for a while. Annie and her mum did it often enough, and it seemed to do them good. His soul belonged in Eden, and if his heart couldn't be where it belonged, then maybe it was time to let his soul, at least, find some peace. Uncle was gone now, and he would no longer have a responsibility to the farm. He was free. He wasn't needed. No one needed him. No one.

Eden called. He had barely spent any time there, not since he was a child and had refused to come home. Not since the day that Annie's mum had found him playing by the sparkling river with Annie and gathered him into her arms. His parents were asking for him, she'd said. They had to go to Melbourne, and wanted to see him before they left. She'd spent almost an hour trying to explain things to him, but a nine-year-old boy with the run of Paradise was hard to convince, and she couldn't use force of any kind. Free choice was sacred in the Garden. He'd seen them later, of course, but by then his dad had been firmly trapped in the clutches of the legal system, unable to speak the truth that would have filled the holes in his testimony and potentially bought his freedom. Some prices were just too high to pay. If only Harry had listened that day. If only he'd paid attention to what Kiah had been trying to tell him. He could feel her, even now, in the subtle way all Cherubim could sense each other—her bruised and fragile presence still played its part to enhance his own connection to the land. The land that was whispering to him that things were not well …

As he raised his head to look southward, time seemed to freeze. All was not well. He was needed. And this time he was not a child, and not distracted by the ambrosial perfection of the River he was playing in. This time, nothing would stop him from saving his family.

The thick column of muddy grey smoke rose up over the trees like a serpent about to strike. If the northerly gusts could just settle a little, then just maybe there would be time to contain the blaze before the column became a suffocating death shroud.

Chapter 30

Lucas must have found his parents' car keys because Annie could hear the rumble behind her as he over-revved the engine and skidded on the dry gravel. Harry's dirt bike was good, but would be nowhere near fast enough to out-run the Gracewoods' Commodore once they made it to the road. So she didn't take the road. Slowing just enough to take the turn safely, she leant over the handle bars so her head wouldn't be removed by the low-hanging branches of the trees in the old laneway. The narrow track was barely discernible these days. Left over from a time when two families had shared the care of one big sheep station, the laneway cut through from one house to the other in a much more direct line. Of course, there was a good reason why a new road had been built once cars began to populate the region. Stock horses didn't complain as much as cars did when the path they were on took them through steep rocky gullies and a natural spring. Lucas lost a precious few minutes finding that out the hard way. Commodores were pretty reliable, but not really designed for off-roading. A few heart-stopping moments airborne reminded Annie that dirt bikes weren't always as foot-sure as horses either. It didn't slow her down though. She was far too terrified to be able to behave sensibly.

Hot gusts of acrid wind whipped the foliage aside for long enough to notice a boggy patch of sand ahead that normally held enough water to entice the sheep out here. Now it was just a flat patch of dead weeds and stubborn sedge that poked up like a traffic warning—so she swerved beautifully and got stabbed in the shin by a stick instead. She sped up again as soon as the sand gave way to rock a moment later.

What had happened? Hay shed fires were an all too common result of storing wet hay. Had the hay been damp? Should they have left it for another day of scorching weather to cure a bit more? With rain predicted for the next few days, they'd decided not to wait, but it had been dry enough, she was certain. She had checked all her bales carefully. Had her mum been as vigilant? Last month she'd accidentally left the garden hose running all night. The veggies had loved it, but in December, after one of the driest years Annie could remember, it had been a disturbing lapse. It was getting steadily more apparent that her mother was finding it difficult to care about her day-to-day responsibilities. Just in the past week, if Annie hadn't written notes on the fridge each day outlining what needed to get done, by now the sheep would have escaped from two new fence holes, the east paddock wouldn't have any water to it, and they wouldn't have had any washing powder, sunscreen or bread left.

Sliding the bike around the bunch of rocks at the top of a small bluff, Annie got her first good look at the conflagration that used to be their main hay storage shed, and the three other spot fires that were just learning to dance, and she thanked God that she hadn't let her mum take care of checking the fire-fighting equipment this season.

Chapter 31

'Stay here, by the water,' Harry directed, looking each person in the eye for as long as his patience would allow. 'I need to be able to find you if anything unexpected happens.'

Naomi Gracewood grabbed her daughter by the wrist and pulled her close, as if she expected Lily to go running off into the bush. 'Are we in any danger?' she asked Harry, not sounding too anxious, but obviously not completely lulled by his gift.

He smiled at her, and looked her right in the eye, hoping the effect would last for a while after he'd gone. 'No. The wind is blowing from the north, so even if the fire doesn't get contained quickly, it will head away from here. If anything changes, someone will come and get you, which is why it's important that you stay where we can find you.'

Kelly's dad piped in, 'Harry, maybe we should all go straight to my place in town. You don't need to be worrying about our safety as well. They're not exactly accustomed to having fires so close—even small ones. I'll come back and give you a hand once they're settled. I think David would like to get the twins and Sarah well away from here.'

Harry looked at the way Dave was pacing along the riverbank, and a sharp stab of jealousy rocked him. What right did he have to fret for the safety of *his* appointed Guardian? Every right. And every reason. It would be hard to convince Sarah to leave. Or would it? Would her mothering instincts outweigh her Guardian compulsion? Could he do anything to soothe her into following one and resisting the other? Perhaps, if he had more time.

'Fair enough,' he agreed. 'But don't head straight there. You don't want to be caught out on the south road. Head north instead, go up to Chentyn and take the highway east, then back down. I'll call you when I can.'

A sharp whistle had Bo jumping onto the back of the ute, and every-one else piled on just as obediently. Both cars made good time getting back to the house.

Sarah was waiting on the front step, and looked like she would have run over to them if she'd been able to decide which of the two drivers to run to. Instead she stood gripping the porch railing, shooting fright-ened glances at Harry while all the passengers disembarked from the two utes. 'I've called it in. The fire brigade's CFA on its way. Annie and Lucas have just gone over there.' If she realised the implications of what that meant for Annie, her steely gaze didn't betray it.

Without replying, Harry drove up to the shed and diverted his attention to loading up all the fire-fighting equipment he had. Peter Gracewood helped him to lift the generator, and then the pump, secur-ing it all in place so it could be operated directly from the back of the ute.

'Could you please take Bo with you into town?' Harry asked him.

'The Ashbrees will take him, I'm sure. I'm staying to help you,' Peter said. 'Just tell me what you want me to do.'

Harry opened his mouth to argue. If he knew Annie, there was a good chance that at least minor healing would be needed before this was over. At the very least there would be some conversations with Annie's mum that they couldn't have outsiders overhearing. And at the back of his mind was the worrying memory of the attack on Uncle Willie, but surely that was all over and done with?

The look in Peter's eyes made him pause.

'My son is over there,' Peter reminded him.

Harry nodded. Arguing would do him no good. 'The more help, the better. Thank you.'

'Then I'm coming too,' a heavenly voice spoke from behind him. Harry kept his eyes forward, wishing he could shield himself from Sarah's emotions the way Annie would have. He didn't need her gift to be able to read them.

'Sarah, you're staying with the twins. David will take you into town with everyone else,' Peter told her in a firm voice.

Harry winced. Never try to tell a Guardian what to do when her charge is heading for danger. That might as well have been his family's motto. He should have had it carved somewhere, in Latin, under a fam-ily crest with a tree and a shepherd's crook. Did Sarah ever get violent?

He turned, breathing deeply at the sight of her gripping her long blond braid and trembling with barely leashed tension. How easy it would be to pretend that she cared about him, but he knew it was just instinct. Powerful instinct, but that still wasn't the same thing.

'Just get in the car,' he told her, nodding toward the passenger side and trying to think past the fact that she was finally meeting his eyes. 'I'll explain to Dave.'

'No need,' she said, heading for the cab. 'I already told him. He's getting the boys sorted. We need to go now.'

She was hurrying him *into* the danger zone? That could only mean that the risk to him was likely to get even worse if they didn't hurry. Or that she wanted to make sure no one had a chance to stop her from tagging along. Either way, the family motto held good advice. He jumped in and started the engine just as Peter squeezed into the cab as well.

'Is Annie's mum home?' Peter asked. 'What do you think's happened?'

'They've been storing hay recently, so my guess is that it's a shed fire,' Harry replied.

Sarah clutched at the dashboard. 'Neither Annie or her mum would be careless enough to do anything that might start a fire.'

Even with her eyes fixed firmly on the road ahead, Harry knew what she was trying to imply. She wanted him to be ready in case the people who had attacked his uncle had returned.

Harry shook his head. 'Hay sheds are notorious for spontaneous combustion. Microbial activity in damp bales can heat up the inside of a large stack to over seventy degrees before starting a chain reaction. Then it only takes a gust of wind at the right time to ignite.'

Peter nodded. Sarah didn't react at all.

The drive down the road felt slow, and yet somehow also far too short. It was hard for Harry to keep his thoughts on the practicalities of what he would need to do once they arrived, because Sarah's thigh and shoulder were pressed up against him. Three people in a two-person cab in an emergency situation made for the perfect excuse to touch, and he hated that he was thinking that way. He knew Sarah needed the contact, and he certainly wanted it, but he sternly forced himself to keep up the speed and not be tempted to prolong the trip, even for a few stolen moments. That temptation fled as soon as they turned into Annie's driveway and hit the thick wall of smoke that roiled toward them, eclipsing the sky and sucking the energy from the air.

As they crossed the cattle grate into the home paddock, ash rained down like evil-fairy dust, filling the air with flurries of sparkling projectiles. Every now and then a flaming ember would drop from above and voraciously attack whatever it landed on. Harry stopped the ute, jumped out and peered through the gloom, his eyes and throat stinging. The small hay shed was a lost cause, and two spot fires had already had time to burn themselves out, having insufficient fuel to keep them from spreading. Annie had kept the place sensibly prepared for summer, but one spot fire had set and was spreading quickly toward the lambing paddock, where clumps of gorse and salt bush helplessly waited to be consumed. Another was devouring the bushes down near the river. Blinking away smoke tears, Harry scanned the place for more evidence of spot fires, and that was when he noticed the smoke curling from the bathroom window of the main house.

Fires generally travelled to the south-east, driven by the hot northerlies that blew in from the desert, so Annie's farm, like most in the area, had been laid out to minimise the risk of embers spreading to other buildings. Their main hay shed had been erected a good two hundred metres south of the house, and it was stacked full of bales from the first cut of the season. They also had a smaller, older shed, much closer to the house that hadn't been used for years. Unfortunately, this year's dry conditions had pushed it back into service to store the smaller bales— the dregs of pasture that they wouldn't normally even bother cutting. That shed was now just a blazing ball of flames and it seemed obvious that the fire had started there, yet it still made no sense. The wind was gusting strongly, in the wrong direction to spread toward the house, only there was no doubt that the house was under attack. Even though there was no sign of any humans or Cherubim, Harry knew exactly where they were.

'Peter, can you take the ute down to the tree line over there?' Harry asked, far more calmly than he felt. He wanted to run. Find Annie and Lucas and Kiah. His stomach was roiling. 'Water down the grass between the spot fire and the paddock as much as you can. Grass fires are quick, so you need to start well ahead of it. If you can't, and it crosses the fence line, just get out of there. I'm going to get Annie's equipment running.'

'Can you see Lucas anywhere?' Peter asked, peering toward the house. Had he noticed the window? From the front, the house still looked perfectly normal, if you didn't know what to look for. Walls of rendered brick could withstand quite a lot, but everything inside was still very vulnerable. It looked like the fire was in the back corner, or possibly in the lounge or bathroom.

Harry gripped Peter's elbow and locked on to his worried face, almost bludgeoning him with his gift. 'I'll make certain he's safe. You can trust me. I know exactly what to do.'

With a disconcerted frown, Peter nodded and took zombie-like backward steps toward the driver's door. Harry didn't waste time watching him leave. He ran to the water tank by the house and flipped a lever that he had helped to install just a few months before Annie's dad had died. '*Someday,*' her dad had told him, '*all houses will have these. They'll make them compulsory. So what if you use up your tank water if it stops your gutters from burning?*'

Had Annie's dad realised his actions would defend his bonded charge even after he'd gone?

Stepping back, Harry watched the sprinklers come to life as they shot precious cool water across the surface of the roof. It turned to steam within moments. That was when he heard the scream. It wasn't a girly squeal or even a frightened reaction to a huntsman spider dropping from the sun visor. The sound was more like a roar of despair and outrage, ripped from the throat of a man who was being compelled to go somewhere he couldn't get to.

Chapter 32

Broken glass crunched under Annie's boots from where she'd smashed the lower pane with a rock and pulled chunks of it out of the frame. She'd wrapped her cotton shirt around her hand so she could work more quickly, so now she shook it out, hoping it was free from glass shards as she prepared to wrap it around her face.

Lucas appeared from around the corner, looking as unstoppable as a cyclone. 'It's not going to happen, Annie,' he rasped, his strong arms like a vice around her waist, pulling her away from the window.

'Let me go. She's right *there*,' she cried, elbowing him in the gut. He grunted, but didn't loosen his grip. 'Mum! Please, listen to me,' she called. 'I need you! I need you to fight this. Please try.' She had no idea if her mum could even hear her. She'd probably been asleep when the fire had started, and yet she could hear the smoke alarm still dutifully blaring in the hallway, so there was no good reason why she would have just sat in the lounge room and let it spread. No sane reason, anyway.

Wriggling against Lucas's tight grip, the only thing Annie could see through the broken window was a thick band of smoke curling across the carpet. Something fell from the ceiling, and she could hear things cracking and breaking up there. It was too dark to see more, and then Lucas hauled her away again, lifting her right off her feet. Suddenly the curtains exploded into bright flame, right by the window she had been attempting to climb through, briefly lighting the scene with an orange glow. There, on the far side of the room, she thought she saw a hand with a golden set of wedding rings on the floor near the edge of the couch, and then the darkness closed in again as the flame light reflected off the impenetrable wall of smoke.

In sheer violent panic, Annie threw her head back and felt it connect with something, then she dropped to the ground like a tonne of bricks, the surprise tactic gaining her a precious moment of freedom. It was enough for her to launch her body through the broken window, kicking backward as she went and trying to ignore Lucas's second grunt of pain.

'You'll get lost in there, Annie.' His voice was even more hoarse than usual. 'You won't find …' The rest of his sentence was lost in the sound of exploding glass as the window pane above them shattered. Pressure around her right calf disappeared and she realised he must have had a grip on her leg.

'I know *exactly* where she is,' she tried to assure him, but her voice was soundless, stolen from her lips by the incredible heat that dried her throat and tongue. Coughing, she tried to keep the bitter smoke out of her lungs and kept crawling.

The room wasn't all that big, and even with her eyes squeezed shut against the sting, she could feel where she needed to go. Surely she was nearly there. Something stung her arm, and the back of her shoulder, but she couldn't even open her eyes to see what it was because she felt as if her eyeballs would shrivel up if she did. Then the heel of her hand caught a melted patch of carpet where an ember had fallen, and she snatched it back just as another burning chunk fell into her hair. She shook it out like it was a spider, trying not to panic. Just a few more feet, surely. Had she passed the coffee table yet? She tried to feel for it, and found only a messy pile of smouldering newspapers and TV guides. To her left she could hear the intermittent bleeping of the smoke alarm in the hallway, now apparently on the floor and melting, still trying to do its job even in its death throes. The one outside her bedroom had taken up the call of duty, so maybe the rest of the house wasn't so bad yet. A few seconds later, her left knee caught on something large and sharp that cut through her skin, but her reflexive cry was cut short by choking fumes. Reaching down, she pulled the object free and found that it was a broken piece of wood, long and squared off—a leg from the coffee table? Why was it broken? She crawled faster, trying to clear a path through the mess of busted up wood and shake free from falling embers at the same time. She tried to call to out to her mum, except all she did was cough again, each intake of breath forcing even more sting-ing fumes down her throat.

Heat from above radiated down like growing tendrils of death, so she knew there was fire in the roof cavity, and that it was spreading rapidly. Bits of burning insulation fell like rain from a spot in the corner where a chunk of plaster had broken away, and she wondered how long the rest of the ceiling would hold.

From just ahead came a muffled groan, and Annie lunged forward, her head hitting the couch cushion. She used it as a guide, crawling around it until her chin slammed into her mother's knee. She wasn't likely to win any prizes for a suave rescue, but that didn't matter. Annie grabbed her mum into a tight hug and refused to let go, even when the door they were leaning against gave way. They fell together into the hallway, and Annie realised that she hadn't known what real heat was until that moment. Always before—even on the most scorching summer days—she had felt somehow comforted by the feel of heat on her skin. Perhaps some part of her had always craved her Guardian's healing touch. This thick air was another matter altogether. Vicious. Tearing and biting and hungry for pain. Death seemed very, very close, and she was more scared than she could ever remember being. She clung to her mother like she was a baby again, burying her face in her shoulder. There was no ceiling left out here, only burning plaster and insulation. Glass smashed nearby, and she knew it was the photo of her parents that had hung on the wall next to the plaster cast of her hand she'd made in kindergarten.

'Keep moving,' her mum rasped.

'I'm not going without you. If you want to die, then do it the right way, not here!' Annie snarled, her stinging lips brushing her mother's ear.

'What? I'm not …' Although her words were lost in the blackness, Annie felt the emotion behind them as clearly as she ever had, and it surprised her. Her mother was frightened, of course, but far stronger than that—she was furious. Then nothing. She'd blacked out again.

In desperation, Annie dragged her back into the burning lounge room to shelter from the heat behind the wall. That was when she noticed that her mother's wrists and ankles were cable-tied together.

Her mother's fury became her own, and Annie used it to focus, and to drag them both back toward the window, toward the promise of delicious air. Her lungs screamed for oxygen but all they got was more chemical poison as everything above them started to melt. She made it almost to the far side of the broken coffee table before something hit the back of her head. Pain stunned her, and even though she was excellent at holding her breath, she found she was no longer able to keep the poisonous fumes from snatching away her consciousness.

Chapter 33

Harry rounded the corner of the house just in time to see Lucas crawl through the lower panel of the smashed window and disappear into the lounge room. Thick black smoke spewed out of the room, all but obscuring the brief glimpse he had of the blood that dripped down his friend's face. There was a burning curtain rod sticking out through the upper window pane, and Harry hoped none of the glass shards had reached Lucas's eyes when it had smashed through.

'Don't even think about it,' Sarah commanded, emerging from the opposite corner of the house with a running hose in her hands. She'd been quick to get organised and find water. She was equally quick to soak him with it, ruthlessly dousing his clothes and hair.

'Forget me! Aim it through the window,' Harry said, stepping back a little so Sarah could concentrate on something other than the danger to him. She frowned, clearly conflicted. 'I won't come any closer,' he assured her with his hands up like she was arresting him. He tried to soothe her, but was unable to focus well enough for it to work. Luckily, her common sense kicked in, and she started to hose down as much of the interior of the room as she could reach. Mere seconds had passed since Lucas had disappeared into the death trap, and already there was no way Harry could see where he was in the gloom. He could guess though.

'Aim a bit more to the right,' he advised, coming to stand behind his Guardian so he could hold her shoulders and guide her to where he could sense the other Cherubim. Steam hissed and sputtered as the flaming curtain was doused, and he hoped that the steam didn't do the people inside even more damage.

A dull thud and a groan issued from inside. Without hesitation,

Sarah dropped the hose and reached in through the window. When she pulled back, her fist was clutching Lucas's shirt, guiding him out. He had his eyes mostly closed and his face was bleeding badly, but he was coughing and swearing like a trooper. Harry started to pull him out, head first, until Lucas twisted around and out of reach. Something exploded from deep inside the inferno, and the brick wall Harry's hand was braced against shuddered as if the house was trying to shake the fire off its back. More cracking noises followed, and then Sarah's shoulder hit him hard at the base of his throat, throwing him backward just as something hooked around his ankle. Sprawled among the trampled flowers and broken glass, he looked up in utter bewilderment at the woman who was not supposed to ever be able to cause him physical pain. Her leaf-green eyes held a frightening combination of resolve and terror against a backdrop of fresh flames.

'Sarah, no!' Realising why he couldn't sit up, he tried to dislodge her foot from his sternum, but she dropped down on top of him, pinned his wrists to the ground and dug her knee brutally into his abdomen. Glass crunched under his back and he could feel a good-sized piece of it slice into his shoulder, yet she didn't let him move. Above him, her face was contorted into such a pained expression that he knew she felt everything that he did—perhaps even more strongly. She still didn't release him. With a sickening lurch, he realised exactly what that meant. He knew he could throw her off. He had the strength, and the will power. Annie was in there, and her mother, and his best friend. He was not going to just lie down and let them burn.

'Wait,' Sarah gasped, tears streaming down her face.

'What? No. Let me go!'

'Just a few more seconds,' she begged, hair like fine satin thread whipping around her face from the confused eddies of hot wind.

A few more seconds? Until what? He had to get them out. Bracing himself against the ground, glass and all, he prepared to throw her off to the side, hoping he could keep her clear of the sharp debris that littered the grass around them, but as he tensed to move, her lips found his in a kiss designed solely to delay any action.

It worked. Stunned by the sudden thrill of the feel of her, he lay there, completely powerless to gather even a coherent thought, let alone movement. Heat flared, and everything hurt, and then the pain was overwhelmed by a flood of other sensations. He wanted her. To touch and be touched, to hold her and know her. He longed to make her laugh and to tangle his fingers in hers. Her mouth was so soft. He'd been waiting for so long, and now she was using his passion against him and they were both burning for it. Even his ears were filled with the sound of the world caving in—as if the Earth had only existed to get them both to this moment and was no longer required. Well aware that she had betrayed him, he still couldn't fault her for it. Not when he could feel the air pressure change and hear everything explode behind her. With a cry of pain, she pulled away, rolling onto her back as flames flicked out toward them. Finally, Harry could see what had happened. Through the blackness of the smoke, the dim view through the window was one of utter chaos. Flames now began to spontaneously appear, showing the devastating truth. He was too late. The ceiling had collapsed entirely.

'Get up,' Sarah croaked, tugging on his arm.

Harry lay dazed, staring at the house, wondering why his Guardian kept hurting him. Surely he was safe now? She'd done her job. If she hadn't, he would have been somewhere in that churning hell, trapped under those burning slabs of plaster and wood with the only people in this world that really cared for him.

'For Heaven's sake, Harry, move! I can't do this on my own and it's hard enough to let you be here at all. Can't you see that I'd rather just let you lie there? Move. Before I change my mind!'

Never argue with a Guardian when her charge is in danger … Rolling onto his side with a groan, Harry did what he was told, and then cried out when Sarah gripped his shoulder and took hold of the piece of glass that was still lodged in it. She threw it away with a fury that made him glad he'd obeyed. She was in no mood to be messed with. For that matter, neither was he. The heat was building even more as the fire found new fuel, and it was relishing the sudden feast of fresh air that it had gained since breaking free from the roof cavity.

'You know where they are. Help me,' Sarah said, coughing as she reached in and pulled away a broken sheet of plaster. Clarity returned as he watched her bravely fight every instinct she had—both natural and supernatural—to save the people trapped inside. She hadn't been cruel, or weak. She'd felt exactly what would have happened if she'd let him go when he'd wanted to. He would have been yet another body to be rescued. Instead, he was whole, and awake, and useful. Or at least he would be if he could just make his brain start working again.

'Don't worry about that one,' he gasped, choking on the burning stench. His eyes stung as he forced them to stay open, trying to discern which bits of broken debris were worth shifting. Annie was not far away, just a metre or two, but she might as well have been on the moon for the impenetrable wall of heat between them. Was the fallen ceiling still shielding his friends from the deadly temperature?

'Get the hose.' He pulled Sarah back and shoved her toward the only weapon they could really use. Luckily, this instruction was close enough to what her compulsion wanted her to do anyway that she didn't hesitate, pouncing on the writhing snake and dousing him from head to toe. With his damp clothes shielding him from some of the heat, he crawled in through the window, shoving as much plaster and burning rubbish away as he could. Palms burning, he almost missed the feel of movement under him. An almighty heave shifted a giant piece of plasterboard just enough to free Lucas's head and shoulders from where he'd been pinned down. He was conscious, and groaning. Sarah must have seen something because water drenched them both, rousing him even more. Flames brightened the blackness every few seconds, and from Sarah's torn cry he knew they had very little time before the room would hit its flashpoint, and then they would all be dead.

For over a year Harry had worked side by side with Lucas, and so now, both knowing exactly where Annie was, they worked in seamless coordination, knowing just when to lift, to drag, to change grip, feeling when the other was faltering, and knowing exactly how to help. And yet the task felt so slow. A wide section of ceiling was wedged firmly between the TV and the side wall of the room, and they needed to break it up in order to have any hope whatsoever of shifting it. The problem was, it was still far too solid to easily shatter, braced as it was with the remaining timber, and they had nothing at all that could be used as a tool. Choking fumes and searing heat made every movement excruciatingly slow and heavy, and it took precious time for Harry to finally find an edge he could lever up. As soon as he did, though, unexpected help appeared. Annie's mother, barely breathing, but astonishingly calm, pushed the remaining half of the coffee table with her feet so that it held up the corner of the slab that the boys were straining to lift.

How she even knew what they were doing seemed miraculous, let alone be able to engineer a solution amid the dark chaos. It seemed to use the last of her strength, because she collapsed with her outstretched hands reaching for Harry's, her lips mumbling a quiet prayer. He grasped for her wrists and felt something thin and tight—a cable tie? Her wrists were bound? At that moment Harry felt something new. A pulse, like liquid power, ephemeral as a word on the breeze, and then gone as her fingers slipped away, and yet it was enough. Something changed in the air, causing his hair to stand on end. Lucas noticed it too, and paused to look around. It felt like the world had been put on hold, and they were the only living things still allowed to move. Unexpected silence fell heavily. Even the voracious flames seemed to suspend their dance as if waiting … listening to a command that could not be ignored.

A Command. Spoken, and felt, yet barely heard because her voice was as weak as her tortured breath. A fragile voice with a crushing authority.

Three living Cherubim. All just moments from death, and none to carry on the line. Harry blinked away the smoke. Had that been trigger enough? Had Kiah felt the compulsion to act, the way the stories always hinted that they could? For years Annie had pestered him with questions and speculations about what they might be able to do, and it wasn't like they didn't *believe* they could—yet no amount of waving their hands about or praying or commanding had ever done a thing except make them both laugh at their own absurdity. Finally, Harry had told Annie to just concentrate on learning to control the gifts they already struggled with and not invite any more drama to their already crazy lives. Now when the drama had gate-crashed anyway, he still didn't know what to do.

Lucas didn't pause for long. He dived under the broken coffee table to grab at the tangle of limbs beyond. Kiah and Annie were both there, Harry knew, and both beyond the point where they could help themselves in any way. Sure enough, when Lucas twisted back, he was pulling Annie's mother by the shoulders, her head flopped to one side. Harry took over as soon as he could so Lucas could go back for Annie, while the fire glared down at them in anger, temporarily thwarted from the feasting it felt it deserved. Even the heat itself felt restricted from reaching them with its full force, and somehow Harry could feel the strain on each and every molecule that obediently refrained from spinning and colliding and breaking and bonding as it wanted to.

A long minute later they reached the window again, coughing and gasping and trying not to succumb to the dizziness.

'I have her,' Sarah said, gasping the words out through smoke and anger and fright. 'Wait, her shoulder is caught on that bit of glass … okay, you can let go now. Harry, let go.'

Oxygen-starved muscles refused to obey Harry's commands, but Sarah somehow managed to take Kiah from him anyway. Harry tumbled out of the window a moment later, falling heavily and barely managing to avoid the mess of broken glass. Lucas fared better, even with Annie in his arms, except he was obviously having trouble seeing through the sting of smoke and blood that he couldn't blink away, so Harry led him over to the grass where he flopped down with Annie cradled in his lap. Almost negligently, Lucas smacked at the hem of his board shorts until the flames went out. When he coughed, little puffs of smoke came out of his mouth, and Harry wondered whether Peter Gracewood would ever forgive him. There were shards of broken glass in Lucas's tousled hair and a large gash across his cheek and another above his eye that were bleeding profusely. His right elbow had clearly been used to protect his face when the window had exploded, because it was also dripping crimson mess onto the grass where he was crouched. His face looked grim and determined as he laid Annie down and leant over her unconscious form, blinking to try to clear his vision. Gentle as a mother cat, Lucas lifted her head and placed a hand behind it. A spasm rocked him, and Harry gripped his shoulder to keep him upright. Annie still didn't move.

'Just focus on one injury at a time,' Harry advised in a barely audible gasp, trying to remember all the things he'd learned from watching his and Annie's parents over the years. There wasn't a lot to go on.

Lucas let out a distraught sob and rubbed his eyes, leaving a smear of blood across his nose. His hands were shaking.

'It's okay, Lucas,' Harry soothed. 'Some injuries just take a little more effort to heal. Calm down, breathe, and try again.'

His friend's obedient inhalation brought on more coughing, but he looked a bit steadier as he supported Annie's head with both his hands, his fingers tangled in her bloodied hair. Her eyes opened a second later, and her whole body went rigid. She opened her mouth to scream, and then gagged as her intake of air pulled the smoke further in. Her eyes locked on to the face of her Guardian, she gave two giant coughs to expel the residual poison from her lungs, and then she threw her arms around his neck. Harry just managed to help her to ease Lucas back onto the grass before he passed out with twitching limbs and a relieved smile on his face.

Chapter 34

The blessed sound of sirens filled the air with the promise of relief. Annie tried to ignore the things that she didn't know how to react to, and focus on the things she was overwhelmingly grateful for. Her mother was alive, although out cold, her grey complexion betraying just how much stress her body was under. Annie chose to ignore the irregular pattern of her mother's breathing that barely made her chest move, as well as the bruise that was forming on her left cheekbone where someone had hit her before abandoning her to the flames. She also chose to ignore the way Sarah was clinging to Harry so tightly, still dizzy from healing his wounds and poisoned lungs and not yet willing to let him go. All of them knew full well that it wouldn't last. What Annie couldn't ignore was the sight of her mum's hands and ankles bound together with cable ties. A nearby shard of glass fixed that problem, and then she shoved the cables into the pocket of her shorts so she wouldn't lose them. At some point she would need to show them to the police, but not until she could be certain it wouldn't compromise their secret. What if they dredged up old questions about the missing necklace? She needed more time to think.

Behind them the hose was still flipping round, exuberantly trying to fight the fire on its own. Her house was burning down. She should probably be doing something about that, but just because she was in sudden perfect physical health didn't mean she had a hope of functioning normally. Not when her mum and Lucas were still unconscious. What she did do was to capture the wayward hosepipe and gulp down a few ambrosial mouthfuls of water before handing it over to Harry and Sarah. After that she carefully inspected every inch of Lucas's face, gently picking off fragments of glass from the many cuts he'd sustained. One of them looked very deep, just under his eye. It would need stitches for sure. The gash along his elbow was a mess of blood and ash, and she drew out a decent chunk of her lounge room window from near his wrist, struggling not to think about the way all those cuts proved undeniably that Lucas was destined to be cursed, no matter how stubbornly she kept trying to push him away.

'My Guardian angel,' her mum rasped, squinting at Lucas through bloodshot, gummy eyes.

Squeaking a little in relief, Annie leant over her, but her mum started coughing and then her eyes glazed over again. Was she lucid enough to realise it wasn't her husband lying there? Had this new trauma pushed her mind too far over the edge to ever come back?

A man appeared from around the corner of the house. He wore a yellow coat with the Country Fire Authority logo and a helmet with the visor up. He took one look at them all and waved to his companions for assistance. Annie saw Harry whisper something in Sarah's ear, and then peel her arms from around his waist.

'No one's inside anymore,' Harry called to the fireman, 'but a quick ambulance would be good. And the police. And there's one more person, fighting a spot fire down past the hay shed. Can you please tell him his son needs him?'

'What injuries are we dealing with?' the man asked.

'Smoke inhalation, possible head trauma and some lacerations,' Harry replied.

And a nasty dose of Guardian healing kickback, Annie added silently.

'I'll get some oxygen for them,' the man said, racing off again.

As if to further dramatise the situation, another window burst, this time in the bathroom, spraying glass across the white azalea bush. Her mum had planted that when they'd buried Annie's guinea pig there. A flash of something large and red distracted her from the memory as the pumper appeared at the back corner of the house, where the fire had probably been started in the gutter to make it look accidental. If she hadn't known better, Annie would have assumed that the hay shed had caught fire and then spread to the house. Someone had planned this. In a way, they were lucky that this attack had involved a potential bushfire—a threat to the surrounding area, including the valley where Eden was hidden. If she hadn't been able to sense that threat in time, would they ever have even questioned these events?

From what she could see, only the back rooms had so far succumbed to the flames. Perhaps the crew could salvage something of her home. She wished they could salvage something of her family.

❧

Luckily, Lucas was awake by the time his dad came running toward them, although he was still disoriented from healing Annie and the CFA captain had told him three times already not to sit up. She realised that meant she must have been pretty unwell. Maybe she should have let him practise more often on the minor bumps and bruises she constantly accumulated.

As Peter approached, his eyes flicked down to where she was gripping Lucas's hand. He didn't comment. Instead, he crouched down next to them and addressed his son in a low, concerned voice.

'Lou, how are you feeling?'

He had the same strong jaw line and fine cheekbones as his son, only his eyes were darker, smoky grey and serious as he inspected the lacerations across Lucas's face.

'Fine. Much better,' Lucas mumbled, shoving aside his oxygen mask. 'She feels like fizzy drink when we touch.'

'They're only giving him oxygen,' Annie said quickly, trying to put the mask back on him. 'So I don't know why he's rambling.'

Lucas batted it away and displayed his adorable but blood-streaked dimples. 'She looks incredible in those shorts, don't you think, Dad?'

'Put the mask on, Lucas,' Annie said.

'And she moves like a whisper. A caramel-filled whisper. And her curves make me dizzy.'

His eyelids were still gummed together and he'd been ordered to keep them shut for as long as possible, but that didn't prevent him from turning his face precisely toward hers. Peter's gaze followed, his eyebrows slightly raised, and that was when she remembered that she'd used her shirt to pull broken glass from the window frame. It was one of those times when growing up around mostly nude people was a disadvantage, because sitting around in just her bra hadn't even registered as being abnormal. Thankfully her stumbling explanation for why she was semi-naked was met with sombre approval.

'Lucas followed you in?' Peter asked.

She nodded apologetically.

'And you both rescued your mother?'

Again, she nodded, unable to decide how much to tell him, so instead she allowed her gaze to be drawn once again to her mother's passive expression, her features completely slack in response to her numb emotional state and all the poisonous gasses she'd inhaled. She was supposed to be keeping her eyes closed too, but she wasn't. With the oxygen mask strapped to her face she looked even less human than usual. It concerned Annie that the captain was still standing over her, while his staff were doing all the fire-fighting.

Peter laid a comforting hand on Annie's wrist. 'She'll be fine. I'm sure the ambulance will be here soon.'

Did he realise how long it took the ambulance to arrive from town? She would have much preferred to avoid the ambulance altogether and take her mother Next Door instead, but that was out of the question. Not only would it have been nearly impossible to carry her all the way upstream—even with Harry's help—but too many outsiders had seen her in urgent need of medical attention, so there was no way she could just disappear without anyone noticing. Not to mention that Lucas still needed the more conventional style of treatment.

Suddenly Lucas sat bolt upright, blinking grit from his eyes and then staring at Annie like he'd never seen her before. Unacknowledged tension, deep inside her, released with the sprung force of a roll of fencing wire, and inappropriate laughter bubbled out of her mouth as an instinctive response to the fact that he was properly awake. Clearly he was still full of adrenaline, only there was nothing left to fight. He opened his mouth to speak, gasping a little in aftershock, then noticed his dad and snapped it closed again.

The captain took a step toward them, presumably to tell Lucas off for removing his mask and sitting up, but Lucas set his jaw and glared at him until he stepped back again.

Peter chuckled. 'He always was quick to recover from things,' he said to the captain, and then leant over to whisper in Annie's ear. 'I won't tell him what he was mumbling if you don't.' With a knowing smile, he stood up, brushing dead leaves from his shorts. 'Captain, just how long will the hay shed burn? What do we need to do? We should talk to Harry.'

He led the captain away to where Harry was washing ash off his arms with the hose, leaving Annie and Lucas to talk in semi-private. He was a very wise and considerate man.

Lucas looked down at Annie's mother, who seemed to have drifted out of consciousness again, and Annie's smile dissolved.

'She looks like you,' he whispered. 'She's so young.'

'We age well. I've been warned to use a bit of discipline as I get older, and not indulge in eating, you know, from the … special tree, too often.' Her voice trembled more than a little, but she was determined to hold it together.

'I'm surprised you age at all then, now that I think about it,' he said.

'People would notice if we didn't. As my grandmother once told me, we age at a normal rate, we just look good doing it.'

He gave a thoughtful nod.

'Lucas, I was kidding. We look like everyone expects us to. We have to.'

'No one could ever expect the sort of beauty you both have.'

She met his eyes, surprised at his bold words, and he flicked his gaze away. 'Annie, I won't …'

Her fingers felt suddenly cool as he pulled his hand from hers.

'I won't ever make you choose between us. I would never do that. Just tell me what I should do.'

'Should?' she puffed, resigned to what had to come. Her mum had been planning to move to Eden. Permanently. And Annie now wished she'd encouraged her to do it sooner. 'Where I grew up, there is no "should". Maybe that's why I've made such a mess of things.'

The welcome song of ambulance sirens echoed off the hills. The paramedics had made excellent time after all. The sound reminded her of the day she and Lucas first met, which made her wonder if she was being given a second chance to do it right, only she couldn't think of how to go about it, so she just kept staring at him.

Lucas stared right back, despite his sore eyes. 'When I saw the smoke, I was terrified that maybe you'd been right to be so worried about her, only that isn't what happened, is it? I mean, her wrists were tied … What I'm trying to say is that I understand why you keep pushing me away. I would have done the same, except now it's getting too dangerous. For some reason, your family is being targeted, and I need to be allowed to keep you and Harry safe. And your mum.'

Kiah Langley's eyes flew open, and she tried to sit up. At last Annie felt something from her, and she embraced it. Her distress felt as acrid as the smoke she'd inhaled, but Annie was well accustomed to drawing it in. Gently, she pushed her mother's shoulders back down onto the grass, but she couldn't stop her pulling the mask off.

'You pushed him away?' her mum slurred. 'Because of me?'

Vaguely Annie noticed that she was crying and told herself off. She should have been trying to find the right words to make things better. She just didn't have any. 'Shhh, you shouldn't try to speak yet, Mum,' was all she could manage. The sirens grew louder as the ambulance came through the gate to the home paddock.

'She can feel everything you feel, Mrs Langley,' her Guardian said. 'Even when it hurts her.'

The poor guy didn't seem to know where to look. For so long he'd done as Annie had asked and stayed away, and now he clearly had things he wanted to get off his chest. She knew because he was projecting a swirling mix of concern and stubborn determination.

Her mum looked up at her, confused and worried. Her bloodshot eyes were still unfocused, and with a sinking feeling Annie realised she might have done them some significant damage. How long until she could take her across the boundary? Her voice, hoarse, shaky and painfully slow, nevertheless proved that she was at least mostly lucid.

'I know that,' she said. 'And for a long time, I tried to keep my distance when it all got too much, but then I realised … when she's around I don't feel so lost. I don't feel the call to … I'm not so lonely.'

Lucas told her the truth then, his strained voice cracking. 'Yes. You are. You're just as lonely, and just as sad. She just doesn't let you feel it. She steals it away—'

He didn't get to finish because Harry was suddenly kneeling in front of them, staring at her mum with his deep brown eyes. 'Kiah, thank God you're awake. I need you to tell me what happened. Who did this?'

Annie laid a hand on his elbow. 'Harry—'

'Annie, we have to know,' Harry insisted. His fists were clenched and he was very pointedly not looking at Sarah, who was hovering nearby to listen in. 'Please, Kiah. The more secrets we keep, the more dangerous things get.'

Her mum shook her head and turned away. 'Safer if you don't know.'

'Kiah, look at me,' Harry said.

'No, Harry, don't.' Annie shoved him aside. 'Leave her alone.' She put the mask back over her mother's mouth again. The up-side was that her mother didn't protest. 'She's scared, Harry. It isn't fair to use your gift to make her talk. She'll talk to the police when she's ready.'

'But, Annie, they haven't called the police yet. I tried to tell them it was deliberately lit, but I didn't know how much to say, so they think I'm just overreacting. I think this has something—'

'I mean it, Harry. *Leave her alone.*'

It wasn't often that the two of them fought, because they could read each other so well that they could usually figure out a better way to resolve things. So when Annie flicked her eyes meaningfully over to Harry's ute, he didn't push the issue. Instead, he got up and headed over to it, knowing she would eventually follow and explain.

A young man in navy overalls appeared from around the corner, carrying a large plastic box that she knew would be packed full of other things that would steal her mum's pain away. He walked very briskly over the crunchy grass.

Fingers that used to untangle her hair on sleepy evenings in front of the telly now dug into her skin as her mum shifted her grip to read Annie's memories. The time for secrets was over, so Annie let her bitterest memories unravel from the tight ball of stress that she had so ruthlessly squeezed them into.

Her mum gasped, and tore the mask away yet again. 'You've been hiding him from me for so long. Why? Why would you do that?' She coughed again. 'You felt how much I wanted you to find him—I can read that … but … you think … I want to … leave you?'

The paramedic was drawing closer. They had no time for this.

'You've been waiting for my Guardian to turn up so you can leave for Eden permanently,' Annie said. 'I stole more than just emotions from you, Mum,' she admitted just as the paramedic approached. 'I stole an extra year with you.'

Her mum tried to reply, but both the poison in her lungs and the sudden settling of the speech embargo left her with only choked-off words and coughing. The ambulance officer crouched down and opened his kit.

'Hello, Kiah,' he said. 'I need you to lie down and let me put the mask back on—'

As the man opened various packets of equipment and checked her mum's vital signs, Annie kept hold of her hand. Her mum gripped back, so Annie closed her eyes and dredged up as many memories as she could find. Of her mum, staring out the window toward Eden, fiddling with her wedding rings. Of times, over and over again, when Annie had drawn in her mum's pain and snuck out of the room to cry. She relived the memory of her mum asking her if she planned to stay on the farm, then asking her to help fake her death. Memories of how it felt whenever her mum left her to cope on her own. The memory of her interview with the school principal, when she'd lied about where her mum was. Assuring him that her mum wasn't giving her too much farm work to do. That wasn't why she was struggling at school …

'Is she on any medication?' the paramedic asked, snapping Annie's attention away from all the painful memories she'd tried to hide for so long.

'No. Not for months.'

Her mum's fingers had gone slack. She gripped them anyway. Lucas had been right. Living with secrets had done none of them any good. If everyone had been honest from the start, none of this would have happened. Harry would never have needed to call Celarsi Holdings to try to find out about the ruby. Annie would never have needed to kiss Harry to push Lucas away, and her mum would have left for the safety of the Garden long ago instead of lying on their lawn, barely breathing. It was time for things to change. She brought her mum's hand up to her lips and kissed it. Then she closed her eyes and played through every memory that she should have let her mum see. How she'd first met Lucas on the beach, and felt his heart stop and then restart. How he'd kissed her and she'd run away. All the times he'd made her laugh. All the times he'd cared for Harry and Uncle Willie. Every dimple-filled grin. Every burning, healing touch.

By the time the second paramedic had finished checking out Lucas and had come over with the stretcher, Annie's mum was awake, and had regained a bit of colour. She watched Annie with glazed eyes and a dream-flavoured smile. When they lifted her into the ambulance, Annie was allowed to give her one last kiss on the cheek.

'All will be well now, honey,' her mum scraped out between laboured breaths. 'Everything will work out fine.'

'I know,' she replied. 'As soon as you're well enough, we'll go on a walk to that pretty place we always talk about. And you can stay there for as long as you like.'

❧

It stunned Annie how rapidly the fires were contained. The hay shed was likely to keep burning for a long time—maybe even days—but the glowing beast looked as if it was cowering in sulky protest of the punishment it was getting from the hoses. Those two pumpers could really dispense a lot of water very fast. They had refilled from the back dam twice already, and would have to move on to the hill paddock dam soon.

The CFA captain praised Annie for the roof sprinklers and short grass and sensible rendered brick farmhouse, and although she wasn't allowed within cooee of it yet, he assured her that most of the front of the house was still intact. The roof would need to be replaced, and the bathroom and lounge were gutted, but the rest of the damage was mostly caused by bits of ceiling falling on furniture. It had seemed a lot worse when she was crawling around in there though, so she reserved her judgment. She thanked the captain and then handed him back the blankets he'd provided for Lucas and her mum to lie on.

Dry leaves clattered across the driveway and piled up like tiny skeletons against the side of Annie's old sandpit, while in the distance a haze of thunderclouds stomped impatiently on the horizon, waiting for enough wind to carry them over for a visit. A tired currawong called, as if to guide the clouds to where they were so sorely needed. Wiping sweat from the tip of her nose, Annie tried hard *not* to think about what she needed to do next, and instead focused on staring down the driveway to where she'd last glimpsed the ambulance as it turned out of the driveway and back onto the road. The vehicle had carried two passengers, one who'd complained bitterly that he didn't need the stupid mask on anymore, even as the doors were being closed; the other drifting in and out of consciousness, but with a ruddier complexion than she'd had when she'd first been pulled from the fire. Annie slipped her hand into the pocket of her shorts. The cable ties were still there. Lurking. She felt as if they were still doing what they were designed to. Tying her in place, preventing her from following the ambulance and being with the people she loved.

A gentle nudge at her elbow drew her attention back. Lucas's dad looked exhausted, streaked with ash and sweat, but he had the sort of steady demeanour that made a part of her wish he would just pick her up like a child and rock her to sleep. Sadly, she didn't think he would appreciate the request, or the weight.

'Harry's going to take Sarah home,' he said. 'I was wondering if maybe I could give you a lift to the hospital, or do you need to sort things out here?'

Without really realising what she was doing, she turned and hugged him. That sentence was exactly what she needed. Peter Gracewood was someone who could think straight and tell her what to do. He held her securely, unfazed by her distress—or by the state of her undress, she realised belatedly. With the patience of a glacier, he waited for her sobs to ease up before speaking again.

'On second thought, perhaps I should take you and Sarah back to her place so Harry can keep an eye on things here. I think you need a bit of time out. Did you even tell the paramedics that you were in there too? Just because you seem to be unharmed doesn't mean you aren't in shock. Are you dizzy at all? Nauseated?'

She shook her head, touched by the guilty concern on his face. He knew she'd been in the house for at least as long as his son, who was being forced to endure a boatload of fuss over his smoke inhalation. It had taken a bit of work to draw away the medical team's concerns for her, and she didn't really want to steal anyone's emotions anymore if she could possibly avoid it, so she tried to sound less tired when she spoke. 'I'm fine, really. Just shaken. And I don't think the fire crew needs any-one here, so I'll go with Sarah and Harry and get cleaned up. You can go and make sure Lucas behaves for the doctors.'

'You really do know him well,' he said. 'I'll meet you at the hospital later, then.'

As much as she wanted to see her mum and Lucas, Annie knew that if she turned up to Nalong Memorial Hospital as she was, with her scorched hair and covered in ash, someone was sure to bundle her off to a quiet room to be checked over by an intern. And something else needed to be done first.

When she joined Harry over by his ute, Sarah was already there, glancing at them both with narrowed eyes.

Annie ignored her and spoke to Harry. 'Mum won't tell you anything because she knows you'll go after them.'

'Them who?' Sarah asked her.

'Mr Durante, and a couple of others, I think. The fool thought he was being clever to turn toward the state park when he left here instead of taking the direct way back to town. I could still sense him heading north when I arrived.'

Harry gaped at her. 'You can sense people *driving* through the park?'

'Not clearly, but I know his … emotional signature, I guess, and when I saw the fire I … searched for him.'

'Isn't that a bit of a hazy thing to go on?' Sarah asked.

'Well, yes, of course it is. Which is why we need to go—'

Sarah's reaction was immediate. She baled Harry up against the door of the ute with one knee between his legs and her elbow against his neck. She shook her head. He stared right back at her.

'What are you going to do, Sarah? Kiss me again?' His gaze flicked over to where Lucas's dad was standing over by the pumper. He'd been thanking the fire crew again, and was now blinking at them in astonishment.

With a furious grunt, Sarah let him go, but tried to grab his keys when he fished them out of his pocket. He was ready for her, though, backing away and then tossing them to Annie, who jumped into the driver's seat as nimbly as if it was an Eden game. Lucas's dad gave them an uncertain wave as she took off down the driveway in a spray of gravel and ash, with Sarah and Harry clinging to the rail at the front of the tray—not exactly legal on the road, but she'd deemed it wiser not to give the grumpy Guardian enough time to get into the cab with her.

Chapter 35

Long shadows made the quiet street look like a ghost town. It matched the feeling of emptiness in Annie's chest, as if some part of her was missing. Lost forever. Her childhood, perhaps. Nalong was a pretty sleepy town to begin with, but on a public holiday, and now after-hours, there was hardly anyone around at all. Everyone was either still celebrating with a game of backyard cricket, watching the tennis on telly, or swimming down at the river. All that was missing were tumbleweeds, although a rogue chip packet was trying hard to set the scene. The ute overtook it when it got caught on a weed growing out from a road drain.

A tentative tap echoed over Annie's head so she wound down the window.

'Are we taking the scenic route to the jewellery store?' Harry asked.

'Just gathering some assistance,' she replied. 'To keep Sarah and Lucas happy.'

She sped up and honked the horn in an offensive continuous blast that lasted the length of the street, and then deliberately slowed down— just as they passed the police station. With the window wound down, she could hear Harry groan. Sarah was laughing. Annie could feel her dancing in the tray, brazenly displaying her illegal mode of transport to the pedantic young officer who was peering out through the station window.

∾

A blue Ford Falcon was parked in the alley between the hairdresser and laundromat. Being a Ford, it wasn't so much 'parked' as it was 'lurking', and Annie wondered if the police would consider the fact that he drove a Ford enough evidence that George Durante was guilty of something. She parked the ute across the road and sat there with her hands shaking on the steering wheel until Harry opened her door.

'Do we have some sort of a plan, or are we just going to wing it and hope he gives himself in after we talk to him?' Harry asked. 'I'm guessing we only have a few minutes until that new constable finds us. How did you know he'd even be on duty today?'

'Educated guess. He's annoying enough that the others would have rostered him on so someone else could have the public holiday with their family.'

'Great.'

She peered past him at Sarah, who seemed frazzled, but not furious. Either they'd had a good chat on the way, or there was no danger that the Guardian could foresee. That would probably change as soon as their intentions were clearer in Harry's head.

'I need to know why he tried to kill Mum,' Annie said. 'And you want the full story about what happened to your parents.'

'And who hurt Uncle Willie,' he added.

'And we need to get him to either admit all this to the new constable or else we need to find some sort of proof that he was involved. We can't leave the police out of this any longer, no matter how uncomfortable it makes us feel.'

Sarah gave them an overly sweet smile. 'And we need to make sure Lucas doesn't go all Rambo at the hospital, so don't do anything stupid. Let me handle it.'

'Wait, Sarah—'

Too late. Armed only with her Guardian reflexes and a compulsion to end the threat to Harry, Sarah ducked across the road and down the alley, leaving Harry and Annie to follow.

Durante Diamonds, like most shops in the area, had an upstairs flat as well as a small add-on unit behind it. The heritage façade was painted pale lemon and white, while all the areas that couldn't be seen from the street remained a peeling grey mess, probably because the adjacent shops and rear unit made it impossible to get any useful access up that high. Of course, Annie only managed to catch a glimpse of the rear of the building before Sarah came rushing back to them, ushering them away. She literally tugged on Harry's shirt sleeve.

'The Mustang,' she said. 'It's parked at the back.'

Annie grinned. 'Excellent!'

'No. Not excellent. Dangerous. We're waiting for the police.'

'And how are we supposed to convince them to investigate this?' Harry argued, flicking Annie a subtle signal. 'We need more information.'

As if they'd practised the manoeuvre a hundred times, Harry jogged back down the alley toward the rear car park and Mustang, while Annie darted around to the other side of the building. Sarah only had one choice about who to follow.

Even in her work boots, Annie found she could climb from the wooden side fence onto the roof of the shed, and then up the drainpipe with hardly any noise. All those Eden hiding games had finally come in handy. Perching under the upstairs window was no problem, with one foot wedged against a metal gas pipe and the other on a barely protruding brick. The sound of a chair being scraped along lino made her quiet her breathing.

'I did what he asked,' a shaky voice insisted from inside the room. 'I could have just let the matter rest. You can *trust* me.'

'You told him she knew his name, not *how* she knew.' This new voice sounded younger, and very smug. Or perhaps just arrogant.

'Because I don't know! Didn't you ask her?'

'She said she was "unable to speak the words I wanted to hear". She was almost as unhelpful as you.'

'I thought you had ways of getting people to talk.'

The sound of skin hitting skin almost made Annie gasp, but she clamped her lips together just in time.

'Please! I just meant that I had no way of finding out. I mean, I could hardly ask her outright, could I? What was I supposed to say? Hey, Mrs Langley, how did you know it was Mr Rosa who sent people to warn the boy away? Did Ruby Doolan tell you before he killed her?'

Killed her? This time, when Annie heard the hit, it was accompanied by the sound of something heavy hitting the floor and she took the opportunity to peek inside, hoping whoever was in there would be distracted. They were. Two men were hauling Mr Durante—and the chair he was strapped to—upright again. The jeweller had a bleeding nose and looked very groggy. She ducked back down below the window sill.

'That was a bad idea,' the smug voice told him. 'No one speaks that name without permission, and to imply that Ruby Doolan was killed?' The man cleared his throat. 'Everyone knows she jumped from that office building. My employer was very distraught when he found out that just anyone off the street could catch a lift to the top floor and find their way up to the roof of his building. He's put in considerable time and effort to make sure such a thing never happens again.'

'But it hasn't.' Mr Durante sounded like he had a cold—or a badly broken nose. 'No one's found out anything they shouldn't.'

'He was never supposed to hear the name of this town again. *That* was your job. And yet, Kiah Langley and young Harry Doolan—both from Nalong—have been leaving messages *with his receptionist.*'

Annie nearly fell off the wall. After all her warnings to Harry to leave the past alone, her mum had left messages? What had she been thinking?

Mr Durante sounded desperate. 'My job was to let him know if there were any more rumours about the missing necklace. I did my job!'

'And are there? Is there any good reason why my employer should risk getting noticed in this backwater hovel?'

No reply.

'You want to say yes because you believe it will mean we need you, only you can't. There's been no sign of the necklace, and there are no more gems.'

'But there might be. Harry said—'

'The guy was trying to squeeze information out of you about his parents. I can't believe you fell for that. There are *no more gems.* Do you know how I know this?'

The sound of scraping and shuffling covered some of his next words.

'… caught her trying to get into his gym. As you said earlier, we have our ways to get information from people, and we can generally be certain that if they won't speak when being suspended from a height by the ankle, then it's because they have nothing to say. Shall we test it to be sure?'

When the window suddenly opened, Annie was caught staring straight into the face of a well-dressed man with pouty lips. How had she not noticed his gun on her earlier glimpse? As much as she would have loved to have said something clever and cool to accompany a nimble escape, what actually happened was that her attempt to slide down the wall was thwarted by the man's painful grip on her hair. Perhaps he would have grabbed her shirt if she'd been wearing one.

Once he managed to grip her wrist and pry her hand from the gas pipe, it didn't take much effort for the man to drag her in through the window. When he looked outside to check if anyone else was around, Annie silently thanked Sarah for obeying her compulsion to keep Harry out of sight.

They had a police scanner on the kitchen bench, spitting out intermittent fuzzy updates from the CFA on how her hay shed fire was going, but Annie was finding it difficult to concentrate on the details. Most of her attention was fixed on the man with the pouty lips and not-so-pouty pistol, who was glaring at her while his co-thug tied her wrists to the back of the chair with cable ties. Ties that were the same as the ones in her pocket. Beside her, Mr Durante was strapped to his own chair, breathing through his mouth and trying unsuccessfully to use his shoulder to wipe the blood streaming from his broken nose.

'You'll answer my questions quickly and honestly,' the pouty man said. 'What's your name?'

'Annie Langley.'

'You're Kiah Langley's daughter?'

She nodded.

'You look like you've been through hell today.' He sat on the edge of the small dining table, and rested the pistol against his knee. 'Why don't you tell me what happened.'

Despite her nervousness, Annie's mind was unexpectedly clear. This man had tried to kill her mother. She refused to give him a reason to try again.

'You murdered my mother and burned my house down,' she lied. Trying to get him to admit what he'd done was probably pointless; it wasn't like she was recording him or anything. She still wanted to hear him say it, and it was frustrating when he ignored her. As if her accusation wasn't even worth addressing.

'Why are you only half dressed?' he asked. From the two men, she only felt annoyance and worry, but the guilt she felt from Mr Durante was almost enough to choke her.

'I used my shirt to break some glass.'

'I was told you weren't home. You mother said you were at a

barbecue. How did you report the fire so fast? We hadn't even left there when it came over the scanner.'

So, he really didn't care about admitting his crime. That was probably not a good thing.

'The neighbours called it in.'

'So you were at the Doolans' farm, to the north. The smoke should have blown away from there, and yet you noticed it anyway. Where is Harry Doolan now?'

About thirty metres to my left, down on street level. She closed her eyes, trying to take comfort in his nearness, and was rewarded with a smack across the jaw. It was even more painful than the one Harry had given her, and only two fuzzy thoughts went bouncing around her brain pan in response. The first was that her own reflexive fury was a lot stronger than anything she'd ever stolen from someone else, which came with the realisation that all the stolen ones were probably dulled by the process. That had some serious implications that she would have to think through sometime when she wasn't pointlessly trying to free her hands to hit back. The second thought was simply, *Sorry, Lucas.* If she survived this she would have to send a big bunch of flowers to the nurses at Nalong Hospital. Lucas would not be the easiest patient to have to deal with at that moment.

'That's what happens when I have to repeat myself. Now, where is Harry Doolan?'

'Trying to convince the police that the fire was no accident.'

The man turned to his colleague. 'Cruise, go and see if anyone else is around. If young Harry makes an appearance, shut him down. Quietly.'

The man named Cruise nodded, and Annie choked back her reflexive cry of protest. Sarah would struggle to get Harry out of harm's way if he heard her screaming. Had that new policeman arrived or not? Would that even make a difference to these men?

The pouty man's smile would have looked flirtatious on a girl; however, when he turned it on Annie it just seemed babyish. 'Who was taken to hospital?' he asked her, but her attention was on Cruise, who was attaching something to the barrel of his handgun. She watched him step from the room and head down the hallway, presumably to scan the street from the front window.

Pain erupted in her jaw again, and the world tilted. With her vision blurred, Annie saw her captor reach for her again and she flinched, yet all he did was steady her chair.

'I won't repeat myself again,' he said.

'One of the neighbours, and … Mum,' she replied around her swollen tongue. 'Why are you killing people? What's this really about?'

'The scanner reported two emergency cases, so I'm thinking she's not dead.'

Damn. She should have thought that through better.

'If she wasn't dead, would I be here or at the hospital with her?'

There was doubt in his mind, which she dealt with easily. Doubt and mistrust were more like thoughts than emotions, but once she stole away his worry and nerves, the drive behind those thoughts dissolved.

A fuzzy message came across the scanner that made her wince. There had been an assault at the hospital. The officer on duty was being asked to ignore the traffic violation he was currently investigating and head there instead. *Damn it, Lucas, what did you do?*

Annie tried to cover the crackled response, on the off-chance that Harry had managed to talk to the policeman about her predicament. 'You murdered Harry's mum too. Is this really all about some ruby?' Her voice came out shaky, full of the nerves she had stolen, as well as her own. There were also tears. She was holding too many emotions at once and it only got worse when she heard a car start nearby and take off down the street. So much for her police rescue.

A moment later, she heard the sound of a warped window being forced open in the front room.

'Please don't kill the boy,' Mr Durante begged.

She'd almost forgotten he was even there.

'The *boy* dug his own grave when he pried into things that weren't his business,' came the response.

Annie couldn't breathe until she heard the familiar sound of Harry's ute start up and then speed off down the road a few moments later. She wondered what Sarah had resorted to in order to convince Harry to leave. All she knew was that she would never resent Sarah's bossiness again.

She turned her swollen gaze back to the man who had hit her. 'I asked you a question,' she said. 'And I don't like repeating myself either. What is it about this ruby that warrants killing innocent people?' Her voice came out much clearer than she expected. It was filled with a deep authority that infused her bones, as if every one of her nerve endings was demanding an answer to her question.

And instead of hitting her again, the man paused. 'Ruby?' he scoffed. 'No. Diamond. My employer had a buyer ready to offer millions, until some farmer from Kangaroo Fart managed to steal it. How did he do it? I was part of that security detail. It should have been impossible. He practically admitted he'd taken it, but wouldn't tell us where it was. Bloody "sacred object" nonsense. So he left us no choice except to take his kid. It should have been simple. His son in exchange for the diamond and the location of where it was mined. Then that bitch interfered. Like I said to George here just this morning, when people don't do as they're told, things tend to escalate quickly, and nobody wins.'

Diamond? Seriously? She'd seen plenty of gems scattered throughout the cave systems Next Door. Any one of them could be worth millions, and yet Harry was selling his farm because he was broke. She could hardly blame his mum for trying to do the obvious, but it had only made things unspeakably worse for them all.

And they had tried to kidnap Harry.

Cruise returned then, looking grim. 'There was a cop car that left, and our young friend and his girl. She practically dragged him by the balls into that ute before taking off. He's going to have a tough time taming that one, although she looks like she might be worth it. I hope she's around when we do catch up to him.'

All Annie's tangled emotions were sucked into a black hole in her heart. That missing part of her was sucking everything down along with it, creating a chasm that was born out of despair for her predicament, as well as her deep love for Harry, who had been abused by these people for far too long. Her fear for him left her voice cold.

'If you let Mr Durante go, I'll show you where the necklace is,' she said.

Chapter 36

No air. Even with the windows down, the hot wind that circulated into the back seat of the Mustang didn't seem to contain any oxygen. Annie started to yawn, and then winced from the renewed pain in her bruised jaw. Was it normal to feel so drowsy when you'd been abducted, or was it the result of too much drama in one day? Or perhaps it was true that she didn't have enough instinctive survival responses to combat even the drowsy effect of the stifling heat. She wondered what her captors would say if they turned around to find her asleep across the sweaty vinyl seat. Probably tell her off for bad victim etiquette. A few minutes later, she found out, when the man named Cruise decided to test out whether a seatbelt buckle really could be used as a branding iron. Annie yelped and jerked as far away from it as she could and the man laughed. Her inner thigh stung, just above her knee, where he'd burned her.

'And what have we here?' he asked, reaching for her. With her hands tied behind her back, she couldn't hide the cable ties that were slipping out of her pocket. 'These should have melted. You got her out, didn't you?'

When she refused to answer, he shook his head. 'Annoying. I wanted to be miles away from here by now. I don't like complications.' He looked to the pouty-lipped driver for advice.

'We stay together,' was the gruff response. 'Deal with one thing at a time. Right now, it would be best to stay out of town until things settle down, so we might as well get this done first.' He craned his head back toward Annie. 'We've turned into the state park, like you said. Where next?'

Her stomach churned, but she forced herself to speak. 'There's a track just past the bridge. It's hard to find because it turns back on itself.

I don't know how far this car will get, though. We'll have to walk a long way.'

'The 'Stang will go anywhere,' Pouty Mouth assured her. 'It's a Ford.'

Annie bit her tongue. No comeback needed. And she really didn't want to get hit again. It was hard, however, not to smirk just a little when less than ten minutes later the car slid into a deep rut and bottomed out. Apparently, no one had taught him to drive along the ruts instead of trying to avoid them. Still, he persevered until the sound of a particularly large branch scraping along the paintwork made them all wince.

Despite her exhaustion it felt good to get her ankles untied, and it was a relief to get away from the cigarette-and-hot-vinyl stink of the car. The thick trees offered much better shade than anywhere in town, and it felt reassuring to be in home territory. Pity about the part where she was feeling crushed by guilt, both natural and supernatural.

'I don't want to be here,' she told them. 'I want to see if Mum's okay.'

'For a captive with no right to bargain, you've done pretty well getting Fourby here to release George. I suggest you stop whining and fulfil your part of the deal.'

The jeweller had been unceremoniously kicked out of his own house. For a while he'd loitered on the footpath, apparently unsure of what to do next, given that he was too scared to ask for his car keys. He'd eventually walked off down the street, still trying to staunch his bloodied nose. If the two men were concerned that he'd go to the police, they didn't show it.

Annie licked her lips. 'You aren't supposed to be here. It makes me uncomfortable.'

Cruise laughed at that. 'Uncomfortable to be walking out in the bush with two armed men, where no one can hear you? Now why would that be?'

'I intend to take you deeper into the bush. To sacred ground. No one is allowed there except a select few members of my mob.' Getting those words out felt like one of the hardest things she'd ever done, but it was important to articulate her intentions. Her palms were sweating.

'Then we should get moving,' Fourby growled, tugging at her elbow.

Annie walked with feet like lead. What she was doing was wrong in every way, yet she couldn't think of anything else to try. Harry deserved a chance to make things right. She had to trust him, and his Guardian's ability to keep him safe.

It was now late enough that the north wind had finally settled, but every now and again Annie caught a whiff of smoke, and she wondered what the fire crew must be thinking about her, disappearing and leaving them to guard the burning hay shed. They probably assumed she was at the hospital. She wished she was. What was her mum going to say about all this? Hopefully she was being sedated, otherwise there was likely to be another security alert as she reacted to Annie's illicit activities.

They walked for nearly an hour, fighting through as many patches of thick scrub as Annie could find after the track abruptly ended. Fear made her keep moving, despite her compulsion to stop and scream at the men to leave. The compromise was to try to lead them by the slowest possible route, but she was beyond exhausted. Shifting hay bales in the heat that morning had already been enough to justify not moving an inch for the rest of the day. Since then she'd raced a car on a dirt bike, fought a house fire, been abducted and was now trying to hike through some of the roughest terrain in the area, hoping for a promised miracle she only half believed in.

All three of them were covered in scratches and flies, and eventually when the sound of running water became noticeable and the ground became steeper, Annie tripped yet again, and was finally too tired to fight for balance with her wrists cable-tied behind her back. Her shoulder hit a rock and her left knee donated a good chunk of Cherub-skin to the dirt as she fell.

'It's all right, love. We can stop for a while.' Fourby hooked his little finger into her bra strap and tugged it off her shoulder. 'We could all use a bit of a break.'

The threat was obvious.

'It would be better if we reached the … the …' It was no use. The words wouldn't come. 'Better to get to where we're going before dark,' she said instead as she struggled to her feet.

Cruise laughed at her again when she stumbled ahead of them, trying to shrug her stupid bra strap back up. When she realised what she was doing, she cursed her own reactions. She'd never felt self-conscious about showing skin before, and she hated that these men were changing that. As if something as trivial as a piece of cloth could protect her from their unwanted attentions. So she left the strap hanging and kept walking, placing one disloyal foot in front of the other, even as every cell in her body screamed at her to lead them away from this place. She had already been sprung once for taking an unnecessary detour—her captors weren't stupid—and it was clear that stopping would be far too dangerous. Once again she paused, feeling for her partner. Harry was still so far away. What was taking him so long?

Fourby reached for her again, and she only just managed to move in time to prevent him pulling down her other strap. Cruise laughed as she hurried ahead.

As she followed the river north, the truth of her predicament really started to hit home. She could never bring herself to lead them as far as the cave, let alone trust them to wait for her to go Next Door and find the necklace. Even if she did, they would kill her anyway, leave her body in the bush, and go and deal with Mr Durante, her mother, and Harry in their own time. Clearly these people were working for someone else. Someone with power and money. How on earth had any-one from Nalong ever managed to get caught up in real-life organised crime? They couldn't even convince the Nalong cinema to show *The Godfather Part III* when it came out.

The bottom line was that her plan had not been much of a plan. Although she'd been trying to convince herself that she had faith in her grandmother's stories, and that either she or Harry would find a way to access that mythical power once Eden was under threat of discov-ery, the truth was that she knew it was impossible. If she was honest, her plan was nothing more than a pathetically desperate and shameful attempt to get her friends to rescue her. Like some princess locked in a tower. Unable to save herself. All those years of denying that she needed anyone's help—let alone some pretty boy who was divinely appointed to become her protector—and then at the first sign of dan-ger she'd thrown away all her convictions as well as her inherited core values, on the off-chance that Lucas or Harry might be able to get her out of trouble. Her role as a daughter should have been to stay with her mum in hospital, not chase after revenge. Her role as a farmer should have been to help the fire brigade defend her property and prevent the fire from spreading. Her duty to Lucas should have been to keep her-self well away from danger, so that he would stay safe too. Her job as a

Cherub was to keep anyone from finding Eden at any cost.

Brutal self-honesty cost her the last dregs of her energy, and she sat down on a fallen log. She could no longer stomach what she was doing, and every step toward Eden was only making her guilt worse. The cave had become like an opposing magnet to her, and if she didn't stop soon, she felt like she would be flung away in some sort of violent backlash.

'Are we here?' Cruise asked, looking around at the egg and bacon bushes as if expecting them to have diamonds growing on them.

'I won't take you any further. I lied. I don't know where the necklace is. I mean, I might have a general idea, but it could take me years to actually find it.'

The two men glared at her, and then Fourby pulled his pistol from his back pocket while Cruise complained about the heat and his shoes and the flies and the bush, using a lot of the same swear words over and over.

'It is hidden out in the bush here somewhere, though?' Fourby asked, waving his gun in the general direction of the valley.

'No,' Annie replied truthfully. She was too tired to block out their emotions properly, but at least their anger helped to dull her fear. She tried to wriggle her fingers to get some blood moving because her wrists were tied so tightly that her hands were totally numb.

'Damn. I knew I shouldn't have left the spade in the boot,' Fourby said. 'Hard to bury a body without one.'

'Ground's too hard to dig anyway,' Cruise argued, 'but there are plenty of big rocks; maybe we can wedge her behind one. I bet there are caves nearby. Want me to look?'

'Sure. I'll stay here with the pretty girl.'

Fourby turned to Annie and crouched down in front of her. His dark eyes were piercing, so she looked away, focusing on his neatly manicured fingernails instead. What horrors had those pampered hands inflicted?

'Not that I don't believe you, love, it's just that I would *really* like to find that necklace. If I can bring it back to my boss, everyone wins, yeah? So think very carefully. Is protecting some Indigenous secret really worth what's going to happen to you?' He tucked a strand of her hair behind her ear and then let his fingers trail down her neck before pushing her other bra strap off her shoulder. Then he pressed his fingers against the red mark on her thigh from the seatbelt buckle.

Annie flinched away from him. She had never been so scared in her life. Ugly tears made it difficult to see, she couldn't stop shaking, and she realised she no longer cared that she wanted to be rescued. She was helpless, and weak, and stupid, and a coward. She was everything she had grown up despising. It was humiliating, and sickening, but she didn't want to die. When Fourby gripped the back of her neck, all she could think about was how desperately she wished that Lucas would rush in and save her. If Harry had somehow managed to spring him from the hospital, they would have come for her, together. They would be on their way. In desperation, Annie closed her eyes, searching for the feel of her partner Cherub. There, to the north of them … and then he was gone.

Hot breath filled her face and she opened her eyes to the too-close sight of Fourby's eyes staring into her own. Despair choked her as she realised that the reason she could no longer feel Harry's presence was because he'd just crossed the boundary into Eden. There was no help coming, and she was out of time.

Chapter 37

Skin on skin. Unwelcome. Uninvited. The man's vice-like grip bit into her neck as well as her pride. What had led this man to this action? Did his emotions affect his values, or the other way around? Either way, Annie, of all people, was certain about the way that emotions affected someone's *behaviour*. So she began to drink his emotions away.

Time passed.

Time enough for a gift to become a curse.

A single gunshot rang through the bush, sending birds into flight all across the valley, and Annie hit the ground hard, unable to break her fall with tied wrists. Too much momentum, rapidly interrupted, from a manoeuvre that had not exactly been well planned. There was no wind at all, which made it feel as if the land itself was holding its breath in shocked outrage. She rolled over and lay on the gun, panting. It burned as it dug into her back, but at least its bullet hadn't hit its intended target.

Shouting erupted from an unexpected direction, and one of the voices was calling her name, frantically, over and over. She knew that husky voice. Lucas sounded so scared, and she wished she could help him, but there was no room left inside her. Too much. Too full. Too painful. Too many conflicting emotions crashed against each other with no room to evade, like high and low air pressures colliding to form a whopper of an electrical storm in her heart.

Her mouth opened to answer him, but no sound made it past her dry throat.

Someone new was shouting too, commanding Fourby to step away from her. She looked up to see the young policeman running into the clearing. His voice was full of authority, but she knew Fourby wouldn't have disobeyed even if he'd sounded like a shy toddler. Where was Cruise? Blinking away her tears, she caught a flash of a dirty white shirt as Lucas ran past her and off into the trees. The policeman was yelling at him to stop, only he wasn't listening. Cruise had a gun too. She needed to let them know, but she was having trouble sitting up with her wrists still cable-tied behind her back.

'Annie, stay down. Stay still,' the officer commanded.

She twisted to see him pointing his gun at Fourby, handcuffs ready. The pouty-lipped man sank to his knees, not even bothering to lift his hands. He looked like a deflated jumping castle. Nothing supporting him. Nothing to bounce off. The policeman dragged him over to a nearby tree and cuffed his hands around it. She noticed that the officer's hands were trembling and she wondered if this was his first arrest.

'Were they armed?' he asked in a hurried voice, looking around for a weapon.

'Yeah.' She wriggled over, revealing the pistol she'd been lying on. 'The other guy has one too. Don't let Lucas get hurt.'

The uniformed cop wasted no time. He grabbed the pistol and took it with him, running for the sounds of the others who were crashing through the trees, not too far away.

Another gunshot made her flinch. She wanted to cry and couldn't because the electrical storm inside her was so dry. Shouts echoed from the rocks, and she tried to distinguish one from another. Was that Lucas? Was he okay, or was he lying in a pool of blood in the dust because of her? Everything she'd done to keep him from her family curse had backfired. He should have been surfing today. Mucking around with his mates. Not running through the unforgiving bush chasing men with guns. More shouting … and grunting. It sounded like a fist fight. And then silence.

Lucas could be dead. It was entirely her fault.

Something flipped in her mind, like switching out a light as her thoughts refused to follow that track.

Annie looked over to where Fourby sat slumped against the tree trunk. His thick eyebrows framed eyes that were empty of all emotion. If the eyes were a window to the soul, then he had lost his soul. There was nothing there. She had left him with nothing. He wasn't just numb, because numbness faded over time, and what she'd done to him might never fade. If that was true, then he was worse than dead. Perhaps she shouldn't have stopped him from trying to shoot himself. In a daze, she stared at the man, trying to feel for something, some residual kernel of emotion to work with, but it was all gone … gone from him, anyway, and she didn't know how to give it back.

An eternity passed as she stared into Fourby's empty soul, while a cyclone tore her own soul apart.

Warm arms lifted her, his touch like fire.

'Annie.' Her name was breathed into her neck as her Guardian drew her close. He was real, and living, and the world began to spin again. He was rescuing her. Too late.

She looked him over, searching for injuries. The cut on his cheek was bleeding. It had been dressed at the hospital, except now the outer dressing was torn half off. It looked like someone had hit him. *Bloody Cruise.*

'Are you shot?' she croaked.

'No. You?'

She shook her head.

'I knocked the other man out,' he said. 'I've never knocked anyone out before, not even by accident. Officer Loxwood is trying to work out what to do with him. He only had one set of handcuffs and so he's trying to figure out how to restrain him in case he wakes up. He's trying to call for backup. Struggling to get reception.'

The Guardian pulled a pocket knife from his belt and cut her wrists free. Pocket knife. He was so country now. She would have smiled if she could.

Healing heat flooded her for the second time that day, which she barely noticed because she was still busy with the storm inside her. *Crash. Boom.* Lightning strikes, laced with pain. She did notice the way Lucas's arms supported her weight though. Beneath rolled up shirt sleeves, his muscles were slick with sweat. His wrist was dripping blood where the lacerations from the glass had opened again, and his breath was heavy from his recent exertion. Violence still showed in the set of his jaw, left over from his fight with Cruise. Violence and lust and anticipation and fear and …

He pushed her away, breaking off her fierce kiss. His eyes were wild, confused, and full of worry. He held her elbows, keeping her at bay, until she twisted away and threw herself at his shoulder, knocking him backward. He was not getting away from her that easily. When he stumbled, she hooked her foot around his ankle, and they both fell. She kissed him again, pinning him down by grabbing his hair in her fist. Those blond locks were hers. Golden, full of sunshine and longing. She'd held back her desire for him for far too long.

'Annie, wait.' He pushed her off and scrambled back, clutching his ribs and then flinching when she tried to reach for his hand. Like he was frightened to touch her all of a sudden. 'Something's wrong with you. I don't understand.'

'Please, Lucas. I need you.' She couldn't hold this in, not for a second longer. She had no control and so this wasn't her fault. If she let this take her over, then she could believe for a little while that none of it was her fault. That endless black hole of molten shame inside her would be covered by a thick slab of ice and fury. She could let go of her fragile control, spin recklessly across the ice and numb the shame. For a little while. She could let her anger and lust rule her because how could it not? It was so strong.

'You're in shock.'

'Harry's gone Next Door. He didn't come for me.'

Lucas glanced at Fourby, who was slumped against the tree, ignoring them. 'I came for you,' he said. His self-recrimination was more than she could handle. He was beating himself up because she was too afraid to let him see the black hole inside her. To let him see that *she* was really the one to blame. She needed him to know how evil she really was. How weak. She could not control this. She would show him how powerful it was, this hunger for physical sensation. She would make him yearn for her as much as she yearned for him, and then they would fall down the black hole together, spinning and screaming and burning, locked together in pleasure and pain.

It was difficult to focus on what she did to him then. When he pushed her away again, he was breathing much harder, and his shirt was missing a few buttons. 'These are not your emotions,' he accused. 'You stole them. I arrived too late to help you, but you didn't need me.'

Annie shook her head, unable to speak. She was too full, and no words existed that would be able to carry what she was feeling. When she stepped toward him, he backed even further away and ducked behind a rivergum.

'You stole all their emotions, and now what has that done to you?'

'Please, Lucas. I can't … You want me. I know you want me, I can feel it. I can always feel it. The things I imagine us doing together …' Bits of bark fell at her feet as she clawed at the tree, stripping its clothes off because she couldn't reach Lucas. He was so close. His heaving chest, his muscled thighs and arms strong enough to hold the shattered pieces of her soul together. She'd felt his desire scorching the air between them for over a year now. No way could she hope to contain it now. Not along with everything else she was holding. A sudden lunge, and she caught the hem of his shirt, but he was too quick, ducking back behind the massive tree trunk. 'Get back here, Lucas. You really don't want to piss me off right now.' Another lunge, and she had his elbow. When he yanked himself free she felt his skin under her nails. She couldn't hold on. 'Lucas, stop. You *want* me.'

'Yes, but this isn't you. And I don't want *him*,' he said, pointing at the broken man nearby. 'I want no part of whatever sick lust he was feeling, and neither do you.'

The rivergum was big enough that when she started kicking it, not even its lowest branches shook. A river of ants became exiled on a chunk of bark, and a huntsman spider dropped to the ground and ran away from the storm that was trying to tear apart its home. Annie's hands beat and stripped and frantically tried to release the lightning, until Lucas caught her wrists again and restrained them, one either side of the tree. He pulled her forward, so that her face rested against the smooth new skin of the wounded trunk. Blood pounded in her head and in her belly. Desire for his touch choked out every other thought.

'Tell me what I can do, Annie.'

'I can't control it. There's too much,' she sobbed. 'I need to let it out.'

'Share it with me.'

'I can't do that—my gift doesn't work that way, and even if it did, I would never …'

'I don't mean using your gift. Do it the old-fashioned way. Let me hold you and help you.' His voice was so gentle. 'Sometimes emotions can't be controlled *or* released. Sometimes they need to be …

transformed, and then they can just fade away on their own. Let me help you feel something different.'

'Something different? I already have *everything*, Lucas. Fury and terror and lust and arrogance and shame and despair … what could you give me that could possibly override all that?'

Warm fingers wove between hers, and her palms tingled where new skin sealed her grazes. 'Try me, and find out. I dare you.'

She had his touch. His healing hands.

Not enough. She wanted his thighs against hers. His mouth and his tongue and his breath and his chest and …

One gentle fingertip traced over her scraped knuckles with fragile care. As if she was a delicate crystal ornament, precious and cherished.

I am a storm, coming to crush everyone I love, and none of them know the truth of what a vile creature I really am …

Warm fingers held hers. Precious and cherished.

The thought of taking in any more emotions made her cringe, yet she didn't have a choice. The emotional barriers she had worked so hard to develop over the years were no match for everything that had happened to her in the last few hours, and her Guardian was throwing everything he felt at her. She could practically see it radiating from him like steam from a hot shower. In another second, she had named it. Compassion. She was *precious* and *cherished*.

'I don't deserve that, Lucas. It's my fault we're here at all.'

'No, it isn't, and besides, what I feel has nothing to do with what you deserve. These are *my* emotions, and I get to choose them.' He let go of her right hand, and then he was gathering her into his arms again, and he laid her head on his shoulder. 'I wish you didn't have this gift. Or, at least, I wish you could learn to control it better. Surely being able to read people's emotions would be enough to be able to sympathise. Why do you need to feel what everyone feels as well? It isn't fair on you.'

'I'm an empath. It's just how it is,' Annie mumbled into his neck.

'Well, I think you should try being a sympath instead.'

'There's no such thing.'

'You're a Cherub. Make it a thing.'

How did he always make things sound so simple?

'I love you, Annie. You are strong and brave and tough and clever. You are beautiful and funny and see the world in a way no one else does. Your gift helps you understand people and gives you insight that's sometimes devastating for you, and yet you're always so kind anyway. You are unique, and powerful, and so, so human, but if I'm perfectly honest with myself, I have to say that none of those are the main reason I love you.'

Annie swallowed down a bitter taste. Had it really taken him so long to work out that he had been fated to fall for her? She could have been a warty stuck-up megalomaniac and he still would have been drawn to her.

'I love you because I *want* to love you. Every passing thought of you thrills me, and you are good for me, and you make me want to be more like you are.'

He still didn't get it. She wished she could hide the truth from him forever, except she couldn't handle this undeserved compassion he was blanketing her with. It broke through her fear and forced her to admit the truth. 'I nearly killed Fourby. I am not a good person, Lucas. Look at him. He still might …'

Her Guardian's mouth dropped open, and he stared at the hand-cuffed broken man as if trying to figure him out. 'He wasn't shooting at *you*, was he?'

She swallowed. 'No.'

'He tried to shoot himself, and you stopped him.'

'I tried to take his self-loathing away with everything else, but it was so much a part of him. He'd held it for so long …'

Lucas looked horrified, and then his face softened, as he reframed his image of the man from 'threat' to 'broken'. After a few moments, he looked back at her. 'What about the other man?'

'Cruise was afraid. When I took away everything else, he was just so scared. I'm sorry.'

He held her while she sobbed, and gave her time. Time to unravel and label and reframe some of the tangled mess of emotions, time to cry and release some of them, time to rest in his compassion and love and let most of the storm fade away. There had never been any need to stay away from Lucas to learn who she was. The honesty of his words and his emotions gave her a polished mirror. She was a frightened girl. She was a Cherub. She was a daughter and a friend. She was often weak and often wrong and sometimes right. And she was so tired.

Chapter 38

After giving Officer Loxwood a very brief rundown of what had happened, Annie offered to return to her farm so she could lead the other police officers to their location. He would need help to bring the two men in.

'That won't be necessary,' the policeman said, just as Lucas barked out a solid 'No'. It was too quick. Annie knew something was up.

'You're exhausted, Annie,' Lucas added, but again his words were overlapped by Officer Loxwood.

'They're already on their way.'

The two of them glanced at each other and then looked away awkwardly.

Lucas took her hand. 'We're close enough to the river that they shouldn't have any trouble following our directions,' he said. 'And as they get closer, Mick's walkie-talkie should work better. They'll work it out.'

The young policeman coughed. 'Mike. Not Mick. Mike Loxwood. Or Officer Loxwood to you, actually.'

Lucas slapped him on the shoulder. 'We're in Nalong now, mate. Time to embrace your inner bogan. Trust me, your name is Mick.'

A request for an update came over the policeman's walkie-talkie. It sounded pretty clear—perhaps they'd started relaying messages via the nearby fire crew.

Annie pulled her Guardian aside while the officer was distracted. 'I can't just let them wander around out here, Lucas. Perhaps we should try to talk your new friend Mike—'

'Mick.'

'Whatever. Perhaps we should convince him to let us bring Fourby and Cruise back to my place with us now.'

'Ha! We've got Buckley's of doing that. He wouldn't dare go against procedure. This is the guy who booked Harry for having a dusty number plate, remember? Look, I know the relief team won't stray. They aren't coming for the scenery. Their youngest officer is stranded out here with two dangerous criminals. Besides, Harry will know if they get too close, right?'

Annie nodded, her gaze drifting to the north. Harry had crossed back from Next Door just a few minutes earlier. She knew he would remain close to the cave while there were strangers nearby. What had he been doing, crossing over the Skin of the World to Eden instead of obeying his compulsion to intercept the approaching criminals? According to Lucas, Harry had said that he needed to find something. Sarah was nearby too; presumably she'd waited in the cave for him. Had Sarah stopped him coming to help her? If so, should she feel grateful to her? Her emotions were already so messed up, she couldn't work out what she felt.

'I think we should get moving,' Lucas said. 'My dad is waiting for us at your place. He'll drive us to the hospital.' He started walking, not even saying goodbye to the policeman, and not looking back. He knew how much she wanted to see her mum.

They passed the two older police officers before they even reached the river, and Annie had to go through her story again, somehow skipping over the explanation as to why she'd suspected Mr Durante's involvement in lighting the fire and gone to see him. She was confident it would be safe, now, to reveal the truth behind Ruby's death, but she wanted to tell Harry first.

'We have officers working with the fire department right now, looking for evidence that the fire was started on purpose,' one of the officers assured her. 'They should be almost done by the time you get there, only you won't be allowed near the house for a while yet, sorry.'

'Done already? I thought Harry said the fire crew didn't believe him earlier. How did you get out here so fast? Officer Loxwood only called for back-up half an hour ago.'

'We've been at your place for a couple of hours, Annie. Standard reporting procedure for any fatality. When your friends arrived, and asked for assistance to find you, I allowed Officer Loxwood to go with them, but I should have taken it more seriously. I'm glad to see you're—'

Luckily Lucas was ready for it, and supported her as her knees seemed to forget what they were for. 'Fatality?' she mumbled, confused. Her lips went numb, and she felt faint. Somehow her body knew the truth before her mind agreed to even go there.

The policeman's mouth opened with a small, silent apology as he looked to Lucas. No one spoke. Why weren't they saying something?

Both police officers tidied their uniforms and stood up straighter, as if they'd been taught to look as professional as possible while performing such a solemn duty. Annie turned away from them, seeking her Guardian's face instead.

Lucas was crying. 'I'm sorry, Annie. I didn't know how to tell you. It wasn't safe to tell you, not when you were already so …'

'Is Mum dead?'

It took him two shuddering breaths to get the word out.

'Yes.'

She kept staring at him. He stared right back, blinking back tears. She needed to read his emotions, but was suddenly too scared. Surely, this was all part of a plan. Her mum had assured her that all would be well. Her mum had called Mr Rosa's receptionist, and he had sent people to murder her. Only, she'd survived. Surely this had been her plan all along. Fake her death and place the blame firmly on Mr Rosa where it belonged. Disappear to Eden. All Annie had to do was to help to get her quietly back across the Skin of the World, and take her home, and then everything would fall into place.

'When?' she asked him. 'When did she … pass?'

'Hours ago. Almost as soon as we reached the hospital.'

Something slammed shut in Annie's mind. That missing part of her. She'd felt it, driving into town. Felt her mother's presence fade, forming a chasm that she'd refused to properly acknowledge.

'I should never have left her,' she realised. 'This is my fault. It's too late.'

Chapter 39

The river sang quietly for Annie and Harry that night. Not sadly. Never sadly, just a little more subdued in its skittering dance than usual. Thunder rolled around the edge of the dark sky, threatening to take away the moonlight, and Annie hoped being out in the lightning wouldn't make Lucas and Sarah too twitchy. Perched on their favourite rock in the river, the Cherubim could see the glow from over the hill where the hay shed was still burning. Annie felt bad for the poor CFA member who was rostered on to guard it.

Her mum was gone. Really gone. She knew her Eden family had a way of telling, of knowing what people wanted. They could check, when someone died, to see if they wanted to come back to their bodies or not. Annie didn't know how to do that, but she didn't need to. Kiah Langley wouldn't have lingered for long. Certainly not anywhere near long enough for them to smuggle her body Next Door, even if they had been able to manage such an impossible heist. When Annie had been allowed to see her, she'd looked flushed, almost healthy, like she had when they'd taken her away in the ambulance. Apparently that wasn't an unusual side effect of carbon monoxide poisoning. She was glad. It reminded her that she was actually healthier now than she had been for years. Healthier, happier, and no longer tied to a body that wasn't quite the right fit. They all knew it. Harry had been the one to put it into words when they were kids. He'd said he sometimes felt like he was just slightly sideways all the time. When she'd asked him if he was hanging left or right, he'd tugged her ponytail and told her not to be so crude, and then explained that he felt crooked, in every direction at once. She'd known exactly what he meant. Cherubim, born into human bodies. Like wearing a snug wetsuit that fits well, but sometimes feels a bit constrictive. Her mum was free of it now, and happy.

Except she hadn't wanted to go.

'I tried, Annie, and I couldn't do it. I'm so sorry.' Anger and frustration radiated from Harry in waves, which felt wrong for someone who had just come back from Next Door. In fact, it just felt wrong coming from Harry at all. He hadn't left her side all evening, abandoning Lucas to take care of his usual evening chores. Apparently Lucas wasn't allowed to leave his mum's sight, but he'd insisted that Annie shouldn't be on her own.

'You should have known it wouldn't be possible,' Annie said, her bare feet dangling in the soothing water. 'I once brought back a wooden carving of one of those whistling lizards, but aged wood is the closest thing to living matter I can manage. And that old feather. No way could you bring out a piece of Fruit.'

'I've seen microbats pass in and out, no problem.'

'Of their own free will. Not ours. Although why they would want to is beyond me.'

'Bat-crazy,' they said in unison, causing a flash of Harry's Eden-smile to escape for a moment. Only a moment.

'I actually made it to the end of the tunnel before the guilt got too strong, but I should have tried harder. I'm sure I could have kept it hidden.'

'Long enough to have a miraculous resurrection at Nalong Hospital? Harry, that's …' she sighed. 'Thanks for trying.'

He took her hand in his. 'I'm sorry about what happened to you. I trusted Lucas to protect you. I shouldn't have let Sarah talk me out of going with him.'

'Don't you dare blame the Guardians. They did their jobs perfectly. We're the ones who messed up today. I deliberately tried to lead people right to the cave and you tried to bring out a piece of Living Fruit, for goodness' sake. We have one job, Harry, and we can't risk that sort of selfish stupidity again. We need to learn from your dad's mistake. Nothing comes out of the Garden anymore, and we don't ever try to contradict our instincts.'

'Does that go for your attitude toward Lucas as well?'

She wasn't ready to answer that.

After a moment, Harry started shifting around, as if he was looking for a more comfortable bit of rock. Then he unrolled and re-rolled his shirt sleeve. Restless. 'About my dad's mistake,' he finally said, pulling something from his shirt pocket. 'I brought back the necklace. I thought I might need it to get you back from those men.'

Annie flinched, yet couldn't resist staring at the long-lost heirloom. Her memories of Harry's mum wearing it were hazy. It was bigger than she expected. Mr Durante had excelled himself, although it was clear that Geoff had designed the style of the setting. The jewel was lovingly embraced by a pair of golden wings. In the dull starlight, the gem looked like it was full of old blood.

'You knew where it was all this time? Wait. I think I've seen it before. Was it on Beltana's necklace?'

'Yeah. Along with a truck load of other things. It took her ages to untie everything else. I recognised it a few years ago—the last time I went. I mean, the last time before your mum and dad tried … you know …' Harry said.

Annie nodded at him to continue.

'When I saw it … for a second I thought she was Mum and I kind of lost the plot. I didn't know what to say when Beltana asked why I was crying. It isn't good for the people there to see me like that.' He blinked furiously at the stars for a few seconds, apparently fighting to control the memories. 'I need to either stay away from this place where so much keeps going wrong, or stay away from the Garden. I can't reconcile them both.'

Annie's hug was fierce enough that Harry had to brace them both to stop them falling into the water. Luckily it was a big rock, and he had a good hold of the necklace.

'This necklace is why you don't go there? Why didn't you tell me?' she asked, feeling a little hurt.

'I didn't want anyone to feel sorry for me.' He rubbed his thumb across the surface of the jewel. 'Actually, I think it's more than just that. I feel uncomfortable even talking to you about the ruby. It isn't supposed to be here, Annie, and I was quite happy for it to remain hidden, only now I'm not so sure.'

'What do you mean?'

'I mean that people don't like loose ends. It's human nature, I think, to keep pursuing unanswered questions. Even I couldn't help digging into the past. Your mum was right to be angry at me for that; I should have left the past alone. This is my fault. All of it. Uncle Willie, your mum, even you. I can never fix what I've done, but I will do whatever it takes to end this threat.'

'What threat?' Annie asked. 'Fourby and Cruise are in police custody, and Mr Durante went straight to the police station to tell them everything he knows.'

'Someone gave the orders, Annie. Someone who really wants this necklace.' He held the polished stone up and they watched the reflected lightning flash from it. 'We can let one little Eden ruby out into the world, I think, if it helps keep people away. At least it isn't a living thing.' He gathered the chain into his fist and started to toss it to her, but she clamped her hands over his before he could, breathing fast. If she dropped it in the river ...

It was hard to think through all the ramifications of what the police were going to write in their reports. If only she could be confident that they would just lock up all the bad guys and store away the file on the Nalong murders in some dusty cabinet forever. Then, regardless of what it was worth, she would be happy to toss the pretty rock in the water and never see the thing again.

She released his hand and rubbed the back of her neck. 'It isn't a ruby.'

'What?'

'It isn't just a ruby. It's a rare diamond. More than rare, here, I guess. Unique. Probably aren't any like it on this side. That makes it utterly priceless, and unbelievably dangerous.'

Harry's mouth fell open. 'Worth killing for,' he whispered. 'They think it might have originated from around here somewhere. And that there might really be more.' His brown eyes sought hers, and they held no hint of their usual calming magic.

No more secrets. She had to tell him what she knew. 'Someone did give the orders. His name is Mr Rosa. I think your mum went to confront him the day she died, to convince him there were no more gems, and that she didn't have the diamond. No reason to come searching, or to threaten you.' She took his hand. 'Harry, they killed her. The fact that she died without revealing where the diamond was is what convinced Mr Rosa that there was nothing here to pursue.'

'Until I started dropping hints. Annie, what have I done?'

After everything that had happened to him, losing his parents, Uncle Willie, the mess with his estranged Guardian—he'd always retained that seed of stirring hope and resilience. It was almost reflexive for Annie to search his emotions for it, like a steady rock to stand on whenever the ground shifted under them. This time, there was nothing. This time, he blamed himself, and shame was all she could feel from him. That was not fair.

'It's up to us now,' she resolved. 'We are Cherubim. We will never let anyone come searching these parts for any form of treasure, real or imagined.'

'Rumours of a diamond, Annie. This is the stuff urban myths are made of. Even if I was to throw the stupid gem in the river, stories of it will stick around. Even if Mr Rosa is charged with murder and goes to prison, someone will eventually get curious as to why this all happened.'

'So we'll give them answers. We'll hand in the ruby as evidence so no one comes looking for it. Mr Rosa didn't exactly make it public that it was a rare diamond, did he? He wanted that juicy fact kept secret until he found out for certain if there were more diamonds to be found. We can use his greed against him.'

'I don't understand,' Harry said. 'If we hand this in, won't they get it assessed at some point?'

With a deep breath, Annie embraced the truth she had denied for so long. Her grandmother would never have lied to her. *When you face your biggest challenge, you will unlock your hidden strength.* 'That isn't the one we'll be handing in,' she said.

Eyes closed, she cupped her hands together.

A taste, like honey and metal on the tip of her tongue. She knew exactly what to do, and what to say. Such beautiful language, glistening and lyrical. And something smooth and cool resting in the palm of her hand. She held it out for Harry to see. The new ruby looked identical to the diamond. Both gems were embraced by matching sets of golden wings, and hung from a golden chain. 'Let's hand this one in instead.'

For a few seconds, neither of them spoke. The air around them felt charged, full of potential. Annie felt like she could use it to blow the whole world away. How would she ever let this power go?

Finally Harry cleared his throat and said, 'Imagine if Lucas had seen that. He was impressed enough with you when you made lambs.'

She laughed, and felt the spiritual atmosphere dissipate.

'I don't suppose you can do it again?' he asked. 'Forget about gems though. Could you just conjure up a bit of cash? Just enough for me to keep my farm. Surely that fits the rules? I'm a Cherub, and I need to be here. I need to keep David Ashbree away from this place.'

She shut her eyes and concentrated, but no matter how she tried to justify it in her head, the buzz was gone. When she opened them again, Harry was staring at her hands. Expectant. 'Sorry,' she said. 'I've got nothing. Maybe you should try. It's your farm.'

The last wisp of tenuous hope faded from Harry's eyes. 'You think I haven't spent the last few years trying?' He looked down at the diamond in his hand. 'I have to face what that means. You conjured up a ruby in seconds. It was effortless.'

'Because Eden needed me to.'

'So Eden doesn't need me to keep my farm. Apparently the secret of Eden will remain safe even if David Ashbree buys it. Trying to use our links to Eden to keep the farm is what started this mess in the first place. Mum should never have sold the gem. And I need to let go of the idea that I can somehow use Eden to get what I want.'

It was time for them both to let go of such selfish stupidity. It was the same selfishness that kept Annie's mind circling back to trying to plot some sneaky way to steal her mum's body without generating all sorts of unwanted attention. And it was far too late for that anyway.

Her mum was not coming back.

'I'm not built like them!' she cried, pointing vaguely toward Eden. 'How am I supposed to be happy that she's gone? She wanted to stay!'

If Harry was confused by her sudden change of topic, he didn't show it.

'That's true. And she did stay,' he said calmly. 'For you. And yet even I could tell that a small part of her also wanted to go. If it had been up to you, how long would you have made her wait here for, Annie?'

'Maybe give me a few thousand more years and ask me again,' she retorted. 'No Edenites ever stay for only a few short decades.'

There was nothing Harry could say to that. It was a futile argument because no Edenites ever lost their love-partners by accident either, and in nearly all cases, they chose to go at the same time.

'You know,' he said after a few moments, typically unaffected by her outburst as he hooked the multi-million-dollar jewel over his head for safekeeping, 'most teenagers struggle to comprehend just how quickly life can pass. They think they have forever to do what they want and yet they still rush through things. They feel like something's wrong with them if they haven't been kissed by the time they leave school, or can't get a job within a few months of finishing their studies, or haven't travelled overseas by the time they turn twenty-five. We've been given a different perspective, Annie. Eden is timeless. We have a far better comprehension of forever, and because of it, we know how to savour every moment for what it is. We don't rush things—and that's good—but just don't forget that we live in two worlds, and one of them won't wait for you. Time here passes so fast. We've been ordained on to a narrow and rocky path, and that path gives us a wisdom that no one in Eden or Earth has. Don't waste that.'

'Stop. Just stop,' she said as she hooked the conjured ruby necklace around her neck. 'This is so typical of you.' She leant down and placed her head in her hands. 'Your arguments are often contradictory when you have a point to make, and still for some reason I always trust you anyway. I know what you're trying to say. Please don't make me feel bad about Lucas because of what's happened with Sarah. I already get that. I do. I am abundantly aware that he could turn around at any moment and leave. Things are complicated in this world and I tend to make things worse than they need to be, but don't you see? We lose *everyone*. The tighter we hold onto them, the quicker they leave us. Harry, today I watched Lucas chase down an armed criminal without the slightest hesitation, because his compulsion to protect me gave him no choice. That same compulsion killed your mum and my dad. I can't do it again. I can't watch Lucas die too.'

Thunder cracked as if backing up her tender plea with violent threat. So many tears filled her that she choked on them. Harry watched, despair colouring the air around him with turmoil.

'Damn,' he whispered, crying with her as the rain finally fell. 'I was afraid you'd see it like that.'

∽

Annie had given her solemn promise to the police sergeant that she wouldn't let anyone near the house until after it had been signed off by them, the CFA and the local council adviser, to be sure it was safe. Harry had backed her up, and his promises naturally—or rather, supernaturally—held a lot of sway, which was why they had been allowed back to the farm so soon. His unnatural persuasion also meant that all three departments converged on the house to conduct their initial inspections the very next morning. Unfortunately, all of them recommended that Annie stay away from it until significant repairs were completed.

While Harry and the CFA captain were inspecting the remains of the hay shed, the Taylors arrived, armed to the teeth with frozen meals, spare clothes from Kelly's wardrobe, and groceries. Ready to turn the old fibro shearer's cottage into something liveable. Vicky went straight to the bedroom with an armload of clean bed linen, and when Annie tried to help, Kelly squeezed her hand and suggested that she go and do some work outside instead.

'I'm here for you, Annie, I promise. We all are, only I don't think we'll be much use to you yet. Let me do the practical things today, and in another day or two I'll be better, and I won't … stress you out even more.'

Annie was stunned. She'd never openly discussed her empathic gift with Kelly, let alone the problems that came with it. And yet Kelly had been right there with her as she'd clawed her way through the brittle months following her dad's death. Her friend's tight hug caught her by surprise, mostly because it came with a surge of resentment, although it was clear to Annie that it wasn't directed at her.

'This really sucks, Annie. You've lost so much, again, and there isn't anything I can do to help.'

Annie soaked in her friend's anger, riding the wave of strength that came with it. 'You do help, Kel. You really do,' she said. 'And you don't need to be so worried about me. I know it's going to be shit for a while, but it won't be like last time.' She gave Kelly a small smile. 'I've learned a lot about myself since then. I can't control what happens to me or to the people around me, but I'm getting much better at sharing the emotions I can't handle, and protecting myself from other people's problems.'

Kelly sighed. 'Slaps, when you master all of that, you can teach me.'

'You already get it, Kel. That's why you always seem to know when I need company and when I need to be alone. It's like you have a super-power.'

Her friend sniffed, and gave her a gentle shove toward the door. 'And my super-power is telling you that you'd better get out of here before Vicky comes back. She cried the whole way here.'

By the time Annie finally ran out of blissfully mind-numbing farm chores to do, everyone had left. She returned to the cottage, letting the fly-screen door clatter shut behind her, and the first thing she noticed was that someone had thoughtfully managed to convince the CFA chief to help to move the kitchen table down from the house. It took up most of the tiny living room, and immediately the place felt more like home. Enough like home that she sat down and cried, and cried.

Naomi Gracewood must have been furious with her son for escaping the hospital, because although Harry assured her that Lucas was feeling fine, it was another whole day before Annie finally saw the Gracewoods' Commodore creep up the driveway. She decided Lucas couldn't possibly be driving because the car was quixotically attempting to avoid all the potholes and stay clean. Sure enough, Peter Gracewood eventually pulled up against the shady side of the tool shed, waited for Lucas to get out and then locked all the doors. Who did he think was going to steal it? The possums?

Annie clinically took note of her Guardian's injuries as he approached. Despite the stitches, the long puckered gash that ran across his cheek looked like it would probably scar anyway, just to permanently accuse her of putting him in danger. Was the cut below his ribs still bandaged? Her fingers twitched, yet she resisted the urge to check.

Peter Gracewood gave her a quick hug and went inside the cottage while his son remained on the concrete stepping stones outside, plucking at the bandage on his wrist and waiting for her to speak first. It was a little bit awkward.

'You look much better,' she said, trying to sound casual.

He nodded an acknowledgment. 'Did you get the flowers?' he asked.

'Yes, they were lovely. I called and thanked everyone. Including your parents. They've been helpful, staying at Harry's place.' She shuffled her feet a bit. 'Are they very angry at you?'

'Angry? Why?'

'Well, how about for leaving home, quitting uni, living out in woop-woop with almost no pay for a year, and then topping it off by nearly getting yourself killed in a house fire, escaping from hospital and taking on two known associates of an organised crime syndicate?'

'Ah. That. Yeah, Lily had a field day when she saw my face. Dad threatened to halve her pocket money permanently if she didn't shut up about it.'

Annie waited, but he refused to address the rest of what she'd said.

'And what about Dave's parents?' she pressed. 'Did the fire, you know … put them off?' Uncertain of what she wanted the answer to be, she was surprised to feel relieved when he shook his head.

'They want to tear down the house and start again, though. Make it more fire-resistant. Clear a bit more around the house. Dave's worried he'll never earn enough to pay them back at this rate. He doesn't want to be indebted to them forever. I told him to get over it. If they want to help, he should let them. They're family.' He grinned. 'And they're loaded, remember?'

Annie wanted to smile with him, except all she could think of was how unfair it all was on Harry. He'd worked so hard—as had every member of his family in their time—but money just seemed to evade him. He'd never asked for much; he just wanted to keep his farm running. Lucas saw her expression and wisely decided to change topics.

'Have you heard about your insurance claim?'

'Yeah. All the paperwork's done from my end, although it will take time to finalise because there's a criminal investigation involved. It's a good thing we have the cottage.'

'You went into the house yesterday, didn't you?'

Damn. If he'd felt that, then it really wasn't safe.

'I'd rather you didn't,' he confirmed, then laughed. 'You don't have to look so guilty. I would have done the same. Maybe just let me tag along next time? Were you looking for something in particular?'

'Yeah, I was. Come on. I'll show you when I find it.'

Half an hour later they sat on the back lawn, in the shade, going through the old family photo album. Lucas's dad had left them alone once he was confident they had no further plans to enter the house again, and gone back to the cottage to make coffee.

Her family had a rich history. Not much of importance was ever written down, for obvious reasons, but there was a simple family tree, and a few old photos. Thin-papered letters and drawings fell out from between the pages every now and again too—loving anecdotes of the men who had been lured to Nalong. Guardians who had been loved so deeply and completely, that instead of just flitting around in Paradise indefinitely, the Cherubim women they were bonded to actually *wanted* to spend their lives toiling away in the dust. It wasn't a bad deal, while it lasted.

It took a little while, but eventually Lucas noticed what was wrong.

'Everyone is so young.'

Three seconds with her eyes closed, to brace herself against the next part.

'I thought you said that you *do* age?' he continued, a slight frown marring his face as he flipped back through the pages again. 'Where are the photos of them all as grandparents? There aren't any pictures of elderly people at all. And what about extended family? There's hardly anyone …'

'They died.'

'Who? Your extended family?'

'No, the couples. Hardly any of us live to an old age. My maternal grandparents both died when I was eleven. My dad's family are still around, but after he died …' Phew, this was harder than she expected. 'After he died, they stopped visiting. They write sometimes, and send me gifts—birthdays and Christmas—Nalong is pretty far away, I guess. They'll come for the funeral. You can meet them.'

'I only have one grandparent left. It's not *that* unusual. You make it sound as if your whole family is, well …'

'Cursed. That's what Harry thinks. Small families, cursed to just breed up the next generation and then die young.' Bitterness coloured her shaky voice.

'*Breed?*' he spluttered.

Annie winced, yet couldn't help smiling a little as she read his startled emotions, because outright panic wasn't his only instinctive reaction. At some point, they were going to have to chat about that, but chances were she was going to pike out and make Harry break the humiliating news to him about their Cherubic fertility traits anyway, so she figured it could wait until then.

For a minute or so he stayed quiet, flipping through the pages as if trying to solve the Mystery of the Family Curse. Strangely enough, he did.

'I don't know that it's as bad as you make it out to be,' he mused. 'I mean, we already know you Cherubim age well, and we also know that Guardians heal fast, so maybe they're not all as young as they look.'

A tilt of her head conceded that probability, though she had to point out the flip side. 'But most families have at least one grandparent who lives beyond, what, seventy? And as you say, Cherubim age slowly because we have supernatural bodyguard-healers and access to the Tree of Life. Guardians never get sick, and heal as fast as it's possible to heal without attracting undue notice. So why isn't great-grandma Sylvia still with us?' He didn't have an answer, so she gave him one. 'Because when she lost great-grandpa Tommy, she decided not to stay,' she explained, pointing to the dates under the old sepia photograph. Sylvia had died just a few months after her Guardian.

They flipped through the pages again, scanning the few dates that were recorded. Most of the time the Guardians died before the Cherubim they were called to protect—which wasn't surprising, but then the women always died within a year or so of their partners. What had she done to her mother? Manipulating her into staying so long?

'Shhh, Annie. No, don't cry. Please don't see it as a curse. Look at the dates again. Nearly all of them got to see their daughters grow up, and meet their grand-daughters. Except George. It looks like he got sent to war. That must have been torture. I wonder what happened to Harry's family at that time?'

Another massive sob erupted from her as she thought about Harry's parents, forced to be apart and exiled from home.

'Oh, sorry! Forget I said that. Listen, my point is that everyone dies eventually.'

Annie glared at him through wet eyelashes. Her mother's body was lying in a morgue, and this was how he chose to comfort her? 'No. They don't,' she retorted through gritted teeth.

Exhaling, he ran his hands through his hair and tried again. 'Well, everyone here does. I will, some day.'

The whole point behind this distressing little conversation was based on that fact. She needed him to be fully aware of what it was he was risking if he tried to stay with her. What she didn't need was for him to be so blasé about it.

'Not helping, Lucas,' she growled.

'And when I do, I want no regrets. I want us to look as happy in our photo as each of your predecessors do.' He turned to the last page in the album, the one with her parents, and her as a toddler. Her dad was holding her high above his head, upside-down and laughing.

Annie cleared her throat in mild warning. 'Our photo? Don't you think that's a bit presumptuous?'

'No. Not at all, and you know it. Right now, I'd say there's a ninety percent chance that I'll agree to marry you.' His voice matched his haughty expression, flawed only by the sneaky smile in his eyes.

Choking a little, she knew she was supposed to feel indignant about that; instead her brain could only seem to focus on the fact that there was a ten percent chance he would leave. Her heart thudded in distress, and she couldn't work out if it was because ten percent was too high or too low. Still, she rallied quickly. 'I'm sorry,' she spluttered, 'did I miss the part where someone *asked* you to marry me?'

He gave her a wry look and pointed to the sky, just like he'd done the day he'd nosed through her schoolbag when the twins were born. She couldn't help but laugh a little.

'So, you believe God Himself is asking you to marry me, and there's only a ninety percent chance you'll agree to do it?'

He nodded so seriously that her heart sank, and yet that was what she wanted, right?

'It depends on you,' he explained. 'On whether you promise me something.'

This couldn't be good.

'If something happens to me, I don't want you to die. Promise me you'll do whatever it takes to stay alive, Annie.'

Her mouth opened with five different responses to choose from, ranging from soppy denial to overt sarcasm, only she was too conflicted to make any sense out of them in her head, let alone articulate anything useful. He'd completely stymied all the arguments she'd practised that might convince him to leave. If she agreed, she'd be telling him she wanted to marry him, but if she refused, it would sound even worse. And what sort of stupid promise was that, anyway?

'You *want* me to go through what Mum did?' she asked instead, latching onto the one question she craved an answer to. She had been fighting for so long to keep her mother from leaving her that she still couldn't decide if what she'd done was selfish or justified. There was still a part of her that questioned how long her mum would have stayed in Eden before choosing to move across to the next life. Even Beltana had implied her mum was preparing to die.

'Yes.'

She blinked.

'No! I mean, of course not,' he corrected. 'But I'm your Guardian and my priority is your safety. If staying away from you keeps you alive longer, then that's what I'll do, no matter how misera ...' He gave a fake cough to try to cover his lapse. 'Besides, I refuse to let you *ever* put our daughter through what you've been through. Good grief, "our daughter". What a thought.'

'I'm confused.'

'It's quite simple, Annie. I don't want you to die, and I don't want our kids to ever think you *want* to die. Promise me.'

'Are you nuts?'

'I've figured it out, Annie. Why Cherubim need Guardians. You're all far too eager to die to fulfil your duty. Although it might seem noble to you, I think it's just a flaw.'

'Are you saying I'm flawed?'

'Big time. Because you aren't ticklish enough.'

'*What?*'

'You can hold your breath until you pass out, you can withstand temperatures both hot and cold that should make you uncomfortable enough to do something about it, and you withstand pain far too well.'

'That was rather helpful when I needed to rescue my mum from a burning building. Maybe I'm built to be brave for a reason.'

'Brave? Choosing to die isn't brave. Nor is it weak. It's a result of a desperation that I never want you to feel.' A shard of genuine concern accompanied his words. 'I don't understand Eden very well, but I'm pretty sure your friends there would agree with me. Not that they would really have any real concept of ... oh ... That's the other problem, isn't it? The more time you spend there, the harder it is to remember how dangerous it is back here, right?'

She let out a sheepish laugh. 'Harry did once try to hold back an entire mob of young steers who were rushing to get through a gate. Came out with some whopper bruises—one was shaped exactly like New Zealand. He'd only been back for a few days and said he forgot they wouldn't just do what he wanted.'

'That isn't funny,' he admonished, going pale.

'What is your point, Lucas?'

'My point is that you aren't fully human. You've been born into a form that's apparently not your natural state, and that has a side effect. You don't have enough survival instincts. Look at these photos. On the two occasions where the Cherubim died first, their Guardians lived for much longer than when it happened the other way around. I highly doubt that all the women in your family just drop dead from grief when they lose their husbands. I'm sure there's always some accident, or emergency, or something preventable that kills them. My guess is that you ladies just don't try hard enough to take care of yourselves. Not without your Guardians to remind you to be cautious.'

'Like I kept reminding Mum?'

'Exactly. Staying so that you're still around to fight for the people you love—that's what's brave.'

Something inside her was released. Like an elastic band around her heart had snapped. A core belief had just been turned on its head. 'So you don't think that they all died young because they were too much in love?'

Lucas made a rather disrespectful gagging sound. 'No. You're not cursed to die of a broken heart. Cherubim would never be that pathetic.'

The long-hidden secret hurt, yet she forced herself to articulate it anyway. 'Mum didn't really *want* to stay. I know, because one of our friends Next Door once asked her when she was planning to move across. They could tell.'

'And what did she say?'

'Not yet. But the point is—'

'The point is that she was grieving, and it's natural to want to be with someone you miss. They probably recognised that. It doesn't mean she was … suicidal.'

'She was just flawed because of her freaky alien soul?' Annie challenged.

'Exactly.'

She waited a couple of seconds, but there was no trace of an apology in his clear blue eyes. She thought about it a bit longer.

'Actually, that does make me feel better. I'd rather be flawed than cursed.'

He took her hand. 'It's still a problem. I won't let you die while there's breath left in my body, and I can't let you get slack about staying safe if I cark it. So if this is going to work, then you need to promise me.'

'You really are nuts.'

'Oh, come on! How hard is it to promise me that you won't die if I do? The idea that you might forget to look after yourself just because I'm not around to pester you about it is utterly ridiculous to begin with.'

'My family history suggests otherwise.'

'You are not your mother, or your grandmother, or your great-grand-mother,' he said.

'Well, how do you know for sure?' She could feel the deep, hot tremble in her voice that only came when her emotions were starting to free-wheel out of control. *Why did he always have to be so infuriating?* 'How do you know I won't be pathetic and weak, and perish of a broken heart if you die?' Her words were coming too fast, tripping over each other. 'Or maybe I'll be a total coward and refuse to make you leave while you still can, even if staying here makes you as cursed as the rest of us. What if I'm as selfish about wanting you as I have been about wanting Mum to stay? What if I decide to agree to your stupid promise just so I can have you, regardless of how much I might suffer for it later?'

Suddenly she found herself virtually nose to nose with him, with the photo album sprawled in a mess on the grass beside them. His electric-blue eyes looked startled. A suspended moment lingered.

'I would kiss you now,' he whispered, his husky voice uncertain. He was so close that she could feel the heat from his skin, calling to heal things that she hadn't even realised needed healing.

'But?' she prompted softly.

'But you always run away when I do that.'

She considered it for a moment, and then smiled. 'Not always.'

Chapter 40

Kiah Langley's funeral was a very small gathering, which she would have approved of, but it was also very sombre, which she would have hated. Yet all in all, Annie knew she wouldn't have really cared because it just wasn't that important to her. The important part came a few days later, when Annie tapped on Lucas's window in the pre-dawn light with an ornamental urn under her arm. Harry was already up and waiting, of course, so without a word Annie led them both down to the river and then started to pick her way southward along the overgrown trail. Early dew soaked their leather work boots, and the warbling sound of magpies and cranky cockatoos heralded their passage.

The light breeze held no remaining trace of smoke and yet somehow the air still felt tainted. Annie walked briskly—as usual when she was headed for home—and she could feel her heart begin to race in anticipation, as if the iron in her blood was being magnetically pulled by the boundary, in a poignant reversal of how she'd felt when she'd tried to lead strangers there. Lucas trailed along behind Harry, clearly confused, and yet too daunted to ask the obvious question.

Guardian. Daunted. She should have known that wouldn't last long. He respectfully waited until someone else spoke first, though.

Harry finally broke the silence when they reached the first safe place to cross the river. 'Are you sure about this, Annie? He doesn't need to come.'

Without looking at him or stopping, she stuffed her socks into her boots and then hefted them across the river one at a time. One of them didn't quite make it, but luckily got wedged against a jammed log in the shallows. She plunged her foot into the cold current before replying. 'He needs to see it. He has decisions to make, and he needs to know how serious the consequences could be if he makes the wrong ones.'

Harry's compassion, like a painful hug, encased her so fully she was glad it wasn't airtight, yet it held a good dollop of doubt too. 'Your mother would disagree,' he said, giving her sleeve a gentle tug to make her stop. 'You know how often she warned us to keep them away from there.'

'Well, she's the one who kept telling me that I was ready to make these decisions for myself, so I'll just have to trust my own judgment from now on, won't I? Besides, you took Sarah there already so it's only fair.'

She held the urn up and began picking her way across the submerged rocks. The one benefit of having such a dry year was that the river was low enough to make it fairly simple to cross the thigh-deep ford. Except when the current pulled them off the rocks. 'He needs to see it,' she repeated, raising her voice above the sound of the water when she noticed Harry still hesitating on the riverbank.

'See what?' Lucas asked, wading in to support her as she wobbled on a loose rock. 'Does it happen to involve finding a hidden stash of warm dry clothes?' The river was about as warm as Annie had ever felt it, and still Lucas's lips were almost as blue as his eyes.

'Sort of,' Harry said with a reluctant grin. 'At least, it involves something that should dry your clothes pretty fast.'

An image of Lucas stripping off his shirt to dry it near the everlasting flames almost made Annie lose her grip on the urn. Luckily, he was still close enough to help her steady it. Annie turned to him with a grateful smile. 'Remember when I first told you what I was?'

He nodded.

'And you said the Bible you remembered had more pictures? It's time to show you one of the pictures.'

Her divinely appointed Guardian literally fell to his knees when he saw the burning sword. It was huge, and very intimidating, and in no way did it look or feel in the least bit safe. It wasn't meant to. Great curls of searing flame writhed fiercely and protectively around the gleaming white blade. If it had been made of steel, it would have been too heavy to wield, but watching the way it spun with such agility, Annie felt like it would be the simplest thing in the world to grab its handle and play out the *Princess Bride* fight scene with it. Of course, its song rang with such purity that the thought of approaching it still terrified her, down to her very non-human soul.

'I knew it was all real, I did,' Lucas whispered. 'I mean, I always believed in God, in my head ...'

'But you never thought about it all that much, right?' Harry asked. 'You grew up believing because people that you trust believe it.'

'Exactly.'

'Well, perhaps they have good reason to.'

'I wish Mum could see this.' Lucas couldn't tear his eyes away from the ancient hidden proof of God's existence.

'Harry, you go ahead,' Annie suggested. 'I'll have a chat to Lucas. I'll find you soon enough.'

'Are you certain you don't need me to help explain?' Harry asked, concerned enough to take hold of her hand. She shook her head and handed him her mother's ashes.

When Harry disappeared between one step and another, Lucas let out a muffled sort of yelp. She let him have a minute to look around, clearing her throat when he stepped too close to the threshold. He stopped walking, licked his lips, and leant toward the boundary as if trying to see across it.

'Squinting won't help,' she told him, taking his hand and pulling him gently back to where her skin could stop crawling. It felt a bit like watching a toddler play near the edge of a busy highway.

'Sorry, I'm just struggling to absorb the fact that the Garden of Eden is *right there*,' he said. 'It's so close. Right on the doorstep ...'

'Repent, for the Kingdom of Heaven is at hand,' she quoted. 'So near, and yet ...'

He sighed. 'There's nothing I can do to be allowed to see it?'

'No. Nothing. If we let just one speck of evil through, it would no longer be Paradise, would it?'

'Are you saying you don't have a single speck of evil in you? I saw the way you coveted your neighbour's last chocolate-coated strawberry at the barbeque. In fact, I distinctly recall you challenging him to a toothpick battle for it.'

Annie shrugged, unable to explain the technicalities of how Cherubim were different. 'The sword knows who can cross and who can't. So do I, actually. I can feel it. I'm sorry, Lucas, but if you tried to get past it, the sword would flare up and burn you to a crisp.' Bile rose in her throat as she remembered …

'Couldn't you somehow override it?' he asked, staring up at the spinning weapon with an awed curiosity. 'Or switch it off? Just long enough for me to have a quick peek? I promise I won't touch anything.'

'Lucas, look at me.'

He turned with obvious reluctance from the glorious flames.

'If, somehow, the sword didn't stop you from crossing into Eden, then I would. No matter what it took. Do you understand?'

His smile faded as the gravity of what she was telling him hit home.

'Only people clean of the taint can enter, and …' She swallowed again. Her voice wasn't supposed to be shaking so much. 'And you can't be *completely* clean of the taint while you live.'

'I have to die to get in?' Then his eyes flashed with unexpected insight. 'Your parents tried it, didn't they? Annie, look at me! Tell me the truth.' Hot hands gripped her shoulders as he spun her to face him.

Tears ran down her face as she remembered. 'Mum sent Harry and me to the other end of the valley, and told us not to come back until she came to get us, but I *couldn't* stay away from the cave that day. Not when I could feel their intentions like acid on my tongue. Harry tried to hold me back, to stop me from watching, except he'd felt it too—the compulsion to act, to prevent the disaster. Mum had been so strong that day, letting the sword do its work.'

Lucas stared at the spinning weapon in horror as she spoke.

'Apparently it was Dad's idea,' she continued. 'Harry and I weren't given any warning, or any say in it.'

How many times had her dad sat and stared at the sword just like Lucas was, frightened, and yet tantalised by the idea of Eden? Paradise, so close, where they could all live safely together.

'They were going to collapse the cave, with all of us hidden away from the fallen world that had stolen Ruby and Geoff Doolan from us. I think now that my dad must have known we still weren't really safe from those people. Guardian premonition of the danger to Mum, perhaps. My parents risked everything on their plan to lock us all away in Eden.'

'But, no. What about …' Lucas couldn't seem to work out how to finish his question.

'What about you? And Sarah? I honestly can't tell you what they were thinking. Maybe they believed we would be happy enough in Eden that it wouldn't matter if we never met you. I do know that Mum refused the whole idea for years. I guess Dad wore her down. You Guardians can be pretty stubborn.'

Lucas finally turned his face away from the spinning flames. Holy fire reflected from his eyes, amplifying their blue sheen, like the quinine glow from tonic water in sunlight. 'They wouldn't have tried something like that without some confidence it would work,' he said. 'Guardians may be stubborn, but we aren't stupid.'

'It did work, partially,' she whispered, feeling rock beneath her fingers. When had they sat down? 'The sword did clean away the taint when it killed him. I could feel it burn away. I watched it happen … his arms batting at his clothes, only his arms were burning too … and he screamed for so long …'

When she closed her eyes, the images were still there in her mind. Emotional memories that her mum couldn't help but revisit every time she'd tried to use her gift on her daughter since that day. Never dulling, never fading. Never healing.

'We lost him, Lucas. The Living Fruit didn't bring him back.'

After crying in her Guardian's arms for much longer than she thought she would need to, Annie gathered herself together and told him not to wait. Now that he understood what would happen, he was keeping his distance from the mighty weapon, eyeing it with a hint of terror, as if expecting it to fly at him at any moment and violently punish him for every bad thought he'd ever had. His emotions were easy to read and so she knew she could trust him here alone. She told him they'd be gone for at least a day, but probably longer, and asked if he could please feed the chickens.

'Chickens?' he asked, apparently baffled by the mundane request uttered in such a holy place.

Annie gave him a grateful hug and then left him to his inevitable spiritual meditation.

The first breath of Eden filled Annie with a joy that transcended even the grief she carried. She'd been expecting to feel a bit guilty about that, but she didn't. Eden was no place for either guilt or grief. What she really didn't expect, though, was the laughter that greeted her when she found Harry sitting among a crowd of people under the gigantic trees of the food shelter. He had the ornate porcelain urn tucked securely in his lap, and seemed to be at a loss as to how to keep everyone from touching and stroking it. His reluctance seemed to be a bit of a game for them, and they were happily trying to figure out what he wanted. Apparently, he had finally managed to explain—to an extent—what was inside.

'Annie, thank goodness. My signing is terrible. I've forgotten everything.'

A dear friend with hair like fine copper thread and the body of an Olympic gymnast explained. *He thinks we don't understand him, which is making him talk like a baby. Your mother chose to Cross Over, but he won't tell us why you brought her dust here. And in such a pretty pot! She would laugh if she knew.*

He seemed so cheerful about it that Annie had to pause for a moment to centre herself. She was ready for this. She had to be, because if she waited, she might never find the courage to do it.

Hello, my friend Tanumi. I wanted her dust to settle here because it is such a beautiful place. This is for me, not for her. My father's dust is here also, and I like the idea of their dust staying together. Don't cry in front of the Edenite. Never do that. You are no longer a child and they won't understand.

Tanumi chuckled. *It is only dust! But I understand. You are still young. We will come with you and sing for her, even though she's already gone. It is what you want.*

Harry let out a tense breath as she took the urn from his hands, and they followed the man through the village.

'Harry,' she whispered, tucking the pot securely under one arm. 'As much as I love the way they view death here, I will *never, never* really understand it.'

He nodded his agreement and gripped her free hand.

As they travelled, the Edenite sang in a steady tenor voice, which seemed to pique the interest of everyone else. Heads kept appearing from above them among the shelter-tree branches, tilting in curiosity as they passed. More people joined them as they headed up the valley toward a thick band of scrub. Birds smaller than rosebuds flitted around their heads with delightfully sweet music.

She hadn't come along when her mum had brought her dad's ashes here. It had been a hideous process, first trying to avoid having the Edenites discover that his permanent death had not been his conscious choice, then taking his body back to Nalong where they'd had to lie about the accident, then the funeral and official cremation. By the time her mum had returned to the Garden with his urn, she'd needed to be alone, and so had Annie. Apparently, there was a place that such things were done though, because everyone seemed to know exactly where they were going. Just as well, because she hadn't really planned things in that much detail. All she'd wanted was for her mum to come home.

It took most of the morning to reach the line of small hills they'd been heading toward. They were so far up the valley that Annie wasn't entirely certain they were still in it. Vast grassy plains stretched out on either side of them, sweet green pasture rippling in the warm wind. They followed an invisible track from one incline to another, which was most likely remembered more than marked. She was grateful for the guidance. Harry reached the last curve at the top a few moments before her, and let out a soft grunt. The second she glanced up, she realised why he was so astonished.

You look surprised. Do you not have such a place close to where you stay? Tanumi asked.

'A place like this? Not very close, no,' she said in a strangled voice, speaking as well as signing so that Harry could keep up. The henge was stunning, formed with multi-hued slabs of rock inlaid with gems and polished ornaments. Each pillar was as tall as a house, and capped so neatly that it looked like the formation had grown from the ground as a living thing. Like a giant, ancient fairy ring, made from the bones of Eden itself.

'Do you always bring the dust remains here?'

It is a good place for a celebration, the man replied.

And it was. More than sixty people had trailed behind them in their pilgrimage to the henge, and each one of them had a story of her mother. Some were long and convoluted, and Annie dutifully translated them for Harry as best she could. Some were just snippets, like photographs, of things they remembered about her. A joke she told, or a strange expression on her face, or a game or song that she'd brought with her from her other home. After a while Annie realised something. They were making a list of things her mother would be contributing to the next place she went. All the things that mattered, and were not lost. Annie found herself feeling a bit humbled by how little she would have to contribute if she was to move on. She was not yet ready to step into that new and exciting existence. Not by a long way. When her time came, she was determined to have a lot more to offer.

'I wish I could share the story of the time your mum fixed the engine mount in my ute using Bo's chain,' Harry said. 'Worked well enough to get me to the mechanic. Saved me a fortune in towing costs. She was very resourceful.'

'She was also more assertive than the people here could ever comprehend. Remember the time she came up to the school and told your teacher off for making you do the "boy" activity instead of basket weaving?'

Harry laughed. 'Yeah. I remember that. The boys had to go bike riding. I hate bicycles. And I wanted to show the teacher how to make a satchel the way they do here.'

'You mean, you wanted to show off.'

'Exactly. Your mum was furious that they gender-biased the activities.'

'Boy/girl day got cancelled after that. My year level didn't get to do anything at all.'

'Still a good memory, though,' he said. 'Not all the best stories are songs and rainbows.'

'That's true. I remember when mum shot the old gelding after that brown snake bit him. Not the happiest story, but I was so proud of her that day.'

For a few minutes they simply stood, side by side, listening to the Edenites recount their memories. Many of them sang, and she wished her mum could hear them. Such honour, respect, such deep unshakable and unconditional love ... and such excitement for all the new experiences they were convinced she would have next. Some of the stories were told in sign-poetry so graceful it might have well have been called dancing.

I will miss racing her down the sun-chute, Ekala said to Annie after one of the poems ended. *Even if it did get more boring recently.*

Boring? Annie asked her.

She refused to go fast. She didn't want to break herself so badly that she would stop. I knew then that she was thinking of moving across sometime this next tree-cycle.

Annie and Harry looked at each other, confused.

It happens like that, sometimes. Ekala continued. *When people break, the Fruit brings them back, but those who are thinking of moving across become uncertain that they will choose to come back when they are fed it. So they avoid doing things that might break them. Until they are certain one way or the other.*

For a moment, Annie couldn't breathe right, until she felt Harry put his arm around her shoulder.

You said you'll miss her? Harry asked the woman in mumbling sign language.

I always miss people when they are not here. I've missed you, Annie. When can we paint again? I've been practising with my toes. I made a portrait of you. I'll show you later.

But my mother is not returning. It is different, Annie said.

How is it different? I will see her again. Just like Tanumi. He once followed a flock of purr-birds because he wanted to find me a blue feather, only he got distracted and didn't return until many tree-cycles later. I missed him, yet I knew I would see him again eventually.

'How long is a tree-cycle?' Harry asked her.

'The time it takes for a sleeping-tree to grow, live and then die,' Annie replied.

'Those trees are huge. They would live for hundreds of years …'

'Which means that it's all about perspective,' Annie realised. 'I'm grieving because it might be a few short decades before I die and see Mum again. My whole life will pass—all my experiences, but it isn't the same with them because they have so much time to share with each other, and are often gone from each other's lives for hundreds of years. They comprehend eternity much better than we do, Harry.'

All evening they sang, and danced, and laughed. And in the morning, when the new sun kissed the valley, Annie watched a diprotodon joey emerge from its mother's pouch to graze. Babies were mesmerising, no matter what species they were. She remembered the look of wonder on Lucas's face when he'd helped her with the lambing. He'd told her then that she spent too much time worrying about everything that could go wrong, instead of enjoying what goes right. He'd been trying to tell her gently, and she hadn't wanted to listen. She had convinced herself that her choice to keep Lucas a secret from her mum had been a strong and noble one. To protect her mum, and to protect Lucas. It was time for her to confront the fact that it had really been based on fear. Eden was so safe. The world outside of Eden was so dangerous. Perhaps growing up in both worlds had permitted her to run from fear too often, rather than learn to embrace life despite it.

Annie breathed in the sweetness of her garden home. She was a daughter of two worlds. It was time to start living fully in both of them, because not all the stories she would take with her when she moved across had to be full of songs and rainbows.

She shook the urn until it was empty, woke up Harry, and they went to find something fun to do.

Chapter 41

They stayed for another night—or was it two? And then got a terrible gut-wrenching call to reality that brought them flying back to the cave, ready to strike out. The last time Annie had felt such sickening urgency was the day her dad had died. Even the race to get back to the farm during the fire hadn't felt quite like this. The feeling was different to mere adrenaline and panic—it was a deep intrusion that threatened something very primal and couldn't be delayed or ignored. In fact, the adrenaline and panic were actually quite minimal, so that when they stepped across the Skin of the World they simply headed out, repressing the usual transitional disorientation to deal with later so they could run like rabbits through the bush.

'Are we certain it isn't just Lucas?' she asked Harry, following his leap over a log tangled with bracken and ground vines. He reminded Annie of the Terminator, coldly hunting his prey, thigh muscles bunching with every easy stride. Their pace was not frantic, but he looked powerful and unstoppable.

'You already know it isn't,' he replied. 'He wouldn't trigger our instincts this way. No. There are two people. Strangers. Both men. I can feel Lucas too, I think. He's farther away, and he doesn't feel … dangerous.'

She overtook him and threw him a glance and a hand signal that let him know how impressed she was, and promptly ran straight through a tangle of blackberries. Yanking her hair free, she ignored the sting as the vines tangled around her legs, trying to slow her down. Something was on the tip of her tongue, an ephemeral whisper that tasted like thunder, ready to be released, and then her skin gave way and the vine fell behind as she kept on running, and she lost its flavour.

About ten minutes later they drew near enough for Annie to be able to discern a bit more information, and she slowed a little. She felt the presence of the strangers up ahead, separated from each other by a small gully that she remembered only vaguely. They hadn't been out this way often, because the terrain was nearly impossible to negotiate. In fact, it was about as far west as you could go without hitting the impassable cliffs along the next ridge that defied access to the valley beyond.

'They want to leave. They don't intend to come any farther south, or at least they'd rather not. But who are they and what are they doing?' she asked, panting.

Harry stopped and rested his hands on his knees, breathing hard. He closed his eyes, head tilted as if listening, so she did the same, hoping it would help. Like the source of a warm breeze, she could feel Harry's presence as clearly as if she was touching him, and extended her senses farther, to where the presence of the strangers clicked like static, or friction. Her Guardian had caught up quickly too, and was somewhere nearby. She could sense him like a subliminal hum, somewhere to the north-east, although she couldn't pinpoint him nearly as accurately as she could Harry. She wondered exactly how far from Eden he could get before she stopped being able to sense him at all. It certainly didn't extend as far as either of their farms. But here, she could feel everyone.

'I see what you mean. They aren't far now,' Harry said. 'They're far enough apart that they can't see each other. Their thoughts are headed away …' A sardonic smile revealed how crazy he knew he sounded, and she chuckled. The compulsion was easier to deal with now that they were close enough to act if they needed to. It made Annie realise just how puffed she was, so when they resumed the chase they kept to a more sensible jog.

Pushing their way into a small clearing a few minutes later, she was stunned to see Lucas standing in the middle of it, his long legs pacing, squinting through the brush to catch a glimpse of them.

'Wow, that was quick! You were much closer to the river last time I felt for you.' She laughed, springing toward him for a hug. 'Your mum was right, you really are stealthy.' She stumbled to a halt and let her arms drop back down as he backed away. The expression on his face looked … devastated. He didn't want her near him. That much was clear, only she couldn't for the life of her work out why. Had they had another fight? She couldn't remember a fight. The last time she'd seen him was in the cave, when he'd come face-to-flame with the holy instrument of death and judgment.

All breath left her lungs in an instant. Too much. The revelation of power and supernatural reality must have been too much for him to reconcile. He was frightened of her. Could she bear this too? After everything she'd done to him, she couldn't blame him, yet she'd lost so much already, to lose him this way …

Harry broke the spell by laughing louder than she'd ever heard him laugh before. Both she and Lucas glared at him in consternation. He was supposed to be the serious one. Why was he acting like this was all some big joke? Obviously Lucas agreed because he started to walk away, clenching his fists and taking short angry breaths.

'Wait! Lucas, please,' Harry gasped, still chuckling. 'Don't start pulling Annie's trick of running off whenever you get upset. I'll leave you to sort this out with her, but first please can you tell me who those people are?'

'People?' he asked hoarsely. 'You mean the surveyors?'

Understanding lit Harry's eyes, then annoyance. 'They weren't supposed to come until Thursday.'

'Surveyors?' Annie asked.

Harry leant his elbow against a tree and took some deep catch-up breaths. 'They're supposed to verify the measurements and boundaries for the adjustment to the land title. So I can give part of the property to you, remember?'

She nodded slowly. An hour ago, she had been exploring an underwater cave filled with tiny fish that glowed in five different colours, so it was a bit hard for her to get her head around.

Lucas lifted his chin. 'Today *is* Thursday.'

Annie frowned at him, and then sighed. They'd been gone for four days? *Ah, crap.*

'Are you sure?' Harry asked, glancing briefly at the sky as if it could tell him the date as well as the time of day. Lucas didn't bother to argue. He stood there with his arms crossed over his chest, scowling at the ground.

'I'd better go and talk to them, then. Thanks for covering for me,' Harry said, striding away.

He got about ten steps before Lucas sighed and called him back.

'Harry, hang on.' Although he sounded resigned, she was getting a strong sense of anger from him, as if he was only just holding onto his temper. There was also something else, an underlying emotion with the flavour of a diabolical toothache. Fresh out of Paradise, she was struggling to recognise his negative emotions.

'You can't go like that,' Lucas said. 'Here.'

To her astonishment, he stripped off his shirt and then proceeded to unzip his shorts, shucking them off and tossing them to Harry.

'Damn!' she yelped, startling them both. Looking down, it finally dawned on her what the problem had been. In their haste to intercept the trespassers, Annie had skipped her all-important 'returning to the dark side' mental checklist—the one her parents had drilled into her that included reminding herself that snakes were not always friendly, and that she should try to retrieve as many of the clothes she had inevitably left lying around as possible. No wonder Lucas was staring at the ground. Crossing her arms over her chest, Annie silently cursed the Australian bush for not containing any fig trees.

Harry grinned, pushed his legs into the borrowed shorts, and then balled up the shirt and tossed it back in her direction before walking away, leaving her to figure out what to say next. She put on the t-shirt. It smelled more intoxicating than the sweetest of Eden flowers.

For a long minute, she and Lucas just stood there, Annie in nothing but his red Ratcat t-shirt, and Lucas in only his navy jocks and Blunnies. There were no words. This had not been the plan. Eventually she noticed that his eyes were fixated on her, but not in the way she expected. He was frowning at her feet, or more specifically, her ankles. Looking down, she could see why. A dotted red line ran from the outside of her right knee, curled around her calf and ended in a ragged strip of bloodied flesh. The track was bloodied here and there with deeper wounds where the thorns had hooked into her skin. Her left leg wasn't much better.

'Oh.' She sat down and held her foot up for him apologetically.

His face flushed, and then completely drained of colour. He didn't move except to cross his arms over his chest. 'I … no …' he stammered, and then he swallowed and tried again. 'It's not that bad. You won't die.' His voice was so husky she could barely hear him.

'What?' she asked, feeling confused, and more than a little distracted.

Every muscle in his torso was tensed, and sitting on the ground at his feet meant that when she looked up at him, she felt that she was gazing up at a statue that would have made Rodin chuck in his carving tools in defeat. Nothing could match that beauty. The statue had sweat dripping from his hair, making it curl enticingly around the base of his neck. One of the drips slid down below his collar bone, and … this was definitely not in the plan.

'Can we just go? Please?' he asked, tight-lipped.

Annie only managed to look away once he turned and started striding back to the river. Following like a hungry puppy, her blood was pounding so loudly in her ears she thought they might burst. She commanded herself not to look at the way his broad shoulders tapered so elegantly down to his hips, and promptly tripped in a rabbit hole. He flinched, but didn't turn around.

'I take it we're not going to Harry's?' she asked, stumbling to catch up.

'My family are still there. I don't think it would be advisable for us to rock up there like this, do you?' His work boots smashed the bracken and dead branches under his feet like he was trying to crush the entire bush into garden mulch.

'You're angry.'

He stopped, breathing hard. 'Really? What gave it away?' he asked. 'Give me a minute to adjust, will you? Did you really expect me to feel nothing?' He resumed his stomping. 'Feel free to take it away if you want. I'm sure you'll do a much better job of controlling it than I am.'

She was pretty certain that if she tried to absorb all the emotions coming from him at that moment, as well as her own, something critical in her brain would probably melt. Again.

'I don't understand why you're angry,' she muttered, not really expecting him to answer, but he spun so fast that she tripped again trying to avoid him. What was it about crossing the boundary that always made her so clumsy? Although, she'd been as graceful as a leopard when they were running to intercept the strangers. Perhaps she had supernaturally used up her quota of coordination for the day.

Eyes like smashing surf bit into hers. Hurt. He was hurting, badly.

'I need time to adjust!' he repeated. 'You took me by surprise. I shouldn't be angry, I'm sorry. You needed him.'

'Who, Harry? Well, yes, but—'

'I understand, Annie. You told me plainly. Openly. And still I didn't believe you. I didn't want to.'

Seriously? This was about Harry? She was used to being confused and disoriented by the intricacies and complexities of this world whenever she returned, yet it had never been *this* baffling before. Then it occurred to her. This was what she wanted. She could go along with this so easily. This could meld with the plan beautifully, except for one problem. The thought of lying to him again, or deceiving him in any way whatsoever made her want to throw up. She just couldn't do it. Maybe if she had more time to acclimatise … no.

'Good,' she told him. 'Because I was lying about having that sort of a relationship with Harry, and I've had enough of lies.' Time for the brutal truth. 'Do you really think that Harry and I had sex?'

He flinched away so violently she nearly tripped again. That toothache emotion hit her again, and this time she recognised it. Jealousy.

'Sorry!' she hissed in a short breath as if she could suck the words back. 'Sometimes I forget that there are things I shouldn't say. Usually I'm in quarantine for at least twenty-four hours before I let myself speak to people.'

'No. You *should* speak. Don't hold back. I'd like to hear you be totally honest for a change.'

And that was the other reason she stayed away from people after returning. No one in Eden would ever say such a thing, with such venom. She needed time to desensitise to even joking criticism, so this, coming from him, was like being hit with a cattle prod. Especially since it was so hideously well-deserved.

'Why would you think we did?' she asked, her voice almost as hoarse as his.

The cords in his neck stood out as he stepped up close, looming over her. 'Four days?' he accused. 'And you lost track of time? He must have been *very* good!'

She choked back a very inappropriate laugh. Had they never mentioned that problem?

'And then you come running out of the bush together *stark naked.*'

'Well, yes, but—'

'But what? Are you going to try to tell me that it wasn't what it looked like?'

She couldn't help it. She laughed. He didn't.

'I really need to find you a Bible with pictures,' she said.

He frowned.

'We were in the *Garden of Eden,* Lucas. What did you think people wear there? Ball gowns and tuxedos?' His mouth dropped open and she smiled in sympathy for his flare of embarrassment. 'You really never thought about it before?'

He gulped and shook his head. 'I was warned not to ask too many questions about what it's like, and the Scriptures are pretty old. I guess I assumed they were a bit out-dated.'

Harry was right. Humans really didn't grasp the concept of eternity very well. Out-dated, seriously.

'So you and Harry …'

'Of course not. I'm about as attracted to him as you are.'

'Oh really,' he snarled, however the venom had disappeared. 'Somehow I can't quite picture myself wishing him a happy New Year with quite as much enthusiasm as you once did.'

Her apologetic smile was so sheepish that he let out a soft laugh. Not a trace of deceit lingered anywhere in her to cause him to doubt. He ran his hand through his hair, pushing back the mess of curls, and then rubbed his face as if getting rid of all his residual tension. When he looked back at her, his eyes were dimmer, and held a hint of self-re-crimination. He plucked at a bit of ti-tree, letting the soft needles drift to the ground. Patiently, she waited for him to reveal his next problem.

'I never asked how it went.' His fingers reached out automatically to brush the hair from her face, but he pulled them back at the last second.

How could she possibly describe the gentle way that they had cele-brated her mother's life? 'The music was incredible,' was all she managed to tell him without getting too choked up. 'We should keep moving. It's a pretty long trek downstream.' She pushed past him through the scrub, paying closer attention to where she placed her feet. 'Are you sure?' she asked a bit awkwardly, 'that you don't want to heal me? It doesn't really hurt or anything, but I don't want you to be grumpy all the way back.' It took a moment for her to notice that he'd stopped again. When she turned around, he was leaning against a gum tree with his head against his elbow and his eyes squeezed shut, like he was counting for a game of Hide and Seek.

'Grumpy is better than … I just can't heal you right now, Annie, I'm sorry.' He peeked at her through one eye, like he was cheating and didn't really care. Her expression held the obvious question, to which he replied, 'because if I touch you now, looking the way you do in that shirt, I might not ever let you go.'

Chapter 42

They both noticed the dusty white Commodore parked by the shed at the same time. Lucas stopped dead in his tracks, his eyes darting around as if searching for a place to hide. The gruelling hike back had left them both streaked with sweat and dirt, despite the frequent dips in the river along the way. As much as she had enjoyed the last hour or so watching her Guardian moving through the trees like a panther, she had to accept that they really weren't looking very presentable. Was she ever going to look respectable in front of his parents? Her track record thus far had not been great.

'I guess Harry must have talked the surveyors into leaving,' he said. 'He beat us back. He would have had to explain to Mum where we were.'

'And what story did you use?' she asked. 'To explain why we were gone for so long?'

'Story? I told them the truth, Annie. Not everything has to be a lie.'

Ouch.

'I told them you and Harry went to scatter your mother's ashes. I may have also hinted that you had a sacred ritual to attend to. I think Mum liked the mystery behind that, because she stopped asking questions at that point.' One corner of his lips curled up at his cleverness. He was right. Lies weren't always necessary.

'I'm sorry it took so long,' she apologised. 'I should have known better and been more careful to keep track of the time. Why didn't your family go home, though? Aren't they supposed to be working?'

Lucas shrugged. 'Dad said he couldn't leave me with two farms to run on my own, and Mum refused to leave without ...'

Without him. She wasn't about to let her son throw his life away on a teenage rebellious phase. As far as Naomi Gracewood was concerned, enough was enough. Annie had read it in her emotions at the barbeque, and she didn't blame her for it one bit.

For a solid twenty seconds, she contemplated just grabbing her Guardian's hand and running back into the bush. They could live quite happily there for a very long time as creepy bush legends …

'Let's get this over with,' she sighed instead, pushing her tired legs up the last stretch of hill.

Lily's face, when they walked into the cottage, should have been framed for its incredible range of expressions. Her emotions were simpler. All she felt was utter glee at the sight of her brother caught pantless with his shirt around an otherwise naked girl. Lucas groaned and tried to duck past her and into the bedroom.

'What are you going to do?' his dad asked, reclining comfortably on the only armchair, with his hands behind his head and a smirk on his face. 'Borrow one of Annie's dresses?'

'It would only be fair,' Annie suggested. 'Since he lent me this.' She plucked at the hem of his shirt. Lily gave them a generous dose of a tinkling sweet laugh that Annie had previously only ever heard from a different race of humans.

'Give him the bag, Lily,' Peter said.

'Already? They look tired, Dad. Maybe he should sit and have a drink and let Annie go and have a shower first.'

Lucas snatched the plastic bag from her hands and pulled out a fresh pair of shorts and a clean t-shirt. His nod to his father was full of gratitude.

His dad, in turn, looked at Annie. 'Harry told us your clothes had seen the rough edges of the bush and were no longer fit for public scrutiny. By the look of those scratches on your ankles, I'd say you must have found the rough top, bottom and centre too. Are you all right? Did you even take supplies with you?'

'I'm fine. We just didn't expect it to take so long, that's all. I'm so sorry we left you with the farms to mind—it was very irresponsible of me.'

Peter sighed, his smile gone. 'Under the circumstances, I totally understand. I'm glad you had the sense to take some time out, and I'm glad Harry had the wisdom to go with you, and I'm proud of my son for not hesitating to step in and help when he was needed.'

She didn't need to see Lucas's face to feel his surprised pleasure at the compliment.

'Still, I think once you've cleaned up, we should probably have a bit of a chat, Annie. Naomi is out watering your veggie patch. It might be wise to go and get dressed before she comes back.'

When Annie came out to the tiny front porch with its sagging tin roof, Peter, Naomi and Lucas were sipping iced water in the deck chairs that had been brought down from the back yard of the main house. Lily was sitting cross-legged under a tree, reading a massive book and clearly no longer interested in them now that they were being all serious. And fully clothed.

Lucas handed her a tall cold glass as she sat down. His face looked calmer than he felt. 'I ordered a water delivery for you,' he said. 'The truck should come tomorrow sometime. I hope that's okay. Your house tanks are nearly empty, and this one ...' He gestured to the ancient corrugated steel drum that only reached a third of the way up the side of the cottage, and was dotted with rust spots. 'I don't think the water is all that clean. I figured it could be a while until your house tanks can refill from the roof.'

Given that she currently had no roof to speak of, that was a fairly safe assumption.

'It isn't the first time we've had to buy in water over the last few years. Thanks, Lucas.'

'Dad and I also fixed the pipe to the orchard, so the cottage grey water will go there, like it used to, apparently. And the other day I moved the lambs back to the gully paddock because their dam was full of ash.'

Annie mentally kicked herself for not having checked that earlier. If she didn't get her act together soon, the place was going to fall apart. Some of her distress must have shown on her face because Peter leant forward with a sympathetic look.

'Are you going to be okay here, Annie? It's a massive place to be trying to look after on your own. I've only been here for a few days and I'm dead on my feet. What will you do?'

'I'll manage. Harry will help. We're both pretty accustomed to the workload.'

Peter looked dubious, but didn't push her.

'I don't know how to thank you for everything you've done. You were supposed to be back at work on Monday, weren't you?' she asked.

Naomi nodded as Peter shrugged.

'I can give you some money to compensate—'

'Don't be ridiculous,' Naomi said. 'You needed help. Besides, now that Lily has had a taste of how much hard work it takes to live out here, maybe she'll stop nagging us to move. You've done us a favour.' Her eyes flicked to where Lucas was sitting, obviously wondering if the same could be said about her son. She was worried for him, and she didn't even know the scariest part of what might happen if he stayed. Suddenly Annie had a vision of herself, facing Naomi and having to tell her that there had been a terrible accident, in that same falsely calm voice that she had been told about each of Harry's parents …

Peter looked at Lucas as well, his serious expression looking very familiar. 'It is, however, time to go home,' he said.

Annie exhaled very slowly.

Lucas stared at his glass and didn't reply. His dad tried again. 'The re-enrolments for your course will cut off on Friday.' No response. She tried to read what he was feeling, but he seemed to have either tuned right out, or somehow learned how to suppress his emotions. How long had he been practising that for?

'It's only a few weeks from when classes start until Easter. You could always come up and visit,' Annie said, trying to sound encouraging. Still no reaction.

Naomi piped in. 'We're thinking of taking a trip to France at the end of the year. You never know what opportunities can turn up when you travel. You could start there and then do some backpacking over the holidays—I know you were thinking of doing that last year.'

For a brief moment, his eyes met Annie's before resuming their ferocious study of the water droplets on the side of his glass. Was he resenting the fact that he wouldn't be able to go with them? She certainly would, in his place. A free trip to France sounded magnificent.

'Or you could come back here next summer,' Annie suggested. 'By then I might be able to offer you some decent pay, if Harry and I can get the place in order.' After all, they both knew he wouldn't be able to stay away completely, at least not without a twelve-step program of some sort. She wasn't totally heartless.

Peter caught on as quickly as she knew he would. 'If the Taylors still have their house at Apollo Bay, we could all meet up there for some beach time,' he suggested. 'Good excuse to get everyone together again. You mentioned Cam's been thinking of flying back from New Zealand for a visit.'

Lucas let out a non-committal sigh.

'Listen, Lucas, I know you like this place, but your options are going to get a bit limited if you don't re-enrol this week,' his dad said.

Annie nearly let a sob escape at his choice of words. He knew his son so well. Good man.

'I'm sorry Harry can't keep paying you,' she added. 'I know he wouldn't have managed for so long without your help.'

Finally, she got a bit of a reaction. 'Glad to know someone needed me,' he muttered. A chink in his shield gave her the tiniest insight ... and she slammed a wall up against his anguish. This was all so hard to do, this soon after Eden.

For a minute or so they all just sat there, until Lily chimed in.

'Can I invite one of my friends?' she asked, stretching her legs out and smoothing the pages of her book. 'To France? If Lucas isn't coming?'

Her mother gave her a disapproving look. 'Of course Lucas is coming. Why wouldn't he?'

'Why wouldn't I?' he echoed softly, tracing his fingertip around the rim of the glass.

Annie wondered what it would take to allow him to go. Somehow, she didn't think it would be easy to board a plane carrying a bottle of someone's blood without an extremely good explanation.

His dad watched him shrewdly, waiting for him to say more, while Annie squashed her own emotions down so hard it made her bones hurt.

Lucas finally took a deep breath. 'Dave will be disappointed. He wanted me to help him start a soccer team. He reckons some of Harry's footy mates might be quite good, if we can convince them that it isn't un-Australian.'

Naomi let out a tense breath, while his dad's face remained unexpectedly passive. Annie used her gift to tune in to him, just a little. Yep. Inwardly, Peter Gracewood was face-palming himself.

Keeping her voice calm, Annie tried to sound casual, despite the tight ball of loneliness that was starting to spin and whirl inside her throat. 'I doubt you would have had much luck there,' she said with a fake smile. 'Even if you did convince them, who would you play against? Half of them already travel from Horsham, and the nearest town after that with a hope of having another team is a three-hour drive away.'

'That's a long way,' he rasped, despair leaking through the cracks as he glanced at her to emphasise his double meaning.

Naomi smiled kindly. 'A bit too far for regular soccer matches, maybe, but not so far to visit. You're welcome to come and see us anytime, Annie.'

'Sure, why not?' she agreed. Standing briskly, she ducked back in through the screen door, muttering something about getting another drink and hoping no one had noticed how shaky she was. Lucas hissed under his breath as he felt her intent, but he didn't move. As quickly as she could, she fled to the bathroom and rummaged through the drawer, trying to find something sharp. Stupid fire. When was she going to be allowed back into the house to get the rest of her stuff? Not that the sewing kit had exactly been a priority up until now. In the end, she had to pull free a tiny nail that had been diligently holding up a calendar since 1982 that one of the shearers had left behind. The semi-naked ladies almost fell off the bonnets of the cars when she tossed it on the floor. A few minutes later she came back outside and handed Lucas a box of matches—minus the actual matches.

'Can you give these back to Harry? He lent them to me the other day. I assume you'll be going back there to get your things.' He nodded solemnly, his fingers lingering on hers for a second too long.

Peter cleared his throat. 'Listen, Annie, I know you don't want to hear this, but I think someone needs to say it.' Her eyebrows rose and she leaned back against the wall for support. He looked her right in the eye. 'There's no need for you to stay here. I know it's your home, and it's been in the family for a long time, but I don't believe that your parents would have wanted you to live here by yourself.'

The tight spinning ball began to unravel into a tangled mess like a dropped fishing reel. He was dead right.

'I think you should follow Harry's example and sell up. Move to Melbourne. From what I hear, you'll do well at uni if you decide to concentrate on further study. I'm sure Lucas wouldn't mind helping you to get started. Find your feet in the city.'

It all sounded so reasonable that she wished for a moment that she could just follow the wisdom of her elders. Only for a moment. She shook her head. 'I can't leave. This place is too important to me.'

Peter gave a sad nod, and she could sense his disappointment. He knew how Lucas felt, and now, apparently, he believed he knew how she felt too. He'd just offered them his blessing, subtly, and she had thrown it back in his face by stating her priorities. He probably thought that if she really loved his son, she would at least consider following him to Melbourne, and yet she hadn't even hesitated to reject the idea.

The inevitable goodbyes were fairly brief after that. It wasn't like they were never going to see each other again, after all, despite the demonstrative hug that Lily almost choked her with. Annie promised to teach her to ride if she came up again, and told her that if she came back at Easter, there would be a foal for her to see. That, of course, delayed their departure for an extra ten minutes while Lily dragged her off to make her show her which of the mares was growing a new stock horse. When they got back, the others were already waiting in the car, and Naomi was nagging Lily to hurry up.

The car drove slowly away while she stood there, waving limply, stricken by how horribly easy it had been.

Chapter 43

As the car turned out of the driveway and onto the narrow bitumen road, Lucas tried yet again to figure out what had gone wrong. The car sped up and trees smeared past the window, blurring his vision and numbing his brain. The hills to the west crowded his window, looming over him in silent accusation. He wanted to scream at them that it wasn't his fault. He'd done everything she'd asked. And hadn't done a thing he'd wanted for himself. Why should the hills frown at him in judgment? She didn't give a rat's about him. How was that his fault? All along she'd wanted him to leave her alone. She'd even shouted it at him, and he still hadn't listened. Stupidly he'd hoped that it was because of her mother, but she was gone now, and still …

'Lucas, what did she mean?' Lily's voice grated at him the way only a younger sister's voice could.

'Who? Annie?' He closed his eyes, trying not to think about the adorable way her nose scrunched when she laughed, or the way her hair fell around her dusky shoulders when it escaped her ponytail. He could still feel the biting sting of her cuts where the blackberries had caught at her. He figured he may as well try to get used to that, somehow. Did she really have any idea how tormented and sick her injuries made him feel?

'Who else?' the irritating voice asked. 'What did she mean by "safe"?'

'I have no idea what you're talking about, Lily. Please leave me alone.'

She rolled her eyes at him and then opened her book, settling in for the long drive. Nearly thirty seconds of silence passed before he gave in and had to ask her.

'All right, explain then. What exactly did Annie say?'

His sister pointedly ignored him, tucking her silver-gold hair behind her ear, so he snatched her book away. She snatched it back, but relented.

'When we were looking at the horses, I asked her how she felt about you leaving—'

'You did not!' he exclaimed. 'You wouldn't dare.'

Lily gave him a sardonic look. 'Of course I would. I'm me. No one expects me to be subtle. I'm just a nosy little sister, remember?'

He glared at her. She glared back. He narrowed his eyes. 'Lily …' he growled.

'Okayyy. She said she was glad you were being reasonable, and that it was safer. That's the part I didn't get, but she wouldn't answer when I questioned her about it. That's why I'm asking you. What did she mean?'

Lucas could feel both his parents listening so hard that his mother's hair was practically standing on end.

'She seems to be under the ridiculous impression that everyone who gets close to her is destined to die young. I told her how stupid that was. If she doesn't grow out of it, she's going to need to buy a lot of cats to keep her company.'

He could practically see the way his mother's face softened in sympathy, even though she was facing the front and he was in the back seat.

'She's lost both her parents within the past three years, hasn't she?' his dad asked. 'It's an understandable reaction. I'm sure it will pass, with time.'

'No,' Lily said, making everyone turn to her. 'She wasn't talking about you. She said it was safer for her. Something about how she wouldn't have been able to promise. At least I think that's what she said. She was actually talking to the horse, not to me.'

The hills sighed, and his world came to a screaming halt.

'Stop the car.' His voice, although screaming inside his skull, came out as a barely audible hoarse cry.

His dad heard it anyway, and didn't even bother to argue. He pulled over so suddenly that he nearly put his wife through the windscreen. Fumbling with the seat belt, Lucas opened the door and started to jump out, but then turned and gave his sister a great big noisy kiss on the cheek. She squealed in genuine fright, clearly expecting a wet willie or other such sibling torment. Instead he just grinned at her.

'What was that for?' she shrieked.

'For being such a nosy little sister.' He laughed and stumbled backward out of the car, hitting his head painfully on the way, yet even that didn't stop him laughing.

His mother jumped out as well. 'Lucas, really. Think this through. You don't need to make any rash decisions right now. You could just—'

'What? Leave my options open? No, Mum,' he said, giving her a swift hug. 'I won't survive any of the other options. I'm choosing this one.'

With the ease of someone who'd spent a year practising the rather dangerous manoeuver, Lucas took a running leap straight over the ring-lock fence using his hand to lever off an old fence post, and made a full pelt beeline across the paddock.

He was a man who knew *exactly* where he was going.

Chapter 44

Check on the chickens. Call the insurance company. Find the cheque book so I can pay for the water delivery. Defrost one of the frozen meals for dinner. Throw the horses a couple of biscuits of hay. Check to see if any of the other dams are contaminated. Make sure the firies didn't leave any gates open and the rams are where they should be.

Annie ran through the list of things she was supposed to be doing instead of standing waist deep in the river with her eyes closed, feeling the tug as the current pulled at her favourite loose cotton dress. Then she mentally drowned the list. Regrettably, it was indestructible so she knew she'd be able to retrieve it later.

Had Lucas taken his shirt back? She wasn't sure. If not, did that give her an excuse to call him? No. Bad idea. Did that mean she could keep it? No. Even worse idea. She could always post it. Maybe she could slip a bit of blood-dosed cloth in with it or something. Somehow, she would have to find a subtle way to keep replenishing the talisman.

She plunged down under the water and came up gasping.

Why hadn't he even said goodbye properly? She hadn't messed with his emotions one little bit, and yet he hadn't even tried to argue against leaving. She'd had some hefty well-reasoned arguments ready to counter his protests with, but they weren't needed because the only thing that seemed to have bugged him was the thought of leaving Dave without someone to play soccer with. After that kiss the other day, and seeing the sword, she'd thought …

Breathing deeply, she stretched her palms out flat on the surface of the water, to let the sweet coolness quench her suddenly burning blood. Why couldn't she shield her own emotions? Every time she'd thought she was, it had turned out to be pure self-deception. Perhaps she could let the water's song take her emotions away instead. It felt good. As soothing and natural as sleeping. Wriggling her toes, she dug them into the sand and pebbles, feeling for every slimy rock beneath her feet. There was life here. Busy and smelly and frenetic, and yet blissfully uncomplicated, too. Rainbow trout and Murray perch drifted languidly among the deeper pools, browsing for food. Downstream a little, a ringtail possum was diving for an underwater entrance to its hollow, with typical possum disregard for its species' official tree-nesting habits. How come everyone else in this river felt warm when she was so cold and numb? It was as if the more life she sensed, the more life was being sucked away from her in return. That was not how the river was supposed to work, but she still wanted the water to just take it all away, because she couldn't stop herself from reaching out … searching …

'Don't you know this is one of the few places in the world that you can't sneak up behind me?' she asked, still with her eyes closed.

A pause, and then there was the feel of warm breath on the back of her neck. His palms stretched out to meet hers just under the surface, offering support as she communed with the river. Heat flooded her hands and wrists and flowed deliciously up her shivering arms. A strong heartbeat joined the symphony of life around her, mingling with the water's song.

'You're really here,' she breathed.

'Of course. Where else would I be?' His husky voice brushed her ear like a kiss. 'I was fearfully and wonderfully made for this place. My soul is aligned to you, and designed for you. Even my body reacts like a petulant child when we're apart. So where else would I be?'

Smiling, she kept her eyes closed, afraid of breaking the spell. She leant back a little and entwined her fingers with his. 'You've been reading your Bible,' she acknowledged. 'There's more to you than meets the eye.'

'And you are the most beautiful thing my eyes have ever seen.'

Then he did what she had been aching for him to do every single moment for well over a year. He wrapped his warm arms around her and drew her close against his body. Healing power, like a small glowing sun, searched out every little flaw in her body, making her gasp.

'I thought you said you couldn't do that for me anymore?'

'No, what I said was that if I touched you, I might never let you go,' he corrected, resting his chin on her shoulder.

Annie opened her eyes and sighed. 'You don't have to decide that now, you know. Your parents are right—'

'My parents are very wise people,' he interrupted. 'Only they don't have all the information they need to get it right this time, do they?'

He had a point. 'All I'm saying is that you don't necessarily have to choose now. I'm not going anywh—' The rest of her sentence was muffled by his fingertip, placed gently on her lips.

'Stop talking now, Annie. You've had your turn, and I listened very patiently.'

'But I—'

'My turn,' he insisted.

He let her go and turned her to face him. Despite his apparent bossiness, he was smiling, the corner of his lips curving in that way that he had …

'You keep telling me I don't have to choose, but I do. Not making a definite choice is still a choice in itself, remember? I won't make Sarah's mistake.'

He had her with that one, and he knew it. Her hefty arguments suddenly sounded very puny, so she didn't even bother with them. She only had one more card to play. 'What if *I'm* not ready? I'm not just breeding stock, you know.'

That got his attention. 'Seriously? You're worried about that?' Then he groaned. 'Dave blabbed about the career counselling incident, didn't he?'

She nodded, biting her lower lip to suppress a laugh.

'Well, don't worry. I have no intention of having kids until I'm at least thirty.'

Annie nearly choked. *Ten years?* The way her body ached for him right then, she wasn't confident she'd last ten minutes.

'Don't worry,' she assured him, a little dizzily. 'I won't hold you to that.'

'What do you mean?'

'I mean that there's one more little Cherubim and Guardian feature that we may have neglected to mention. You know how Sarah fell pregnant despite the precautions they took?'

His face blanched.

Annie waited.

He took a careful breath. 'So you don't want to just be breeding stock, but your body has other ideas?' he clarified.

'So does yours,' she defended.

He grinned and pulled her tightly against him. 'Well, in that case,' he said, running his fingers down her back, 'I'd better make the most of this freezing river. It might be the only place I can trust myself.'

Feeling the way her skin hummed wherever it touched his, she doubted even that would help them much. Not even if they waited until the river was supplemented with Eden's spring snow melt.

'Lucas,' she breathed into his warm neck. 'Do you trust me? Do you trust how much I love you?'

River light danced in his serious blue eyes as he pulled back to look at her. 'Trust you? You're a liar, and a thief.'

She opened her mouth to assure him that she hadn't broken her promise to leave his emotions alone, but he cut her off.

'You lie, you steal, and you do whatever else it takes to protect Eden, and protect the people you care about. And that's why I trust you with my life.'

Chapter 45

Mr Rosa stood by the floor-to-ceiling window, looking out over the city skyline. From there he could just make out the docks, stacked with shipping containers, many of which he had a vested interest in. It had been a long time since he'd been down there himself. Not since the days before the nightmares. These days he preferred to leave the messier details to others. Others that were supposed to be reliable, and loyal. Fourby had been one of his longest serving employees.

'Yes, we can get at him, although I'm not sure there's much point,' the lawyer said, drawing a cigarette case from his pocket. 'Apparently he had some sort of nervous breakdown and told the police everything within the first half an hour. Cruise managed better—too terrified to talk, but also too terrified to be trustworthy. I've already made arrangements for him. He won't be around to testify.'

'You'd better make it clean, Mr Johnson.'

'I know my job,' the lawyer said. 'Cruise has enough history on record that an old vendetta will be blamed for the fight. I can get a weapon into the right person's hand at the right time. He'll be dead by the end of the month.'

'Good. And your suggestion for Fourby? What deal did he make with the police, exactly?'

'He didn't. As I said, he volunteered everything—even details they didn't know enough to ask about. It's as if he just doesn't care anymore.'

Mr Rosa glanced down at the top of the neighbouring apartment building. The sight of the swimming pool on the roof made him shudder. Why would anyone choose to swim for fun? 'So, Fourby has agreed to testify?'

'He's mentally unstable. I already have two independent psych reports. He won't even make it to the court room.'

A single thin cloud stretched around the top of the Rialto building, reaching toward the group of hot air balloons that drifted in the morning haze. A clear day ahead. Good. He hated rain. The whispering voice was angrier when it rained.

'Tell me more about my necklace,' Mr Rosa said, taking the cigarette lighter from the lawyer's hand and striking a flame. Instead of igniting the man's cigarette for him, he picked up the photo of Fourby from the desk. As the flame caught, the colours of his employee's face melted together and then bubbled away into nothing—just like the man's decades of loyalty. 'When will I get it back?' he asked as he watched the photo burn.

'Harry Doolan has agreed that he has no legal right to the gem. After he handed it in as evidence, it was assessed by three of Australia's top jewellers. They all agree. It's just a ruby. It even has a minor flaw. The thing is worth about thirty grand, that's all. Your claim to it is legal, and the valuation reflects what you paid Ruby Doolan for it.' The man hesitated.

'So what's the problem?'

The lawyer stood very still, as if he'd seen a snake in the grass. His response was carefully enunciated, his tone overly soothing. 'The police are questioning why you had such a large insurance policy for it. There may be fraud charges involved.'

Moments passed in silence as the chemical scent of burnt ink drifted around the two men.

'Sir … Mr Rosa, sir?'

The man was staring at the burning photo, looking horrified. Mr Rosa looked down to see flames wrapping around his fingers. As he noticed the sting, he let the remaining bit of paper fall.

'Do you believe in miracles, Mr Johnson?' the businessman asked, feeling the whispers grow louder in the back of his mind.

The lawyer frowned, and didn't answer.

'Turning a ruby into a rare diamond—sounds like a hoax. But turning a diamond into a ruby? Now that sounds like a story worth investigating.'

Don't fret now, Mr Rosa, the voice whispered. *I'll take care of the court case, and then it will be time for us to part. I have no use for jail time.*

Panic rose like a scream in the business man's throat. The whispers had never been so clear.

I will even leave you to choose if you will live or die, the voice whispered. *So long as you stay out of my way, I don't really care. I have a story worth investigating. A frightened jeweller to whisper to. And a town to search.*

Epilogue

A gasp, crisp with night-chilled air, filled Annie's lungs as her hands fell away from the standing stone. She gulped down air and tears as if she'd forgotten what breathing was for. It took her a few more seconds to remember where she was. Eden. This was Eden. This was real, and where she had been was only wax vapour, memories drifting away as they burned. The standing stone had unlocked them for her. Unlocked and then folded them into its crystalline matrix for safekeeping. And it had granted her a gift. Looped around her own memories were those of her mother, as well as Harry's, and Lucas's. As each of them had crossed over into death, Annie had come here to share her memories of them, and it seemed that the stones had used those connections to gather and guard their memories in the process. She had seen their memories as if they were her own. And not just theirs. Mr Rosa, Director of Celarsi Holdings. The man Ruby Doolan had caught a single glimpse of during her husband's trial, and been obsessed with until the day she'd broken into his office and been killed by his staff. Mr Rosa, the man who had eventually been convicted of insurance fraud, and of Kiah Langley's murder. He must have died now as well, and the stones had granted Annie the gift of his memory thread, tangled with her own. That couldn't be a coincidence. It felt more like a warning.

Goosebumps rose as Annie recalled the sound of that voice, whispering its chilling threat. A voice that had searched her home town and found nothing, because Lucas was gone, Sarah had turned her back on her role as Guardian, Harry had stayed away from Eden, and Annie had been hiding from her past. There had been nothing for the dark presence to find. Until now.

How much time had passed since Jake had stolen the sword? Time in Eden ran the same as in Nalong, and yet it always felt skewed, Annie knew. Had it been a day? A week? Either way, Lainie and Noah must be warned. This threat was not new. It wasn't about Jake running off with an intriguing artefact. This was an ancient evil that had lurked in wait for years, and had now found what it had been looking for. The solution to the threat was there too, somewhere in her fragmented and damaged memories, she was sure of it.

Annie looked up at the moon and breathed in the scent of the Garden that had sheltered her. She wasn't ready to leave Eden. She'd tried, and hadn't coped, and yet she also knew that the time for hiding from her past was over. She had made a promise to Lucas, and had kept it for years, but perhaps it was approaching the time to break it. She was still a Cherub, and still had work to do.

SHAMAR

THE SENTINELS OF EDEN

BOOK FOUR

CAROLYN DENMAN

Chapter 1

Annie felt burdened by a memory that wasn't hers. It belonged to someone she'd never even met. The man responsible for her mother's murder, Mr Rosa, had died in jail. She remembered the day her partner Cherub, Harry, had raced up from the cottage to switch on the news report so she and Lucas could hear it for themselves. While Harry's face had been cast in a sturdy mask of passive contentment, his heart had been full of sorrow and longing. Was there anyone left who could see through that mask? No. Wait. Harry was gone now too. If only he'd listened that day when she'd tried to convince him to move to the Garden. Instead, he'd insisted on remaining in the place where rubies and diamonds were valued more than lives. A place where those whispers would continue to haunt her, even without Mr Rosa. Chills chased the memory of that voice around her mind and down her spine. It hunted for a clue. Hunted for her. Relentless.

I have a story worth investigating. A frightened jeweller to whisper to. And a town to search.

There had to be a reason the standing stones had revealed someone else's secret, and now she had to choose whether to allow Eden's perfection to soothe away her sense of urgency, or to follow the thread of her flawed recollections. After spending the night reliving her past she was exhausted, yet too afraid to sleep. Too afraid of her dreams, in case they forced her to remember even more. Why couldn't her story just have ended there? Why couldn't she have stayed locked away in those first few years after Lucas decided to stay in Nalong? That town was not timeless like Eden. Events kept ticking along, counting down from one disaster to the next.

Beside her, a silver tree dropped a ripe piece of Fruit that rolled gently to a stop within arm's reach. Its ambrosial fragrance made her mouth water and her fingertips twitch. One bite of the Living Fruit would dull her memories and cure both her tiredness and anxiety. Sadly, there were ramifications for her. She wasn't ready to unravel all the tangled emotions that were wrapped around her past. Enough shame still haunted her that eating from the Tree of Life would infect it with an illness it couldn't heal. Besides, she had work to do and couldn't afford to get lulled by the Garden's autumn somnolence. Nor could she continue to hide from her own memories. She turned from the Fruit with a sigh.

There was only one person in Eden who might understand, and she finally found him with a group of five others, grinding various coloured rocks to make paint. Nayn came over as soon as he noticed her waiting under a nearby tree. His unruly white curls were streaked with bright orange where he'd pushed it out of his face with dusty fingers.

You are not happy, he signed as he approached. As if she didn't know.

Just tired. I've been up all night. Remembering.

He gave a solemn nod. *The standing stones can hold many memories. They act like the planet's own consciousness. Stones, gems, some metals. The bones of the Earth have ways of keeping hold of memories, and what is consciousness if not memory with emotion?*

Annie grabbed hold of Nayn's wrist, inspecting the orange stains on his hand. *How much of this ochre have you been breathing in?*

Enough to give me heightened powers of deduction. You are not just tired. Dallmin has hurt your heart, and you are angry, he persisted. There was no sign for angry, but he used his facial expressions to convey what he meant. If she hadn't been feeling so miserable it would have been comical.

He is gone now, so how can I be angry at him?

As easily as breathing. You feel what you feel. That is the way we are built, even here.

Pressing her lips together, she looked across to the people mixing paint ingredients. They were laughing at Bungee, who'd tipped a wooden bowl of powdered lapis lazuli over himself and was now sneezing out blue dust. Their carefree laughter at the dog's antics only made her feel jealous. Her anger at herself and at Dallmin had no place in Eden, no matter what Nayn said.

I should have known better, she signed. *Have I lost all sense of reason? Have my memories of Nalong slipped so far away that I've lost touch completely? Lainie was so shocked when she discovered he had left, so why wasn't I? I've basically killed him, Nayn. By letting him leave the Garden I've doomed him to an early death. What will become of him? And what does that make me?*

Nayn wrapped a strong arm around her shoulders and gave her a quick squeeze. Then he picked a bunch of tiny yellow flowers and started to weave them together with some long grass strands. *Dallmin is not dead, Annie. He is alive and burdened by knowledge he should never have had to face. It is important you remember this. He still loves you. What that makes you … is a beloved one.*

And what use is it to be beloved if I cannot love back? He can never return here.

When Nayn frowned at her she realised how bitter her words were.

Perhaps you should get some rest, he suggested. *And we can talk later.*

Why bother talking more about this? The outcome won't change whether I'm rested or not. Dallmin is lost. No one ever returns once they have been outside.

Finishing the tiny floral crown, he placed it on her head. *Except us.*

Yeah. Except Cherubim.

And one other … that I know of.

Annie gaped at him. *Really? Who?*

He laughed and refused to answer, despite all her cues telling him how badly she needed to know. Instead, he jumped up and trotted away to join the paint-makers. Unless she wanted to make a scene in front of the innocent humans, she would have to wait for him to return.

With Thanks

Turning an Empath into a Sympath is no easy feat. What started as an exploration into Annie's character quickly became an intrinsic and necessary part of Lainie's future. After all, the wise people of this world know that past and future are so interconnected that they might as well be part of one eternal dream. They also know that sometimes the most valuable things in life take a cohesive community effort to achieve. So this is where I get to thank my community. To Alex, Brian, Jen, Lily, Nickie and Vron, thank you for pandering to my perfectionism while still being gentle with your feedback. To my editor, Sarah Endacott, thanks for being more of a perfectionist than I am, and for not being gentle at all. To Michelle at Odyssey Books for working tirelessly to get the books out into the world, and still finding time to give us authors those precious words of encouragement we need to keep believing in our stories. To Elijah Toten, for yet another soul-grabbing piece of cover art. And to my family, for keeping me balanced and prying me away from the keyboard at all the right times. Yeah, I know eating is important. And yes, enticing me away with doughnuts will *always* work. Lastly, I'd like to thank all my readers, especially those who have taken the time to write me a review. I know it's bad etiquette to respond to reviews in any way, but how can I read such lovely things and not say thank you? All feedback is helpful, good and bad, and I truly value every word. Without you, that great marketing machine of wheels and cogs would never even begin to roll.

Blessings on all of my community. May you never step on a poisonous animal, never cop a burger as dodgy as the ones at Nalongest Yard Fish & Chippery, never lose your soccer ball to a swan, and never lack for affection even when covered in blood and birthing goop. And may the River always sing for you.

About the Author

Carolyn lives on a small hobby farm on the outskirts of Melbourne. She has a science degree, far too many pets and a fear of the ocean that makes her Mauritian mother roll her eyes. Somehow between her mortgage-broking job, driving her kids crazy (mostly by asking their friends' opinions about the Singularity) and feeding sixty-three baby axolotls, she has managed to write short stories for *Aurealis* and *Andromeda Spaceways* magazines. She is currently working to complete the fourth and final book in *The Sentinels of Eden* and after that she has promised that she will finally vacuum the bedrooms.

www.ingramcontent.com/pod-product-compliance
Lightning Source LLC
Chambersburg PA
CBHW032209180726
48284CB00001B/249